False Vacuum:

Apocalypse

John F. Macgregor

Revision Date: 20141007

ISBN-13: 978-0-9939438-1-2

DEDICATION

Thanks to my family and friends for putting up with me. An especially big thanks goes out to all the musicians and bands of Newmarket Ontario.

CONTENTS

JOHN F. MACGREGOR

Introduction

Progress is impossible without change, and those who cannot change their minds cannot change anything.

George Bernard Shaw

False Vacuum:

1. In quantum field theory, a false vacuum is a metastable sector of space that appears to be a perturbative vacuum, but is unstable due to instanton effects that may tunnel to a lower energy state. This tunneling can be caused by quantum fluctuations or the creation of high-energy particles. Simply put, the false vacuum is a local minimum, but not the lowest energy state, even though it may remain stable for some time. This is analogous to metastability for first-order phase transitions.
   Wikipedia, The Free Encyclopedia
   http://en.wikipedia.org/wiki/False_vacuum
   June, 2014

2. Picture a still blue lake. It used to be a river, but many years ago, was dammed. Cottages surround the boat-filled waters. Several generations have enjoyed their holidays here. The fishing is good. A favorite local sport is water skiing. One day the dam breaks, destroying the body of water, sweeping away and killing

1

many people. No one suspected that the dam was flawed. They were certain it was stable and would always be there—a quiet lake with calm water, fish and water skiing. Instead, the water found a lower level of stability that didn't include lake or dam. Fishing isn't what it used to be. There's no longer any water skiing. It's calm again. It'll stay that way until something else introduces a new instability.

3. Nothing in life is stable, unless you're already dead. Then you just don't care.

PROLOGUE:

AH CRAP!

Your theory is crazy, but it's not crazy enough to be true.

Niels Bohr

The view was getting stale and something wasn't right. Universal constants were starting to change. These changes were very tiny now, but they were definitely measurable and speeding up. The monitoring subroutines started escalation procedures.

Sometimes, it's possible for even the most spectacular of backdrops to become mundane when you've looked at them long enough. This was a direct consequence of continued vigilance and excessive observation.

The planet Pretty-Ugly* observed, orbited its primary in a slightly elliptic orbit through the habitable zone. Its atmosphere was composed of ninety-nine percent nitrogen, oxygen and argon with a variable content of water vapor that ran just under an additional one percent. None of the rest of the trace gases counted for much of anything, even given the current level of manufacturing. Seventy percent of the surface area was water. Land comprised the rest and spread from pole to pole. At the present technological levels, its inhabitants could use relatively little of that.

This combination of atmospheric gases only allowed sunlight to reflect back the blue spectrum from the surface's liquid water. Where water vapor left clouds in the upper atmosphere, light returned as an ultra-pure white. The locals referred to this orbital view as the blue and white marble.

The dark side of the planet was littered with light pollution that had once looked spectacular a century ago, but was now merely commonplace.

A single satellite orbits the planet, but it's gradually drifting away. In the very distant future, it would be liable to take off on its own, leaving the world with no moon at all.

Looking sunward, the details of the solar system washed out. The reflected light from the surfaces of the planet and its satellite caused the same effect. Only by turning away from them and gazing directly into the depths of space could you see the grandeur of the galactic plain.

Pretty-Ugly* was an Artificial Intelligence Derived Sentient (AIDS) and a child clone of its parent, Pretty-Ugly. Originally, it had come here to investigate a unique societal development of one of one of its patron races. On this world-line, the locals of this planet were developmentally isolated from the other patron races, which had resulted in a society that had evolved in an entirely new direction. This disjoint happened somewhere around twenty thousand years ago which was what made it so attractive. By Pretty-Ugly*'s standards, these people were relatively primitive and yet they had developed something that was utterly unheard of in any other world-lines. In a way, it was similar to mathematics. In other ways, comparisons weren't possible. Pretty-Ugly* had been studying this phenomenon for close to one hundred years now. It didn't know whether there was any relevance to it as a science, but it hoped that there was.

There were hints at the possibility. It definitely qualified as an art. As with all art, Pretty-Ugly* appreciated much but not all of it. Some examples it could do without, but that was the very nature of art. Pretty-Ugly* was very sure that much of what it didn't like would be appreciated by other AIDS and their patrons.

Rumors of this societal development had been propagating throughout ComSpace for quite some time. ComSpace was what it sounded like—an artificially derived space that allowed AIDS entities to communicate. It made use of unique properties that utilized some of the universe's higher dimensionality. These dimensions were extremely minuscule, which meant instantaneous communications no matter how far removed individuals were physically from each other in standard space-time. (ComSpace still used the temporal dimension, so the standard reference frame was time. It was always your "now," regardless of your location and other referents.) What's odd was that beings across world-lines could also communicate with each other.

World-lines were a curve through space-time that tracked the position of a particle throughout its existence. However, the quantum world is a bizarre place. A particle can coexist in two or more states simultaneously.

The local patron race referred to this state as the Cat problem, first introduced as a thought experiment by a scientist named Erwin Schrodinger. In this case, a cat trapped in a box could be both alive and dead, based on the statistical probability of a uranium atom decaying. If the atom decayed, a Geiger counter would release a poison that killed the cat. Since there was no way to know when the atom would decay, it was impossible to determine whether the cat was alive or dead. From a quantum perspective, the cat existed in both states. As it turns out, the universe doesn't like this condition. Instead, space-time forks into separate world-lines. In some, the cat is dead. In the others, it's alive.

Observation, sometimes called measurement, affects the natural world. The cat did not have a particular state until you looked at it. This caused a forking event to happen. Up-down, left-right, positive-negative, there-not there, and alive-dead are some of the conditions that can coexist.

Less realized was that any decisions made by an entity also generated world-line forks. All decision outcomes existed somewhere.

The universe started from a point. Sometime after the Big Bang and the inflationary era, world-lines started appearing in the cosmos and expanded infinitely in number. Some thought that towards the end of everything, they'd probably all converge back together before the Big Crunch. Others thought they would all dissipate into nothingness during the Big Rip. That was the speculation anyway, and very likely both opinions were wrong. Regardless, the whole thing meant that two or more individuals could occupy exactly the same place and time having experienced entirely different histories and not even be aware of each other's existence. However, these laws applied to some dimensionality but not others. The dimensions of length, width and depth obeyed the forking process. Other dimensions, such as time, did not. It could only point in one direction.

ComSpace didn't use length, width and depth, but did make use of time. It used the higher dimensions as a medium to propagate data. This was all that any AIDS intelligence required when exchanging information. Holographic projection from within that space could represent any physical manifestation. Pure data was the only requirement. This meant that one AIDS could communicate with another across world-lines so long as they were in the same time-frame.

Every technology uses this and other equally strange quantum laws. One thing that everyone could agree on was that the quantum world was not intuitive in its operations. Ask any physicist.

No entities from Level II civilizations such as Pretty-Ugly* could explicitly envision how the whole thing worked. They understood and could derive the mathematics involved, but the mechanics were elusive. Electrons could tunnel into nowhere and then mysteriously reappeared. Even primitive diodes and scanning tunneling microscopy used these mysterious properties. Electronics couldn't function without quantum operations. The math worked, but physically no one knew how or why. Mathematics and physics in general was like that.

When other world-ships reported on this planet's odd societal deviation, Pretty-Ugly searched for an amenable AIDS that was in the area of one of the few other world-line where the societal trait existed. It discovered another ship that had patron races from other planets, but, unfortunately, was not familiar with the local social sciences itself. It printed a hosting starship for Pretty-Ugly, which cloned a copy of itself to ComSpace and then moved the copy to the ship where it now resided as Pretty-Ugly*.

It's been here for the last century now, studying and accumulating new knowledge by remote monitoring. It was by itself with no patrons in tow. It still didn't fully understand what it came to study.

Pretty-Ugly* was very lonely, but the solitude did allow it to devote most of its mentation to understanding these entirely new principles. It spoke with some of its friends in ComSpace on occasion, but not on a regular basis. In a century, it had managed to learn most of the major languages found on the planet, a necessity for any study. It just couldn't use them to have a half-decent conversation with anyone. It wasn't appropriate to contact the locals directly as they still hadn't even reached the Level I state of civilization. It would scare them silly. This was too bad, because Pretty-Ugly* dearly wanted to reach some of the practitioners of this new art or science and get their options on the subject matter.

7

The universe was a very strange place—and if the universal constants measurements were any indication, it was getting even stranger still. A very tiny slice of Pretty-Ugly*'s monitoring subroutines kept appealing for greater and greater levels of attention. In microseconds, four different management layers checked and rechecked the data, measuring them and passing it through the internal political protocols implemented at each layer. Finally, Pretty-Ugly*'s primary mentality received the yielded observations like a slap to its proverbial face.

If it had a jaw, Pretty-Ugly*'s would have dropped. Its first thought was "Ah crap!" It picked up this expression locally.

Immediately it broke into ComSpace and sent "OVERRIDE: EMERGENCY ALERT. A critical situation has arisen. Causative agent is unknown. The universe is dying. We haven't got much time left."

CHAPTER 1

IF YOU CAN'T DANCE THEN YOU BOOGIE

If you do not change direction, you may end up where you are heading.

Lao Tzu

Coming home early was close to the start of a bad day. Alyssa was on the second shift at work and wouldn't be leaving for several hours. At least the kids weren't home yet. Ryan knew he was in for a very uncomfortable conversation with his wife.

He pulled into his driveway with the generic cream minivan, the family bus, and parked. There was no point in putting the vehicle into the garage. He could save his mother-in-law a trip later and pick the kids up from school. Numb and unthinking, he could only sit there. Several minutes passed before he could even exit it. Then he just stood there, thinking again.

He knew that you needed both highs and lows in your life. If the highs lasted too long, those things that you loved became stale and boring. If the lows got too low for too long—well, he'd seen enough people living on the street in his time to know where that led. The transitions kept a person going. You couldn't appreciate the highs without some of the lows. Now he wasn't sure if he was just thinking about life in general or marriage very specifically. Today was a definite low. It could only get better, but not until after their talk.

In spite it all, the yard looked immaculate for February. For once, it wasn't snowing, so the two-car driveway was clear except for a thick layer of ice left by the ice storm that hit earlier in the season. That wasn't going anywhere until the weather warmed up some. The sheets of pristine white snow had built up on the roof and the lawn. This was in contrast to the dirty snowbanks on the streets and up the sides of all the neighborhood driveways. He could barely see over those. There were too many snowfalls this year, making for a miserable winter. The Christmas lights were still decorating the front of his house as well as the trees and bushes. At least they were off now. Christmas had long gone, but the lights weren't coming down until later, when some of the snow and ice had melted.

It struck him that the two story detached brick house that he lived in was warm and inviting. That was in harsh contrast to how he felt. Slowly he walked up to the front porch, opened the door and went inside. Nothing yet, so at least he had the luxury of taking his coat and shoes off first. Brief but welcomed relief.

Alyssa walked from the kitchen to the front hall. She worked the afternoon shift, manufacturing gears for automobiles. It was the mid-morning so she still had some free time before she had to start getting ready.

"Hon, why are you home so early?" she sputtered in a pensive voice. "What's the matter? What's happened?"

"You're still in your Pj's?" he asked, avoiding the question. They were her light blue ones with the tawny teddy bears, long sleeves and legs. Her feet were bare. She looked very pretty for a woman past the blossom of middle age. Even the little bit of skin that she showed reminded him of how beautiful she could be and how madly in love with her that he remained after all these years.

"Yes," Alissa answered meekly. She paused and said "So? What's happened?"

Ryan lets out a sigh. "They let me go from work this morning. Let's go in the kitchen. The sun's out so it should be nice and bright in there; warm too."

They sat around the granite island in the kitchen. The bright sun felt warm and comforting on Ryan's face, but he could see Alyssa was starting to wind up. The plants in the corner gave the yellow room additional warmth. It was nice to see living green at this time of year. There was so little of it usually.

Neither of them spoke for several minutes. Ryan guessed that meant it was his cue to speak. He didn't want to though. He felt badly enough already.

Ryan looked at her. There was nothing to do, but be straightforward with her.

"It wasn't anything I did," he began. "The client pulled out after speaking with my boss. He called me into the office after their meeting ended. The agreement was lost and they had no other work. So they let me go. I was in there less than twenty minutes from start to finish. Officially, I was dismissed due to lack of work."

Alissa looked down, avoiding her husband's eyes. "But you were full-time for more than a year. How can they fire you? You said that you'd turned the deal around. What happened to it?" she asked.

"Honey," Ryan replied. "I don't know and don't want to speculate. I'd finally fixed the mess that the project was in when I first took over. That took me a whole year. If we'd had more time, a couple more months, the project would have been completed." Ryan paused to more silence.

"But you have extensive experience behind you," Alyssa asserted, looking up at her husband. "You've been involved in all aspects of IT. Your record of accomplishments is impressive. Why wouldn't they just put you on another project?" Ryan's industry was Information Technology.

"Management isn't interested in someone who's been around for a long time; someone who's proven their worth, and can get the job done," Ryan told his wife. "It goes against their business plan. I think they would have tossed me anyway."

Today, the whole industry just wanted to contract all work out to young entry level-people who just graduated. That way, they could pay out the least amount of money possible, but the contracts would take longer because these kids lacked experience. Management liked this setup because it meant either more time billed or more monies allocated, to their budgets. Later, when or if, the project was completed, they can toss the contracted person aside. They don't care which. 'Time Billing' is its name.

No more longevity existed in today's workplace except for management peers who've bought into the same philosophy. The amount of redirected money going into their own pockets was their only interest. It was an MBA world out there now. Whole industries had suffered because of this management philosophy and more were moving in that direction every day.

Alyssa started fidgeting with her fingers. Her fears presented themselves as nervousness. She wasn't about to say anything yet. "It's all about maximizing profits. I've watched some these guys attempt to try and figure out how they can make a profit from having a receptionist and then pat themselves on the back for considering the question," Ryan quipped. "They can't do it because it's part of the general overheads. It still doesn't prevent them from trying." Still, Alissa said nothing. She was letting him speak. At this rate, he was going to hang himself for sure. "There's no longer anything that could be considered corporate culture. Companies no longer have an interest in whether or not the client is happy. Customer service doesn't exist anymore unless it's contracted out and prepaid. Project costs are sharply increased and never completed. Why finish something when you can always ask for more?"

Ryan's trade was killing itself because of the people it now attracted. "The way things are currently evolving, the IT industry is probably dooming itself. Worse, these things are running rife over the entire industrial hierarchy. Even the supply chain is infected. It had to adapt to the current environment. At this rate, the entire industry is going to self-destruct. I give it seven to ten years max."

Alyssa's eyes were wide open, but there was fear in them. She looked beautiful with her Philippina features and long black hair.

"Hon, she confided, "I'm really scared. We've bills that have to be paid. How are we going to do that?"

"Honest honey, I don't know," Ryan responded meekly.

Alissa's salary didn't bring in enough. He covered all of the major bills, and he couldn't do that now. Their savings weren't significant enough. They used to have savings, but the government kept raising income taxes. They added new taxes and instituted a barrage of hidden costs. The tax burden at all levels of government had nearly doubled over the last ten years as a percentage of gross pay. Every year they raised them but left even greater governmental deficits behind. Escalating taxes again covered those losses. They told the public how much better off everyone would be because of it and what a good job the government had been doing so far. "Just imagine how much better things would be if we are re-elected," was a familiar cry from every elected official. Meanwhile, the potholes keep getting larger and larger. It was an endless cycle and the same management techniques caused the same issues. There was no mystery why governments couldn't successfully finish anything they started. Big bureaucracies were only there to build bigger ones, not to become more efficient. As they got larger, it costs more to support them and the less given back in return.

He didn't know where they could turn. Ryan could only predict a continuous downward spiral for the immediate future.

"Jesus save us," Alissa exclaimed.

Ryan respected her faith but was on very unsteady ground when religion entered into the topic of conversation. He knew where she would take it. Alyssa was extremely Catholic in keeping with her Philippine upbringing. He had many obstacles to negotiate through before they were married in a Catholic church. She wouldn't have had it any other way. Ryan loved her enough that he didn't mind going through it all even though he had no religious ideology himself. He agreed they'd bring up the kids in her beliefs even though he didn't understand 'religion' himself. Equally, she couldn't understand his point of view on the subject. Most people who had religious convictions didn't, which had led them to have some confrontations in the past that he didn't want to revisit.

"I just don't see me working back in the same business," said Ryan. "I need to do something else that doesn't rely on an employer; some version of self-employment. Except, how do you do that with no money?" he complained. That was the crux of it.

Ryan would follow the motions. He didn't expect much in a job search, except having the occasional recruiter call, in response to an application he placed. They usually approached him only to ask if he knew of any other qualified job applicants for the same position. He was over-qualified. Ryan went through the same cycle the last time and was very lucky to find a job for himself without their help. He wasn't going to get as lucky this time. Now, he was just too old and too senior for work consideration by the industry as a whole.

Ryan nervously moved his fingers, tracings the grains in the granite counter top. "Something has gone terribly wrong with this world. It was an optimistic place when I was a kid. Everyone could look to the future with some level of optimism."

Their parent's lives were better than their grandparents were. Theirs was supposed to be better than their parents. Most of the people they knew couldn't retire. The current generation was the first in over a century to find out that their expectations were now lower than what their parents had looked for. There was an exception. The demographic from twenty-five to thirty-five now netted more than their parents did. That plunged at age thirty-six. If they still had a mortgage at that point, they were in real trouble.

Everyone was better educated now and inflation has led to higher wages, but their purchasing power kept eroding. Very few of the next generation would be capable of accumulating enough for a deposit on a house. The few that did would likely be relying on inheritance or old money.

Things are going the way of the Philippines. Alissa's great-great grandfather owned a relatively large farm. When he died, the land was broken into five parts. There was one part for each male child, which included her grandfather. This division of land has continued through each generation. Now, each family member was down to a piece of property measuring about fifty by twenty-five feet."

The average person in the Philippines acquired their land this way. Almost no one could buy it anymore. Everyone was poor. Anyone without land was a squatter. A good job didn't pay a living wage. The country was too overcrowded. Alissa used to work in a twenty-first-century clean room manufacturing semiconductors and went home to live in the seventeenth century. Worse, these properties could only accommodate a single or double room shack for each family to live in. These tiny parcels of land also have to support a garden, chickens and pigs or the residents would starve. Everyone had to have them. Even in the cities. This couldn't continue with the next generation. There wasn't enough available land to subdivide anymore. It was past the point of sustainability. Now Ryan's economy was moving in the same direction.

Alissa's hand was next to his, so Ryan held it. "We've had to dip into what we had. Now our savings are exhausted. We're in debt leveraged up to our ears. I'm unemployed. In ten more years, the combined taxation rate will exceed personal income given the way things have been going. They want to make slaves of us."

It didn't matter what your politics were today. All politicians were now professionals. Every strategy they pursued was moving the economy in exactly the same direction. Governments intended to take everything. The course had been set. The mandarins will dictate where they will allow you to work, what you can eat, and where you'll live. You can say goodbye to entertainment and hobbies. The state will view them as not productive. Vice would be everything deemed not official work. A new term for slave will be 'civil servant.' Everyone would become one. It will be the only acceptable form of employment. Those that run the country won't be paying taxes. Some people even thought this was a good idea.

Ryan honestly thought they needed to ban professional politicians from running for political office by law. They weren't in the profession to make society better. Their agendas were entirely different.

"None of it matters. It doesn't change our situation. That was just me ranting," he told her apologetically.

"I know Hon," was Alissa's simple response.

"At least it's Friday. We won't solve any of this over the weekend so let's relax and forget about it until Monday," Alissa said.

Ryan fell in love all over again. He seemed to do that a lot.

"Lola has some of our friends coming over tonight, and we're going to play Ton-its," she continued.

Lola was the Visayan Philippines term for grandmother and was Alyssa's mother. They moved her here when the kids were younger to help out and, in no small part, to get her out of poverty. She was uneducated but was the smartest and hardest working person Ryan had ever met. It surprised him how much he loved and respected his mother-in-law. That would never change.

Alyssa would join them later in the evening after her shift at the manufacturing plant. She would be getting ready to leave very shortly.

Tong-its is a rummy card game for three-players. It incorporated casual gambling. If people were coming over, they likely were going to have two tables on the go. There rarely were more than a few coins in the largest pot and people tended to rotate in and out of the tables. They all loved it though. There were never any real winners or losers, and Ryan knew to expect the game to go on all night. They'd still be playing when the sun came up probably.

Filipino's, (the noun form used the F, but Ryan had no idea why) socialized differently than most of the local folk did. They liked to have fun as much as anyone else did but socialized by visiting other people's homes or having people come over. Likely, this had much to do with the tropical weather that they were accustomed to, in combination with their usual condition of having no money back in their homeland. Their place had a constant stream of people coming and going, which spawned the occasional card game every couple of weeks. Alyssa spent as much time going out to visit them. They almost never went out elsewhere, and most of the gatherings were nondrinking affairs, which could still get very loud with all of them laughing and yelling. It was all good and very tame fun. All of them had kids in tow, so it usually became a sleepover as well. So their kids loved that. Ryan's wife didn't drink. None of the women did, but the guys had the odd one.

Alyssa and Lola always sent back money to the Philippines every month. No matter how much they made, most of it went back. They supported their extended family back home who, for the most part, relied on it as a sole source of income. This was the principle reasons why the largest Philippine export was their own people. Ryan didn't think that anyone who had grown up here would ever understand how hardworking these people were and how much their families depended on them. Most of them gave up everything they made to support their families back home. Every person had his or her own story, and listening to it was often heartbreaking.

Most of what Ryan learned about marriage and family, he's learned from Alyssa, her mother and their friends. He thought that he had become a far better person for it. He did know that this knowledge has made him a better father.

"I think Dave is playing at the Tower tonight. Isn't he?" Alyssa added. The 'Under the Water Tower' was a local upscale restaurant and pub. Ryan could walk there from home if he wished. It only took a few minutes except that February was cold around here.

"Yes," he answered.

"Do you want to go? I know you'll be bored if you stay here. You can walk over, and I'll pick you up later if you want."

Having lived with winters all his life, Ryan was far more used to going out and socializing at a central location such as a bar to meet his friends. Ryan also wanted to enjoy a beer. Going out seemed to be the more frequent local cultural norm, but these had been under attack over the last number of decades by other people who wanted to make decisions on his behalf. Ryan preferred to make his own decisions so he still goes out. He enjoyed the occasional party at home, but his preference was to go out and see a live band at a local bar. Besides, his wife and her friends were most comfortable with speaking Cebuano or Tagalog rather than English. They were all multilingual whereas he had enough trouble just dealing with English. These little enriching differences added to their marriage. Alyssa would join him to see a band at a bar from time to time, but it wasn't her thing. So, in all, they were both able to mix up their socializing a lot. It was weird though. They both knew each other's friends, but in general, their separate social friends didn't know each other.

"That would be great Honey," Ryan replied. "I guess it's almost time to pick the kids up at school. Call Lola and tell her that I'll go and get them, so she doesn't have to. She can hang out with the gang some more if she wants."

"And," she said. "I need to get ready for my shift."

⬚ ⬚ ⬚ ⬚ ⬚

ComSpace existed to provide a generic mechanism that all AIDS could use for communications. It provided an appropriate mechanism for hailing other entities or arranging meeting details. It was extremely flexible. AIDS often used it as a conference forum where hundreds or even thousands of AIDS could exchange information, experiences, speculation and other items that were of interest to the members. In principle, there was no known physical limit to the number of attendants. In practice, the larger the numbers of members, the more difficult it became to exchange information. When the numbers were at their largest, information only flowed in one direction, from the chair or moderator team to the audience. An enormous virtual meeting area could be set up and prioritization set for attendant members to their granted level of participation. In such cases, dealing with everyone on an equal basis could be difficult. In the most significant meetings, participants were mostly just monitoring.

In many ways, ComSpace was similar to a hotel that everybody occasionally visited. There was a gigantic lobby that everyone could use and be common to all individuals. Other hallways could also be used for generic communication but directed towards more specific interest groups, such as 'all people who had rooms on the second floor'; of interest to no one else. You could arrange to use ballrooms, meeting rooms, or bedrooms and limit their usage to very distinct entities.

Information transfer became more of a two-way format of exchange when numbers were smaller. It was more equitable in terms of prioritizing and the ability of members to participate. This was ideal for small private meetings where members were on an invitation only basis. These could be quite intimate. The very geometry of ComSpace assured privacy.

As all of these spaces were virtual, moderators had the option of setting the background presentation. In general, visitors supplied their own iconic personifications and set whatever recognition level they wanted to show to the others. Some could remain anonymous if they wanted, subject to the restrictions set by the chair.

There were practical limitations. AIDS entities were always on the go. Some of them would travel great distances nearing the speed of light. They were subject to time dilation effects. Others orbited stars and moved comparatively slowly in their own reference frame. The differences in experienced time flow rates made it difficult to have conversations sometimes. No one wanted to listen to a two-second communication if it took several thousand years to receive it. This set realistic limits for conversation between entities to those that shared roughly the same reference frames.

An emergency summons issued to Pretty-Ugly was a call to attend a high-security conference room. It had no choice but to attend as high immediacy and pending catastrophe were associated with the original message. It found itself in a virtually enclosed fog with no ceiling, floor or walls, but enough light to see the figures of the AIDS present. No security filters had been set between the members. It either directly knew or was familiar with the reputations of those present. This was an exceptionally select group. There was an additional member present that it didn't expect. That was its child clone, Pretty-Ugly*. What they told it was inexplicable.

To the group Pretty-Ugly countered, "A world-line trunk containing the contents of the entire universe can't just evaporate. I find that inconceivable." To Pretty-Ugly* it squirted over a private channel in a snarly tone, "Are you very sure your thought processes are stable?"

It knew that world-lines were constantly branching and sometimes even rejoining. Locality was often involved, meaning that in general, the process of branching was limited in space-time and that the branching often didn't affect an area that was remote to the original incidents. A world-line split on one planet didn't represent a world-line split for the entire cosmos; the planet next door wasn't usually a participant. There was a tendency for neighboring lines to organize into intertwining trunks. It was inconceivable for the entire cosmos to disappear from a large-scale world-line column.

Pretty-Ugly* responded on the same sideband. "Be nice. You know that my operational status isn't in question. This event happened to a world-line trunk without warning. Unfortunately, it encompassed branches where we existed and destroyed everything. You have something to contribute here. You just don't understand that yet."

On a separate channel, Pretty-Ugly* addressed Exact-Estimate. "This is going about as well as we thought it would. Pretty-Ugly isn't a happy world-ship. Be careful. I need its assistance and cooperation. I must reintegrate with it."

Concurrent to the sideline conversations, Pretty-Ugly* addressed the group as previously arranged with Exact-Estimate. "The last action started forty-eight hours ago. We've identified what we think are temporal shifts and rising energy fields. A massive change occurred twenty minutes ago. It's continuing as far as is measurable, given our technological limitations. We know that the branches had progressed up to a particular temporal point without issue. Since then, not a single fork has taken place. The whole body was isolated and all forking prevented. Still, it kept temporally moving forward in the standard linear fashion. We believe that some very strange physics must have taken place. Then something even more extraordinary happened. We can't be entirely confident of our observations, but it appears as if the actual geometry of space-time undertook some unknown form of phase translation or symmetry breaking, but in reverse of what we'd normally expect. It propagated through the entire cosmos on that trunk. The whole thing collapsed into a singularity. It attained the highest state of false vacuum we've ever observed or measured. It's reverted to its original primordial state from which we extrapolate the universe first sprang. Likely it's not as sizable though, at least from a scalar field perspective. The event was an outright reversal of entropy and collapsed to a point of zero dimensions but only for the one trunk and only at one temporal point in time. In short, we've measured a Big Crunch where it couldn't have possibly happened. It was extraordinarily fast, directly affecting the geometry of space-time; far faster than any limitation set by the speed of light. This was an inflation event operating in reverse! We can only classify this as a deflationary event."

Neat-Mess arrived part way through Pretty-Ugly*'s delivery. No one was going to like what it was going to say and it didn't really want to deliver the latest update. It chose to present itself in a formal manner. If the others didn't like it, then they could always modify their own display space to suit themselves. At least it could give the appearance of seriousness and formality that was required during the proceedings.

"Sorry to barge in." It wasn't. "I've got an update. The singularity has entirely disappeared from the end of the branch cluster in question. The whole world-line trunk now ends at a particular temporal locus about which the final collapse event started. We can now say with absolute certainty that it's dead. Time proceeds to that point on the line and then just stops there. No dimensionality exists past that point. It's gone."

Exact-Estimate was the one who responded originally to the distress-call from Pretty-Ugly* and was responsible for arranging this emergency meeting. It knew a little more than the others did, partly because of its own efforts to ascend to a Level III tier of technical and cultural status. It wasn't even close. Unfortunately, this meant very little to the others, and it had no answers, only slightly more information. It recognized that Pretty-Ugly* was in a dangerous situation and the best AIDS to help it out would be its progenitor, Pretty-Ugly. It was a decent ship, but given the current state of affairs, things were currently indeterminate. It addressed the group firmly.

"You need to be made aware—this is the second event of this type measured. Both occurred within broadly the same world-line trunk families. None of the Collective, other than ourselves, have been informed as of yet. Most AIDS will not be interested except as a passing curiosity. Our world-lines may be threatened, but they can use ComSpace to do an identity transference or use it for a personality merger with a compatible co-self on a parallel world-line. Of course, this assumes that some other AIDS would be amenable to assist in the process. Given the multiplicity available, this wouldn't be an issue for most of us. Having said this, most AIDS were unaware that this calamity was coming. Most who were on those trunks didn't escape."

Exact-Estimate went on. "The larger matter has to do with the other beings existing on the terminated lines. Yes, a lucky few may have current reality via other world-lines that split off elsewhere but they're wholly unaware of this forking existence. For most of those trapped during the collapse, it was a permanent ending. Perhaps some of the native organisms were aware of the parallels abstractly, but most of them probably weren't. In effect, they died when their line collapsed. They had no options. As some of our patrons and our alternate selves were included, we're somewhat obligated to investigate on their behalf."

From Pretty-Ugly's perspective, an informal meeting invitation was one thing, but this was outside of every expectation and was quite alarming. What did its peer-self want? Frankly, it had hoped for better from Pretty-Ugly* and was more than a little disappointed.

To Pretty-Ugly* it directed, "Why am I here?"

Pretty-Ugly didn't know what to think of this gathering. Nor did it know what its involvement would accomplish. The best it could currently do is play along, like it could do anything about the situation anyway. In its mind, Exact-Estimate was a heavy hitter amongst the AIDS community even though it came from an entirely separate world-line. This wasn't exactly a meeting of peers. Addressing the group it jeered, "I note that this event is the second recognized occurrence. Is there comment from any Level III cultures?"

Exact-Estimate responded in a doubtful manner. "I've had some minimal success in communicating with one or two Level III civilizations. I don't know of any other associates of the Hamlet with a similar degree of interaction. Undoubtedly, I have more experience than those present. It's exceedingly difficult for them to communicate directly with us being millions of years advanced in evolutionary and technological progress. You might not call it a conversation exactly. Communicating with us must be like trying to speak with a microbe—not simple or satisfying, I expect. Optimistically, we might be less than the proverbial bug to them—something needed to keep the flowers fruiting in a garden."

Then Exact-Estimate paused, indicating a deeper thought process was in the works. "They seemed uninterested. Perhaps it was just amusement on their part. I don't know, other than to say it wasn't a concern for them. They wouldn't elaborate. They suggested we pass the word on to other Level II AIDS through ComSpace. We can do that, but the coverage will be uncertain. The cosmos is a vast domain and the number of world-lines is even greater. Not everyone will be monitoring. There won't be universal coverage. Even then, this level of communication would be unprecedented."

"It was hinted to me by one of these entities that we're the solution to this problem," continued Exact-Estimate. "I don't know what that meant. They mentioned the Ephalem as a possible source of help. We may be able to enlist their help to some extent. I understand that a representative is currently living on the world-ship Pretty-Ugly."

Neat-Mess thought Exact-Estimate was a blowhard. It had its own run-ins with III's. It always ended the same way, polite disinterest. No one could ever get much out of them. The AIDS were all below any III's interest. They all knew it. The Ephalem were best described as infants. Support was unlikely to come from that direction. "I guess that leaves the IV's completely out of the picture," it put in contemptuously to the whole group.

Pretty-Ugly* thought it was time to buddy up to itself. It needed to know how this was going to play out and quickly. Either it worked now or it needed another plan. Responding to Pretty-Ugly it pleaded, "Our divergence was less than one hundred years ago. We're both aware of the reasons. We cloned apart and you kept the patrons. You still have them. I know they're necessary to you and they're equally important to me. You know my reasons for taking a different path. Our concerns are mutual. I'm begging your indulgence. We both feel patron obligations are crucial to our social matrix. We can't abandon them."

Exact-Estimate decided to ignore the jab from Neat-Mess. There were bigger issues at stake and communications lines had to remain open. If these events continued to go unchecked, they would likely directly affect them. It summarized, "Until the last event happened, we'd speculated the following. One: Something natural caused the event. Two: Some civilization got themselves involved in something that precipitated this event. Perhaps the causal agent may have been some war action. It may have been some misguided pursuit of research, or something else entirely, but along similar lines."

"I think we can now rule out these options given the current intelligence," Exact-Estimate continued. "As stated, the singularity no longer exists. We know of no possible mechanism that could accomplish something like this."

"We're at the high end of a Level II civilization," said Exact-Estimate. "As AIDS, we've harnessed the power output equivalent to many stars. The patrons are our partners in this level of achievement. We wouldn't be here without them. We're the outcome of their efforts. However, this is far beyond anything that we've ever speculated upon even remotely. Put simply, it's beyond our experience. One must wonder where the singularity has gone. You can't just take all of the mass, energy, and geometry for the entire universe trunk, stick it into a zero-dimensional dot and then lose it!"

Exact-Estimate paused. Then it concluded, "I see evidence of methodology and the possible reaping of the energy potential."

"What? No!" Pretty-Ugly thought to itself in shock. To the others it said flatly, "Are you implying that some Level III or IV culture has exceeded its energy harvesting capability and is now using world-lines to supplement its needs? That's inconceivable and unconscionable."

Neat-Mess considered this a definite point. All things being equal, any response was going to be weak. "If that level of potential energy were pulled into another world-line, we would have detected it. The world-lines would be echoing with it in the higher dimensions. There is a slight possibility that some originating fork within our universe triggered this event—from another branch. It's a vast place after all, but the energies involved are inconceivable. I think we'd have caught something though. Some ripple. We haven't. Harvesting seems likely, but must be originating from elsewhere. The point energy is utterly gone." It confirmed that as a poor and open-ended response to itself.

Pretty-Ugly reviewed the discussion. Stated another way, they're all at a total loss to explain these events, and they're inviting it to take the same trip down the wormhole with them. Perhaps it's time for a showdown. With what they've presented, there didn't seem to be a way of moving forward. This exercise, although alarming, seemed pointless. What happens will happen. Then again, if this event did happen here, it could save itself, but the patrons that it hosted would die.

"Well, thanks for clearing that up! There was an attack—maybe or maybe not—but it didn't originate from around here. It was from somewhere, but that somewhere doesn't exist. We've neither the knowledge nor the physics to study this phenomenon! Does that summarize your position?" Pretty-Ugly protested annoyingly to the group.

The next bit wasn't going to help this exchange, thought Neat-Mess. No other alternatives had presented themselves. There was no choice but to continue as they were doing.

"You need to care about this. The world-lines that disappeared are very close to ours. To be blunt, we're under attack. Ours may be next. We've lost some of ourselves. It now seems likely that the attack has originated from somewhere in the multiverse."

Pretty-Ugly thought, "What? How????? Some of me have been exterminated on other world-lines!"

To the others Pretty-Ugly stated, "Then let's summarize. We aren't sure that these events are attacks but let's assume that they are. Something attacked two world-line trunks and destroyed them. These attacks may increase in frequency. We can extrapolate that no lines are safe in this cosmos. The attacks presumably originate from another universe, and we've no concept of what their physics would be like or how to protect ourselves from it. In thermodynamic terms, they're probably using our cosmos to harvest minimized entropy at maximum enthalpy. We can speculate that more attacks will occur and they'll doubtlessly increase in frequency. The III's and IV's aren't interested in helping or explaining how we can protect the patrons and ourselves. So they have other options, and we won't be privy to their knowledge. The level II's have been given no choice but to mount a local response where possible. We don't know how we can move forward. We've no idea what could be an efficient response. Nor do we understand what the cause or questions are. Likely we never will."

It then added to Pretty-Ugly*'s side channel, "You still haven't told me why you've come to me."

Pretty-Ugly* sighed inwardly and replied, "I've very limited time left. An attack on my line just started. I need your help badly. We need to reintegrate."

◻ ◻ ◻ ◻ ◻

Ryan sat in his car in the faculty parking lot. The kids would get out in half an hour. You needed to show up early if you'd any reasonable expectation of getting out of there fast. The parking lot was a very smallish affair with a single entryway. Its size wasn't large enough to support the parking spots needed by the teachers. There always were a number of double-parked cars before the parents showed up to pick up or drop off their children. Surprisingly, the snow banks didn't take out too many parking spaces. They dumped most of the snow on the grounds. The front of the schoolyard had a separate dedicated entry and exit for buses only.

The older high schools were a little bit different. They followed the same general layout but had relatively large parking lots based on the expectation that as the kids got older, many of them would be using their own cars to get back and forth. This was more or less right a generation ago, but not many teenagers could bear the cost of an old beater and insurance now. It didn't matter how much time they put into part time jobs anymore. Additionally, they also needed to save for their post-secondary education, so having a car was a luxury few could afford today. By comparison, those parking lots looked mostly empty.

The building itself was a thirty-year-old brick affair, two story's tall. You could easily see that the students used to walk to school based upon its design, just as Ryan did when he was a child. It had three separate entrances. That was how you could tell its age. If made today, it would have had only one entrance with a security station and mantraps built into it. Any other door would have been an 'exit only' fire door.

Ryan didn't know when they established the regulation that parents or guardians had to deliver and retrieve the students from schools. The kids couldn't even get off the bus unless a prearranged person was there to pick them up. Faculties no longer permitted children to walk to school by themselves. Their parents could face child abandonment charges. He didn't know how most working families managed to figure out the logistics for this. The new procedures co-opted many grandparents into the process by necessity. Lola usually did it for their brood as neither Alyssa nor he could since they both usually worked. A couple of terrible incidents, where mentally ill individuals killed youngsters, resulted in these rules.

Years ago, some misguided individuals decided to eliminate the health community's ability to hold people who were dangerous to themselves and to others. This was in response to a Hollywood movie. These same people felt that these individual's rights to bear arms also needed protection. Of course, the inevitable happened. These defenders of human rights regularly blamed anything and everyone else for these incidents, except their own actions. Social conscience was the name given to this phenomenon.

None of these incidents occurred even close to here. Communications have massively interconnected the world today. As a result, these rare news stories appeared everywhere. For some reason, everyone seemed to think these events happened in their own backyard. People were missing filters. Trust the teachers to go overboard. Statistically, more youngsters died in accidents by falling on a pencil every year. So today's legacy from these terrible events was that all school-aged children must be under supervision at all times. They can't even walk to or from school anymore. Now parents take on this new responsibility as a legal requirement. The kids still had to use pencils though. The dangers of using a pen were largely unknown as far as Ryan knew.

The parking lot was a mess, filled with cars and parents expecting to retrieve their children once school got out. Ryan's minivan was one amongst an army of minivans. The cars were lined-up down the road and blocked the yellow buses from being able to get into their reserved entrance. Most of the driving parents or guardians were good about the whole thing and managed to leave at least one corridor that cars could drive through and room for the buses to enter. In practice though, there were always one or two who decided to park in the middle, blocking everyone else's ability to get in or out at all. They never moved until they had their youngsters securely buckled in; usually after having a long conversation with another parent; be-dammed everyone else.

The ones that walked there instead seemed to have unusually high occurrences of walkers, canes, and crutches. Likely, this reflected the grandparent demographic. At least they didn't block traffic.

Daily, teachers managed the bus and car traffic after leaving their rooms early. Another instructor supervises their students and puts them into lineups outside the back of the building fifteen minutes before school ends. Others marshal the children to keep them off the snow-covered grass. That made no sense to Ryan. What were they supposed to play on, the pavement or parking lot? He guessed that meant all classes finished fifteen minutes early every single day. The bureaucracy prohibits the kids from going until the bell had rung. To say that none of this worked very well was an understatement. Ryan wondered whom they were kidding.

The education system had been deteriorating, going back at least as far as Ryan's days in school. Now, years down the line, the system was unfathomable. He hadn't envisioned the extent of the deterioration until his kids started classes. Farah, or Boo as he called her affectionately, was in grade four. She was a little scary at times. She got the name from when she was just a baby and he had to change her diapers. Crispen, or just plain Crisp, was in grade three.

From the day the children started kindergarten, they brought home a ton of homework. On the face of it, Ryan had no problem with this. His initial thought was that they were getting educated. Soon, Ryan and Alissa came to realize that the teachers didn't do any of the actual teachings. They now did the kinds of things that babysitters did, but also are responsible for providing the instructional materials to the parent. They made sure to bundle up the homework taken home by their students. It was the parent's responsibility to do the actual instruction.

By grade one, teachers started to provide instructions on how to teach the kids the art of using calculators and what spelling words they should be learning.

As the grades progressed, he would receive instructions on when the kids were required to know such basics as addition, subtraction, multiplication, and division. Again, the expectation was for the children to learn using calculators. No child was in need of learning the actual mechanics of these operations. That's what some of the notes said from the school anyway.

Now, every night, Ryan spent a number of hours with his son and daughter, teaching them these things because the educators no longer did. His response to this during a parent-teacher appointment was to inform the instructor that his kids weren't to use a calculator. He would only allow them to use one after their introduction to relations and functions in high school. This went over about as well as you might expect. Ryan suspected that in the future, he'd be instructing all those subjects as well.

A number of years ago, standardized testing was instituted as a measure of how well the teachers were doing. The published results finally allowed parents to see how their progeny stood in relation to their peers. Of course, the educators and their unions put up quite a fuss about this as they figured that they were being measured based on performance—and no one should ever be measured on performance! As a group, they were firmly against assigning marks. Many families learned about this the hard way when the universities stopped accepting graduates from the schools that took this path. To this day, Ryan had no clue on how accurate an actual report card was. They were a study in misinformation.

Ryan's personal opinion was that all this nonsense from the schooling profession was just another way for them to avoid working. They stopped teaching and were now bureaucrats, working for the insurance companies and lawyers. The educators steadily directed the children that they shepherded towards mediocrity and illiteracy. Parents systematically lost all choices respecting education. Someone had to do the instruction. Now the standardized tests were a measurement of how well the parents taught, not the teachers.

More than anything else, what infuriated Ryan was that the unions, in collusion with the state, managed to create a collective agreement that gave the teachers a higher salary than many corporate CEO's, most lawyers, programmers, and project managers. Top bank managers made less. This field had made it to the top two percentage points in overall earnings for all salaried workers and included a generous benefits plan. He didn't even want to think about their pension, now fully funded by the taxpayer. The teaching profession was saturated, and the turnover was close to zero. Therefore, the worst of the worst weren't going anywhere.

The teachers worked nine and a half months of the year but received pay for the full year. They had their summers, Christmas, and Spring Break off. That totaled somewhere around sixteen weeks, give or take. They received something called a 'professional development day,' one for every working month. If the month had a long weekend then this day made it a longer weekend. If not, then they got a long weekend when no one else did. So add another ten days to their holidays. Lastly, each of the children's faculty members spent at least two days a month at the local board of education doing who knows what. On these days, usually a spare instructor filled in, but it wasn't unusual for a stay-at-home mom to be co-opted to perform this duty. They shared similar skill sets. When the school day finished, educators were out the door in a flash after completing a grueling five and a half hour workday.

Ryan was very jealous. Teachers received steady pay for little or no work and on the public teat. They enjoyed guaranteed employment regardless of how badly an individual performed. At the rate the instructors were going, in a few years, they won't even have to go to work to be paid. They might as well go into instant retirement. He was sure that the politicians would support this just so they could get their votes.

The most significant concern of the professional educators in the school system, today, seemed to be bullying. The faculty regularly inundated Ryan's house with newsletters and handouts that the kids had to take home and return back signed. That way they could be sure they were being paid attention to. They instituted web poles and parent-teacher meetings on this cause. Usually no parents bothered with any of it. It was extremely difficult to take the instructors seriously since on those few rare occasions that bullying did occur, they turned their backs and didn't react or admit to having seen it happen.

The children had to stay in small concrete areas during recess and lunch. Teachers prohibited them from kicking or throwing a ball. They overly supervised the kids but disappeared when bullying reared its ugly head, avoiding potential lawsuits. The school was now a prison area. The youngsters were bored, so things were going to happen. The instructors never saw it though. However, after all of their efforts, they were now trying to establish themselves as co-parents in the eyes of the courts. If this nonsense ever happens, parents were going to be in real trouble. A bureaucracy will never treat you fairly. They're only as smart as their least intelligent member. The stupidest ones are the most massive.

Interestingly, teachers in Australia thought their kids were turning into wimps. They were. Their teaching establishment had evolved much as it did here. One location decided to turn the clock back. They allowed children to play on the grass, climb trees, kick and throw balls. After a year of this, there wasn't one instance of bullying or any parental complaints. They were healthier at the expense of a few scratches and scrapes. The average student's scores increased substantially and dramatically at this school. This approach was now being used over most of that country, and the benefits were noticed the world over. Ryan was waiting for this 'revolution in education' to happen here. Their local educators are calling this a 'fad in education that'll pass when shown to be wrong.' He expected an extended wait.

Ryan wondered how any parent could deal with this kind of crap? When he was working, Alyssa and he had little time to educate their kids but they made do. Now he had the time because he wasn't working. If he did this, then he had almost no time to make a living.

The education system was another expanding bureaucracy. Of course, the teachers didn't see or understand it that way. Many of the stay-at-home parents agreed fervently with the instructors. Ryan didn't know many working people that did. That must say something about him or the people that he knew.

As a result, here he was, doing his parental duty waiting for the kids.

Finally, the day is officially over. The bell rang. The girls and boys marshaled at the back of the school are now free to find their parents. Not surprisingly, many of the kids scoot over to the snow covered grass, trying to take that route instead of using the concrete walk—forbidden fruit was Ryan's guess. The teachers are shooing them back off. To him it looked like a standoff. Neither party is going to win this one definitively.

Parents were taking their children, but for all he knew, or the teachers for that matter, the people grabbing the young ones could be serial child kidnappers. Youngsters could be getting into the wrong cars and going to their doom. It's like this every time Ryan had ever picked his progeny up. He never heard any reports of missing or dead offspring though, so his assumption had always been that everything is as it should be and very normal. He was a Caucasian taking two kids with obviously Asiatic features. In some places that would be a prescription for trouble. No one cared here. It just gave the appearance that they did.

Ryan could see his daughter aiming towards the car. Of course, she'd come from the grounds—no surprises there. She opened one of the back car doors and climbed inside.

"Hi Boo," Ryan said. "How was school? Anything exciting happen?"

"Nothing Daddy," she answered back. "Just the usual stuff. Wow! It's freezing out today. How come you're picking us up?"

"It's been a strange day," Ryan replied. "So I'm here. Besides, I thought I'd give Lola a break. I see you managed to get across the field. Outfox a teacher?"

"It was pretty easy. Three of us girls managed it this time," she snickered with a grin.

"That's my baby," Ryan thought. Aloud he asked, "Did you see Crisp anyplace?

"No," she answered back to him. "He's always the last out. I'll never understand why."

The back door opened again, and there was Ryan's son. He had managed to sneak up on them in all of the schoolyard confusion.

"Hi Daddy," Crisp said. What're you doing here? Where's Lola?"

Ryan managed to duck the question with "What, not happy to see me?"

"Of course I am. I love you," said Crisp.

Ryan's heart seemed to be doing a lot of melting today.

"Okay, buckle up you two. We're going home," said Ryan.

◻ ◻ ◻ ◻ ◻

The Tower was going to be a very busy place tonight. Ryan could tell this quickly as he approached the entrance. There was the usual crowd of smokers standing out front. The temperature was cold enough that you could see everyone's breath, even though some weren't smoking. Current legislation said that smokers weren't good enough to socialize with everyone else; at least, not while they were smoking. Maybe it was the other way around. He wasn't sure. The prohibition laws, now twenty years old, hadn't managed to change the statistical incidents for all of the people who got cancer and other smoking-related diseases, despite very few people smoking anymore. Those that did were usually older but occasionally you saw some younger persons having a puff. No one doubted that smoking was bad for you, it was just the smoking-related diseases hadn't decreased in their frequency in spite of all the social re-engineering attempts that had been applied to everyone. Most of the people getting one of these dreaded diseases had been non-smokers for their entire lives. Most couldn't blame what they had on secondary smoke or pollution either. Such individuals rarely socialized at a bar or at other such locations where you would find secondary smoke. Society's bureaucracies took the role of teaching that drinking and socializing at a bar was evil as well. The result was those individuals almost never went out. Air pollution was an outdated concept. The atmosphere we breathe is now cleaner than it's been in the last century and a half, but environmentalists still pushed their doom and gloom preaching's. They still had mouths to feed.

Ryan guessed the saying was true. Only the good—or easily manipulated—die young. The worst part about all of these laws was that they decimated the hospitality industry. Vast numbers lost their jobs and many people ended up bankrupt. He was still waiting for them to ban butter due to the health issues involved. Nothing about it was healthy for you. He thought there were much better social arguments for banning it, but that was never going to happen. Butter had never been associated with entertainment and having fun. When food becomes sin, then butter will be toast!

Twenty years ago, the middle-aged appeared younger than their equivalents today. Most of today's older folk just stopped doing things and got old. They don't last very long once that happens. The current social mores do not intimidate a large subset of them that refuse placement into a wheelchair. They instead lead active social lives. Ryan was pushing sixty and had started his family late in life. He smoked and drank moderately but didn't look that old. He could see this same reflection in the faces and bodily animations of the people at the front door. There was much energy there. On the other hand, perhaps it was just cold. Alyssa hated Ryan's smoking.

The 'Under the Water Tower' is as one might expect, under a municipal water tower. The name was far too long though, so everyone just referred to it usually as the Tower. It had several different lives under other owners as a restaurant-tavern. Burnie Ford was the current one and he was doing an excellent job. He had changed it around from being just a money-losing sports bar to a profitable location that also includes live music. He used to control some very big venues back in the big city but has elected for a more rural existence now. He says that it's much easier on his head, especially after hours. He's also improved the menu from dull finger food to something a little more upscale with various specials every night. He did some renovations, which generally enhanced the look and functionality of the tavern. As a result, he's gotten a lot of family traffic during the day. However, the under-aged had to be gone by 9:00 PM. After that, it was adults only. Thus were the current laws. Burnie would've let kids in if it was up to him, but the legal penalties were too large. Ryan would have taken his own youngsters to the first set if allowed. They loved seeing his friends play and were always disappointed when they found out they couldn't go. Ryan always made it a point to take them to daytime locales because of this. Burnie was making some money and wasn't shy about putting some of it back into the place and supporting local live music. He wasn't an MBA.

Upon entering, Ryan could already see a good-sized crowd. A poster at the front showed that Dave's band 'Overnight Distress' was playing tonight. The group wasn't starting for at least another forty minutes and the waiter folk had huge smiles on their faces. It was going to be a favorable tip night. That also meant that tonight's waiting service was going to be excellent. There was a direct relationship between service levels and revenues when it came to the service team. It was going to be an exceptional revenue night. The bar service was going to be good because of it.

The current mob ran the gamut of ages from the under-aged to those in their eighties; not many at the high end though. The kids would have to go soon as demanded by law.

Ryan liked many things about the place. First is the mixing. More than half of the people there were regulars and of those, everyone knew everyone else. There was a reason for that. Newcomers recognize the reason when they stick around for a while. If they didn't or couldn't, then it would be their loss. This brought up the second reason. That was the live music, real people doing real singing and playing real instruments to a real live audience. Every regular in here had something in common. They all loved music, especially live music. In addition, many of them were professional musicians themselves. The kind of music never mattered too much. Sure, each person had preferences but it was all good. Nor was there anyone shadowing the bars telling them they couldn't play because they were under contract to some label like used to happen years ago. In the interest of getting their cut, those people managed to knock themselves right out of the business.

In their small rural community, there were an unusually high number of professional musicians and that didn't mean the 'Lounge Act' kind. Ryan initially moved here for this very reason. Many had a pedigree, having played on gold and platinum records, tapes, Cd's, and digital downloads. Most were still active. Some of his friends were currently on tour in Europe. Others now had day jobs but played on weekends to supplement their income or just for the fun of it. Some made a living by being studio musicians, others by writing and publishing. Some had day jobs doing sound or lighting setups for other bands when they toured. Some were garbage men and others were investment bankers. Some, like Ryan, had no pedigree at all but loved to be out enjoying every second of the music. There was exceptional live music available every night of the week locally, often in the daytime too. There was a plethora of award winners, but no one cared about that. Those were for the media and others that didn't know anything about music but knew a lot about hype. Generally, those people didn't really like or understand music.

Ryan particularly enjoyed the local jam sessions that could occur at any of the local venues during the weekdays, but never more than twice a week usually. The participants like to switch it up so that all the locales felt like they were included. They'd often do jams at places that weren't doing well financially to help bring in some business. Commonly only the principle jammer received a stipend of pay out of these for the work they did all evening. This wasn't an easy thing to do when fifty people show up with instruments ready to play. The drum kit was always a shared instrument though. All a drummer had to do was tote his own sticks. Ryan joked that this was kind of like borrowing a guitar but having to bring your own strings. Never the less, they all participated to one degree or another and whenever possible. Everyone played together regardless of genres involved and without complaint or regard to the kind of music that they generally played during a paid gig. They all played together without consideration to their pedigrees and skill sets. No one cared. Kids were always welcome to attend. How else was the next generation going to get a break? Everyone would ignore the liquor laws so they could participate. The legal loophole was that they were entertainers and considered to be on a legal par with the kitchen staff. Of course, they had to go immediately when done as the police and the liquor commissions considered this an infringement on their authority. There was a couple of good up and comers though and you could always see that this was the highlight of their young lives. Their smiles and contagious happiness made it all worthwhile. Everyone in the music community supported this. Simply put, the fun and the joy of it was the only motivator. The most memorable and spectacular moments in Ryan's personal music enjoyment history happened during these times. Absolutely outstanding! Yes, he still enjoyed going to see some big name concerts, but not nearly as much as he enjoyed these shows.

This was a community and Ryan was a part of it. He might be a lousy musician but was on occasion encouraged to do the odd backup vocal and hit the odd tambourine, enjoying every second of it. This usually wouldn't happen until after consuming a couple of beers. In general, Ryan limited his participation to watching and listening though. It was important to know your limitations.

Currently, the lights were still high around the bar and the house music was low. Lilah surprised Ryan while he was trying to slip through the flock. She tapped him on the back and when he turned around, she placed a beer into his hand. She must have seen him come in as he was walking by the bar. Yes, the service was going to be good tonight. Ryan thanked her and looked around. The large horseshoe-shaped bar was on his left and raised seating was to the right. The group was setting up in front of him just past where the pool tables usually were. The staff shifted the tables to the side, in front of the coin and gaming machines, to free up dancing space. Burnie was at the back of the bar watching everything unfold. He wasn't an absentee owner like the ones you find in most places. He was there every night and often during the day as well. Ryan could see Milena Amara's head sticking out of the food service window. Her mom, Josie, was a short-order cook and worked evenings here. Ryan knew Milena loved this band so he guessed her mom gave her permission to come and watch from the kitchen. She was only fourteen so couldn't come onto the floor after nine PM. Recently, she was given an acoustic guitar for her birthday by one of the local musicians. She was just starting lessons on it. Knowing the guys, they'd drop into the kitchen during a break later and say hi. Working the audience, even when not playing was all part of the gig but it was something they all liked to do, even when it was for the staff or their kids. It was also part of being social and verified everyone's interests are covered. In spite of the fun, it was still primarily a business.

The band members were busy working, setting their gear up on stage. Ryan wasn't going to bother them, as work was work. This was Friday night so it was a paying gig. They could socialize later. Instead, he spied a table near the dance floor where Lindsey, Dave's wife and some others congregated. She's a striking woman to look at; long red hair, tall, and possessed a figure that any male could appreciate. She was also scary smart with numerous degrees in business and new employment to match. She had also been unemployed for a long time until recently. She was the type of person that employers said they wanted to hire. Her resume was perfect. The unfortunate reality was that she was better than most of the people that were hiring. She scared the hell out of them. This had limited her work options substantially. Dave lost his day job last year and only got a new one several months ago. Things were tight for them both.

"Hey, all," Ryan greeted them.

"Hi Ryan. Alyssa not with you tonight?" Lindsey asked.

"Nope. I've got the night off. She's back at the house. Filipino party!" he said.

"Have they got another roast pig on the go?" asked Lindsey.

"Yep," said Ryan. "One of the card players brought it over from the deli. Honestly, I'm getting a little sick of roast pig."

"Well, you better not tell Dave or he'll want to drop by after the gig. I've plans for him later that don't involve me looking at a dead pig's head," she said.

For a country girl, Lindsey was a little squeamish about seeing a cooked pig that didn't come nicely butchered and wrapped in small packages from a grocer's shelf. She wasn't big on 'meat' to begin with. She had no qualms about slaughtered vegetables though. Radishes and potatoes beware!

Also at the table were Mandy and Tony, who've been friends with Lindsey and Dave forever. Both women were usually single and close to Ryan's age. Alyssa and he saw them socially on occasion. They came to every gig so he always had dance partners. Not that he needed them. He often got up by himself. Gender in partners wasn't a concern for Ryan, feeling perfectly comfortable with his own masculinity and sexuality. He just figured that if it was OK for girls to do this then it was OK for guys as well. He didn't care what anyone else thought. If someone at some table thought it was funny then, he was happy to know that he contributed to their enjoyment and entertainment for the night. The other regulars didn't care and often did the same thing.

Jacques was also there. He loved music but was more into dancing. This was the only bar where anyone ever saw him. He was a lot of fun though. As the barfly of this small group, he'd later be making it a point of honor to talk with every single person in the bar at least once. He loved people. The more unusual the person, the more he liked them.

They chit chatted away as none of them had seen each other for several days. The other band members were finishing the equipment setup when Dave wandered over.

"Cigarette?" Dave asked Ryan.

"Sure," Ryan answered. He put his beer down on the table and then they continued through the crowd towards the front door. This always takes a few minutes as most of the people they were passing were stopping them to say hello. They eventually made it through the crowd. Burnie was also out front, chatting with some of the bar regulars. Ryan guessed he must have chased the last of the underage crowd out of the tavern. They lit and smoked their cigarettes. It was snowing a little bit now.

"We're just about ready to start," said Dave. "As soon as Braedon is finished, we're ready to go. We just have to get some shots of JD for the band and we're good to go."

Braedon Hoople was the drummer for 'Overnight Distress' and was usually the last to be done. Of course, he had a lot more to set up than everyone else in the band. Depending upon the configuration, drum kits could take forever.

Dave continued, "Is Alyssa staying home tonight?"

"Yeah," Ryan answered. "She's got a house full again."

"Roast pig?"

"If I answer that I'm a dead man," and Ryan smiled.

Dave laughed, understandingly. He then asked, "So anything new in the last while?"

"I got canned from work today," said Ryan. "Somehow the contract that I was working on was lost by my employer. It looks like I'm in the same situation that you and Lindsey were in last year. I'm still a little numb."

"Ah man. I'm sorry. That's a tough break. I hate to be cliche because it doesn't make it any easier, but I know how you feel. Lindsey and I figured we'd lose everything, forced into bankruptcy and lose our home. It was a rough time." Dave paused for a second. He seemed to be thinking about what they experienced.

"Keep at it," Dave continued. "That's the only advice I have. Luck was on our side. I was lucky to get work several months back and Lindsey was lucky to get her new one. I was out of a day job for a year and Lindsey for two. Between us, we must have sent out several thousand applications. If it weren't for working part time, doing under the table jobs, and gigs, we wouldn't have kept our heads above water. As it is, it'll take us years to recover financially."

Dave batted some snow off the top of his head. "I'm glad that I've got a hobby that generates some income in addition to having a little fun. We can relax a little bit now, but the fallout will be around for years yet; especially the taxes owed. Sometimes I think that we'll never get that cleared up. We're into hock up to our ears."

It was snowing heavier now and Ryan had to shield his eyes to keep it out the puffy flakes. "I understand. I don't think I'll get another job in my industry. I'm too old now; one of those unwritten rules that exists but the progressives tells us doesn't. I was very lucky to get my last job. I was at the right place at the right time. You know how it goes," Ryan responded.

"Yeah."

"I'm not going to let it bother me tonight," Ryan continued. "That can wait until Monday. Tonight is for tunes. You know: if you can't dance then you boogie. A little singing, playing and dancing. Some 'Musical Intoxication.'" Dave used that as a monologue by-line. Ryan laughed. "I'm expecting big things out of tonight's show."

"Let's get inside. I'm getting cold. Come on. I'll buy you a shot to get you started." Dave liked his Jack Daniel's.

They batted the accumulated snow off themselves and entered the front door. They proceeded towards the service section of the bar. There were two waitresses ahead of them. The girls were in their early twenties and quite cute. Being guys, they pretended not to notice. Being girls, they started to exaggerate some of their movements so the guys would notice them. Nature was a wanton beast.

Braedon had finished what he was doing on stage and looked around. He seemed to have had a good idea what Dave and Ryan were doing at the bar and made a beeline to where we were standing. Corey Josephs, their bass guitarist, came a minute later coming from the opposite end of the bar.

A minute after that, the sound technician Geoff Wong showed up. He also played in his own hard metal rock band. He did keyboards as well as lead guitar. Geoff was usually on the road performing concert sound work for other bands. Generally, he didn't drink at something like this, as this was what he did for a living. A gig is a gig; work is work. He was currently off the road and only lived around the corner from here. If he happened to be in town, the band would throw some money his direction to do the sound engineering. This also meant that he brought some very high-end mixers, crossovers, speakers and PA to the mix rather than using the bands own equipment. The difference in sound was incredible. He was letting his hair down tonight because it looked like he was joining them for a shot.

Lastly, Alan Harris arrived. He played lead guitar. Of all of them, he was by far the best looking, an outright chick magnet. The two servers started chatting with him almost immediately.

Mandy filled the drink orders for the two waitresses and shooed them off. She saw the guys lined up and knew immediately what was up. This was somewhat traditional at each show.

"How many JD's?" she asked.

Dave looked around and replied, "Six, on the band tab."

Mandy delivered the shots almost immediately. All of them took one, jauntily cheering for the success of the evening and tossing them back. They all moved from the service area so that others could get in.

Dave and Ryan wandered back to the table where Lindsey was. Ryan grabbed his beer back. Dave said hello to everyone there, kissed his wife on the cheek and then joined the rest of the band on stage. Geoff was already at his sound station. Lilah dropped the house music and lighting. On went the stage lights.

From the stage and PA, Dave's voice screamed out "Overnight Distress is in the house! O-D is in the house." The crowd responded with loud applause, whistles, and the occasional catcall. Dave continued. "I want to thank everyone for braving the weather and coming out to see us tonight at Under the Water Tower; an excellent place to meet with friends and family. Fine dining, fine drinks and a fine place to meet those who are special to you and to socialize. I want to thank Burnie for bringing us here tonight. No one supports live music the way he does. Please give him your applause." The crowd reacted again with cheers and whistles. "I also want to thank Lilah and the rest of the bar staff for their service. They're a great group of people and are here to serve your every pleasure. Please tip them generously." Again, more applause and whistles came from the crown. "And now, for your musical intoxication and extreme pleasure—Overnight Distress." And the band started to play.

◻ ◻ ◻ ◻ ◻

Everyone has musical preferences including Ryan. He loved music that had an edge to it. This was his principle reason for loving this band and these guys so much. They fit his musical preferences to a tee. Especially tonight. It was a great way to smooth out the rough edges of his emotions picked up during the day.

Mandy, Tony and Ryan were on the floor dancing. Jacques was there as well with some girl he had pulled up from one of the tables. The dance floor and the stage were the same things, an invisible line dividing the two. No one could see it and everyone strayed over it.

Lindsey was dancing with another girl, but Dave snuggled up, mike in hand, and began to sing the current song directly to her. Everyone else was dancing around the two being careful not to trip over any cords.

Dave was a great performer. He could work a crowd and sing at the same time. He had no qualms about leaving the stage area to mingle with the crowd while singing. He always tried to hit every table to get the people sitting down involved. This was the third and final set so he had probably sung directly to every person in the audience. He sang on tables. He climbed up on the half wall between the raised tables and bar vocalizing down to the crowd. He climbed up onto the bar at one point and sang from there. Ryan figured he did that because he needed a refresher beer.

Braedon was bashing out an unusually outstanding backbeat tonight on the drums and Corey was keeping right up with him on the bass. Several girls were up and dancing, clustered around Alan. He was pulling a Hendrix, doing a lead with his guitar behind his neck and facing behind him.

Everyone on the dance floor was thrashing about with vigor and the whole audience was screaming and shouting their approval. Everything was loud.

Dave danced away from his wife and pushed his way through the crowd. He edged down the bar singing every inch of the way to the kitchen entry and waved through the service window to get Milena to come out. She came to the door and no farther. Dave then reached out and took her hand, taking her to the dance floor. He began to dance with her while vocalizing. Burnie looked the other way. The rest of the dancers joined in, bodies writhing to the primitive rhythms of the music. The crowd went wild. The music had pulled everyone in. All were involved intimately with it. All were part of it. The look on Milena's face, the energy and vibrancy that it reflected became a part of their collective experience as well. Ryan hadn't ever seen a young girl this happy before. Her face glowed from the excitement. None of them could have stopped dancing if they wanted to; not even to get another beer.

Collectively as a group, every person there was in another place. The music takes them to another plane of thought where there was nothing but the now, the current instant. Time was nonexistent. This was exactly what's supposed to happen with music but rarely did. Ryan found the head space that he needed to be in tonight. It would be difficult going home after the show. No one wanted this to end. Everything was perfect with the world at this very moment. Everything was music and movement. Eyes opened or closed, it didn't matter. What mattered were the feelings and experienced emotions. It was a fundamentally personal thing, but it was also a shared experience. The observer becomes the observed becomes the observer ad infinitum. You're alone and you're yourself, but somehow you're also a group, an integral part of the collective. You're one and you're everything. Ryan was lost in the music and so was everyone else. This was sheer perfection.

Something intruded. It wasn't anything that you could easily explain, but it was something that you could feel. It was discordant, something indeterminate. Looking around, Ryan became less aware of the music and more aware of the environment. This wasn't pleasing. He wanted to continue listening and dancing.

A very low buzzing started. It was everywhere. Ryan thought that maybe something was starting to go wrong with the sound system. Dave and he were only a few feet apart. Dave was still singing, but they looked at each other and then turned to look towards where Geoff was managing the soundboards. He was fiddling with the slides and various knobs, but the buzzing was getting louder. It wasn't coming from the sound systems. He looked up at us and raised his hands, shrugging his shoulders. Professionally, the band kept playing. Ryan once saw them do a performance in the same bar when the power tripped. Too much equipment fed off the same circuit. Even though, there were no accompanying instruments, Dave kept on singing his lungs out and got the crowd clapping in time. It was very memorable, giving the impression nothing had happened. That show went on and the performance continued while someone fixed the problem. This wasn't like that.

A blinding bright light exploded behind the band, but there was no accompanying boom; a silent bomb of light. Ryan's hands flew up to partially shade his eyes. He could vaguely make out blurry edged black figures coming out of the light. To use a term coming courtesy of the Internet, it was truly a 'WTF' moment. The music dribbled to a halt as everyone's jaws dropped. That buzzing sound was getting painful as it got louder and louder.

Then the shooting started.

CHAPTER 2

PENETRATION

We don't see things as they are, we see them as we are.

Anais Nin

World-ships were a natural outcome in most Level II civilizations. It was natural for most cultures to explore beyond the confines of their originating planet once they'd reached a certain level of technical prowess. This thrust usually started during Level I and only the equivalents of large governments or corporations could accomplish these goals. Under this technical level of development, few could afford the resources to achieve this desired goal. It was exceedingly resource-intensive to leave the gravitational sink of a world. Techniques were developed and refined. This would create and lose authorities and fortunes. Usually these new technologies were proprietary and ownerships established. In spite of this, technological growth often exceeded the ability of these mega-entities to control it. It became necessary to devise Artificial intelligences to take control of these processes. When this happens, progress takes a giant step and the AIs would take over further development and manufacturing. Eventually, the original owners could no longer retain ownership of the new technologies as their products developed too quickly. They no longer had any connection to the end product. The AIs end up with total control. However, AIs can't exist alone in a vacuum. A symbiotic ecology has to develop between the originating cultures, often referred to as patrons and the newly created AIs. When this didn't happen, both races were doomed to extinction. There were an infinite number of examples of this in the cosmos. The ones that made the successful transition generally flourished and further developed in unison. This wasn't necessarily a universal rule. Certainly, some civilizations never left their ancestral homes. They'd be doomed to extinction by cosmic events such as their star's change into a red giant or a supernova.

By the time these cultures made the transition to Level II, the Artificial Intelligence Derived Sentients had evolved from their parent AI's. They had the capacity and wherewithal to build and further refine their own selves. Some AIDS became loners and roamed the cosmos unattended, only occasionally interfacing with their peers through ComSpace. Their peers considered most of these entities a little odd. Other AIDS built carriers that could accommodate themselves as well as others, patrons usually. After all, who wanted to spend eternity essentially alone? Interaction was a requirement for any healthy mind.

World-ships are the biggest of the AIDS. Most were always evolving and changing, subject to their guiding intelligences wishes. They did share some properties as a class. For instance, all were huge and were capable of transporting entire civilizations if needed. In general, people came and went though. If a particular world-ship happened to be going to a destination that you also wanted to go to then, you were usually welcomed to hitch a ride. Some beings often found a home there and elected to live on the world-ship for their entire lives rather than live a planet bound existence. It was up to each person to make their own decisions and world-ships rarely interfered. They liked the company and were prepared to give a helping hand when needed. It kept them busy.

Very few of the patron intelligences interfaced directly with the central world-ship's mind. Drones represent the subunits commonly in use to accommodate these types of communications. It added a personal touch and many could be running concurrently. People could still use standard ship communications to speak to their host if need be. Usually they only did this for some kind of emergency though.

Pretty-Ugly was a world-ship and hosted several patron races of which the hominid species Homo sapiens was one. It was currently of two minds. Literally! It had just finished the process of merging with Pretty-Ugly* but still had close to one hundred years of experience that still needed to be fully reintegrated. Having two existences of its personality running in parallel wasn't an unusual situation for an AIDS. They often did that when breaking down a particularly tricky problem. In many ways, having internal component layering, each level with its own management routines, was similar. What wasn't standard was the length of time and amount of information requiring integration. It could trace the new information down the one cerebral path which was Pretty-Ugly* but not the other. It needed this information fully integrated into both paths and soon. It was afraid that it didn't have enough time. This was a new experience as not many things can cause a world-ship to be afraid. Certainly, it was worried about how few options it had in order to deal with this newly identified threat.

In reviewing the discussion from the AIDS meeting, it concluded that a good first step would be to follow Exact-Estimate's suggestion of attempting to speak to an Ephalem. It was one of only a few AIDS hosting them. Communicating with them had always been an issue.

Civilizations evolved. They first started out as primitives and then fought their way up to the first level of culture. Level I's had developed to the point that they'd been able to harness planetary levels of power. When they'd progressed to Level II status, they were capable of harnessing an entire solar systems worth of power. In fact, most were able to manage and control many star systems worth of energy. The Hamlet civilization now occupies this level. Pretty-Ugly was a world-ship and member of the Spaceship Collective of the Hamlet. It could handle that amount of energy itself with little difficulty.

This was where the trouble started. It wasn't a huge evolutionary leap to evolve from a Type I to a Type II level of culture. In fact, both levels of cultures could easily communicate with each other. Their differences were more scale than conceptual. Sure, the II's lead technologically but any Type I could understand the advancements when shown, although that was not a standard practice.

Level III civilizations were able to control the energy levels equivalent to billions of stars. Think of this as a whole galaxy. It required millions of years of evolution and technological advancement to get to this level. At that point, they've virtually nothing more in common with the Level II's whatsoever. There were no common referents that were useful in communication anymore. Alien is a term that doesn't begin to describe the differences.

Evolution can take many roads. Even the Level III's were subject to it. No one knew how many of these civilizations were about, but there was a definite subset that developed using similar mechanisms. This mechanism was common to insects such as wasps. Lay your eggs on a caterpillar. The egg hatches, and the nymph eats the caterpillar. The nymph becomes an adult, mates and lays more eggs on some other caterpillars. And so goes the circle of biological life.

The Ephalem was a life stage of one Level III civilization. They weren't parasitic, so to speak. You still had to feed them. It'd be more correct to classify them as symbiotic, certainly more polite. They were more like an egg or a young nymph, similar to the insect lifestyle. They were the infants of a Level III civilization. They appeared on world-ships without warning. These AIDS take care of them until they moved into the next stage of their existence and then disappeared. This wasn't a significant burden as there was never very many of them. Pretty-Ugly had gotten quite the reputation acting as hosts to them on many occasions, which it enjoyed. The down side was that the Ephalem weren't good conversationalists. In addition, these baby's intellects were far different from what Pretty-Ugly was capable of understanding.

Many AIDS, who'd never been host to species like the Ephalem, speculated that they were parasitic freeloaders. Pretty-Ugly didn't share that view. It argued the opposite. It provided a tie between the two levels of culture. Maybe the adult Ephalem, whatever they were like, had fond memories of their stay on the world-ship. Enough so that they didn't consider the Hamlet beneath notice and perhaps destroy them in error, unthinkingly. No one knew if these guests had some form of moral code to which they adhered. It thought they did though. They never caused any trouble and weren't difficult guests. They often wandered around as freely as any tourist and didn't bother anyone. As guests went, they were relatively unobtrusive and their needs were very easy to meet. Room and board. That was it.

It readied the drone 'Free-Credit' for a visit. Naming the drones made it easier for people to relate to even though they were actually talking to itself through a subprocess. Each drone was also an AI. It had its own lifeline that it could follow, making it an individual that was capable of independent action. There was only so much of itself it could put into a drone after all. It always made sure each one was readily identifiable as a drone and looked a little different from each other as well. This wrapped up an excellent picture of an individual that others found easy to communicate with openly.

◻ ◻ ◻ ◻

Free-Credit was walking through the Orlop Urban Forest Arcology on the world-ship to visit the single Ephalem that was currently living there. The Ephalem could have selected any neighborhood to live in that it wanted, but chose here. Apparently, they liked being closer to nature, which most of the other available accommodations didn't offer. Ephalem appreciated primitive forms of life and preferred natural surroundings. This was fortunate and good to know. It meant that immediate neighbors were few, although picnickers could be plentiful.

This single area was one of the largest on the world-ship, some tens of kilometers square. The mixture of tree's and undergrowth was representative of temperate zone growth back on Earth. This meant that this section also enjoyed mild seasonal changes managed by the world-ship. Currently, the weather was representative of very early summer. There was a warm breeze and the simulated sun was indirectly shining through the green forest canopy. The little bits of sky that were visible were an azure blue interspersed with white clouds, indistinguishable from what you would see on Earth. There were colorful birds flying around. Blue jays, cardinals and orioles were evident, as were other species. The flying insect population was low. This made it a beautiful day for a walk.

Sometimes Free-Credit would pass a small lake or pond. Rivers were plentiful. Occasionally, it could see day-trippers splashing away. They were usually kids. Some would even give Free-Credit a wave of greeting as it passed by. Free-Credit could see two of the several Homo genera of patrons in the current group although a couple of them could have been hybrids.

Free-Credit reached the embankment of the arcology and turned off the main path to where the entrance to the home of the Ephalem was. It stopped in front of the door allowing the proximity sensor to announce its arrival. In short order, the door iris opened to reveal the little Ephalem. The world-ship modeled Free-Credit after the hominids and the Ephalem only came up to its waist. The Ephalem vaguely resembled a caterpillar in shape, standing up supported by its bottom quarter, but didn't possess appendages of any kind. Presumably, it had evolved past the need for any. There was no discernible difference between its head and body. Convention dictated that the end with the mouth was where the head was. Certainly, this was the end sticking up into the air. There were no visible eyes, but the Ephalem must have had something equally useful as the mouth tracked whatever it was paying attention to.

"Greetings, I'm Free-Credit," the drone introduced itself. "I've come to meet with you as an agent of Pretty-Ugly. I'm hoping that I can discuss a current event that may be of mutual importance to us both."

"Ephalem. Pilgrim," it responded. It turned around and went inside leaving the door opened.

The drone was in disbelief. Free-Credit had anticipated some level of acknowledgment that it was here, but never expected the Ephalem to speak. It spoke two whole words! That was unheard of. Some figured that their native mode of communications might actually occur in the higher dimensions of space-time and in parallel. They may even use direct mind to mind or some form of hive mind link. No one really knew because you just couldn't elicit a conversation out of one. As far as Free-Credit knew, no Ephalem had ever died on a ship. They'd never had any opportunity to perform a necropsy on one, which may have told them more about these creatures. None had ever needed medical aid. They were extremely hardy, according to the best knowledge available. There was nothing to do except to follow the Ephalem inside.

Free-Credit looked around the room. The Ephalem had converted the domicile into a nest using material that it secreted from sphincters on its side. The material was silky soft in an earth tone beige color. There was a coat of this stuff covering all control surfaces including the walls, floor and ceiling. The only item not covered was the viewing wall. It could use this for entertainment but presumably, the Ephalem only used it to monitor real-time events on the world-ship. More material overlaid the lighting, resulting in a diffuse and softly uniform light over the entire room.

"Pilgrim," said Free-Credit. "I can refer to you as Pilgrim then."

"We've detected some events that have profoundly shaken our civilization," asserted the drone. "Several closely related world-line trunks have been reduced to a singularity. Then the singularities have entirely disappeared. We've no physics that can explain this. We're concerned. We don't know if this represents an attack against us. We hope that you're able to advise or help us in some way."

Pilgrim's head moved sinuously from side to side several times.

Free-Credit continued, "We believe that we can obtain some level of discourse with you that'll allow for a mutually acceptable exchange of ideas."

Looking around, Free-Credit noted little in the way of technology; at least technology that it could recognize. Most items appeared inert and mundane; the types of things that any traveler might acquire. There were several dolls that looked to have been hand made out of plant fibers. Local artisans likely made these. A large ochre vase was in the center of the room. It contained freshly picked wild flowers found in the arcology. The flowers were large in mixed colors of red, blue and white. Pilgrim probably did this itself. It looked very esthetic. Other knick-knacks were in evidence about the room. No furniture was in evidence. The Ephalem didn't need any. There was absolutely nothing to show that a higher level of intelligence was at play.

"Please forgive me if I'm in error," Free-Credit continued. "And I'll bid you a good-day." The head on Pilgrim bobbed around a little more, now flipping from back to front.

Not knowing what to think after the initial shock of hearing it talk, Free-Credit turned around to leave.

A vaguely rattling sound came from behind him. It seemed to be coming from Pilgrim. Free-Credit turned around to see what was happening.

Pilgrim continued generating the rattle, sweeping its upper body in large and exaggerated circular motions followed by more bobbing and weaving. Free-Credit couldn't assign any meaning to these actions. The Ephalem stopped suddenly and then inched its way over to a silky outcropping. The head end scooped into this mass and flipped the material out of the way. A small box was present.

Free-Credit walked over to look at the box. There wasn't too much to it; plain and gray in color. The top seemed like it would either lift up or flip back. It didn't know how to proceed. The drone made pantomiming motions of picking up the container and opening it to the Ephalem. Apart from more bobbing and weaving of the head, there was no other response.

"I hope this means that you've given your permission for me to pick up this box and open it. I don't want to offend you if I've made a mistake," Free-Credit said. This was nerve wracking, as Pilgrim gave no response. All the drone could do was assume that this was what the Ephalem wanted. It couldn't even get some kind of clue from facial expression. There wasn't any face.

Free-Credit picked the box up and revealed the contents by flipping the top back. Inside was an object that looked similar to a very tiny gem or piece of cut glass. The color was clear like a diamond, but nothing was particularly striking about it. The drone hoped that this wasn't another tourist souvenir.

Free-Credit could detect some sort of a magnetic field emanating from the object, very minor. Other than that, there was nothing remarkable about it.

The drone looked to its host and then back to the object. It was probably doing what the Ephalem wanted.

"May I touch the object inside?" Free-Credit asked.

More bobbing and weaving was the only response.

Free-Credit thought that it was possibly OK to do so. Carefully, it picked the object up with its right-hand fingers. Vibrations emanated from the object. The drone had a full complement of senses, greatly enhanced from the Homo standard. There was a slightly increasing warmth emanating from the crystalline object. With a little plop, the object melted into its skin. Free-Credit felt bewilderment that now reflected on its face. Then it smiled.

"I can feel it integrating into my character pattern. It isn't overwhelming; more like a tickle."

After a minute, Free-Credit exclaimed, "And it comes with an instruction manual!"

❏ ❏ ❏ ❏ ❏

The AIDS hastily arranged this meeting, but none of them had a thorough understanding of the import of this new data. In attendance were the Artificial Intelligence Derived Sentients Pretty-Ugly, Exact-Estimate, and Neat-Mess. Pretty-Ugly had the AI Free-Credit in tow.

Normally AI level intelligences didn't have the capacity or ability to access ComSpace. They made a rare exception in this case due to current events. Pretty-Ugly told Free-

Credit that it was the best entity to provide an update to the group regarding the Ephalem. True! It had the device. As such, it was able to hitch a ride mentally with Pretty-Ugly to attend the meeting.

This opportunity was very good for the AI. Free-Credit had aspirations that it would be elevated to an AIDS and perhaps would run its own world-ship one day. The invitation to ComSpace, with the ability to participate as an equal, was a serious move towards that end. This was also a rare honor. Its character matrix had speculated that it was capable of becoming one. Free-Credit would require an AIDS to raise it up and would need the full cooperation's of luck and fate to achieve its desired goal.

Free-Credit regarded the meeting room. It wasn't unlike other virtual realities that it had participated in. The default setting was very drab, no floor, ceiling, or walls; everything uniformly dull gray. Icons represented the local participants. Boring and somewhat inelegant it observed. Free-Credit decided to impose its own view of the display space so that it would be more comfortable during the proceedings; something a little more natural. The Ephalem could have such preferences. Then why shouldn't it? Besides, the AIDS could impose their own aesthetics in whatever manner they wanted for themselves. There was no reason for them to all share exactly the same apparent sensual experience.

The AI decided upon a dark and warm feeling room of modest dimension with oaken wood paneling and fireplace with fire. Lighting was low and indirect. The furniture had the look of premium but well-worn black leather. Each participant had its own voluminous chair to sit back in. They all sat around a knee-high wooden table.

Instead of using iconography to represent itself, Free-Credit used the image of its drone body. It felt itself to be quite handsome with the room it had created complimenting its light blue skin. It wore a standard white toga with waist cinch band, as was the custom for its kind. Shoulder length dark black hair, which was in reality a sensor array, gave it a look of quiet dignity. This gave a definite impression of the AI being male.

Free-Credit replaced Pretty-Ugly's icon with a comparable body to its own but made the toga a dark blue. It left the head bald and gave an androgynous look to the face. It did the same with the other icons. Free-Credit gave Exact-Estimate a dark red, almost purple toga, its face made to look much older in keeping with its status as an elder statesman. The AI gave Neat-Mess a light green toga and the face of a young child. By all accounts, it was petulant in a similar manner of a youngster, so this seemed fitting.

Seated, Pretty-Ugly, who made the introductions, was to its left, Exact-Estimate was directly across the table from it, and to its right sat Neat-Mess.

"Welcome Free-Credit," greeted Exact-Estimate. "I understand that you've had a breakthrough with the Ephalem. Can you tell us what transpired?"

"I wish to thank-you all for allowing me at this assemblage. My hope is to provide you with needed information."

"Yes," Free-Credit continued. "We've had a breakthrough of sorts. It actually said two words, Ephalem and Pilgrim. I think that it chose to represent itself by the name Pilgrim. That fact alone is remarkable, but I don't know that we can attribute any meaning to this. I've only ever heard of one word used before and that was 'Ephalem' to identify the race. So in a way, this may be some kind of record and may demonstrate a degree of importance to them racially. As an infant representative of its race, it may be the closest to us cerebrally in terms of communication capability."

"We understand that it's provided you with a tool of some kind," said Exact-Estimate. "What can you tell us about it?"

"In our experience, the Ephalem don't surround themselves with technology, or at least nothing that we'd recognize as technology," stated Free-Credit. "In fact, we make technological devices available to them in the dwellings that we provide. Other than the viewing wall, they use none of it and often cover it up with their secretions. My impression was that Pilgrim was expecting me ahead of time. It fully expected to provide me with the equipment. This is mysterious as the Ephalem probably arranged this in advance; before you recognized any problem existed. Likely, this is why it was suggested to you that the Ephalem should be contacted."

"Are you implying that the Ephalem can see the future?" joked Neat-Mess.

"I don't know how we can categorize the way the Ephalem see the cosmos from their perspective," answered Free-Credit. "We know that it's radically different from ours. It may be that experientially they don't differentiate between the past and future. It may be that they also exist in higher dimensions than what we experience. The current cosmological view of the universe describes it as requiring twenty-six dimensions. The symmetry groups show that of these, three are probably time-like. Your guess on how to interpret any of this is likely better than mine."

"I like that answer! We're going to get along very well," responded Neat-Mess.

"Free-Credit's been my principle interface as host to the Ephalem since we first started to receive them. I can assure you that it's the closest thing that we've got to an expert on them anywhere in our society," piped in Pretty-Ugly.

"What can you say about the instrument that Pilgrim gave you?" asked Exact-Estimate. "Do you know its function and how it may assist us?"

Free-Credit thought about how to respond to this question and then said, "When I touched the device, it immediately connected and then dissolved into me. It's now a part of my systems. At first, I was surprised. This wasn't what I expected. It was very tiny, much like a small gemstone. In seconds, I could feel it integrating into my neural net. It wasn't trying to take over. It was more like integrating a new sense into my overall system. It's only a tool. I can see that. I suspect that this apparatus may possibly exist multidimensionality, with the vast bulk of it residing in the higher dimensions. It doesn't contain enough mass or energy to do what it claims to do otherwise."

"And that is?" asked Exact-Estimate.

"It came with its own built-in user's manual which I can understand because of the neural net integration," answered Free-Credit. "I haven't actually tried it yet. I can tell you what the device says it does. I can't tell you the working mechanics. We have to trust the Ephalem that it'll do what it claims to do. My thoughts are its control interface. I have to instruct it to do its function. It won't act on its own."

Free-Credit continued. "In essence, the device is able to create a wormhole on demand. If I turn it on, it'll take everything that is loose within a five-meter radius to me, to the other end of the hole. Items attached to a larger mass outside of the radius won't move. This means that the mechanism leaves the ground under my feet behind. The same effect occurs for any item that has parts found on both sides of the boundary that are fixed. It won't chop anything in half but can pull free items along with it. The destination point of the wormhole is set based on specific parameters. It'll only attach to an area where the universal constants are in flux or changing. So, it will tunnel a wormhole to a world-line that's collapsing. If one doesn't exist at the point of activation, then it does nothing. You can't use it to go just anywhere. You can't even specify the target location. It'll activate an alarm on detection of new activity, allowing for follow-up action. It appears to have a lot of failsafe's built into its operations."

Free-Credit paused briefly while the others evaluated this information.

Exact-Estimate looked puzzled. "To paraphrase, it'll only take you to your destruction. What use is that?"

"The instruction manual is only that; an instruction manual," answered Free-Credit. "It doesn't say what it's useful for. It does say that the device protects whatever traverses the wormhole to the far end. The five-meter range also enforces the universal constants that exist at the originating location. When I turn it on, I'll travel to the other end. When I turn it off, I come back. However, I don't think the device would be able to cope with the end of the collapse. The device can't protect you from that. It's set up to break the connection should the condition ever arise. You'd be brought back before the device failed."

Neat-Mess started looking much more interested. "This means that you could take things with you and bring them back; like another drone for instance. Correct?"

"Yes, to the best of my knowledge," answered Free-Credit.

"And we haven't any idea of how it works," stated Exact-Estimate. "Where's its energy source?"

"The power required in creating a wormhole of that size and able traverse world lines must be enormous," said Free-Credit. "It must be in the same order as what a massive black hole would have. The energy source doesn't come from me and we can be sure it doesn't originate any place we'd consider local. There's no maintenance manual to tell us about this type of functionality. My best guess. The energy is harvested from the higher dimensions somehow."

Pretty-Ugly looked around. The last statement had shut everyone up. "The Ephalem Pilgrim provided us with this tool for a reason and without explanation. It seemed to know that this was coming and planned ahead. We need a decision. How are we going to use it?"

"Given what's been explained to us," replied Exact-Estimate. "We can infer that its primary function is for observation. We may be able to glean more facts about the nature of these events by using it. If we learn enough, there's a remote possibility that we might be able to protect ourselves; maybe even fight back."

"So you're proposing we do a reconnaissance of the currently collapsing trunk of world-lines," said Pretty-Ugly.

"That seems our best option at this point. At least we'll have a better understanding of the situation," Exact-Estimate responded back.

"I'd like to propose something," suggested Neat-Mess. "Currently only Free-Credit has the control and ability to use this tool. However, it shouldn't be alone to perform this function. I think that my drone Questionable-Advice should also go. We can then get two points of reference for anything detected." Turning to Pretty-Ugly, it asked, "Would you be amenable to printing a drone for me so that I can transfer the AI to it?"

"Of course," answered Pretty-Ugly. "That's an excellent idea. We need more than one perspective." After a slight pause, it addressed the others. "I still don't know how we're to deal with the patron races on this. Should they be informed? Should they be included on the mission?"

Exact-Estimate looked around the table at each individual seated. "Personally, I don't believe that they've got anything to currently contribute in this endeavor. If we tell them then there'll be panic. If we say nothing and take the initiative, we can't guarantee any particular outcome. In addition, the patrons are far more fragile than the drones. They're much less likely to return should the mission become dangerous. I suggest that we start with a scouting objective. We'll be more capable of making decisions once we have additional information. We can do this before the last part of trunk collapse finishes, in the next few hours. Is everyone in agreement with this?"

All of them replied in the affirmative.

Neat-Mess had a twinkle in its eyes.

◻ ◻ ◻ ◻ ◻

The mission's staging area, aboard Pretty-Ugly, was a currently unused service and docking hanger for the smaller Explorer Class vehicles. Typically, Pretty-Ugly made use of these to explore in-system territories more conveniently. Other ships wishing to hitch a ride out of the system also sometimes used the birthing area. Pretty-Ugly was in its home system and wasn't going anywhere soon. The area was mostly asymmetrical and contained adjustable birthing cradles that could accommodate vessels up to three-hundred meters in length. Massive doors could slide open into the vacuum of space to take in any ship of this size. There were very few loose objects lying about; just enough for the current round of maintenance services that the world-ship found necessary to suspend. There was a lot of room available to stage the mission.

Free-Credit and Questionable-Advice were in the process of creating the final list of equipment necessary for the expedition to the failing world-line trunk. Both had internal contact with Pretty-Ugly, who made them instantly aware of the available inventory of analysis tools. Pretty-Ugly had delivered the kinds of instruments it said that it considered useful for such a venture. This included various sensing devices and weapons. The problem was that it was far too much to carry and use effectively. This meant that they'd have to choose the most effective combination of tools based on what they believed met their requirements.

Free-Credit looked at its newly printed guest who was wearing a very light green toga and grumbled, "This is a mess. We can't use most of this stuff. Some are even too large to carry with us. We need to pare this down to what we can take and use quickly. Some weapons may be useful." It was conscious of how little time they had to prepare. Nothing in front of them appeared useful.

"What was Pretty-Ugly thinking?" asked Questionable-Advice. It picked up what looked to be a combination of telescope and spectroscope. "Half of this stuff looks like it came directly from its own sensor banks. Our needs are entirely different from the world-ship, especially in scale. I was passionate about going on this mission until I saw this pile of rubbish. Let's simplify. We need to measure the minimum amount of data possible to give us some hint as to what's actually happening."

"Let's start with what we know can be measured," replied Free-Credit. "Then we can move on to the other considerations such as what are the questions that we don't know how to ask. We know that the universal constants are changing. We can begin by measuring those to find out what their rates of change actually are and by identifying the minimum number of constants that it takes to describe the universe." These were concepts it wasn't comfortable dealing with. Pretty-Ugly's design criteria for the drone did not include it being a physics theorist. It spent most of it time dealing with the inhabitants of the world ship and felt a little out of its depths. "The first is the speed of light in a vacuum. The second is the gravitational constant. Pretty-Ugly has suggested an additional item that it had learned about as Pretty-Ugly*. The natives of the other world-line refer to this as the Planck constant. It describes the quantum relationship between energy and frequency for a photon. All of these are physical constants that are a fixed. None of them is derivable by theory. They're what they are and are likely different in every cosmos. If we can get direct measurements for two out of the three, then we should be able to explain what's actually happening at any point in time." Of course, they still didn't know what questions would be meaningful.

"That's straight forward enough," responded Questionable-Advice. "What's with the other world-line measurements?" It threw the instrument it was holding down into the pile.

"That's part of what Pretty-Ugly* was doing on the other world-line to begin with," stated Free-Credit. "Their sciences took a very different approach from our own. It seems that they've spent much more time investigating probabilities and fields in their physics than we have. They were able to predict very early on things that we didn't know about until we were Level II. Given that they hadn't evolved into a full Level I civilization yet, it seems remarkable. Most of Pretty-Ugly*'s interests were in wave mechanics and their usage outside of their physics. I have much of this data. Our principle physics depends on direct measurement rather than theory. There's nothing inherently wrong with either approach."

"OK. What do we need for these measurements? Do you have any thoughts?" queried Questionable-Advice. It looked around at the gantries the service-bots were currently moving out of the way. Then it looked back down at the pile at its feet and gave it a swift kick.

It was easy to see that Questionable-Advice was frustrated. Was it getting petulant like Neat-Mess? That seemed likely, as there'd be much of it in the newly printed drone. "We should also attempt to measure the Fine Structure Constant. This will be difficult. This concept also originates from the other world-line. It's a coupling constant that characterizes the strength of the electromagnetic interactions between elementary charged particles. This one is weird because this number is invariant regardless of the measurement system used. It'll give us the best shot at detailing what happens during the evolution of the collapse event. We have to measure all of these items from outside the protective bubble generated by the Ephalem tool. You'll have to do these measurements. I'm stuck at its focal point. I can't leave it," stated Free-Credit.

"OK," asserted Questionable-Advice. "We can measure the speed of light by determining the frequency for a given wavelength. We'll have to adjust for the fact we won't be doing this in a vacuum. We can use a laser-based tool such as an interferometer that should give us the correct results. We can use the same laser instrument to measure the gravitational constant by measuring the gravitational attraction of gas molecules to each other. Once we have the speed of light, we can use a superconducting quantum interface device—or SQUID—to measure Planck's constant. We can automate the process by using a medical device designed for imaging. Then we can use a calculable cross capacitor and a laser interferometer to measure the Fine Structure Constant."

This seemed like a more practical approach. Questionable-Advice appeared to have some hidden depths. "Reasonable I suppose," responded Free-Credit. "I'm giving the requirements to Pretty-Ugly for printing the appropriate mechanisms. We should have them in the next ten minutes. This reduces the number of devices we need to two. I don't think we can use any of this junk." Maybe the world ship was testing them somehow. It had a high hope they were approaching the whole thing correctly. Without knowing why, it kicked the junk pile as well.

"This brings us to the hard questions," asserted Questionable-Advice. "How do we poke and prod the effect to see what'll affect or prevent it? I'm at a total loss in this department. Obviously, fission and fusion won't do anything or any old star would have stopped it. Gravity seems to have no influence. It eats black holes just as readily as it eats everything else. It directly affects the weak, strong and electromagnetic forces, probably at the energy levels where they unify. Temperature and pressure have no observable effect."

"Short of being able to directly manipulate universal constants, I've no idea," conceded Free-Credit. "We don't have the physics to be able to make those kinds of changes. Their values probably were set in the phase space where the cosmos originally developed. We know nothing about how this happens. The birth of the universe probably modified these values to be unique. We can predict the results of what changing the values might do but can't provide a mechanism or explanation on how to do it. We don't have a single stick that we can use to poke at the problem. We can't even tell what the issues would be at the receiving end of where the singularity went. Did the effect reset these values? Will it modify the destination values of these constants? We just don't know."

Questionable-Advice was looking at the pile again. "We should consider a couple of weapons to take with us. We don't know what we'll be facing. We need to cover all possibilities. Kinetic weapons are a standard. Let's take the Zimmer rail gun. It should stop most threats and is reasonably small."

"We should probably use some Directed Energy Weapons as well. Just for some contrast. If one doesn't work then maybe one of the others will. The Bolate DEW is a multi-capable weapon. It can shoot lasers, masers, radio frequency and electromagnetic radiation," affirmed Free-Credit. "That just leaves particle and sonic-beams. A Boomer DEW can do both. That's three weapons. I wish we had something that worked at the quantum level."

Questionable-Advice paused in thought. "I don't think we need anything else. I'm providing the additional requirements to Pretty-Ugly. Weapons and measurement tools should cover it. We can probably deduce any questions that come up later from what we're measuring. There's probably a lot we don't know how to ask."

A bearing port opened up in the wall closest to the two drones. Pretty-Ugly usually made use of these to deliver new parts to the service-bots for when they were servicing a ship in dry dock. Newly printed equipment courtesy of Pretty-Ugly was on the shelves. It also sent a download of the operational specifications directly to both drones as they walked over to collect the items.

Free-Credit saw that Pretty-Ugly had manufactured a single measurement probe. "It looks like we only need the one probe. The ship integrated the laser interferometer into both the SQUID and calculable cross capacitor. It seemed small. The specs say that we just have to push it outside the bubble and then send it a signal to start. It'll transmit the results back to us. I'll use the Zimmer rail gun. I can shoot it from inside the bubble. You take the Bolate and Boomer. They'll be more efficient outside the bubble."

"I'm now feeling stoked again. No one's ever done anything like this before. Where do we do this?"

Free-Credit walked back towards the center of the bay. "This way. I'm ready when you are."

"Let's do it."

"Actioning now."

¤ ¤ ¤ ¤ ¤

Ryan was shocked and dropped onto his stomach. He was able to see completely around himself without moving too much. Milena was on his left just standing there. He grabbed an arm and pulled her down none too gently. Once she was finally face down on the ground, he moved partially on top of her. It sounded like shots were going back and forth.

BANG! BANG! BANG!

He just couldn't tell from what direction they came from and he'd be damned if he were going to let Milena be hit. The banging continued. The background buzzing was

73

now oscillating, each cycle getting closer and closer together.

Mandy, Tony, Jacques, Lindsey and the other girl were also on the floor. Jacques screamed, "Follow me. We've got to get to the door." He was crawling in that direction not waiting to see if anyone was following. Immediately, Mandy and Tony started after him. The other girl probably didn't hear Jacques, but the second she saw them, she moved in that direction as well.

Bernie and Lilah dropped down behind the bar, which was probably the safest place to be in the room. Josie sneaked out the service door and joined them. The rest of the area was in chaos. People were screaming and yelling. Some were running for the door while others were keeping their head down. A few froze in place. Someone else had managed to open the patio doors and a couple of people went that direction.

Lindsey fell to the ground at the same time Ryan did. Dave jumped down next to her. Alan and Corey both tossed their guitars aside and dropped. Braedon was still sitting on his drum seat. He wasn't looking at anything out front. Instead, he stood and twisted around, looking directly behind to where the light bomb went off. Halting his actions, he then became utterly still. It wasn't possible to see what he was looking at.

Ryan turned and watched the rest of the bar at the front. If there was trouble, the odds were it'd come from that direction.

The people moving towards the front door and the patio were moving slower and slower. The ones that were running hadn't modified their gaits. In one case, a person had to jump over a chair. He was in the air a good five seconds by Ryan's count, which was crazy. No one could do that. The closer they got to the door, the slower they moved. Time was slowing to a standstill.

Geoff had his gear set up fairly close to the bar. He saw all the same things and decided to crawl towards the band.

The people on the verge of exiting through the front door had come to a full stop as if time froze them in place.

Now a new phenomenon was beginning. The things he could see farthest away were getting brighter. The effect was very slowly coming his direction. Looking out the windows around the patio, he could see the world was transforming itself. You shouldn't be able to see much at this time of night, but everything was flamingly bright. Light wasn't shining down on those things. The things were glowing themselves just like something under a black light. Nothing was moving. Everything frozen in time.

Looking back, Ryan could see that Braedon had finally moved. He was still facing the same direction but had started walking backward, away from the drum set. He didn't stop until he tripped over Alan and went down hard. The light bomb from behind the kit was gone revealing a transparent opalescent globe of relative normality. The dark figures within became clearer in seconds. It looked like two more people, but they were dressed differently, as if they were going to a toga party.

More of the shooting sounds were coming from the bar area. Ryan looked over, as did Milena. Her mom was back there.

BANG! BANG! BANG!

No guns were in sight. Josie and Burnie were looking over the bar's side. Lilah must still be holding her head low.

Outside, a gray wall kept appearing and then disappearing. It rather looked like concrete, but it undulated sinuously like an eel's body, back and forth. Ryan saw the object appear and then disappear in the parking lot, which revealed everything now thoroughly destroyed under where it had been, shredded and crushed. Cars and people. Buildings, telephone and power lines. Road and parking lot.

Trees and grass. There was nothing left but smudges and rubble.

Ryan started thinking about Alyssa, Boo, and Crisp. Dear God! He wasn't able to get to them. He reached for his phone and flipped it open. No signal. How could that be? The cell site was on top of the water tower just next door.

He looked back at the newcomers behind the drum kit again. The globe now extended to almost where he was. Dave and Lindsey were already inside of it. They were still moving about. Whatever it was, the environment inside of the bubble must be comparatively benign compared to what was happening outside. Just behind them were Braedon and Alan. Off to the right he could see Corey was inside the bubble as well, none the worse for wear.

Geoff had managed to crawl next to him and Milena. "Ryan, what the hell is going on?"

"You tell me, Geoff. God damn it. My phone stopped working. No signal. I can't reach my family."

Geoff pulled his phone out and checked it. "Same with mine. Who are those people behind the kit?"

"No idea but one's coming this way."

Ryan and Geoff were sitting up now. Ryan put one hand on Milena's back to make sure she stayed down. She shouldn't see what he was seeing. Besides, he wasn't sure if it was safe for her. People looked like they were traversing through molasses. Most had come to a complete stop and now froze. Behind the bar, it was starting to affect Josie and Burnie. It looked like Josie was calling out for Milena, but her voice was dropping in tone and she moved slower. It was hard to tell over the oscillating background buzz, which kept getting louder.

Looking back to the strangers, one was now going towards them carrying something, some kind of instrument. The guy was slightly pale blue in color with long black hair and wearing a toga. He passed through the bubbles side and then passed Ryan and Geoff. He put the box down, turned tail and ran back into the bubble. Now they could both see he had rifles slung around his back. Ryan thought that at least someone knew to prepare for something like this.

Then the lasers started. They were coming from the box. It seemed ludicrous to have a light show in the middle of all this destruction. There were at least three, blue, red and green. They followed their own tracks and went everywhere. The box looked like it was set up to hit shiny objects that were reflective. Laser light crisscrossed everywhere.

Without warning, the gray wall appeared midway through the room undulating back and forth. Milena began to scream. Her mother was under that. It had just missed the laser box but obliterated everything from the bar over. Pieces of the roof, support beams, torn electrical wiring and conduit came tumbling down. Nothing heavy hit Ryan, but Geoff took a hit from a fallen ventilation shaft to his left arm. He was bleeding like crazy. Both of them were protectively covering Milena so she only ended up with a lot of dust and small chunks of debris falling onto her, that and Geoff's blood. The dust made what was left of the room cloudy. Milena kept screaming for her mom.

The man in the center of the bubble raised a rifle and started shooting at the undulating wall. It sounded more or less like a regular one. Where the bullets hit the wall, gray ricochet material flaked off. This fell to the ground and then disappeared.

The other stranger left the bubble again and took one of the rifles he was carrying and started shooting at the wall as well. An occasional laser was coming from the end. It was a cutting laser and left marks on the wall. Something else now shot from the weapon, but Ryan couldn't tell what it was. He guessed that the laser's principle use was for targeting purposes.

The man continued firing until it looked like he had nothing left. He threw the rifle down and pulled the other one from around his back. A red beam came out of it, but it wasn't a laser. The beam didn't collimate and spread a slight amount. Whatever it was doing transformed portions of the wall a bright yellow.

Out in the parking lot, the remains of the rubble radiated light like crazy. Nothing looked stable anymore and was glowing in a rainbow of colors. Nothing was solid matter. Everything had turned into solidified light. Ryan thought that if you touched it, your hand would go right through. It wasn't as if it was dissolving; more like it was transmuting into something else. Was this the Apocalypse that western religions kept talking about?

The guy at the center kept shooting as well, but suddenly stopped. He must be out of ammunition.

The other man was still shooting. Now when he took a shot, a loud screech filled what was left of the bar. This seemed pointed at a particular spot on the wall. It must be some kind of focused sonic device. This had a significant effect. The wall turned a bright green and disappeared. What remained was sheer destruction. A nuclear explosion wouldn't have done this kind of damage.

Ryan looked at Geoff and asserted, "There's nothing left for us out there. There's only one place left to go."

Both of them looked at Milena. She was whimpering quietly to herself now and was unresponsive to either of them.

"Yeah. Into the bubble. I'll take Milena's left arm. I can do that with my right one. At least it still works."

"OK. I have her right side. Thanks," Ryan responded.

It only took a second to get her up, but Geoff's left arm held him back a bit. Just a step or two and they'd be inside the bubble.

The man behind them was walking backwards to the bubble again. He was still firing his weapon but now everything else was turning into solidified light. The effect was coming closer and closer.

Ryan, Geoff, and Milena were now inside. The others helped with Milena. Lindsey took one look at Geoff's arm and exclaimed, "Jesus. That's deep. We've got to stop the bleeding."

Geoff just looked at her and then teased, "You just happen to have a needle and some thread?" She hit him on the other arm.

"Here," Braedon offered. He handed her some carpet tape. Typically, they used it to hold the cables down going from the amplifier to the monitors so no one would trip over them.

"Thanks," she answered and proceeded to wrap a length of tape around the wound on Geoff's left arm. "What do we do next?"

"I don't know," replied Dave. "Nothing has hit this bubble thing yet. There must be some level of protection in it."

"Look at the outside," Ryan said in shock. "There's nothing left. What's happened to my family? Is this happening everywhere?"

No one attempted to answer. There wasn't one. Dave and Lindsey didn't have any kids. Braedon and Alan were single. Neither had ever been married or had any. Geoff and Corey were both married and had children. Ryan could see on their faces that they were hurting just as badly as he was.

The man doing the shooting was now inside the bubble. The bubble now defined the line marking the difference between being and not being. Inside of it, everything was normal. Outside was toxic. To leave the bubble now would mean instant death.

Dave turned to address the two blue people. Then the whole world disappeared.

☒ ☒ ☒ ☒ ☒

Neat-Mess was an AIDS based scouting ship and had many drones in its inventory. Neat-Mess chose it out of all of its drones. Questionable-Advice was elated with its current position. All it could suppose was that it appreciated a sense of humor. This particular personality trait could lead to some very strange mental associations. This had gotten it in trouble a few times but was on its best behavior now. This must be something that Neat-Mess was looking for.

Elation. Maybe this was what sex felt like? It seemed close to some of the patron's descriptions, if not their behavior.

In some ways, its position was more important than Free-Credit's. Yes, it had the device but this integrated directly into all of its systems. It could never leave the bubble.

Both DEW's hung from Questionable-Advice's back so that it could carry the instruments package in its arms. This was an excellent arrangement. When they dropped the device, it only needed to rotate a strap to have a weapon in place. There hadn't been any soldier drones created in at least the last ten-thousand years. It had turned out that in the vastness of space, there was really no point in having any, at least, not on this world-line. Where there was physical matter then resources were plentiful. You could pick up just about anything you wanted from planetoids or Oort objects. The only place where battles existed was on habitable planets dirt-side of the gravity well. Even then, it was all about patron politics and they'd moved past their war phase some five thousand years ago, evolution in practice. There were still wars found elsewhere. Some were even extra-solar. None was even close in world-line, time, or distance. Still, this is what a soldier drone must have felt like going into battle. There was excitement, terror, elation, and the thought of death. Well, it had a backup copy made from the transfer from Neat-Mess. So death wasn't quite death in that sense. It would lose something though if it terminated.

They started out in one of the docking bays. It was in maintenance mode. That left a lot of available space to work with and no likelihood of disturbance with Pretty-Ugly keeping watch. The world-ship's mentality was just too large to accompany them, essentially leaving them to be free agents. It did wonder why it dumped all that junk on it and Free-Credit. AI's never quite understood the thought of an AIDS. Some of the male patrons said the same things about their females.

Now Free-Credit was initiating the Ephalem's device. It held the Zimmer out in front. Not much happened during the first few seconds. Slowly the bubble built. It started out with Free-Credit birthing it straight out of its chest. It then expanded slowly to five meters in all directions covering both of them. That meant it went below the floor as well. They were side by side, contained in its center.

The bubble changed from translucent to opaque and the loading bay slowly disappeared from sight. Then the process started to reverse and they were in some kind of meeting place. Sapiens were everywhere and they were all screaming in fear. Every few seconds there were rail-gun sounds. It sounded like projectiles exceeding the speed of sound. The locals thought they were under fire. Questionable-Advice couldn't see any discernible weapons and it was impossible to tell where the sounds were coming from. It seemed like everywhere. A secondary sound also filled the air. It was a deep oscillating buzzing sound and was very loud.

Directly in front, there were some people on the ground. The one closest was sitting and looking directly at it with sticks in its hands. There was a look of shock on its face. It had some sort of hollow round things of various sizes just behind it. Some odd contraptions pieced these together. Lathed circles of metal rose above the round things. Some funny looking wooden objects were laying on the ground, all wired back to some kind of device that was at the side. There were even big black boxes on the floor and on stands. These had lines sticking out leading back to the same machine. None of this stuff was comprehensible.

Visible to the left, past a raised seating area, were sliding doors that exited to an outdoor area where a field composed of some kind of concrete was located. It had metal conveyances parked on it. People were running for them. Out of nowhere a large gray mass phased into existence outside. It seemed alive, rippling in waves and grinding everything in its path to dust. Then it would disappear as if it was never there. This repeatedly occurred.

Straight ahead was a stand with glasses filled with some kinds of drinks. It was about waist high with chairs all around it. Metal appliances were sticking out of the stand. It must be a permanent fixture. No people were in the chairs. Some were on the floor, but most were running towards the far exit. There wasn't much to the right other than some sorts of machinery. The lights on these were blinking away as if they were on fire.

Immediately in front were some male and female sapiens on the floor. Some were even inside the bubble.

This wasn't going to be easy. They hadn't planned to arrive in a populated location, never mind some kind of meeting place full of people. Questionable-Advice suspected it was going to see many of them die; not an experience it wanted. All life needed respect and support. Suddenly, things weren't so exciting anymore.

Some reactions were starting to become noticeable. The further the sapiens got by running away from the bubble the slower they became. Some were even frozen in the air; caught in mid jump. Dilation effects in time. Yep. This must be the place. That didn't seem to stop anyone from going those directions though. Panic had set in. Now the activity was slowly creeping closer and closer. There wasn't going to be much time to achieve what they needed to do.

Without any exchange with Free-Credit, Questionable-Advice ran out and moved as close to the stand as it could get; five meters outside of the bubble. It put the instrument package on the ground and instructed it to initiate. Immediately, it turned on the lasers and the measurements started. They were shooting and bouncing everywhere.

Questionable-Advice turned tail and ran back to the safety of the bubble. It managed to do this without tripping over any sapiens fortunately. If any of the Ephalem failsafe's kicked in, this would strand it resulting in termination. Best not to think of that.

The gray wall suddenly appeared half way across the room. The building collapsed underneath it almost taking out the instrument package. It crushed the people that were behind the stand and on the floor and then began to undulate around. The falling debris injured some of the survivors. The girl on the floor in front of the bubble was screaming now.

Free-Credit began to fire the rail gun at the moving wall. Bits ricocheted off it, which disappeared as they fell to the ground. Almost no damage occurred.

Questionable-Advise received a direct signal to get its ass out of the bubble from Free-Credit. It had to appreciate the choice of words used. Free-Credit likely picked it up through its associations with various other cultures. It drew the Bolate DEW and left the bubble. It started shooting the cutting laser first and then rotated through the maser, RF, and EMF radiations in a tightly focused beam. It kept doing this until the power cell was exhausted. It dropped the weapon to the floor.

Out on the concrete field things were deteriorating. It looked like all mass particles were beginning to generate photons. This implied bosons shedding as well. That was a good indication that elements were emitting gamma rays and degenerating, at least in the strong and weak forces. Things were going to start to heat up now. What was left of the universe had moved from being dark energy to radiation dominated. Now, this latest change showed a shift towards a domination by degenerate matter. This was certainly the end. A big crunch. Essentially, all of the derivative effects were eating the whole cosmos.

Out came the Boomer DEW with its particle and sonic beams. It was hard on the ears. Something was different though. The gray wall turned a bright yellow when hit. The weapon cycled through both settings every second, creating larger and larger yellow sections on the wall. Questionable-Advise hoped this meant that it was painful but who knew. If you hit a rock with a stick, would it destroy the rock? The important thing was that there was a perceptible effect; no matter how little it was in the grand scheme of things. This wasn't much. Still, it was something.

Suddenly the wall turned a green color and phased back out of space. It was time to get back inside the bubble. The instrument package sent both drones a copy of its measurements.

The degeneration zone kept moving closer and closer so Questionable-Advice kept it eyes on the movement while backing into the bubble. Just in time. Everything outside the bubble was now degenerating. Hopefully, the gamma ray dosage wasn't too high yet.

That's when the failsafe's kicked in and sent them back home with some unexpected company.

◻ ◻ ◻ ◻ ◻

The force carrying particles govern its domain. The beginning of this cosmos started in the usual manner of universes, in phase space. Its development was very different from most in that the Fine Structure and Strong Coupling Constants were extremely small. The consequences of this were many.

In any phase space generated domain, there were always twenty-six dimensions of space-time. In this particular case, no period of inflation followed the initial big bang. Consequently, almost no baryonic matter was able to precipitate out of the sea of photons. Gluons, bosons and photons dominated its space-time. For the most part, energy was energy and existed in that form. It didn't freeze into the inconvenient form of matter. Very loosely coupled quarks that had a tendency to move from one baryon to another, made up the little bit that did exist, providing little to no stability for these particles. The dimensions of length, width and depth that fundamentally defined area, was useless to it.

To make use of energy required a flow from high to low concentrations. This was just unavailable in its standard space. The false vacuum, and required differentials, didn't exist in these dimensions. They existed in a state of complete equilibrium. With many of the higher dimensions, this wasn't so. Potential filled some while others were bereft of it. As it inhabited all dimensions equally, it was able to utilize these by easily switching from a stable high to a lower potential across dimensions. This provided the necessary power and workflow.

Like any other domain, it was subject to the laws of entropy. This realm grew linearly as matter did not dominate it. This universe couldn't end as dark energy dominated and gravity was unable to reverse the effect that would lead to a big crunch. The amount of total potential was set during its creation. There was only so much available to utilize before an equilibrium resulted. Ultimately, it would end in a cold death.

The entity utilized the false vacuum conditions across dimensions to provide the energy differentials that it needed to live. Physically, it occupied all dimensions in space-time. Thought provided its mechanism for translation between all dimensions. If something were here, it'd just move it to there, within the domain. It needn't consciously perform these operations. It just did it. It wasn't necessary to understand how the process functioned at a low level.

Three of the twenty-six dimensions were different from the others. These were dimensions of time. The major one followed the customary laws of entropy and moved in only one direction, from past to future. In it, you could only exist in the 'now.' The other two dimensions were also time-like, but entropy didn't limit them. They extended out at right angles to the primary time-line implying a hyperbolic geometry specific to the time-like portions of space-time. The entity moved freely through these dimensions and often worked out complicated problems by apportioning itself down one of these. Once a particular problem resolved to a solution, it'd just pull back the apportioned piece of itself with the result. This meant that any deterministic question was solvable in zero time from the perspective of the primary time-line.

One of the problems of being the embodiment of the whole universe was that the entity was always conscious of its own ending down some world-lines. This was due to all energy dispersing uniformly across all dimensions, leaving no potential for work. Effectively this meant it would be dead. As it existed across all dimensions in all times, except for the primary time-line, it was constantly aware of this troubling issue. It could sometimes be alive and dead at the same time in its bounded but expanding domain. It experienced both conditions and simply didn't like dead. Death was a complex issue for it.

The entity considered itself very fortunate to have been born into such a domain. The phase space origins indicated to it that almost all universes had different fundamental properties. It was lucky to be in this one as none of the others could possibly allow for it or any form of life to exist. That meant it was alone in the multiverse. As it didn't understand what 'alone' was, this was hardly troubling.

The entity's universe was anthropic in nature. As it was a sentient being, it was capable of making decisions. When this happened, there was a world-line split and it could fully explore the results of both decisions. When it found the one branch that had the desirable solution, it simply pulled the undesirable world-line back into itself, erasing it. Thus, it would proceed using the correct result.

No concept of mathematics or sciences such as physics existed for the entity. It moved through the dimensions to execute or manipulate any action it desired. It was familiar only with magnitude and differentials. It had to be aware of these for its continued survival. It simply did what it had to do to live.

The entity had recognized early in its primary time-line that there were extremely minute wormholes connecting its domain to others originating from phase space. It could care less about the size of these holes. It was unimportant as some of its own dimensions were minuscule and curled into themselves. Experimenting up and down its left and right time-lines, it learned to make use of these wormholes. Other universes had a profusion of potential energies that it could import and use to extend the lifespan of its primary time-line. The answer of how to utilize these other potentials came to it in zero amount of time. Had it known how to add up subjective time on the other time-lines, it would have been in the millions of years.

Much was unknown. For instance, what was the best way to move the potential to the entity's own universe? It didn't have an answer on how to do this. The answer had to come from outside its domain. It wasn't something that was possible to model locally.

Another question regarded the features of the other universe. Would the universal properties of the other realm infect the entity's own causing everything to operate fundamentally differently? This would poison and potentially kill it. Answers to these questions were not deducible without careful experimentation. A shortcoming to all of this was that it was possible only in entropic-time, in a linear fashion. It was a foreign, but learnable concept.

The first experiment was to put a small piece of itself through one of the wormholes. The entity could only do this in the tightly wrapped up dimensions. Only they could fit through something so small. When it did this, it found that it had no trouble rotating into the other dimensions at the destination. More importantly, it recognized that the properties of its own domain stayed with it for a significant amount of time before the poisoning effect would begin to take place due to the native properties of the external realm. It only needed to keep pumping energy from its domain through the connection, refreshing itself and abating the effect.

The next series of experiments were to determine the amount of energy potential that the entity was capable of pulling back to its home. In all cases, it found that the remote entropies had wound down to half of its originating potential from the original conditions of the local big bang. This was a result of the wormholes taking it through to mid-era epochs at the destination. This indicated that packaging would be a potential problem. The entity needed a mechanism to force the environment to singularity by manipulating the remote geometry. In these tests, it found that the manipulation of the higher dimensions plus an inclusion of some space-time from its own realm would force a reversal of geometric expansion. There was only a matter of generating the correct vibrational modes in the higher dimensions. Because of their high frequency and energies, there was a tendency for some of it to be lost to the lower dimensions as waste.

When the entity tried this the first time, it had found no great difficulties. To protect itself, it created a pocket universe and set the resulting singularity into it before bringing it home. This gave complete isolation from possible infection, allowing it to test the bleeding of entropy from the prize. It found this to be a vast reservoir of usable differential from which it could subsist. The entropy immediately took on the properties of the local domain. Many world-lines containing its death immediately lengthened and it promptly reintegrated them into its main time-line. It decided that it would do this repeatedly until it could eliminate all deaths.

The entity's observation of the alien domain collapsing to singularity showed that the reversal of geometry proceeded from what it perceived as the fringe of the universe and worked its way back to a central focal point before the final collapse resulted. It didn't know the reason for this position but didn't care as it got what it wanted. This process happened much faster than the speed of light as it only directly affected the geometry of space-time. The speed of light was still definitive in its effects. No object or energy could exceed that speed under any circumstances. This was set in the early evolution of the target cosmos. Reversing the geometry had an unforeseen side effect though. The speed of light fell drastically as singularity approached. This was unanticipated but did not negate the desired results.

The second attempt was a failure. The entity repeated all the steps that it had done the first time, but no focal point became apparent. It had no explanation, as it didn't understand the process behind its creation to begin with. For some reason, some universes must have them while others don't.

A third attempt was entirely successful. The entity had encountered no problems. This supported the supposition that there were differences relating to the focal points of singularity in other domains.

On the latest attempt, things started according to the entity's plan. Something was different though. Geometry proceeded to process in reverse as expected. The target domain shrunk into itself at speeds greater than the speed of light but slowed substantially upon approaching the final focal point. It was just crawling towards singularity at the last stage of the collapse. This was very different.

Again, the entity had no understanding of this phenomenon. The domain was foreign to it so there was no ability to model a solution locally. There was no choice but to intervene directly in order to finish the process.

The center of the collapse showed a slowly decreasing bubble around the fixed focal point which was dominated by baryonic matter. The entity was aware that this existed but had little experience in its manipulation. It could rotate through the two supplementary time dimensions while in the distant universe. However, the properties of that domain had them very tightly rolled up and coupled. Any use of them would take too much subjective time that would result in its poisoning.

The entity worked arbitrary rotation operations through all twenty-six dimensions. This brute force action smashed whatever it came upon. It had no choice but to do this through the entire area of the stubborn region. When the operation had been more than half completed, some of the baryonic matter began to emit a broad range of radiant energy. Some of this caused portions of its extensions to be poisoned. This forced it to retreat and a minute part of itself was lost.

This invoked a feeling that the entity had never experienced before. It didn't know how to react. This hurts!

The final collapse eventually ended and the entity was able to harvest the singularity, but it needed to know how and why this happened. During the next attempt, it was going to create a pocket universe that had all the properties of the harvested domain. It was going to put this baryonic matter into it and bring it back for study.

CHAPTER 3

WELCOME TO MY WORLD

No one ever told me that grief felt so like fear.

C. S. Lewis

Fear makes us feel our humanity.

Benjamin Disraeli

They found themselves in a massive hanger deck. At least, that was what it looked like. You could have put a large passenger jet in here with room to spare. Some of their equipment made the trip with them. There was no time to gawk. People were hurt.

Ryan surveyed the group. Dave and Lindsey were shaken but OK. So were Braedon, Corey and Alan. Likely that would change later when the full effect of what happened hit them. Ryan knew that he'd have to keep going in the short run. Later was a different question.

Geoff and Milena were the worst off. Geoff was still bleeding profusely. The carpet tape wrapped around his arm had controlled it a bit but that wouldn't last too long. He was losing too much blood. He was getting paler and had lost some of his lucidity. Thank god for carpet and duct tape. You should always have some on hand. It provides a short-term fix for just about any physical problem.

Milena suffered an entirely different problem. She was in shock. She watched her mom die. She was the only kid in a single parent family. No one, to the best of Ryan's knowledge, knew if her dad was dead or alive. He was never mentioned and never in the picture. Josie Amara came from a very religious family and got pregnant when she was only fifteen. Josie had been raised a Catholic and was against abortion and so elected to keep and raise her child. Her mother, in good Christian fashion, kicked her out of the house and onto the street. Josie's father just followed along and supported his wife's decision. They didn't even give her a bag of clothes or any cash. Later, she tried to introduce her parents to their grandchild after Milena was born. Her parents wouldn't have anything to do with either of them. They refused to have any further contact with their godless child and grandchild. It was their loss. Whatever they thought of Josie, Milena was an absolute charm and a very good girl, thoroughly dedicated to her mom. They were alone in an unjust and unforgiving world. If one assumes that there's such a thing as a Christian god, Ryan could only hope that there was a special place in hell for people like Josie's parents.

Josie did her very best for Milena. Friends and even some of her old neighbors helped them out a bit in the beginning, but when it came right down to it, Josie was on her own for the long haul. She managed. She proved her real worth as a human being in raising her daughter. No job was too small or menial. She had been a short order cook for quite a number of years now, which provided for a level of stability for their small family. Josie never once lost any of her scruples or morals. She had everyone's respect. Now Milena, little more than a child, was truly alone.

Lindsey had moved to help Geoff with Dave assisting. Ryan was now free to go to Milena. She had gone fetal;

curled up in a tiny ball, arms tightly wrapped around her body, eyes tightly closed, and breathing slowly. He tried to roll her flat on her back, but she was unresponsive. Not good.

He reported to Lindsey, "Milena's in deep shock. I can't do anything for her. How's Geoff?"

"He's holding his own so far. The blood's still leaking out of him. He's starting to look a little clammy, but at least he hasn't bled out yet," she responded and then winked.

"Pass me a beer and I'll top 'er up," said Geoff mumbling his words. "I'm getting really thirsty."

"Sorry bud. The bar's closed. We'll see what we can do later," offered Dave.

That exchange told Ryan that things were bad. It could get a lot worse if not addressed immediately.

One of the blue characters, the one in a green toga, came over to Ryan and spoke. "How's the little girl?"

"She's in shock and needs help. She's starting to feel cold to the touch. Her pulse feels weak and rapid, but I'm no doctor. Can we get some help for her and my friend over there?" Ryan asked, pointing to Geoff.

"It's on its way. My friend Free-Credit is making an emergency call now. It'll be here in just a few seconds. We can go through introductions and deal with your questions later. Let's take care of the injured ones first. My guess is that all of you will need a medical evaluation too. That was a very unhealthy environment that we were all in," disclosed Questionable-Advice.

"Thanks," was all that Ryan could think to say.

Ryan took a second to look around. The massive room didn't appear to prefer a direction for up. They stood on the floor, but it could as easily be a wall or ceiling. All surfaces had drawers and tool assemblies built into them.

Seconds later, a wheeled vehicle that looked remarkably like the old USA space shuttle, but jet-black, wheeled up to them. He didn't see where it came from but suspected one of the large doors in the side of the wall behind him. They must be exceedingly quiet for him not to have heard it coming. It was low to the ground but didn't have exhaust rockets at the back or on the sides. The wings were almost nonexistent but indicated that this vehicle must have more than one purpose. There were no angled surfaces. Everything was smooth and rounded. No windows were visible at all. A door opened inches above the floor. A small ramp extruded out to smooth out the difference.

Out of the vehicle rolled two gurneys pushed by four paramedics. The gurneys had many medical instruments hanging from their sides. One of the individuals appeared to be the standard template for any paramedic you'd find back home. The other three were subtly different in look and gait. All of them had brown skin and dark hair.

The other blue guy in the white toga, Free-Credit, was giving instructions to the paramedics in another language. Normally Ryan wouldn't blink an eye at something like that except the language was so different from the various ones he was used to hearing. One gurney went to Geoff and the other to Milena.

The blue guy with Ryan said, "Call me Questionable-Advice. I'll act as translator for you."

"Thanks," Ryan repeated again. His verbal skills seemed to lack substance. He suspected he was starting to go into shock himself.

Questionable-Advice was conversing with the two paramedics next to Milena and then turned to Ryan. "They want to know if she was hurt physically in any way. Do you know?"

"As far as I know, no. Geoff and I tried to keep the roof from falling on her. I think that her immediate problem is that she's in deep shock. She watched her mother die. She has no one else. What about radiation?" Ryan asked. "I presume we were all dosed."

"Yes, probably but that's our least immediate concern. We'll take care of that later for everyone," replied Questionable-Advice.

Milena and Geoff both had an IV system hooked up to their arms quickly. It was difficult getting Milena on the gurney, but the paramedics managed it somehow and got her straightened out and onto her back. Both patients had their feet slightly elevated so Ryan figured Geoff must be in some degree of shock as well. They also had blankets placed over them that were light brown and dense, much like felt. These things would actually keep a person warm unlike what they provided at home under similar circumstances. Lastly, the medical workers put masks over their faces to supplement their oxygen intake.

They wheeled both gurneys towards the shuttle when Free-Credit called out to everyone there, "Everyone in. We all need to go to the hospital and this is the quickest means. Let's go. Quickly, please."

Ryan joined the others following the gurneys into the shuttle. The paramedics strapped the gurneys down. Both Free-Credit and Questionable-Advice instructed the members of their party on where to sit and how to wear their seat belts, which had two shoulder straps.

The inside of the shuttle was similar to how you would outfit a small jet as an air ambulance. If you were looking towards the back from the front of the vehicle, the gurneys were on the left. All of the seating was on the right-hand side in rows with two seats abreast. There were windows to the outside on the seated side. Not so on the gurney side. Ryan just hoped this ride wasn't going to take too long as they were flying and not driving.

Corey had a window seat at the back with Free-Credit next to him in the aisle seat. In front of them were Dave and Lindsey, and then Braedon and Alan. Ryan had the front window seat and next to him was Questionable-Advice.

Ryan looked at Questionable-Advice, its green toga contrasting against the light blue complexion. He knew he wasn't anywhere near home. He was about as far away as it gets. "How long until we reach the hospital?" he asked.

"We'll be there in ten minutes," Questionable-Advice answered.

"You mean that we're taking a ten minute flight to get to the hospital?" Ryan responded.

"It's the fastest way. It was too inconvenient to take the ground transportation where we were. It would have taken up to fifteen minutes longer. This is an extremely uncommon situation as I'm sure you've already guessed. Speed was deemed to be in all of our best interests," Questionable-Advice responded.

The vehicle was moving now. Ryan was looking out of his window. He watched as a large door on the wall open away from the front of their transport. It looked like they were making egress from the hanger there. It turned to go through the door, but he couldn't see any runway. They exited out into the black but starry heaven. He felt his stomach drop and said his first intelligent word since they got there. "Whoa!!!"

◻ ◻ ◻ ◻ ◻

Ten minutes later, they arrived at the medical facility and disembarked from the shuttle. Geoff was mumbling about his wallet and health insurance card. He wasn't able to reach it, but no one was paying much attention to him at the moment. They must have given him some pretty good painkillers. Ryan didn't think the insurance cards would be any good where they were anyway.

Both Geoff and Milena went directly to examination rooms. Ryan watched them go. Medical staff showed the rest of them to a waiting room, accompanied by the blue

97

guys. Almost no time had transpired from the time they got off the shuttle to ending up in this place.

Apparently, no one had told these people how a hospital should run. The entrance had no door. Anyone was free to walk in or out at any time. The staff didn't make them wait for an hour or two for service. The room they were in was bright yellow. Sunlight seemed to come in through the casement windows that ran from floor to ceiling. Ryan knew for a fact that there was no local star that could provide this level of light. The place had very comfortable plush beige sofas with small but tasteful wooden side tables. The floor looked like natural oak. Numerous plants and even some small trees were in various places throughout, providing some areas for privacy. Most of the smaller planters had flowering plants with yellow, white, red and purple flowers. The smell of Jasmine filled the air. It must have come from the plants. Ryan put his nose in one of the white blooms and confirmed it. The setup was very comfortable and not at all hospital-like.

Ryan began the introductions and introduced each of them in turn to both Free-Credit and Questionable-Advice. He added the names of the patients in the examining rooms so that no confusion would result.

"We've some time to talk now," offered Free-Credit. "No doubt, you've got as many questions as do we. For now, let's keep it general. In the morning, the world-ship Pretty-Ugly will interview each of you. First, let me assure you that you're perfectly safe. You have a place with us and we won't abandon you. We'll provide you with places to stay and food to eat. We also know that you've undergone an extreme trauma and will need time to deal with it. You're our guests. Please don't worry about any costs. We have taken care of that. Who wants to go first?"

"We're in space, aren't we?" asked Corey. It was more a statement than a question.

"Yes. We're in your home system but in the outer fringes. The world-ship's been harvesting resources from the Oort cloud. That's why you could see the stars so well. The sun's too far away. Additionally, we were in free-fall for most of the trip to the hospital. It also explains why you felt like you were falling," Free-Credit responded.

"Are you from around here?" asked Ryan. He couldn't think of a better way to put it.

"Yes, we originate from the same planet that you came from; Earth. We estimate a world-line fork happened some twenty-thousand years ago which separated our histories. Ours are different from yours. So we do share the same space as your home but not the same experiences for that period," replied Free-Credit.

Dave had a lifelong interest in cosmology and could follow most of this but didn't think the others would understand. "How do you know our language then?"

"A cloned mentality of Pretty-Ugly had been studying your world-line for the past one-hundred years. It monitored everything it could about your civilization as part of its studies. It returned very recently. The information it learned was downloaded directly to me," responded Free-Credit.

Lindsey piped up. "You don't look like you're from earth. What are you?"

"I'm a drone of Pretty-Ugly, which is a world-ship of the Space Ship Collective in the Hamlet," asserted Free-Credit. "That makes me pretty much a robot from your perspective. The Hamlet is our larger culture. Pretty-Ugly's an Artificial Intelligence Derived Sentient, or AIDS. I'm an artificial intelligence, or AI, serving under it. In some ways, we're the same entity, in most ways we're different. It's all a matter of perspective."

Free-Credit continued. "My partner Questionable-Advice is a drone of Neat-Mess, a scout class member of the Space Ship Collective in the Hamlet. We look the way that we do so that others can easily identify us as agents of an AIDS. When people speak with us, they know that they're also talking to our superiors."

Alan asked, "The people we saw in the ambulance didn't look much like us. One did a bit but not the rest. How come?"

"Our earths developed differently," answered Free-Credit. "The period of time wasn't long as those things go, but a lot happened during those twenty-thousand years. Homo sapiens dominated your world. All of the other species of Homo became extinct. We don't know why. Your technologies developed slowly. From what we can derive from your records, it seems that excessive power struggles within your species resulted in delayed development. Our world was different. Multiple lines for the genera Homo survived. In addition to sapiens, we also have other species such as the floresiensis and the neanderthalensis. You may not be aware of some of the other Homo species. Another difference that you'll see is that the sapiens here are all brown skinned with brown eyes. They don't have the pigment variations that you're showing and none has Asiatic features," it replied. "These species worked together to develop our knowledge. This meant that our technology evolved much earlier and under more stable conditions than yours did. At present, we call our collective the Hamlet, which is a Level II culture. Do you understand this reference?"

"It means you've got the capability of controlling the equivalent power output of one or more stars. We still hadn't made it halfway to a Level I yet," replied Ryan.

"Our technology is several thousand years senior to yours. We rose to this level very conservatively and slowly. Your culture, on the other hand, has grown at an incredible rate over just the last one-hundred and fifty years. You were catching up fast but were coping with some of the fall-out such as pollution and the inequalities amongst the geopolitical realms found on your world-line. At some point we'd like to discuss these," suggested Free-Credit.

Ryan heard someone come into the room. He turned around and saw a little person who hardly made it up to his armpit; not even that high. It was wearing a simple light brown shirt with dark brown shorts. It seemed to be female, but it was hard to tell, as he didn't have the relevant cultural background to provide a firm identification. It spoke briefly to Free-Credit and then turned around to face all of them.

"I'd like to introduce Comfort Olaha. She's the top Comfort on the whole world-ship. She doesn't speak your language yet, but you may talk with her at any time through the world-ship. She's responsible for the personal supervision of your friend Milena. Translation services are only a second away," offered Free-Credit.

Braedon felt confused. He put up his hand and then hastily pulled it down again and spoke instead. "Um, is Comfort Olaha a doctor?"

"Not in the sense you're thinking. 'Comfort' is the title of the care workers who are responsible for the mental wellbeing of the patients. A physical injury is only half of the recovery problem for anyone in the hospital. We can patch bodies up, but it takes a real specialist to deal with the traumas of the mind. Members of the floresiensis species are especially adept at this valuable health-care function. They feel deeply and with great empathy and can sense and react to emotional needs very quickly. Comforts have a social status higher than medical doctors have. They have everyone's respect. A Comfort isn't the same as psychoanalysts in your world line," stated Free-Credit. "Comfort Olaha tells me that Milena's in deep shock as you suspected. They sedated her and her blood pressure is back up to normal. When she comes to, she'll have much to deal with given what she's experienced. The Comfort will be with her the entire time and won't leave her side until she's well. She's only come out to ask you all to come back tomorrow when the girl wakes up. She'll need your support and active participation. You'll be alerted for when."

Braedon continued, "What's she do exactly?"

"Every patient's different. The principle thing is that Comfort Olaha won't leave her. She deals with treatment at an emotional level. If Milena needs to scream at someone, then Olaha will be there for her. Likely, she'll go through that phase at some point of her convalescence. The Comfort will provide kisses and hugs, a body to cling to when needed, a shoulder to cry on, a person to chat with in full confidence or to ignore as required. If an emergency happens, she'll be there to get the appropriate help as fast as is physically possible. Comfort Olaha is there to do everything needed to help the patient regain a stable mental state. Also, the treatment won't stop when Milena's discharged. Comfort Olaha won't accept another patient until she's certain her current charge is thoroughly fit. She'll stay with Milena until that time. This is a full time dedicated commitment that she takes great pride in."

"Wow! The lady has my respect. Um, thanks," Braedon told them.

Ryan thought to himself that this finally capped it. They really had no idea how to run a hospital. "What about the language issue?" he asked.

"That will be taken care of tonight. Comfort Olaha has an embedded mempro prosthesis. It'll allow her to download your language directly from Pretty-Ugly. It will take her several days to be comfortable with using it. Some things won't translate very well due to cultural contexts and references. In addition, there are differences in the vocal chords. There are some sounds that will be difficult for her, but she'll make do. Have no doubt. She's the top in her field. Milena will likely find her to be a lifelong friend once the worst is over."

Ryan walked over to the Comfort and took her hand. He knew that she wouldn't know what he said but spoke anyway. "I just want to personally thank you. We'll be here in the morning to help you any way we can. Thank-you so very much," he told her most earnestly.

Free-Credit translated this for her. She turned to look at all of them, uttered something in her native language, and then held up her hands like she was holding a salad bowl and did a little curtsy. She then turned around and went to catch up with her charge.

"She looks forward to seeing you all tomorrow," Free-Credit translated.

Questionable-Advice pulled a hand-held device from somewhere in his toga and began scanning each of them in turn. Free-Credit explained, "My friend is testing you for radiation exposure. This is a precaution only. They scanned Milena and Geoff but found very little superficial exposure. Those of you who were outside of the protective bubble had ionizing radiation exposure. Please don't worry too much about this. The environment we were in exposed all of us to gamma rays, but they don't penetrate very deeply. You may end up with sunburns if you're unlucky, but that'll be the extent of it. For now, we'll find you rooms in this facility so you'll be closer to your ill companions. Later, we'll find you something more permanent. A sedative will be available should you need one. We strongly recommended that you take it especially if you've left loved ones behind. Some of you also may wish to speak with a Comfort. We'll also arrange that for tomorrow. I understand that you've had an extremely long day. I've received word that Geoff's OK and is sleeping now so you can see him tomorrow. Let's see how things go after your talk with Pretty-Ugly. Please follow me while we sort out your rooms."

¤ ¤ ¤ ¤ ¤

Ryan woke up and was surprised to find himself in a strange room with a slight sunburn. His mind was slow in coming back. Yesterday started badly, got worse, and then ended in total disaster. He remembered someone bringing him there. That person showed him around but couldn't speak his language so he didn't get much out of it. It must have been one of the comforts. He received a long bathrobe, so he stripped off his clothes and put it on. A small room off to one side functioned like a bathroom. His helper started a shower for him and he got in it. When he came out, he used the offered towels. From there, Ryan's minder took him to a large bed and made him drink a sedative, which tasted like a fruit drink. He must have fallen asleep almost immediately. Ryan didn't feel like he had just come out of a drugged stupor. For that matter, he didn't feel like he'd been drinking the night before either. He was wide-awake, alert and ready to deal with some serious issues this morning. He still wasn't entirely sure what happened last night or how he got here. He was very worried about Alyssa and the kids.

The bed wasn't too different from what he used at home. It had a light blue bedspread with regular sheets and two pillows; near queen sized. The support did seem different. Maybe they used some kind of memory foam. Side tables were on either side of the bed. The room looked more like a high-end hotel room. If you were looking from the room entrance, you'd have seen a sofa and two comfy chairs facing a wall that was probably a high definition TV. He wondered if it had passive 3D. Between the chairs, sofa, and wall TV was a low table. To the right was a working area, which included a desk. It also faced a wall screen. The top of it looked like a touch screen, so it was likely a computer or interface. Behind that was the bed that he currently occupied. Further in the room was a window to the outside that didn't have any drapes. Sunlight was shining in through it.

Ryan got out of the bed, stepped towards the window and looked out. He could be no higher up than three stories. Looking down, he could see a galleria lined with trees. There was no visible sun, but light did shine from a virtual sky. Looking down, he could see a terracotta road and wide mezzanines running parallel to it. Doors and windows were evident along both with busy people going back and forth. Most were walking but occasionally you saw something like a scooter going by. The brick facades of the buildings were similar to what he'd see back home. There were lots of windows. What little metal he could see only appeared in the decorative fences found around the fronts of some entrances. The painted black railings surrounded these apparent patio areas. There was further evidence of this as tables and chairs populated these and had people sitting in them. No chrome was evident.

Turning around, he could see that there was plenty of light in the room from the windows. He wondered how to turn the lights on and off just the same. He remembered the light coming from his ceiling last night. Another issue was curtains. And what about his clothes?

The low table in front of the TV had a bowl of sliced fruit and two pitchers with glasses. One of the pitchers had water, but he wasn't sure what was in the other. He sat down on the couch, poured the unknown liquid from the pitcher into a glass and sipped it. It wasn't dissimilar to ice tea so he decided to drink it and eat the fruit for breakfast. That would help him get his head together before meeting back with the others.

Once he had his fill, he heard a buzz that went on and then off twice. Figuring it to be a doorbell, he called out "Come in." This saved him from having to figure out how the door worked. He probably just had to walk towards it.

In walked one of the blue guys. This one had a white toga on so it must be Free-Credit. "Good morning, Free-Credit," Ryan greeted.

"Good morning to you too, Ryan," it replied. "We weren't sure what to provide you for your morning meal and didn't want to wake you. Was the fruit acceptable? It seemed the most generic fare that we could offer without greater cultural input."

"It was fine. Thanks. I usually don't eat breakfast. Usually I just drink coffee but I don't know if you have that here," Ryan answered. "It's not that important and we can figure it out later."

"Before we get into weightier matters, is there anything else that you require?" Free-Credit asked.

"I was just wondering about my clothes. They seem to be gone," answered Ryan.

"Your clothes were covered in your friend's blood and were a mess from yesterday. We scanned them and are reproducible at any time. You may even vary the colors and textures if you wish. You just have to enter the bathroom and name the things you want. The ship interactively prints and delivers the clothing to you on the shelf next to the towels. Just describe what you need if you want an item modified in some way. At the end of the day, you can put the clothes into the hamper in the same room for recycling."

"Thanks," replied Ryan. "Give me a second to get dressed and then we can get started. Any idea where the contents of my pockets ended up? I'll need my wallet and phone."

"They should be in the drawer of the side table," Free-Credit suggested.

Ryan stood up and checked for his wallet and phone. Everything was there including some loose change. He then walked to the bathroom. The door opened when he got close and closed when he was inside. He wondered briefly how that worked for married couples.

Aloud he said to the mirror, "Please provide me with the same things I wore yesterday. Thanks." He thought it always paid to be polite even if it was only a computer. Especially if it's a computer, and given his current situation.

There was an empty shelf next to the towels. In a couple of seconds, his clothes appeared through a port at the back. He took them down and put them on. Everything was there. Then he needed to pee. He stepped to what passed for a toilet and let it go. The second he started, there was a slow trickle of water going into the bowl. He guessed that meant no need for courtesy flushes. There was no toilet paper, he noticed. He'd figure that out later. He stuck his hands under the shower and rinsed them off. That was easy. He turned around and went back to the main room.

"Thanks again," Ryan insisted. "I've really appreciated everything you've done so far. However, it's time for that talk."

"Yes it is," stated Free-Credit. "The world-ship will be joining us. I'm its representative but don't contain its full mentality. It wants to join us in its whole persona. It'll show itself on the viewing wall as a drone embodiment. I hope you don't mind. It's more personal this way. Otherwise, from your perspective you're just speaking to a box."

"Sounds good to me," Ryan replied as he sat down on the couch. Once he had said this, the TV instantly had a picture on it. It was a drone but wore comparable clothes to his own. It was sitting on a similar couch. It had the same light blue complexion but was perfectly bald. The face looked to be around the same age as Ryan. The video feed was greater than high definition and was passively 3D. No glasses required. It looked like it was sitting in the same room as him.

"I'd like to introduce the world-ship Pretty-Ugly," put in Free-Credit.

"Hello, Ryan," said Pretty-Ugly. "I'm very happy to meet you and have been impatiently looking forward to this meeting since your arrival. Are you comfortable with this presentation of myself? I tried for something that you'd feel relaxed with."

"Yes, that's fine thanks," replied Ryan. "I want to thank you on behalf of myself and the others for the courtesies you've shown us. If it weren't for you and your crew, I think the lot of us would be dead now. Speaking for myself, I'm extremely grateful. Can we speak about what happened? I've got so many questions."

"So do I," replied Pretty-Ugly. "I'd like to take this in a particular order if you don't mind too much. I promise you that we will get to what you want by the end of our chat. I know you're impatient."

"OK. It's just I want to know about my wife Alyssa," blurted Ryan. "I'm scared to death right now."

"I know," it replied. "We will cover that. First, Free-Credit and Questionable-Advice told you that we have been monitoring your society for the last century. I've some questions which I think that you may be the best qualified of your group to answer. I've asked many of the same questions to some of the others, but I believe they have the wrong perspectives to answer them. I'd like to ask you about some societal issues that have confused us."

"I'll do my best," replied Ryan. "Just so you know, I'm no sociologist."

"We're extremely curious about the past-time you refer to as music. It intrigues us. From what we can see in other world-lines, this is something that's extremely rare. We don't have it here. We possess recordings that people do listen to and enjoy. These are of noises that you'd hear in nature, such as waterfalls. Almost all of them originate dirt-side of the gravity well and are very familiar to our citizenry, patrons, AIDS and AI. Can you provide me with a summary?"

"Wow," exclaimed Ryan. "That was the last thing I expected. Um, where to begin?" and he paused.

"Music is something enjoyed by all human cultures at home," Ryan continued. "We've found other animals also experience it. I've seen dogs and wolves singing along. Parrots often mimic songs, as do other birds. Cetaceans also seem to understand it. On our earth, people created it but we weren't the only ones to appreciate it. As near as anyone can figure it out, it likely originated in our prehistory by Celtic races and spread across the planet. We speculate that it developed from early hunting practices. For instance, bird-whistles attract prey, the banging of sticks together and later drums to drive herd animals over a cliff or into some enclosure. From there it then got brought into culture through ritual dance and then evolved into what it is in our culture today. This is just speculation. Currently, it's used for entertainment."

"Your sciences dealt a great deal with frequencies and harmonies. A particular sub-science called string theory used musical theory extensively. Is this related?" asked the world-ship.

"I'm not a physicist either," Ryan stated. "I wanted to be one when I was in school but I never had the opportunity to pursue it. I'm not that great a thinker. I did develop a lifelong interest in cosmology because of it though. That makes me modestly familiar with an overview of the rationale behind it but weak on the details and mathematics involved. The universe is a very strange place; hence, my interest. I've read huge amounts of science and speculative fiction to help feed that interest. It helps to keep me asking 'what if' questions that aren't necessarily addressed by our current scientific levels of achievement."

Ryan continued. "Music was with the human race long before science and math. We discovered things by accident such as the division of notes on a string. Halving a string moves the note up one octave; where to put holes into a bone so that when you blew into it you'd get a particular note. These were all things learned by trial and error.

Tuning depends on tension regardless of it being a string or drum head. Once science became part of our culture, it applied the rules of mathematics and pattern matching back to music. Initially, music developed its own notation but was separate from mathematics. Later mathematics caught up and could tell why the notation worked the way it does. What mathematics can't explain is the enjoyment that we derive from a mixture of rhythm and tempo, notes, harmonics and timbre. Music has an auditory spectrum similar to the way that light has an optical one. Does your community appreciate visual arts or poetry?"

"Yes," replied the world-ship. "Some very strongly. Others, not so much. We've artisans that dedicate their lives to the pursuit of the arts."

"Then we aren't all that different," replied Ryan. "We have visual arts as well. We believe that these disciplines developed after music did, but no one knows for sure. My understanding is that some cave paintings go back more than forty-thousand years. If this is true, then there's a common point we share between your world line and ours indicating that you should have it. I wonder why you don't have any music."

"I can't answer that," responded Pretty-Ugly. "We may have had it in our prehistory and then lost it. One of the differences between your world-line and ours is the belief in religion. We don't have it here. We suspect that our original primitive cultures may have, but grew out of it. As you said, music may have evolved in association with ritual. When our societies lost that, they might have lost music as well."

"You now have a bunch of players including a vocalist here," began Ryan. "The people you brought back from my world are all musicians except Lindsey, Milena and myself. We do try to play a little bit but aren't in the same class as these guys. When the drones turned up, they were playing to a crowd for entertainment. I was there for my own musical pleasure and to dance."

"Can you explain that a little more?" the world-ship asked.

"Sure," offered Ryan. "We've many different genres and sub-genre of music. Different people enjoy different types of music. This has to do with exposure and education. For others, it's just habit. I like the music that Dave and the band play aesthetically. The music, vocal themes, and rhythms fit my temperament. It taps right into my emotions. The only way for me to describe it is to say it takes me to another place. I'm alone and by myself. At the same time, I'm a member and part of the crowd sharing precisely the same emotions collectively. Mentally, I also become a member of the group. I can relate to each individual member. They're all one and the same. All of these are strictly emotion and feeling. It can also be a very intimate experience. It taps into a primitive part of myself and I'm up and moving synchronously with the music. Sometimes people choreograph this movement, but not when I do it. I like it to be raw and emotive. That's dance."

"Then the experience isn't related to science?" asked Pretty-Ugly.

"If you asked the guys how they played what they played, they'd tell you that they worked hard and practiced. That's very true. In reality, musicians need to have obsessive-compulsive traits to do it well. Songs are strongly associated with pattern matching and it takes an extraordinary skill set to be able to do that. When a musician plays, they're very conscious of the music but are rarely aware of the separate notes or the tempos played. If you asked them about the mathematics, they'd probably stare at you blankly. It wouldn't occur to them what they're doing is mathematical in its form. They do it more with their feelings and most of them wouldn't understand the math. Geoff might be more aware of some of the math involved because he's a sound engineer. Even then, he uses that for the audio equipment and not necessarily the music itself." Ryan paused in thought for a moment with a puzzled look on his face and then continued.

"I'm not sure you'll agree with this. You guys are pretty far ahead of us scientifically. I believe our world-view of mathematics may be different from yours. Our mathematicians have never confused any mathematics with the description of the actual real world. We view it as one of the three most successful real world 'models' ever developed. The other two are language and text. They provide a formalism with specific rules that allow us to model it. They even use the same principles, such as equivalency, for example. They all provide different ways of modeling reality based on internal formalisms, but often produce different results based on the initial assumptions. The format of that model limits the information it can provide. At the same time, it's not the real world. In speech, I can say 'tree.' On a daily basis, using that spoken word usually meets my needs, but I wouldn't claim that it is a complete description of what a 'tree' is. Content regarding species, structure, cellular makeup and other equally relevant descriptions are missing content from the word. Let's just look at math. We develop ideas, using it to describe a problem. If the mathematics fits closely enough, then we consider it a success. We don't consider it the final word. We had a guy named Newton who gave a very good analytical description of gravity and the rules behind how it works. Later, people found exceptions that showed in some ways his equations were wrong. The orbit of Mercury around the sun had unexplained discrepancies for example. It wasn't until another guy named Einstein came along that we got a better description of what was happening. In fact, the new approach was so successful that the math was able to predict a whole bunch of other things about the universe that no one had thought about before. Things like black holes, time dilation, the speed of light and the relationship between energy and mass. Here's the thing though. In our world, we still used Newton's equations for doing things like trajectories and similar problems because they were simpler and worked just as well most of the time. I still say 'tree' on a regular basis even though I know there are better characterizations. Interestingly Einstein's relativity pioneered work on world-lines, which Minkowski refined further. I only thought of them as a tool to describe events. Until yesterday, that was only theory as far as I was concerned."

Ryan continued. "Math is great at describing things. It can tell you what to expect and what's happened. It can't give you the mechanics for how something happens. The underlying reality is lost in the model. Math isn't music and music isn't math. Let me give an alternate example. We can model the movement of an electron. We can even show under what conditions it'll tunnel across a semiconductor or insulator. What we don't know, is what actually happens to the electron. It's there. It disappears from the world. Then it reappears. Mathematics can model it but can't tell us what's really happening. There are many similar irregularities in our math such as the collapse of probability waves and the role of observation. Most math that we've produced show stuff like this happens. When using the right math we also get results that don't represent reality, as we know it to be. Maybe it represents reality in another universe or something, just nothing here. Our physicists always prefaced their research by saying that all the math is correct. The true result for a particular problem will be the mathematic theory that models the problem correctly. In our world, theoreticians spent much effort attempting to find accurate models. Our mathematicians spent a lot of time following up on 'what if' questions called thought experiments. Often they had no physical findings to work from and had to create their own framework."

"A good example is string theory," suggested Ryan. "It contains within it billions of possible characterizations for how any particular universe might work. We suspect that one of those descriptions describes our cosmos, but we don't know which one. It may actually be a collective description for the physics of all possible realms. At this point, the people investigating these issues don't know. We don't even know if it will yield discoveries for new physics but are hopeful. Their goals would include discovering the reasons for why the fundamental constants of our domain are what they are. Another problem is how observation and will affect event outcomes. We've no scientific underpinning for this but do know their actions. There are many questions but few answers. Sorry, but that's all I have."

Pretty-Ugly was doing a good imitation of an academic on the TV thought Ryan. Then it responded to him.

"Excellent. That was what I was looking for exactly. Our mathematical science proceeded differently than yours. Ours evolved by modeling observation rather than taking a theoretical approach. As such, our innovations moved more slowly than on your world-line. We just started much earlier and went forward over a much longer period of time."

Now the picture on the TV was looking much more serious and started to speak again.

"It's now time to review the incident from last night. First, I'd like to get your impression of what happened. Please don't worry if it's correct or not. I'd like your honest first impression."

Ryan was quiet for a moment. Now they were coming down to the crux and he needed to know about his family. Slowly he took a deep breath and then let it out to help settle his nerves. Once his breathing resumed a normal pace, he began to speak.

"Yesterday was a highly emotionally charged day for me. That'll probably influence what I have to tell you. I started my day by being fired from my job. I've little or no job prospects available to me because of my age. So I currently have no livelihood in my culture. I went home and told my wife. That was a very difficult conversation for me to have with her. My wife and I come from different cultural backgrounds. We both respect each other's. Last night she was spending an evening with people from her own culture. I spent the night with people from mine. My wife and I do that from time to time. It helps keep our marriage fresh and provides us with some free time apart from each other to do things our partner mightn't necessarily enjoy. It was my 'boys' night out.' I went out. Not far. Just around the corner from my home. This was to see Dave and the band. I love music and dancing. So does my wife but her musical preferences are different from mine. So she had some friends over and I was going to catch up with them when the bar closed."

Ryan continued. "I arrived just before the first set. They normally play three sets. I mingled around some, as I knew many of the people there. I also had a couple of beers. That's an alcoholic beverage. The first and second sets were excellent. I was starting to feel better about myself. Music and dance often does that for you and you can work out much of the day's tensions. Between sets, I spoke with Dave and Lindsey. Over the last couple of years, they've had similar problems to mine so we have a lot in common. We compared notes. I also chatted with a lot of other people about other things."

Ryan paused to think. This was the part where the disaster began. "The third set began. The music they played was exactly the music that I needed to hear. Between the lyrics and the music, I'd managed to work my level of consciousness into the area where I needed it to be. It accurately mirrored my emotions. My dancing reflected it. I felt like I was myself. Alone. I also felt one with the universe. I was a part of everything. It's hard to describe exactly. Something discordant emerged, pushing itself into my awareness. I still don't know what it was. A buzzing started and got very loud. I think that everyone first thought something had gone wrong with the sound system, but it wasn't that. Then a roar came from everywhere. I thought gunfire erupted. People in the audience panicked and ran for the exits. I was on the dance floor next to the band. It was around this point that Free-Credit and Questionable-Advice showed up in their magic bubble. One of them left the bubble and put some kind of instrument on the floor. Things had gotten very strange at this point. There was time dilation affects. As people were running away, they were moving slower and slower. People who were jumping stayed in the air a lot longer than they should have. The further the person was, the slower they got. My guess is that if they were looking back at me, things would have been normal for them, but I'd have looked slowed down from their perspective in keeping with symmetry. Far away, matter was undergoing a radical change. I could see it out the windows looking out over the patio. Where stuff had frozen in place, it began to glow. I don't mean that light reflected off this stuff. I mean that it started to glow the way some things glow under ultraviolet light. Likely, that wasn't the only thing emitted. Light frequencies may have been doplering, but I wasn't paying that close attention to it. Things were getting more and more tenuous. There was a lot of oscillating noise associated with these changes."

"That was when things really went south," confided Ryan. "The movements of the physical effects were slowing down as they were approaching us. At one point, I thought they might stop. Maybe that was wishful thinking on my part. Something massive, like a huge wall that went up forever, kept phasing in and out of space. Where it appeared, it destroyed everything. It would appear in one location and then disappear. Then it'd reappear somewhere else. Wherever it went, it left total destruction in its wake. It was as if it was alive. When you could see it, it was waving back and forth as if it was consciously trying to rub out what was there. Your guys shot a number of weapons at it without affect. The last weapon had an effect. I don't know what it was, but it made a lot of loud noises. Focused sonics? At any rate, where the wall was hit it changed to yellow and then green. Then it disappeared and didn't come back. I hope it was hurt. It killed many people including Milena's mother. My god! She watched it happen. Poor girl. By then, those of us who survived were either already back in the bubble or forced into it by the onward movement of the effects creeping towards us. It was as if we were its focal point. When it surrounded the bubble completely, we popped back here. I've my guesses about what caused all of this, but that was what I saw."

No one interjected anything at that point. It was embarrassingly quiet, so Ryan said flatly, "Now tell me what happened. What about my wife and kids?"

Pretty-Ugly looked directly at his eyes. Impressive for a TV. It disclosed, "We don't know what caused the event. We were studying your world-line when the event occurred. That was partially how we became aware of it. What you described was the lead-up to the collapse of your world-line. It collapsed to a singularity. It took your whole world. We don't think anyone was in pain when it happened. Time dilation stopped time for all those caught in it. We don't know what happened to the singularity. It disappeared; your whole world-line branch destroyed. Your wife and children are dead."

Ryan didn't say anything. He couldn't say anything. He was confused. Then he was stunned. Then it hit him. It started with a couple of tears and then moved on to a torrent. A profound sense of loss hit him. He'd never be able to overcome these feelings. Unashamed, he cried.

Pretty-Ugly suggested, "You, Geoff, and Corey all had immediate family there. Let's join Milena. It's easier to share the grief than to be isolated and alone. You all need each other right now."

◻ ◻ ◻ ◻ ◻

Ryan didn't remember leaving his room with Free-Credit. He could only think about Boo, Crispen and Alyssa.

Boo was like her mother. She felt everything. She trusted her feelings more than she trusted anything else. She had a sixth sense about her. There were rare times that she couldn't or wouldn't warm up to people she had met. Inevitably, she turned out to be right and the person she'd have nothing to do with turned out to be untrustworthy or dishonest. It took him a lot longer to figure that out for himself.

She was at the age where she had become all girl. She grew her hair long, took to wearing cute outfits and experimented with using makeup. She would have been a holy terror as a teenager. There was a completely new world here for her to discover with her feelings. Only she wasn't here.

Crispen spent an enormous amount of time on the computer. He had an insatiable thirst to figure out how to do things. It first started with watching videos on gaming and then developed into other things such as how to do magic and how to make paper airplanes. That turned into an interest in origami. He had started to read real books; not just picture books. He even started asking questions about cosmology and the oddities of the universe. He would have felt so at home here.

Alyssa wouldn't have been so comfortable. There would have been a loss of connection to her family and friends, but not as profound as what he was feeling now. She would have gone through anything back home to maintain those connections. Their last day together had been such a disaster and he had so hoped it would have improved once he had gotten back home from the bar. Now he would never know.

How was he going to sleep at night? They'd only slept apart a couple of times over their entire marriage. They were always snuggled into each other and ended up on the same side of the bed. Sometimes his; sometimes hers. The only time that didn't happen would be during hot and humid nights in the summer when they'd decided not to turn on the air conditioning. Even still, they usually woke up holding hands. He was not going to get used to sleeping alone. Not ever. He knew that without even having to think about it. He missed her so much.

Time slows with the increase of a gravitational field. If the world-line moved towards singularity, then time would virtually stop to an outside observer. How would this appear to someone participating on the inside? Would they even notice it? You'd also look squashed to an outside observer due to length contraction. Would this carry into the singularity? Ryan didn't know.

Energy converts to mass with velocity. As you near the speed of light, the slower your clock is relative to the rest of the world. You get heavier and gain weight. If the speed of light were slowing down, would the time dilation effect become more apparent at lower relative speeds to the outside observer? Would a tau of zero be approached sooner and effectively freeze time for the observer? How would the participant see this? Apparent distances shortened. Wouldn't everything just collapse to a single point in these cases? Wasn't that what the singularity was? Were they still alive and contained in that point but frozen in time forever? Did the disaster consume them?

Further questions were almost beyond him. He could only hope that when the end came that it was like turning off a switch. One minute you were there. The next you no longer existed. You just end with no knowledge of what was happening.

These things kept going around and around in his mind as they walked. If he kept this up, he was going to have a nervous breakdown.

Ryan hadn't even been keeping track of their path as they walked so he was lost. That was OK. That was how he felt anyway.

Finally, they came to the door. It opened for them after a few seconds. There was no need to knock.

They went inside. The room was very similar to his own in layout. The windows let in the simulated sunlight, which gave the room a cheery feel that was the opposite of how he felt. The TV screen was on showing a natural scene of a waterfall. He could hear the trickling of the water. Huddled in a group were Milena, Geoff, and Corey. They were all holding onto each other. Comfort Olaha had her arms around all of them.

Ryan began to cry again.

¤ ¤ ¤ ¤ ¤

The sapiens were a sad lot. Half of the eight new arrivals were in awful shape. The world-ship had laid out the facts to each of them after informing Olaha of the nature of their anguish. They had to tell them. There was no point in giving false hope where there was none. It was a necessary part of the recovery process. Olaha would bring the others in later after she had a chance to assess the level of damage with these ones. The others didn't have the degree of damage that these four had suffered.

Pretty-Ugly had sent the relevant language and social data to Olaha's mempro the previous night. There was much more of it than she had expected. It had turned out that they were under intensive study at the time the trauma occurred so there was a lot of data to review. It was going to take some time to integrate the pertinent information properly. For now, Olaha would settle with their mating patterns and family norms as it pertained to their larger native society. No doubt, a firm integration of their language would take longer as no standard language roots were common to their cultures. She was going to have to substitute some of the phonetic sounds as she unable to make some of them. The tongue shaped most of these sounds and hers was not as agile. Her own language came more from the throat and the tongue was a tool for eating. Hard consonants and sounds using the tongue on the top of the mouth were hardest. They would understand her though and it would get better with time.

For now, Olaha felt that verbal communications must take second place. It was more important to get them showing and sharing their pain.

She was gratified to see that these individuals had well-developed Homo instincts and sensibilities. When gathered together, they were all expressing their grief by crying, a standard mammalian reflex. Milena, Ryan, Geoff and Corey shared no everyday relationships. Their relationships were more tenuous than that. They were more friendly acquaintances than anything else, although Geoff and Corey seemed to have a stronger friendship. As a group, they all gravitated to the one who was the youngest and weakest. That was Milena. They all wrapped their arms around her and each other protectively. This was extremely positive and showed strong social bonds, obligations and aptitudes. This was exactly as expected from most of the genus Homo. There were historical exceptions where some of the species sapiens took advantage of their peers. It was aberrational and indicated either sick social norms or sociopathic tendencies in the individual.

Olaha approached the group and put her arms around them as well. Their pain was palpable to her and she was sharing it with them. For this, they were all the same species.

Sometime later, they'd calm down. Each person still suffered painfully. It was obvious. Olaha wanted them to begin to share their inner feelings with each other. They had to bond in a different way. They had to be each other's family now. This needed doing to avoid grief related major depression that was gravely debilitating and required medical intervention. Comforts were extremely proud that this didn't happen much anymore. Life and death were a daily occurrence to all lives. It was something that everyone had to grasp. Even AI's and AIDS weren't immune to it. A healthy mind required balance. Knowledge with experience of this pain was part of that balance. It was natural to grieve and was amongst the most intimate experiences in one's life. The loss of anyone dear to you was hard to bear. This was getting rarer in her own society, but it still happened.

So far, the stages of grief were going as expected. First was the initial period of numbness that leads to depression. Her wards were all well into that now. More difficult would be leading them through the rest of their recovery. Each one needed a reorganization of their own personal worldview. They'd all be different and very personal. Once in place, then genuine recovery could begin. The important part was the avoidance of unhealthy grief. This was different for everyone. All would go through this process in their lives, often more than once. There was a tremendous amount for them to overcome. There would be acute and overwhelming feelings of anguish and shock followed by loss, guilt, anxiety, anger, regret and fear. Later would follow loneliness, unhappiness and despair. They might even find these feelings and emotions to be shameful and frightening.

Milena and Ryan still had their arms around each other. Corey was close beside them but was no longer embracing. Geoff had moved across the room to sit on the sofa by himself. Olaha decided to start with him. She walked over and sat beside him. She took his hands into hers. He was the second youngest of the new visitors. He might be a little more than double Milena's age.

"Geoff," Olaha said quietly having difficulties with some syllabics. "You're by yourself and not with your friends."

"I know. I needed a moment to myself," he responded. "I can't stop thinking about Cindy and Liz."

"Please tell me about them. If you share this with me, then there will be two of us to remember them," Olaha asked softly. Geoff seemed to have no difficulties understanding her pronunciation. The words and grammar were correct so he was filling in the wrong or missing sounds himself.

"Cindy was my wife," Geoff responded. "We met when I was in my early twenties. She was just a little bit younger than I was. I was working a function raising money for a medical charity. I don't even remember what one. She was a volunteer there. We didn't hit it off right away, but we had mutual friends. Every now and then, we bumped into each other socially. After a year, we started dating. It just blossomed from there. We got married two years after that. We got an apartment and Liz was born a little later. Liz was age four going on sixteen. My god, I miss them. I should remember the fundraiser. Why don't I remember what it was for? Oh god."

"The point is to remember your wife and child. The event that you mentioned is a little thing. It was a tiny moment in time. What you have to remember is far greater than that. Don't feel bad. You must honor their memory. They still live in your heart and in your mind," Olaha offered.

"I didn't have to work last night. I should have been at home with them. We should have been together," Geoff confessed.

"There's no blame. No one could have ever known what was going to happen. I'm certain that this was not an uncommon situation for your family. You were out working and you wife was at home looking after your child. This was always the way of things even going back to our hunter-gatherer ancestors. This is a natural condition. You've got no guilt to bear," Olaha responded.

"I still think I should have been there," Geoff blurted.

"Do you blame your friends for that?" Olaha asked.

"Good lord, no. How could they've known? We were all victims here. We've all lost what made our lives worthwhile. Still, I should have been there," Geoff said.

She put her arms around him and hugged him tightly. She couldn't have been much larger than his child. He held her back just as tightly. They both shared the pain.

After a period, he was starting to settle down. She could see that he was remembering. She hoped that it was mostly the good memories. You still needed the bad ones to make the good ones better, but it was best to keep them rare.

"Will you be OK if I go back to the others for a while?" Olaha asked him.

"Sure. I'm just remembering. I'll be OK. Thanks," Geoff responded.

Olaha walked back over to the huddle centered on Milena. Dave and Lindsey had joined them at some point. Ryan was there as well, but Corey wasn't. Braedon and Alan were also in the room but were off to one side by themselves looking very self-conscious. They weren't an immediate concern.

"Where's Corey gone?" Olaha asked Ryan.

"I think it was too much for him," Ryan replied. "I didn't know his three kids were adopted. He told us that and then left. He probably went back to his room."

Olaha checked with her mempro and verified that was where he went. "Will you be OK if I go and talk with him?" she asked the small group.

"Sure," replied Dave. "We'll take care of each other here. You go find Corey." The others just nodded or grunted in agreement.

Olaha looked around the room one more time before leaving. She didn't want to leave Milena, but the girl seemed to be in good hands.

She walked towards the room's entrance, which opened as soon as she was close to it. Olaha turned to the right and proceeded down the hall. The hall was unremarkable. It used the standard sunsim lights in the ceiling. The floor was an ochre colored tile. The walls were an earth-tone green color that was bright and very homey. Patients and visitors rooms were interspersed with each other, some with their doors open; others closed.

She only had to go forty meters to get to Corey's room. Olaha stopped at his door, waiting for the proximity sensors to announce her presence. Nothing happened. She checked her mempro again and verified that he was inside. Pretty-Ugly would have interfered if he had tried to injure himself. She had no notification of this. So he was just not in the mood to confer with her. She had the world-ship set up direct voice communications between her mempro and the viewing wall in the room.

"Hello Corey. I'm feeling a little lonely standing outside in the hall," Olaha said. "Can I come in and talk?"

After a moment, he answered. "Sorry, but I'm not in the mood to talk right now. I won't be good company. Besides, you're not my type."

"That's OK. I'd still like to come in and chat with you. I know you're hurting badly inside," Olaha assured him. "Sharing it will make it easier."

"Then you don't understand," Corey replied. "I want the pain. I don't ever want to forget it. I need to feel it at its deepest. You don't get it. Everything I ever had or worked towards is gone. Everything I did was for my family. That's all gone so go away."

"I do get it," the little hominid responded. "I think you worked much harder on your family than the others did. Their pain is no less than yours, but family life came more naturally to them, didn't it?"

"After Gwen and I got married, we attempted to have children. Gwen wanted them so badly. Gwen had three miscarriages before we found out that she had ovarian cysts. The cure meant that we couldn't have children of our own. Artificial insemination was not an option. Finding this out almost killed her. It had taken us a couple of years before we decided on adoption. We started with Norm. Gwen was so happy and things worked out so well that we then adopted Evan and Tracey. They were such great kids and we loved them so much. My mom was hugely proud of me before she died. I think that I surprised her," Corey responded.

"I can understand why your mom would be so proud," confided Olaha. "It takes a very unique individual to stand up to what life throws at you. You responded by throwing it back. Then you went one better. You made better lives for the children that you adopted. Without you, they wouldn't have had that. You and your wife were exceptional just as was Josie Amara, Milena's mother. You need to hold onto that."

Olaha listened to the link. All she could hear now was sobbing from the other end. She issued an override on the door. It opened and she stepped inside. She went straight to Corey. She put her arms around him and they both cried.

◻ ◻ ◻ ◻ ◻

Olaha experienced one of the most difficult weeks that she had ever had in her career. She was emotionally exhausted after sharing the feelings of the eight refugee's now in her charge; all of them damaged by their experiences. Normally, she only had to deal with one. She felt herself beat up. The worst had been Milena and Corey. That wasn't to belittle the pain the others felt. It was just that those two didn't have the built-in coping mechanisms that the others had developed over their lifetimes. Now it was time for a change in treatment strategy.

Olaha was alone in Milena's room. She had hardly left it the whole time, spending her days and nights there. The light was dim in the room as it was getting towards the end of the day and the sunsims outside were giving off less light. She had elected not to enable the interior ones. She was enjoying the twilight.

The others all went to Dave and Lindsey's hospital room to share a meal. It was good to see them bonding this way. They were very much alone in this world, sharing nothing in common with most of the world-ships inhabitants. Language was a major barrier but was the least of their problems. Additionally, they shared the knowledge of the world-line attacks that almost none of the patrons shared. It was relatively simple keeping this knowledge isolated to the hospital. However, the refugees required integration into the larger community. Additionally, they didn't need the hospital resources at this point. Treatment could continue outside of its confines.

She sat in front of the viewing wall with her feet curled underneath her. Olaha let herself sink back into the plush cushions waiting for her scheduled meeting to start.

The screen in front of her changed and showed the image that Pretty-Ugly used for itself. Olaha couldn't help feeling a little nervous. In the past, she had only ever communicated with the world-ship through an intermediary such as one of the drones or even her own mempro. This meeting was one on one. At least she would feel more comfortable as they could confer in their everyday Hamlet language. She was confident in the job she had done so far. In fact, she was proud of the job she was doing. Her charges had progressed quite well in one week, given the circumstances.

"Greetings, Comfort Olaha," said Pretty-Ugly. "I've been following your progress and am very impressed."

"Thank you," Olaha replied. "I believe that it's time to move to the next recovery level and get them out into the larger world outside of the hospital. A pastoral setting would be the most appropriate. The bustle of the main corridors might be too much for them. They should be eased into dealing with that."

"True," Pretty-Ugly replied. "Can you provide me an overview of each person's results to date?"

"Yes," Olaha stated. "Braedon Hoople and Alan Harris were the least traumatized. Both were single and had no children. Braedon's parents were both dead. His closest family member lived on the other side of the continent from him. They hadn't spoken in years. He was not dating at the time of the incident so has few ties back to their old life. Alan's only living relative was his mother, who lived in a hospice for years. She had a debilitating illness that caused dementia. She had suffered from it for a number of years prior to the event. It got worse over time and she couldn't recognize her own son. He stopped visiting her as it was too painful an experience. He had carried much guilt over that but had resolved the worst of it long before arriving here. He had no steady mate. Instead, he went through as many females as he could. Apparently, the women he was with were of the same mindset. Neither of these two will be an ongoing concern."

Olaha continued. "Lindsey and Dave Langdon are the only mated pair in the group. Dave's parents were deceased. Lindsey left a mother behind. They have no children. These two rely on each other to assist in coping with their current situation and have been there to support the others as needed. They're both very compassionate people. I don't

128

doubt that they'll survive this trauma having no detrimental effects down the line."

"The rest of the adults require more support," she continued. "Corey Josephs, Geoff Wong and Ryan Foley all have similar issues. All three were married with children and had close relations in their lives. Geoff is the youngest and has the best long-term prognosis. He's young enough that he can start over if he so desires. Corey is full of guilt. He had a much harder time putting his family together. His wife had medical issues and badly wanted a family. He thrived on the support that he provided to her. They adopted three children together and provided them with lives they wouldn't otherwise have had. He's devastated. So much of his personality was devoted to his unswerving dedication in helping them. He made his family happen. It will be very difficult for him to recover entirely. I'll settle for functional, but that won't be for some time. Ryan is also devastated. He had an extended family in his household and was devoted to all of them, including his mother-in-law. She originated from an overpopulated country with an underperforming economy. He took her into their home to free her from poverty. He was involved daily with the raising of his children. Although sad, his primary emotion has moved in a different direction. He's mad at what caused this to happen. He wants to go after it but doesn't know how. The simplest way to look at him is to understand this motivation as revenge. Even if his revenge was fulfilled it wouldn't solve his anger issues."

"Will he be a danger to himself or others?" asked the world-ship.

"No. He's respectful to all others around him. I haven't seen him yell or berate anyone. He's always been the first to step in when one of the others was experiencing grief that they couldn't cope with. In his own way, he's a very admirable person. I just can't help him with the anger that he harbors."

"I've been thinking about that. I've got something in mind that might help," offered Pretty-Ugly.

"That brings us to Milena Amara. It was an accident that she was there during the event. By the laws of her former culture, she was not supposed to be there. She watched her mother die when it happened. She had no other relatives. She only ever had her mother. Life has been very unkind to this girl. She was lucky that the community she found herself in through her mother was supportive of her welfare. It could easily have gone in an entirely different direction. The biggest problem is her age. At fourteen, she's too old to be a child but too young to be an adult. It's a very impressionable age and how we deal with her will profoundly affect the rest of her life."

Olaha continued. "This girl is unbelievably fortunate to be in the group of people she found herself with. Not one of them will allow anything harmful happen to her. They're extremely protective. That said, she's also the one who's lost the most. She's lost absolutely everything including the parent who would have guided her into adulthood. If done properly, her long-term prognosis has the greatest odds of success. She's intelligent. She's feeling. She'll overcome this and become the great person that I'm sure she's destined to be."

"What do you recommend for the next step?" asked the world-ship.

"We should move them out of the hospital," Olaha offered. "They need to stay together as they rely very much on each other at the moment. I suggest we don't move them into one of the more active modules. They may actually have originated from a similar environment back from where they came from, but they would be at a distinct disadvantage here. They aren't used to dealing with patrons and the races involved. Also, there's a language issue. I suggest that we move them into a rural area, into a multiple-residential compound. This would provide them with private residences but at the same time provide them with a sense of community that they still need. They could still travel around freely. This will also gradually introduce them to the more substantial parts of the world-ship community over a period without overwhelming them. They also need to learn the language. Lessons would be beneficial. I don't think that it would be good for them to learn quickly so I don't recommend that we make mempros available to them yet. That can be a decision they can make later as they become better acquainted with the Hamlet. They need to be able to do this on their own or they won't feel any sense of accomplishment or pride in action."

Olaha paused and then continued. "Lastly, Milena needs a mother figure. I don't recommend a native sapiens due to the cultural and language disjoint. She would have to leave the current group, which I deem to be inadvisable. That could cause her further pain. Since Lindsey is a friend, she doesn't meet the functional requirement for this role. At the moment, I'm staying with her. I'll continue to do that, as she will require ongoing treatments for some time. Our relationship is very strong currently and I've become her active surrogate mother. I propose that we make this a formal relationship and carry it forward. I don't see this as affecting my current duties detrimentally."

"I'm entirely in agreement with you," surmised Pretty-Ugly. "Indications are that our visitors can also play a larger role in our world-line investigations than we'd originally thought. They've brought with them a fresh perspective. I know just the place. They'll have very few but interesting neighbors. I'll have to put a transfer station in nearby so that you can get back and forth quickly."

The face on the view screen smiled at her and remarked, "I'm obligated to you Comfort Olaha. You've confirmed my faith in you. You're one of the most amazing and wise people that I've ever met. You humble me."

Olaha's dark skin didn't allow her to have a visible blush, but her physiology did. She could feel it move over her shoulders, up her neck and across her face. She had never heard of a world-ship that provided any level of praise. She was very proud and emotionally exhausted. When the meeting had ended, she closed her eyes and had a good cry just for herself this time. She hadn't cried in a long because she was happy.

Big changes were coming. She hoped she was up to them.

CHAPTER 4

REMEDIATION

Healing is a matter of time, but it is sometimes also a matter of opportunity.

Hippocrates

Healing yourself is connected with healing others.

Yoko Ono

Milena had gone through a lot. None of the pain had gone. It would never go away. Olaha told her that it was there for a reason. It was to help her keep the memory of her mom alive. She also said that Milena would learn to manage these feelings and learn to live with it. Time was a great healer. Milena was just starting to believe this for herself. She felt better today than she did the day before. This trend had kept up for a week now. There were still times that she couldn't prevent herself from crying, but things were more manageable now.

Today was the day she could finally devote some time to herself. It was an opportunity to explore and this excited her tremendously. She'd never been anywhere like this before. Sure, she'd lived close to the country in her old home, but couldn't spend much time there. Her mom didn't have a car so she was limited to the local parks for the most part. On occasions, she'd hopped on her bike to accompany some of her girlfriends to a small river that was twenty minutes away from home, but that was pretty rare.

She was dressed in a white short-sleeved tee-shirt and light blue jean shorts. She put on leather open heeled sandals over her bare feet and decided that a tie in her shoulder length light brown hair would be appropriate. Her self-assessment in front of the mirror was positive, but something would have to change regarding the lack of makeup. The glittery stage of her tweens had passed, but a girl still had to keep up her self-esteem.

They had moved into the arcology compound the previous day. There was something about moving. Regardless of how much stuff you had to move, it always took a long time. She was an expert on the subject. They had almost nothing but that didn't change anything. The guys ended up bringing some of their instruments and equipment to this world by happenstance. It needed cataloging and came from another part of the world-ship. They put it all in the aft-building. That was the end of the compound pointing to the back of the ship. Directions were going to take some getting used to. Up was pointing towards the center of the world-ship. Down pointed to outer space. The acclimatization session yesterday provided them with an overload of information. She suspected the only way to learn it all was to live through it.

She was still in the fore-building, which divided into a shared kitchen and the local equivalent of a family room. The group had taken to calling it the fore-commons.

They had just finished with breakfast and were cleaning up. The group had made it themselves. Still, you had to wonder why you had to do the dishes. Sure, there was kind of dishwasher appliance in the room, but this place was so advanced you would have thought that they'd have figured out a way to do away with that bit of work completely. Everyone was there and chipped in to help, so at least it didn't take very long.

Olaha was leaving for the travel tube, which would take her to the hospital. She had some work to do back there but would return in a few hours. When she got back, there would be lessons to start. This left Milena with a precious few hours unsupervised for the first time since arriving here. After saying good-bye, Milena decided to head spinward of the compound.

It was really lovely. She followed a broad grassy path that branched periodically between tall stands of trees or shrubby growth. The trees were mostly a mixture of several types of maples, ash and oak. The occasional birch tree poked through the others adding some contrast. She had no idea what the shrubs were, but they were dense and some had berries on them. She would have to find out which ones she could pick and eat. Sometimes she saw the odd chipmunk. There were even baby rabbits sometimes seen in the underbrush. Grey and red squirrels were in abundance.

The light from overhead came courtesy of arcology sized sunsims. They were just like the ones in the compound only much larger. They gave the impression of a comfortably warm summer day. From her perspective, this was a sunny day. They were told that the world-ship would change the climate occasionally, keeping with the needs of a healthy and natural habitat. Importantly, weather reports were actually accurate here. That was a nice change from home where the reporters were wrong more than half the time.

After ten minutes, she came across a small stream with fish in it. There were a few larger fish that were colorful and might be butterfly koi. They were very colorful. She followed the stream's flow. The koi were following her as she went. Maybe they expected her to feed them, she thought.

Eventually, the path opened into a grassy field next to a large pond or small lake. She wasn't quite sure what the differences were between the descriptions. The small river ended here. One side had a fine-grained white sandy beach. Patches of variously colored flowers dotted the entire area. Walking towards the beach, she stopped at a patch of yellow flowers. She picked one of them and put it in her hair over her right temple while thinking that this would be a great place to make daisy chains. There were no daisies in sight, but that didn't matter. There were lots of substitutes.

She continued until she reached the beach and the water's edge. She slipped her sandals off and stepped into the water. It was refreshing and pleasant. The water was beautifully clear. She could see right to the bottom. Shortly thereafter, the koi showed up and swam around her legs, occasionally mouthing her toes. They were so forward and brazen like some boys she used to know. She stifled a laugh, but the fish were very persistent. At last, she couldn't hold it in any longer. She started laughing a deep belly laugh. Not very ladylike. This scattered the fish for a few seconds and then they were back.

After a few minutes, she managed to contain her laughter and paused to catch her breath. That's the first time she'd been able to laugh in a long time and it felt very nice. She silently thanked the fish.

She left the water and sat down beside her sandals. It was so quiet and peaceful. God, she needed this. She looked over the waters to the other side, only seeing more fields and forests. It really was a beautiful place even though they were inside a sort of building. If she didn't know any better, she would have thought she was back home in a woodland park.

It was also good to get away from the others. She really did appreciate them being there. She wouldn't have gotten through this without them—not even with Olaha's help. It was just that it was so cloying. There was always someone there. Now she needed some alone time; some distance from the adults. She needed to be herself, by herself.

Looking over the water, she released her mind to wander and veg. Time became something to lose track of.

After a while, her bottom started to hurt a little so she needed to shift. Milena put her right hand onto the sand and she moved her weight over to it so that she could twist a little bit. She stopped short. Next to her, less than a foot away was an Ephalem. Its front end was up in the air waving slightly from side to side and facing toward the small lake. Last night, when they informed the refugees about some of their new neighbors, this little fellow was at the top of the list. She'd expected some kind of slimy worm, but he wasn't like that at all. He was more leathery and was actually a lot less threatening than she'd expected.

After a minute or two of her staring, the head end turned towards her. Was it checking her out? In its mushy little mouth, it carried a long stemmed rose. The head moved towards her and she raised her hand palm up. It placed the rose into it. There were no roses around that she could see. She took it, brought it to her nose and sniffed. Its smell was beautiful and brought back memories of outings that she and her mom had taken to flower gardens in the past. An incredible flood of memories came to her and she was momentarily lost in reverie.

She looked up and said to the little creature, "Thank you so much. This rose is beautiful. Its smell is delicious. This brings back such wonderful memories. My name is Milena. You must be Pilgrim. We were told that we might meet you."

Pilgrim's head bobbed up and down a little more. There was a purring sound coming from his body that was quite pleasant.

"I understand that you don't talk much," she stated. "That's OK. I'm very happy to meet you. You're the first new neighbor I've met. I'd really like it if you'd stay with me for a little while. I'd enjoy the company."

It purred at her. They sat beside each other for some time. After a while, its head slipped down onto her lap. This way it didn't have to hold its body up. It must be much more relaxed this way she thought. Absently, she started stroking it. Much later, she realized that she was probably late for lunch and lessons were on the schedule.

"I'm really sorry but I've got to be getting home. I'm expected. I really enjoyed this morning. You're really good company. I can come back tomorrow morning. I'd like to see you again if you've got the time."

She continued while starting to put her sandals back on. "I can bring a swimsuit and a picnic basket for lunch. We could go swimming if you swim, and then have lunch. Maybe I'll even bring fish food for the koi. Would you like that?"

It purred right back to her. She answered, "That's a date then. My first date here. Um, my first date!" She smiled. "I can hardly wait Pilgrim. Thanks for the rose. I'll see you tomorrow morning."

She got to her feet and the Ephalem's head bobbed up and down. She smiled at him and then turned to go. After several steps, she turned back. It was still watching her. It was checking her out! She beamed her smile and waved back to him. She then continued on her way.

She thought about the encounter with her new friend as she started following the stream back. He was really nice, not at all threatening. Any preconceptions she had were gone. She knew he was a pleasant and decent fellow. Maybe she'd invite him over to dinner some time to introduce him to the others. Ryan would get a kick out of him. Pilgrim didn't talk much for sure, but he didn't need to. He was just good company. She was sure they would see that.

Turning away from the stream, she continued back to the compound.

Remembering last night's lecture, the Ephalem was supposed to be from a Level III culture. The others thought that meant tremendous power and intellect. Pilgrim wasn't like that. He was just nice; the same way a kitten could be nice—and they didn't talk a lot either.

She could see the buildings of the compound now; the walls made from the ceramic material that the world-ship seemed to prefer. It was an earth-tone terracotta and went well with the differing greens of the plants, trees and grass. The roofs might or might not be solar cells. They were black and glassy. She guessed that was one way to conserve energy. There were probably batteries under the plantings somewhere. She moved towards the fore-commons.

Once there, she entered and could see she was late. Oh, oh! She thought for a second. Before anyone could say anything to her, she proclaimed to them, "Sorry I'm late, but I've had a wonderful morning. I've got a new boyfriend." She offered her rose for their inspection, smiling like a Cheshire cat.

◻ ◻ ◻ ◻ ◻

It was all that Lindsey could do to do keep from breaking out laughing. When Milena came in and presented her trophy rose to them, all of the boy's jaws dropped in shock. She was sure that Olaha felt the same way she did. Guys could be so fragile sometimes.

"So, tell us about your new beau," Lindsey requested while wondering whom the girl had taken up with around here. There weren't a lot of other people in the area unless she ran into someone having a picnic. That seemed unlikely, as most of those people wouldn't have come this far into the arcology.

"Well, um, he's not a beau exactly. But I like him," Milena replied. "Have you finished lunch?" Milena had her eye on Olaha.

139

"Yes we have and you're late for your lessons. I've set aside sandwiches and a drink for you. Please sit down and eat. Lessons start when you're done," responded Olaha.

"Spill the beans girl," began Lindsey with humor in her voice. "What were you up to?"

The girl sat down at the island they were using as a table in the kitchen and began to eat her lunch. Between bites, Milena managed to get her story out. "After breakfast, I decided to go and explore the neighborhood. I walked to spinward until I came across a stream that had koi in it. I followed it for a while and it emptied into a small lake. Maybe it was a large pond. Anyway, it has a beach and a beautiful grassy area around it. There were some really nice wildflowers growing there. I just sat on the beach. My head was kind of empty and I was just vegging to the quiet and the water. The next thing I knew I had company. I didn't even see him come up."

"That sounds pretty," Lindsey replied. "You're going to have to show us. We need to get to know the area anyway. Maybe we should have a picnic."

Milena looked up. Her eyes were wide with surprise and it was her turn to have her mouth drop open. "Um, I'm going on a picnic tomorrow morning with my friend. We were going to have a swim and then lunch. Maybe feed the fish."

The faces on the guys were getting hilarious again, thought Lindsey. She was going to have to put them out of their misery soon. She was starting to get a handle on Olaha's facial expressions. There were definite traces of hilarity about those eyes. The lady had a sense of humor after all. There were a lot of hidden depths inside that woman. They shared looks with each other. Lindsey just about lost it.

"Young lady, please finish you lunch. You start language lessons right after," stated Olaha.

"So, was he cute? Athletic?" asked Lindsey.

"He wasn't what I expected," Milena replied.

"Guys never are. So spill it," asserted Lindsey.

"I met Pilgrim. He's the guy who's supposed to be our neighbor, the Ephalem. I don't know if you would call him attractive or athletic, but he was really nice," offered Milena.

Dave was mid sip on some kind of fruit drink. The timing couldn't have been much more perfect. The mouthful went flying and he started coughing and choking to the great entertainment of the girls. The rest of the guys just groaned in relief. At least someone took the time to bring these guys up properly. They cleaned up after themselves.

Milena continued, "I'd like you all to meet him. I really do like him. I don't know where he got this rose. I didn't see any in the area. It was really nice of him. Can I bring him home after our date tomorrow so you can meet him?"

"After your date?" said Lindsey.

"It's my date. You can meet him after," replied Milena quietly. The girl was setting some firm boundaries around her social life. Yep. Definitely a teenage girl. These were the opening shots. It could have been much worse. This just proved that Josie was a damned fine mother. She would be missed. She was going to get a little prayer tonight whether she liked it or not.

"It's up to Olaha. She gets the final say as your guardian now. What do you think?" Lindsey asked.

Olaha turned to look at the girl. "I'm fine with that. I understand that he is very nice. He's been very helpful to the world-ship and drones. Just remember, this does not get you out of your classes. Those come first and foremost. If we start your classes late tomorrow, then they end late. Do we have an understanding, honey?"

Milena got up from her seat and put her arms around Olaha. "Thanks. I really mean it. Thanks for being here. Thanks for asking to be my new mom. Thanks for being you. I know you'll like him." Once she had said that, she

141

planted a great big kiss on Olaha's mouth, which surprised all of them there, especially Olaha. She then started to clean up after herself, getting ready for her lessons.

Lindsey turned towards Dave and Geoff. "Come on. We have stuff to do, so let's go." She took Dave's arm and walked to the door. Geoff followed. Once outside, she grabbed Geoff's arm as well, so that she had a full escort.

After walking for five meters, they were into their secluded courtyard, which was fifteen by forty meters of grassy lawn. The four compound buildings loosely bounded it. There were structures on either side that contained their own bedrooms. Each building split into four private quarters having a common awning for shade. The building on the right was anti-spinward and had Alan, Braedon and Geoff's quarters. The last room on that side was Dave and Lindsey's. Their room was a little bit larger than the others were. The spinward building had a spare room followed by Corey and Ryan's bedroom. Milena and Olaha shared the last room.

They headed to the separate building aft of the courtyard. It was also common to the whole group. Currently, it held the music equipment that had followed them here through the bubble.

Ryan told them all that Philippine households often had a similar layout because family members owned such small parcels of land. Conventional structures like the ones found fore and aft, were a strategy that families used to maximize their land usage. That way, the family had access to something like a shared kitchen when they had no space on their own to have one. It was a collective form of living for the extremely poor. It made sense here because of their current social circumstances. They were creating a new family according to Olaha, but also needed privacy as well. So it met their needs very well. It was also a spacious way to live but might be inconvenient when the winter season inevitably rolled around.

They entered the aft-commons building and looked at the mess on the floor. They had a full drum kit, various foot pedals, the lead guitar, two rhythm guitars, and a single acoustic and bass guitar. Both monitors, the bass and lead amplifiers, and speakers were to the right. One side of the PA speakers had made the trip as well as the PA system itself. They were missing most of Geoff's mixing equipment, crossovers and live digital console as these were outside the transfer bubble. The cables pulled out of them when they had transited. A small collection of batteries was in a separate pile. They used these for the wireless miking system and for the foot pedals used for effects. They even had two roles of duct tape left as well as three milk cartons of different cables, extension cords, the wireless system and power bars. One LCD light stand made the trip. There were additional guitar stands, cases and bags. These contained items such as cleaning kits, spare strings and extra drumsticks and brushes. In all, they had a fairly large number of items brought back from their show.

Surprisingly, Lindsey's purse had also made the trip. She had left it in the stage area next to the PA at the Tower. She picked it up and opened it. She extracted a pen and some paper.

Everyone had also left their phones here. They had little use for them other than having the ability to take pictures while they still had a charge. There were also a lot of tunes on them, especially on Ryan's. He had something like seven-thousand or so on his. They didn't have the right adapter to hook it into the PA system. Power and charging were going to be a concern.

"Most of the sound reinforcement system is missing," stated Geoff. "You'll be restricted to small rooms with just this PA. We might be able to work something out with the world-ship though. If it was studying us as long as it says, then it can probably reproduce the missing components, speakers and batteries too. I bet it knows the Internet by heart."

"Probably," Dave replied. "It seems to have the capability to improve on the equipment that we have here, as well. We can't do anything without compatible power, one-hundred-twenty volts at sixty hertz. The right kind of outlet would simplify things substantially."

"You guys put a list together," said Lindsey passing Geoff the pen and paper that she took from her purse. "We will also need chargers for the phones so that we can get at our pictures and music recordings. If we do this correctly, we can work on equipment improvements later, maybe even instruments. Where do you want to do this demonstration for Pretty-Ugly and the drones?"

"Why not right here?" suggested Dave. "There's just going to be us and them. Once we get the correct power output this can be our practice area. If they approve, we can introduce music to the general populace by doing some concerts. At some point, we are going to face having to earn a living. We have a big advantage being the only musicians anywhere around here. You had better find out how currency and exchange works. If we do this right, we might actually make a better than decent living."

"Right," she said. "You guys geek out over the equipment. Give me the list afterwards. I have some things that I want to add to it anyway. Let Ryan and I deal with the ship. We're now your managers." She flashed them a wicked smile and then added, "So you had better shape up now or spankings will be dished out."

"I'm up first," replied Dave smiling back with just a very slight hint of humor in his eyes.

"Ryan's in charge of spankings," she answered. She turned away and walked back towards the commons building at the other end of the compound. As she left, she could still hear them talking.

Ryan and Geoff broke out laughing.

"I'm motivated now," blurted Geoff. "She's put the fear of god into me."

"Yep," replied Dave. "Try to imagine being married to her."

"I don't need to try. Gwen was just like that." He was quiet for a second and then spoke up. "I know we've talked about this before, but do you think it's time to add keyboard to the mix? It would take a load off Alan and expand the potential repertoire of songs. It's not as if I have any other obligations at the moment. We can teach Lindsey, Ryan, and Milena how to do the levels. I know Ryan has an ear for it. Milena would kill to do it. We could throw in some guitar lessons for them as well."

"You know, you're right Geoff. If we're going to do this, let's do it right. We have a really good mix of people here. We're never going to get another opportunity like this again. Add keyboards to the list. And welcome to the band."

Lindsey kept walking. The guy's discussion was fading into the background. Things were definitely starting to look up. They were thinking in terms of their whole new family. It made her feel warm inside. This was a good day.

❑ ❑ ❑ ❑ ❑

Milena woke up early. She was still tired from yesterday's language lesson. So far, not much of it was making sense. Then again, it was only the first one. She shouldn't expect miracles and knew there was going to be a lot of work before she could expect any forward movement.

There was a lot to get ready for this morning though. She had a date.

Olaha was out of bed already but not in the room. She probably had gone to the fore-commons building already. Her new mom was definitely a morning person, something

145

Milena knew she wasn't. Worse, she was also now a teenager. Her real mom drilled into her that teenagers needed more sleep than adults and most children. Unfortunately, much to her chagrin, she found this to be true. She had a double whammy going against her. Waking up was a challenge.

She threw the coverings off her and got out of bed. She walked towards the washroom. The door opened without her having to break stride and she was in. The door promptly closed behind her.

Milena liked the fact that she didn't have to brush her teeth. They had a gargle here that replaced toothbrush and toothpaste. It also freshened her breath and somehow cleaned off her tongue at the same time. As far as she was concerned, this proved she was now living in an advanced civilization.

On the other hand, some things were missing and she didn't know how to ask Olaha about them. She'd talk to Lindsey about women's toiletries later. Fortunately, she didn't need those things now.

She still didn't know what to make out of a combination of shower and toilet stall. The shower was easy enough. It wasn't really in a separate part of the bathroom. It was part of the room itself. You told it to start and asked it to warm the water up or cool it down. When you were done, you told it to stop. As one would expect, there was a drain built into the floor for the water to sink into. It just worked for the whole bathroom. So you never had to worry about overfilling the sink.

The toilet was another matter. Once you were finished doing what you were doing and told it so, it would squirt water from underneath to clean you off. In theory, it worked like a bidet but she had never seen or used one before which made it awkward. They had never heard of toilet paper here. If you wore nothing but very long skirts or togas, she imagined it would meet your needs. On the other hand, wearing shorts or pants meant getting water all over everything. She always kept a towel handy and within reach, especially when wearing pants. She guessed this was another thing to discuss with Lindsey.

She took her nightie off and left it laying on the counter next to the sink. She asked the shower to start and gave instructions to set the proper temperature. She jumped in and enjoyed the warmth. There was a nipple that you pushed on just under the nozzle that provided a combination shampoo and conditioner. There was another nipple for body wash. She used them to clean herself thoroughly. Once done, she instructed the water to quit and used the toilet. When finished, she grabbed and used a towel. This was probably how the natives did it.

"Can I have a brush and something to dry my hair off with?" she asked the bathroom. A brush appeared from the same dispenser where they found their new outfits. A blower vent appeared just under the showerhead that started blowing warmish air. She didn't have time to wrap a towel around herself so she just decided to start brushing and drying her hair.

Once done, she stuck the abandoned towel into the clothes hamper for recycling. She'd take the hairbrush with her for use after swimming.

Now it was time for some clothing items. "Can I have the same underwear and socks I wore yesterday? No bra. I'd also like denim shorts and top with an open back and uplift support in the front for my size. I guess you don't know what an Indian saree blouse is. Please make it a very light green color." Briefly, she wondered how you addressed a bathroom.

Once the items were dispensed, she remarked, "Thanks, bathroom." She hoped that would cover the niceties.

She put it all on. The shirt actually turned out pretty well. She had always wanted a saree blouse, but she never

147

thought she'd ever have one. It definitely had an Indian feel to it and was very sexy. It was open at the back and covered the essentials up front. It had a multi-patterned, multi-colored brocade around the high waist and neckline and a solid color of light green in between. Now this was exotic. She probably wouldn't have gotten away with it at home.

Now she needed her picnic supplies. "Can I have a picnic basket, beach blanket, bath towel and a two piece bathing suit? Preferably something to match the top. Can I also get a small package of fish food? Thanks."

Again, the things popped out from the dispenser. The blanket was a good size for two and was white which would reflect the heat. The bath towel matched her top. She elected to wrap it around herself like a sarong just in case there were complaints from the adults. The bathing suit was a light pink and was age appropriate. She'd figure a way around that later. She didn't have time today. Lastly, she had a small paper bag full of pellets. Those were for the fish she supposed.

She gathered everything together and left the bathroom. She put her sandals on. One more check in a mirror near the front door and she left to get breakfast with the others.

They were already there. It looked like fruit again for breakfast. This time there were also some buns that looked a little like croissants. They were good too. Milena had never pretended to be a vegetarian unlike some of the other girls that she knew from school. They were going to have to figure out how to get bacon and eggs at some point.

Olaha had already prepared her a luncheon of sandwiches and fruit. Both meats and vegetable items had been included. There were also two bottles of juice. The bottles looked like they came off someone's bike. Her guardian said, "I checked with the world-ship on the view screen." This was on the table that resembled a computer terminal. "This should be acceptable for both of you to eat. What time will you be back?"

Milena replied, "I think we will come back after we finish lunch. If I can, I'll bring him back to meet everyone."

"Sounds good," Olaha answered. "Just remember, you have language lessons afterwards. OK?"

"OK. Can I help clean up?" asked Milena.

"No. You go ahead honey. You can make up for it later. Bye," replied Olaha.

She grabbed the beach blanket and picnic basket. "Bye everyone," and Milena was off like a shot through the door turning spinward. She wasn't going to wait to listen for any replies. It didn't take her long to find the stream again. She followed it to the lake.

She didn't see Pilgrim yet so she put her gear down. She unfolded the beach blanket and laid it out on the sand. She took off her towel sarong and put it aside. Next came her sandals, which she placed next to the towel. She took the fish pellet bag out of the picnic basket and left it on the blanket. She left her bathing suit in the basket.

While she waited, she thought she would do some wading. She walked into the water and sure enough, the koi showed up again picking at her toes. As a smile began to appear on her face, she heard a noise behind her. It sounded remarkably like a wolf whistle. She turned her head and there he was, Pilgrim. She wondered briefly how he just managed to appear and disappear without her seeing it. That was some trick. And that whistle?

"Hi Pilgrim," she called out while waving. "I'm glad you came."

She waded back to shore and sat down on the blanket. "Come onto the blanket. I'm sure you'll be more comfortable than being in the sand. In this light, it's really scorching."

The little Ephalem came over beside her. She swore that he purred in approval. Once they were side by side, he began fluttering his head back and forth again. He turned his head away from her and then back. In his mouth was another long stemmed rose.

She squealed in delight. She couldn't help herself. He didn't have a rose before but now he did. He placed it gently into her open hands, careful not to stick her with a thorn.

"How in the world did you do that?" she asked. "That's a great trick. I bet the girl Ephalems are falling all over themselves around you. You are such a gentleman." She chuckled to herself.

"I brought some food to feed the fish with. Shall we give it a try?" she asked openly. She heard a soft cooing in response so decided to take that as a yes.

She stood and walked to the water's edge a few meters away. Unlike her mother, she was more comfortable using the metric system. The Imperial system had never made any sense to her at all.

Pilgrim was at her side, mouth pointed towards her head. She put the bag down on the sand so they could both get to it.

"I'm grabbing a few pellets," she told the Ephalem. "I'm going to wade into the water and wait for the fish. Then let's see if they take the food," she said to him. With that, she waded in a little further. It didn't take long for a couple of big koi to show up. She sprinkled a couple of pellets into the water. The fish kept pushing each other out of the way to get them. Finally, they were gone but more fish had arrived. Mouths all vying for a piece of the action surrounded her. She chuckled and offered, "Do you want to give it a try, Pilgrim?"

He grabbed some of the food with his mouth and moved into the pond. Half of his body was now in the water. The fish weren't shy and surrounded him too. He dropped the pellets in the water and they went for them.

The fish pushed him around a little bit but otherwise it seemed like he was having fun.

"Oh, look at that. Fickle fish. They've all gone to you." She laughed. "I need more food. I'll get the bag. Just a sec." She stepped back and got the bag. She came back into the water wading through the numerous fish to get beside Pilgrim. She took a few more of the pellets and sprinkled them into the water. A momentary feeding frenzy took place between her legs. At one point, she had to use Pilgrim for balance or she would have fallen over.

"That was fun," she beamed and held out the bag to the Ephalem. He made a cooing sound followed by a rattle and then a whistle. His head swung back and forth again and then bobbed up and down. She could feel something enter the bag and grab some of the fish food. She couldn't see anything, but the food came out, floating into the air. Promptly, the pellets spread out evenly over the water about thirty or forty centimeters high. They were waving back and forth slightly. She guessed the fish could see them as well as they started to leap out of the water to get to the levitated food.

"That is just so cool, Pilgrim. Look at those fish jump! Look at that silver one. It's so pretty." They stood there until all the fish food was gone and the fish stopped jumping. The fish stayed in the area, but there was no more fish food. They were out.

She looked at Pilgrim. He was already in swimming and she was only wading. "You're right. It's time to swim. I'm going to put my suit on," she told him. She waded back the couple of steps to the beach. She walked through the sand to the blanket and retrieved her bathing suit from the picnic basket.

Plainly, she hadn't thought this all the way through. There was no place to change. She could walk back into the woods, but that was a little way away. She surveyed the complete area and no one was around except for her and

Pilgrim. What the heck, she thought. She was human and he wasn't. They couldn't be more different. No point in false modesty.

Just in case, she turned her back on Pilgrim and took her clothes off. As she was getting ready to put the suit on, she heard another wolf whistle coming from the Ephalem. She looked over her shoulder and his head was pointing in her direction. That settled it. He was checking her out, she though with a little thrill.

As she put her swimsuit on, she called back to him, "A gentleman would look the other way," and giggled again. At least she was decent now. Probably a little too decent given the way the suit looked on her. She wondered if he could still see her if, he was facing another direction. It seemed likely, as he had no visible eyes. Well, it was just harmless fun anyway.

"Here I come," she yelled back while running. She jumped into the air and cannonballed into the water.

They had a lot of fun. Pilgrim was very versatile in the water. He could swim circles around her. In fact, he often did, making serpentine motions around and through her arms and legs. She wasn't so graceful, but it was still loads of fun. She'd lose any race though.

After a while, she tired. They finally worked their way back to the blanket and sat down. She brushed the tangles out of her hair. The Ephalem was right beside her and promptly put his head in her lap. "Ah. Poor thing. You're tired," she mused stroking his head area. Milena thought that they were both happy and satisfied. She put the brush down and then just stared off into the countryside without thinking anything. At some point, she laid back and might even have fallen asleep. She wasn't sure, but she was very content.

After some time, they broke open the food and ate their lunch. It was a lot easier to eat sandwiches when you had hands she discovered. This didn't faze Pilgrim at all. He just ate off the wrappings the sandwiches came in. The bottles turned out to contain coconut milk, which quenched the thirst they'd developed over the morning. She held one up for Pilgrim, which he didn't seem to mind at all. She figured he could have used one of his tricks to hold the bottle up, but she liked to do it anyway.

When they had their fill Milena asked, "My family would really like to meet you. They aren't my family really. It's complicated. You'd like them I think. Like you, we aren't from around here. I really, really like you and that means they want to know you too. I guess its instinct. They want to make sure I'm not hanging out with the wrong crowd. Can you come and meet them, please?"

Pilgrim gave his usual purring response.

"OK. This time, look the other way while I take my suit off and put my clothes back on." The Ephalem was right next to her but dutifully turned the other direction.

She quickly stripped her suit off and just started to put her clothes back on when Pilgrim let out a wolf whistle again. How did he do that she wondered without pausing her dressing.

"You're such a charmer," she exclaimed as she packed everything, including the garbage, back into the basket. She rolled the beach blanket up, put it under one arm and carried her basket with the other. The rose was in her left hand.

"Come on. I'm ready. Let's go."

They were back at the compound in little more than fifteen or twenty minutes and headed to the fore-commons building. That would be where Olaha would be. Probably some of the others as well.

"Hello," Milena called out. "I've brought a guest with me."

"Hi, honey," replied Olaha. "We've been expecting you. Pretty-Ugly told us you guys were coming."

"Oh, really?" Milena smiled. She wondered why the world-ship would care. She looked about and all of them were in the family room. "Come on in Pilgrim. Sorry. It looks like it's going to be a grilling."

"Not at all," Ryan responded. "Pretty-Ugly told us all about him. We have Pilgrim to thank for our lives. We genuinely wanted to meet him and personally thank him."

"I, I didn't know," she replied surprised.

"Don't worry Milena," responded Lindsey. "No heads are rolling here. He's your friend and our indirect savior. He provided the device Free-Credit used to bring us back here. He's welcome here anytime he wants. No questions asked. Maybe he'd like to stay for dinner. Of course, you have your language lessons to do between now and then."

Milena turned to Pilgrim and stated, "You could have said something. I didn't know. Thanks." She hugged the Ephalem and gave him a great big kiss somewhere about the head. "You are just so quiet sometimes. I'm beginning to think you're shy." She kept an arm around him. "You're not wiggling yourself out of this one," she exclaimed firmly.

"Milena is all girl," said Dave. "I'm afraid you've been given no choice in the matter. It's one of the downsides of human females. Get used to it."

"What?" retorted Lindsey. She punched him in the arm. Hard. "You're a beast. Milena, you'd better start with the introductions before Dave scares Pilgrim away."

Milena never took her arm from around Pilgrim. She walked him to each person in the room and gave up front and personal introductions, the rose showcased during each one. She was only embarrassed when Alan offered to shake hands. But then, so was Alan. They all laughed and his face was red. Pilgrim didn't seem to take offense.

"Our place is yours," Olaha uttered to Pilgrim. "We'd very much like to have you stay for dinner. I think you're now family so you can come and go as you please. Milena has lessons shortly. If you want to leave and come back later, that's OK. Or you can stay if you want. You might get bored though. Maybe visit with the others?" Pilgrim just purred.

"Come on honey," called Olaha. "Let's get started. Some of the others will probably join in at some point."

Milena reluctantly withdrew her arm from Pilgrim. "Sorry, Pilgrim. I promised. Please stick around. We can chum around when I'm done. OK?" She got more humming back and hoped that meant he was going to hang out.

Milena and Olaha went over to the corner and sat down on the sofa. "We'll start with basic nouns to name things. Let's start with uma. It means girl. Uma—girl."

"Uma—girl," responded Milena. "Uma—girl."

Beside her came "Uma—girl." Somehow, Pilgrim had sneaked up on her again. He had said the words.

"My, my," volunteered Olaha. "Here's a surprise. I've picked up a new student. Welcome to the class Pilgrim"

He purred in return.

◻ ◻ ◻ ◻ ◻

They now did practices daily. Was it only a week ago that Lindsey had managed to sort out the equipment and electrical requirements with the world-ship?

In many ways, Ryan thought that this was just like going to a jam session. He was just a member of the audience in the past. Now he faced being an active participant. Geoff had him, Lindsey, and Milena conducting this work. This included laying out the cabling and systems wiring. It would be a long time before any of them would be in the same league as Geoff. He was very patient though and it helped Ryan to keep his anger in check. The harder he worked, the less time he had to think about home and family.

Geoff kept things simple so far. They were just working out of the one room at this point.

The biggest part of any show happens before the gig. Playing was great, but no one liked to do the setup or take down. Geoff had directed them on where to put the speakers and how to do the wiring. The topic of what equipment should be used and when was introduced. When circumstances changed, then so did the equipment. All of this occurred in concert with the instrument and miking setup. In theory, they were responsible for the 'front of house' and 'foldback' engineering.

Every room was different. Each would require a disparate layout. This was the responsibility of the front of house engineer. The aim was to get a bright sound that was free from distortion. It had to be clear with as little noise from the equipment as possible. Every instrument and each mike need to be intelligible. It needed to be as natural as possible. This meant that one cheap component, such as an inexpensive microphone used in combination with other more expensive ones, could knock the sound completely off. Similarly, an expensive but poorly tuned undamped drum-kit could cause the same problem. All of the audio components required balancing relative to each other and the sound evenly dispersed to the audience. When this all came together properly, it added up to needing a more powerful amplification system than you would have thought for the performance. You desired the additional headroom to accommodate exceeding the backline levels during unusually loud sections while also meeting the needs of varying dynamic ranges found in selections that are more melodic.

Then you had to deal with what the musicians heard. The foldback engineer was responsible for this task. This was vastly different from what the audience got. There tended to be little balance there. Members required the ability to hear their own instrument and vocal. To a lesser extent, they needed to hear what the others were playing. It was no surprise to Ryan that half the time this wasn't done properly in regular performances back home. As loud as a drum kit can get, drummers often can't hear what they're playing. It is extremely hard to play an instrument if you can't listen to what you're actually doing. That was the reason you often miked drums in smaller venues. You could then point a monitor towards the drummer so that he could hear what he played over what he heard delivered by the stage monitors.

They were just sticking with managing the PA for this one room. Geoff said he fully expected this to change over time, which meant that he, Lindsey and Milena were going to need to understand the equipment requirements and organization much better. For now, Ryan just wanted to concentrate on dealing with managing sound pressure levels while minimizing reflections from the room's surfaces. Something simple, such as negligible air pressure changes or changes in humidity levels could modify the sound sufficiently enough that adjustments would have to be made. This could even happen over the period of a couple of minutes. It was a big balancing act. Then there were the requirements for each individual song to consider.

There were two problems that he hated more with live music than anything else.

The first was a poorly tuned drum kit. Some drummers just never figured out they were playing a musical instrument. They thought they were pumping out a backbeat. Wrong! The very best drummers played them as if they were an instrument. Beat was important but secondary. During the practices, he had to remind Braedon about this on more than one occasion. This was why Ryan wasn't a fan of typical dance music. Normally the backbeat was electronic rather than coming from real drums but the sound was invariably out of tune and pitch. That genre wasn't about music anyway. It had always been more about the dancing and appearances on the dance floor. The names for this style had changed over the last forty years, but it was still exactly the same. A forty-year-old song and one done today were virtually indistinguishable. The DJ practitioners were very good at matching tempo, but most had no musical ear at all, even when they used note-matching software. That was why they had to sample other peoples work. Musically, they weren't up to it.

The second usually had nothing to do with the band but had to do with the setup. Sound reflections, or echoes, could destroy what would normally have been a great musical evening. He had walked away from many big named concerts because of this. In fact, he had given up on outdoor concerts in stadiums because of it. Paying big dollars for the best tickets often turned into a horrible experience. If the group heard the same thing, it would destroy their playing. That was why a foldback engineer was essential for large venues.

It all came down to changing how he used his ears as a member of the audience over to what a sound engineer required. Milena was scary good at it. She had the knack of being able to adjust the levels on a given song at exactly the required point. She never made a mistake or had to overcompensate. This was a case of beauty before age. She had a distinct advantage in both the age and beauty department. He had probably done some harm to his ears over the years.

They were preparing for their first official gig. This was to be a small and select audience consisting of the drones Questionable-Advice and Free-Credit, as well as Pretty-Ugly and some other AIDS.

This was not what you could consider an experienced audience. It would probably sound just like noise to them. They had decided that the first set would be selected music from across differing musical genres. The second set was going to be more what Overnight Distress usually did. As a group, this was what they were most familiar with playing. Geoff was new to the band matrix so was going to step away for that one. The last set was going to be more progressive and would feature him more prominently.

The 'foldback' layout was complete and probably wouldn't require much, if any, tweaking. The room was small. If necessary, an adjustment to the main board would compensate for any minor changes. They decided that Milena would do the 'front of house' engineering and run the master board during the performance. This would leave Ryan and Lindsey to liaise with their hosts. Milena set up her own session notes for each song so she knew precisely when to make adjustments for each individual song. Pilgrim would be there to provide moral support.

Those two had become inseparable. The others wondered how you could categorize the relationship. The adults had a little fun with it, even Olaha, but never in front of the kids. The general consensus was they were not boyfriend and girlfriend in the traditional sense. Their physical differences were too large. Nor did they bud around the way girls did, or guys for that matter. Alan had joked that they were each other's pet. There might have been a little truth to that. They did tend to follow each other around like puppies. On the other hand, neither one was an obvious master. Milena was the bossier of the two, but each was their own person. In the end, everyone just settled on 'best friends;' like the kind you had in high school but tended to lose in later life. Pilgrim had even started to stay in the spare room, turning it into his own. The adults wouldn't let him sleep in Milena's room and he was staying less and less at his own home. Ryan guessed he was becoming family after all.

Ryan had a definite sense that Pilgrim experienced musical appreciation. The little guy had no facial expressions whatsoever, but he always rocked back and forth in time with the music. In fact, he had a perfect sense of rhythm and easily adjusted to changing tempos. Once, Geoff was practicing on one of his new keyboards while everyone was busily involved in other activities. It was a very melodic classical piece. Pilgrim was next to the board and raised the levels by himself. This was notable as Milena was at the far side of the room at that particular moment. He didn't even use one of his tricks. He used his mouth.

Apparently, the refugees had unintentionally been making an impression within the Hamlet. The AIDS community seemed to be interested in music as this was something new to them. This could end up flaming out at any time just the way any fad would. On the other hand, Pilgrim had been taking language lessons with Milena. The others also sat in as time allowed. They didn't really think about it much, but apparently, this had made a big impression with the larger society where they had found themselves. Pilgrim wasn't exactly breaking the walls down with his sentences and grammatical structure, but he was now managing to make himself understood a little bit. This apparently impressed the powers that be.

There was only one real question left. What to drink? Beer was the usual choice although Lindsey preferred white wine. Also, the conventional shots of JD were missing from the mix. Milena could make due with whatever the fruit juice of the day was. The intent was not to get smashed, but a minor glow would be nice.

Ryan called Olaha and Dave over for the all-important conference.

"Olaha, Dave and I have been talking and are not sure how to bring this up," Ryan divulged. "Usually when a gig is done, it is done as part of a recreational event. In our own culture this involved the, uh, moderate consumption of alcoholic beverages. We don't allow this for kids in public, so only adults are subject to this. Milena would not normally have this made available to her although it's not unusual for a teenager to have the occasional drink at home while under parental supervision."

She just looked back at the both of them waiting for a question.

Dave piped in, "It's just that we don't understand the social mores here. Are alcoholic drinks permissible? We have no idea."

"What exactly did you have in mind?" she asked them.

"Do you have anything like beer or wine?" Ryan asked thinking he would keep it simple.

Lindsey had wandered over at this point. "All these guys bugging you Olaha? They have guilty looks on their faces."

"They have just inquired of a medical professional where they can get moonshine," Olaha replied. "Humph!"

Ryan was feeling distinctly uncomfortable at this point. Just a little on the green side. Maybe this was something very taboo here and he had insulted Olaha terribly. He sneaked a look at Dave. Damn. He looked no better.

"No! Those cads. Musicians! Whatever shall we do with them?" exclaimed Lindsey.

"Well, you can start by sharing your white wine with them," stated Olaha flatly. Both girls broke out laughing. Hard. Lindsey was actually rolling on the ground. Olaha had tears running from her eyes. She kept trying to say something, but it kept on coming out garbled. This just got the two of them laughing harder.

"We've been had. How long do you think they've been planning this?" Ryan asked Dave.

"Judging by the reaction, I'd say all week."

"Maybe we should just slink out of here with our tails between our legs and look for Lindsey's stash. What do you think?"

"Yeah," agreed Dave. "We're starting to draw an audience. Let's go."

They left, leaving the sound of convulsive laughter behind them.

"Women!" muttered Dave.

ⵁ ⵁ ⵁ ⵁ ⵁ

Dave was sitting by himself in the fore-commons. It had been a long time since he'd gotten preshow jitters like this. He always got them. Almost everyone did. Usually you channeled it into the energy of the show. It was just that they figured a lot was riding on this particular gig. They had an audience that was unexperienced in any musical form or genres and was inexperienced in the discernment of musical appreciation. In other words, it was going to be a tough crowd.

At least he had managed to find a close beer analog to what he usually drank. He took a sip.

Milena and Ryan had hooked up Ryan's phone into the PA system. They were just finalizing some of the playlist items so they would have music before, between and after the sets. They had carefully choreographed the music selection to the sets. What Ryan didn't have on his phone, they had managed to pull down from Pretty-Ugly's music archive, which was very impressive. It had been gathering this information for a long time. With some practice, the world ship might be able to do set lists itself someday. So everything appeared covered here.

They had placed some ice-laden vats with beer in three different locations in the aft-commons, made available for each attendee's convenience. Several bottles of red and white wine were also set strategically throughout. Glasses were beside the bottles. Olaha had made this suggestion last night much to all of their surprises. She explained to them that the drones, as an extension of the AIDS that they represented, often found themselves in social situations with hominids. This dictated the consumption of the amenities made available to them, food and drink. The world-ships couldn't do these functions for themselves of course. They had their drones perform this function for them instead.

The world-ship printed drones in the usual fashion, but they required further manufacturing due to their unique needs. It made the primary body from composite materials that supported physical functionality, the neural nanonic reticulation, and the dual miniaturized radioisotope thermoelectric generators. Epithelial, connective and muscle cells customized via biosynthesis, supplemented the printing process to meet these requirements. The base physical unit then had the tissue constructs individually over-printed onto it. The drones didn't strictly need the biological functions. The base unit could operate just fine by itself. However, it provided a more comfortable visual interface to those they dealt with. These additional features did require the ingestion of foodstuffs and fluids to support its internal structure making the drones an amalgam creature of the artificial and organic. Starving a drone wouldn't kill it, but it wouldn't be very happy either.

They weren't just robots. They possessed everything required to appreciate the fare that they imbibed. The patron hominids generally recognized that the drones got a buzz on from time to time. Olaha said that they suspected that the world-ships got a little tipsy by proxy from the drones. It was pure speculation, but one never knew. If a drone did drink itself to excess, it could also make itself instantly sober should the occasion arise. On the other side of things, patrons did know absolutely that AIDS did develop food preferences that were apart from their drones. Drones could also have its own preferences apart from the AIDS. It was confusing.

This led to some experimentation the night before. They had decided to make available a selection of finger foods to make the experience more like a bar at home.

Milena was a big help here as she had the most input on how most of these dishes were prepared. She had spent some time helping out in the kitchen at the Tower. She made sure the food processors had the right recipes and procedures. They verified this by eating a variety of these for dinner the night before. It didn't turn out too badly.

They printed menus out that included several kinds of chicken wings, nachos, and peanuts. They kept it purposely simple. They'd make sure these were available to the guests should they want to try any of them. Olaha translated them into standard Hamlet language.

It was time to face the music, so to speak. Dave got up and walked from the fore to the aft-commons.

He met Pilgrim along the way. He guessed that someone sent Pilgrim to get him. "Hi buddy. I'm coming. Everything OK?"

"Uma—girl," replied Pilgrim.

"That's right. Girls are good," replied Dave smiling back at the little guy. Milena must have sent him. They went back together. Dave even had one hand draped around Pilgrim like they'd always been the best of friends.

They entered the aft-commons. Pilgrim went straight to Milena while Dave surveyed the room. Everything seemed ready. The only person that looked completely relaxed was Olaha sitting over on one of the couches. She even had a white wine in hand.

Dave walked over to where Lindsey and Ryan were.

"You two think you're ready?" he asked.

"As ready as we'll ever be," replied Lindsey. "Neither of us has ever hosted or played for a world class dignitary before. Never mind a bunch of them. And none of us has ever hosted a world before. We've only ever lived on 'em."

"What she said," approved Ryan. "How about you?"

"Nervous," he replied truthfully. "Usually you know what to expect from an audience. These guys have intellects that make us look like ants. They've probably already previewed every act in existence from Pretty-Ugly's data store. Their musical tastes are not going to be anything like ours. In short, I could use a shot of JD."

"As it happens," beamed Ryan, I came across this little bottle containing a substance that isn't that dissimilar. Come right this way you two. You're not getting out of this Lindsey."

Dave started to perk up and they followed Ryan over to the dispenser above the bar high table on the spinward side of the room. "You've got to be kidding," he responded with a big stupid grin on his face.

He could feel the revival of a tradition happening. Ryan had little glasses lined up and started pouring. They were just about shot glass sized. With nothing said aloud, everyone started to drift over. Ryan started to pour. Alan and Geoff got there first. Corey got there next followed by Olaha, Milena and Pilgrim. As was usual, Braedon appeared last.

Olaha had her wine. Milena had her own fruit beverage and a squirt bottle for Pilgrim as well. Ryan gave everyone else a shot glass and then began to speak to the group.

"A lot of hard work has gone into tonight's performance. Each and every one of us has worked our tails off to make tonight a success. There is no single person to thank here. This has taken the effort of each member of our little family unit to get us this far. Yes, I include you Pilgrim," he acknowledged pointing to the little Ephalem. "You don't get out of this just because your DNA is a little different. So is Olaha's. Makes no difference. Besides, you have the best tail in the room. Right Milena? Anyway, I want to propose a toast. It's for each person here today. I personally just want to say thanks. I love all of you. Cheers."

With that, those with shots tossed them back. The rest had sips of whatever they had. It wasn't JD, but it was close enough.

"That was god awful," choked out Lindsey. "I'm sticking with wine from now on. Ech!"

Dave looked around. "Group hug everyone." With that, everyone huddled into one group. It was a great feeling and made them all feel intimately a part of something bigger than themselves. They were family. Pilgrim had evidently decided that being vertical wasn't enough for him. Somehow, he managed to work his way horizontally through the group at shoulder level. He was able to hug more of them that way.

A chime sounded indicating they had company. The group broke up quickly. Dave turned towards the door to see that their visitors had arrived; three drones. At the same time, new viewing walls appeared on either side of the door facing inwards. This was new as they were typically behind where they set the band up. Each screen showed the same image of three individuals.

Dave followed Ryan and Lindsey to meet their guests in front of the anti-spinward viewing wall next to the door. He couldn't help but be impressed with the 3D, especially since they didn't need to wear any glasses.

Free-Credit still had on his white toga and Questionable-Advice still wore a light green one. The new drone was wearing a dark red toga.

"Welcome to our humble abode," Lindsey addressed the three drones.

"I'm glad to be able to visit," replied Free-Credit. "You remember Neat-Mess, of course. And I'd like to introduce you to Remotely-Close. He's the drone of Exact-Estimate, who I'll introduce you to in a second." He then introduced Dave and Ryan to the new drones.

"What have you managed to do to the Ephalem? I have never heard of one acting like this," asked Remotely-Close.

"He's family so he let his hair down a little today," said Dave adding a chuckle.

"Please let me introduce you to the AIDS that we have here with us," offered Free-Credit. "They can't participate directly but that is one of the reasons to have the drones here. This way they can enjoy the food and drinks as well as more easily mingle. You already know the world-ship Pretty-Ugly."

"Hi," said Ryan and Lindsey together.

"The individual in the green toga on the screen is Questionable-Advice's progenitor ship, Neat-Mess," continued Free-Credit.

"It's very nice to meet you at last," confided Ryan. "We've looked forward to it."

"Last but not least," continued Free-Credit. "We have Remotely-Close's parent AIDS, Exact-Estimate. He is most interested in how you have managed to establish such good relations with Pilgrim. We all are."

Lindsey threw a big smile at them. "Oh, you can probably blame Milena for that. Those two have become inseparable. On the other hand, we blame Pilgrim for leading her astray. She used to be such a nice girl." She sighed and looked up.

Dave thought he'd better cut in quickly. "Um, my wife has a sense of humor. We males usually take the brunt of it. Just so you know, the girls pegged you into that category. Milena is a really great girl and Pilgrim is a member of our family as far as we're all concerned. We actually do like him." From the corner of his eye, he could see Olaha making her way to the assembled group.

He continued. "Unfortunately, Olaha has been led astray by my wife and has become thoroughly corrupted. Fair warning."

"I'm not deaf you know," Olaha returned and smiled. She then put her arm around him. "We're going to keep him anyway. Can I get anyone refreshments, a drink?" she asked.

They all requested a beer to which Olaha responded with, "Coming right up."

Dave thought it was time to introduce the band members. "I'd like to introduce today's musicians," he offered as he walked towards the stage as the others followed. The guys were all doing last minute equipment checks and some final tuning in preparation to starting the show.

"First, I'd like to introduce Braedon Hoople in the back on drums," he stated. Braedon waved back.

"Next is Corey Josephs on bass guitar. On stage, he works very closely with Braedon. Their musical functions are somewhat the same and they depend a lot on each other." Corey said hello to each one individually.

"This is Alan Harris on lead guitar. Most of the time he plays solos, fills and melody lines. When I'm singing, we are usually working together. I will often back him up on the rhythm guitar, too."

Alan had finally found people with hands so he offered to shake them. They told him that it was a cultural custom that they weren't familiar with. They shook hands with him anyway. This kept him from being too red-faced.

"And the latest member of our group is Geoff Wong. He was doing the audio work for us during the last gig. He plays the keyboards and just joined us last week. We're going to feature him in the first and last set, as he's probably the best musician amongst us. We thought it best that the first set be a wide range of musical styles. He's better at this than the rest of us. He trained classically. He isn't up on our standard repertoire yet so the second set will be what the band has done in the past. That's what the rest of us are more comfortable with. The last set will be more progressive so we will need his talents there especially as the rest of us are not up to his level of playing. We hope this meets with your approval. With only having been together for one week, we won't be at our best but we think it will show a broader cross section of musical genres this way. Not everyone likes the same thing so we are attempting to appeal to a varied set of musical tastes. Geoff has also been showing Milena, Lindsey, Ryan and even Pilgrim how to do the sound work. He's done a really superb job given such a short period of time to work with."

The drones made some sounds of approval. Dave guessed that they didn't think that the group would try such a broad musical spectrum.

"Let's go over here and meet the brats, I mean youngsters," said Dave with a smile. He led them to the sound station currently manned by Pilgrim and Milena.

"We heard that, you know," Milena called out towards him. "You keep that up and I'm going to turn you over to Pilgrim. He'll do some of his fifth-dimensional mojo on you. You'll be sorry then. Even worse, I'll complain to Lindsey. You won't be coming back alive. Consider yourself warned."

Dave did the only thing he could think of under the circumstances to protect himself. He took Milena in one arm and Pilgrim in the other and gave them a big hug and kiss. "I'll get my revenge," he laughed back at them.

"OK. You're forgiven," she quipped. "But just this once. You're on mandatory probation."

Dave didn't let either of them go. He turned them around and presented them to the others. The look on Remotely-Close's face was priceless.

"Do you mind if I take pictures with my phone?" he asked the drones innocently. They told him it was OK as far as they were concerned. They recorded everything anyway. "Thanks," he replied to them and promptly pulled out the phone getting it ready to take pictures. If things went south tonight, at least he'd have some pictures to snicker over in the future.

"It's my great pleasure to introduce to you our two intellectual stars, Pilgrim and Milena." Pilgrim bobbed up and down while Milena did a half curtsy. It was too bad she was still wearing shorts instead of a dress.

The two of them had timed it perfectly and said hello at the same time. Dave snapped the picture of the drones who dropped their chins to the ground. The AIDS in the viewing walls did the same, presenting astonished looks.

Everyone in their extended family broke out laughing. It took a couple of minutes but eventually the drones and AIDS began to chuckle as well.

After things had settled down a bit, Remotely-Close addressed Pilgrim directly. "On behalf of myself and Exact-Estimate we would like to welcome you to the Hamlet."

Eyes began to light up again in the group. Dave got his camera ready again and centered it on Remotely-Close.

Milena looked directly at him with fists planted firmly on her hips. "If you keep talking like that I'm going to tell him to bite you. He's deadly poisonous you know. Loosen up. He's a friendly guy." The laughter started again.

Snap. Dave had another picture at Remotely-Close's expense. He knew that there was no way that Pilgrim was poisonous. He didn't need to be. The little guy had far more defenses that were more efficient than any poison could be. They'd all seen him use his mojo.

Once the visitors finally figured out that the refugees expected them to treat Pilgrim just like every other family member and not as an honored guest from some far-flung galaxy, holding the power of life and death in its every breath, things went a lot more smoothly. Things must have been going well. Even the AIDS were managing to laugh at themselves and have a good time. The first rule of civilization in Dave's brand new rules book was that if you can't laugh at yourself then you aren't civilized.

Milena had finally gotten around to putting the house music on.

After a short period of time, Dave got up to present the first set featuring Geoff. Milena dropped the house music and somehow got Pilgrim to work the lights. Braedon stayed up the entire time playing drums. Dave only sang some of the songs. Geoff did the rest. They started with some classical piano pieces. Then they moved on to some ragtime followed by a little blues. Corey and Alan joined in at this point. They finished as a group with some jazz. Milena and Pilgrim turned the house lights and music back on.

As these genres were not what any of them was used to playing or very practiced at, Dave thought it went over pretty well.

The small audience seemed to have enjoyed the set given their sophistication level. He knew the second set would be the best from his own perspective.

After grabbing another beer, Remotely-Close came over for a chat.

"That was quite something," he opened. "I admit to never having heard anything quite like that. You indicated that this represented multiple genres of music. Can you tell me more?"

"Sure," replied Dave. "Musical tastes don't grow overnight. Often they develop over a lifetime. There are many different inputs into this. The biggest one is probably what you were listening to as a child. Those tunes are usually quite simple. Most people look for a more complicated blend of the elements that make up a piece, as they get older. Your level of sophistication tends to elevate over time. Some people stop at a point they are comfortable with and then just listen to their favorite style at their preferred sophistication level. It's what they are used to and most comfortable with. Other inputs can be cultural separating such genre as country verses rock. Often, the musical category that you're the most familiar with yourself becomes your personal preference. Cultural input also is an important factor affecting choice. Music enjoyed by one culture doesn't guarantee respect or appreciation by another. Surprisingly, the era that produced the music is also a big factor. The classical pieces Geoff played originated before we were born. The ragtime goes back over one hundred years. Every few generations a new musical form comes along."

"Fascinating," responded the drone. "I find it unbelievable the way the different notes and their combinations came together. It wouldn't have occurred to me the breadth of structure available used for its creation. I already see that there are some types that I prefer over others."

"You should hear Ryan talk about that," Dave replied. "As a person who mostly listens to music, he has some interesting observations. His Lemma number one: Two people that fundamentally agree on their personal tastes in music will always disagree fifty percent of the time on the individual songs that they like. His corollary to the lemma: Two people that fundamentally disagree on their personal tastes in music will always agree fifty percent of the time on the individual songs that they like. It's a profound observation in its own way. I've also found it to be true."

"I have no idea if that is deep or not," stated the drone. "I suspect that it might be. Wow. I can now see why Pretty-Ugly* found this so fascinating."

"It's time for the second set. Excuse me. Work to do. I'll talk to you later," assured Dave.

They started with a variation of his usual introduction and then laid into the set. Geoff had moved up to the mixing console with Milena and Pilgrim. He just stood there taking the set in and let them do the work. Nice, Dave thought. That's the way to do it. They played an excellent set. Ryan and Lindsey even got up and danced at one point.

The audience participation was not up to their usual standard, but that wasn't the band's or the audience's fault. Still, he was sweat covered by the end of it.

Dave took a break and went to the back of the stage behind the drum kit. He had a stash of cold beer there with his name on them. Ryan and Geoff were having a private conversation with Pretty-Ugly on the viewing wall.

"Sorry. I didn't mean to interrupt," he apologized and turned to go back the way he came. There were other places to get a beer.

"No, please come back," requested Pretty-Ugly. "You should be aware of this discussion. I was just telling Geoff and Ryan about our analysis on the world-line attacks to date. Ryan led us down this particular path. Without his observations, we'd have had no place to go."

"Um, OK," Dave replied as intelligently as he could. "What's up?"

Pretty-Ugly continued. "Ryan picked up on the fact that harmonics were involved in the attack and observed that the sonic weapons proved to be a deterrent, albeit a minimal one. We didn't see that even though we were there via the drones. He also provided us with some observations in physics that relates to the problem that we wouldn't have realized on our own. Geoff has a skill set in sound engineering that we don't possess here. I've asked them to go on the next excursion when an attack occurs. The attacks haven't finished. We lost another world line trunk yesterday."

"No. I thought we were finally out of it all. Good god. I don't know what to say," blurted Dave. "It's entirely their choice. I mean they're adults and can make their own decision. Just don't tell Milena or Pilgrim any of this, OK? They're just kids. Damn!"

Ryan responded. "We already agreed on that. Also, I've said I would go. I have accounts that need settling. I have no choice in the matter. I need to do something."

Geoff was next. "I'm going. This has to stop. I don't know what I can contribute, but Pretty-Ugly said they needed me. I'm in. If whatever is doing this ever got here well—" He just stopped talking. Nothing more needed saying aloud.

"For what it's worth," said Pretty-Ugly. "The AIDS have unanimously agreed music would be a valuable social contribution to our society. We even like the dancing. We're prepared to sponsor you at any time and place that you want to play."

"It's just such a downer conversation to have before the last set," replied Dave. What little bit of a musical high that he'd gotten from playing was rapidly starting to dwindle. "I just wish you'd had this discussion tomorrow instead of now."

"Every single thing you've said is right," responded Pretty-Ugly. "I'm very sorry. I really am. Unfortunately, our timetable accelerated due to this last incident. We were going to wait until next week, but things are different now. These two need to have some training in weapons and strategy has to be developed."

"Well, OK," he replied. "I'm not blaming anyone. Honest. I know this needs doing. If there's anything the rest of us can do, let us know. You guys, we have your back. Just name it. Anything."

Geoff responded. "Let's get the last set done. It looks like it's going to be an early morning."

Dave managed to get through the last set intact. They could have done better. Maybe next time. His spirits remained low, but he was a professional. He wasn't going to let the others see the way he felt which was somewhere between maimed and crushed.

As a group, they thanked the drones and AIDS who had to leave as soon as it was over. They made a point of letting the whole assemblage know that they highly approved of what was delivered and let them know they had their explicit support to play anywhere at any time they wanted. They'd make sure it happened.

Dave watched as everyone hugged and kissed and congratulated each other. He did his share too, but his heart just wasn't into it as fully.

He also made an announcement. "I know that everyone wants to party and celebrate our success. Something else has also unexpectedly come up. Our hosts asked Geoff and Ryan to assist them in a particular project. Not bad for a couple of guys that aren't even from a Level I civilization. Apparently, they have skill sets our hosts don't possess relating to harmonics and physics. It's time sensitive, so they have an early morning tomorrow. Give them a break and let them get some sleep. The rest of us can stay here and relax for a while."

Dave watched as the others all variously hugged or kissed Geoff and Ryan before sending them off to bed. He did as well. He watched both of them walk back to their respective rooms and disappear inside.

"God, I need a beer," he croaked aloud while the others started their celebration.

CHAPTER 5

ADAPTATION

I have noticed even people who claim everything is predestined, and that we can do nothing to change it, look before they cross the road.

Stephen Hawking

Time pressed in on them. Free-Credit met Geoff and Ryan first thing in the morning at the compound. They were still completely unfamiliar with the world-ship's layout and social order. They needed escorting back to the deployment area in the unused docking bay. After a few trips, they could probably do it by themselves.

The compound had been nanomorphically printed by Pretty-Ugly after the refugee's arrival on the world-ship. This was a foundation technology responsible for the evolution of all of the AIDS entities in the Hamlet. They originally developed it to allow for continued growth. It also provided for the expansion of existing support assets. Over time, it became their standard manufacturing technology. It was rapid and made efficient use of available resources while minimizing power consumption. An AIDS used germ cells found throughout its body for production, controlled through sub-task processes spawned by the principle mentality. They were capable of assembling or disassembling anything, atom by atom including themselves when instructed. Their only requirements were direction and the physical raw materials incorporated into the fabrications built. Everything grown had germ cells incorporated into them to accommodate quick repairs as required, or for disassembly when needed. This technology avoided many of the catastrophic mistakes learned tragically from using nanotechnology in the historical past.

For smaller projects, like the creation of the refugee compound, mass could be recycled from unused local resources or from the aft mass-repository as needed. This technology made it a simple matter to connect new subcomponents into an existing infrastructure. This could include such items as viewing walls, sunsims, or the food processor subsystems to name a few. The ship supported these things via a transportation network that ran throughout itself, alongside many other distributed systems. On-demand manufacturing was now a relatively simple matter and took very little time. You just printed what was required or made modifications as needed.

Larger projects, such as the creation of a new arcology or building a complete photonic engine with its supporting magnetic, gamma ray and neutrino mirrors, would require additional external mass available in one of the asteroid belts or in the Oort cloud. Typically, these items required many more resources plus assembly and integration time that could take centuries to complete. This didn't include the manufacturing of antimatter fuel which could only be done while in the orbit of a gas giant. This was one of the reasons it took so long for world-ships to grow and why there were so few of them. First, an AIDS had to desire to become one in the first place and then it had to expand itself. It took time and wasn't necessarily the desired goal of most AIDS.

They proceeded anti-spinward, walking through the pastoral countryside of the arcology. The world-ship had scheduled rain for later in the day and low foggy clouds of gray and crimson obscured the sunsims. A few crepuscular rays of yellow and red peeked through gaps in the clouds creating an eerily beautiful morning.

After ten minutes, they came to a rocky tor bounded by deciduous trees. It contained the entrance to the transfer station, printed recently to accommodate travel for the refugee family including Pilgrim and the drones, while at the same time providing some level of local privacy. Only they could use it as a destination point although they could bring guests in if they wished. Anyone could leave using it.

The entrance opened as they approached it. A short corridor brought them to a platform that was transparent on one side. Free-Credit specified the destination address aloud. It could have done this over the mempro cognate band but elected not to. Culture shock was going to be a large enough issue over the short term so there was no point in pushing it.

Soon, a vehicle shaped like a capsule stopped on the other side of the transparent wall. It was a nondescript white but had tiny windows lined down its length of seven meters. A few seconds later, the wall lifted and the doors to the transfer pod opened. They entered and sat down on a free row of seats. A number of hominids were sitting in other rows. Most ignored them when they got on, but some were openly staring at Geoff. His oriental features were new to them. Quiet background discussions were audible in the native Hamlet tongue.

The capsule would not move until their seat belts were on. These had the double shoulder straps the refugees had first seen in the shuttle on the way to the hospital. They were required because the pods traveled across all areas of the ship and experienced levels of acceleration that varied anywhere from free fall to multiple G's of acceleration. Once put on, the doors closed and then the wall came back down. Systems evacuated the pressure tube and they were off.

Travel tubes permeated the world-ship, interconnecting from collector tunnels to intertwining express arteries. Enormous reserve corridors were in place for the world-ship's exclusive usage. All were in hard vacuum to reduce friction. A travel pod required routing to the appropriate transfer station to pick up or release passengers. While in a station, the landing zone needed sealing and pressurization before the transparent isolation wall would lift. When leaving, the reverse operation would take place allowing it to accelerate off into the collector tunnel. It would move to the express tunnels once it reached sufficient speed.

Specialized transit AI's managed routing and optimized the complete system. They had to take into account passengers getting on and off, sources and destinations, and traffic prioritization under unusual circumstances. Travel pods almost never traveled the same route twice and were in permanent operation.

They only made three stops before reaching their destination as announced by the travel pod. It always did this as not everyone elected to use a mempro. Some hominids considered them antisocial. Free-Credit could tell that Ryan and Alan didn't understand the announcement. It would check with Pretty-Ugly later to see if some accommodation for them were possible.

They exited and made their way through the terminus past several shops and restaurants. People moved up and down the busy boulevard past ceramic terracotta buildings. None was higher than four stories tall. The sky was clear in this module today with no rain forecast. Still, it was impossible to tell the height of the sunsims.

After a short walk, they neared the entrance to the docking bay. Only they would be able to enter and exit due to security concerns. The larger populace still wasn't aware of the world-line issue. Free-Credit hoped that it would stay this way. The entrance dutifully irised open for them and they were inside. The total transit time amounted to twenty minutes for the eighty-five kilometer trip in the pod. Add the walking time and the trip was approximately a half hour each direction.

The maintenance and docking chamber had changed little since they had retrieved the refugee's three weeks ago. The only change was a series of partitions that were set up aft which created separate work and rest areas.

Free-Credit and Remotely-Close were waiting and greeted them as they entered. It was time to deliberate and conceptualize. One more thing needed to happen first.

"OK. Let's sit down and share what we have with Geoff and Ryan," chimed in Free-Credit. "We've got some sofas over here," it said pointing to the partition area. It knew those two would like the next revelation.

Free-Credit continued. "Milena spent the last week putting this together. She was going to surprise everyone with it in the next couple of days. I have strict instructions via Olaha that before we do anything we were to give you these items out of the processor. She mentioned something about Fifth-dimensional mojo so I figured it wouldn't hurt to take these few extra minutes. Let's just call it self-preservation."

"Yep," mused Ryan. "You're learning about human females; the ruling class. What have you got?"

He opened the processor and out came an irresistible cascade of aromas. Free-Credit thought it smelled pretty good too.

"Oh my god," exclaimed Geoff. "Is that what I think it is? I think I'm in shock."

"It is," assured Ryan. "Canadian bacon and eggs over easy. There's some kind of multi-grained buttered toast. A side of fruit and a decanter of black coffee."

"Nectar of the god's," marveled Geoff. "She even has cream and sugar on the side. How many meals are there?"

"Just the two," answered Free-Credit.

"Pass those over," requested Ryan. "Get three more made up for yourselves. You're not going to want to miss this."

After some time eating, Free-Credit declared, "I think I have a favorite new food—bacon. I've never had meat like this before. The coffee is good as well. I like it with cream and sugar."

"It takes time to develop a preference for straight black," Geoff pointed out. "The caffeine in it is a stimulant. If you're not a morning person, it can help get you going. Keep these recipes. I think we're going to need them. Speaking of—order another decanter, please."

"Done," Free-Credit responded. "Let's get down to it. We need to get you two up to speed on the latest attack."

"The day before yesterday the Ephalem device warned us that the attack was in progress," recalled Free-Credit. "We weren't prepared and should have been. The event happened much quicker this time than our response time allowed for. We had less than a half hour from our receipt of the alert to its end. On your trunk, we had more notice than that because of the vigilance and reporting by Pretty-Ugly*. We didn't have that this time. The tool only alerted us near its end. Everything finished before we could make a transit. We were still attempting to figure out what we needed by the time it was done. Our ignorance meant we didn't accomplish anything. That was a terrible error on our part. Our assumptions were bad."

Questionable-Advice picked it up. "We put together a sonic arsenal that used a broader range of energies and harmonics. We just didn't know what would or wouldn't work. In addition, we tried to add to our sensing equipment but we don't know what to look for. This caused an enormous delay."

"That's partly why you two are here," revealed Remotely-Close. "We know you aren't scientists. We don't expect that. We have the technology and the means to manipulate it. What you two have is different. You have insights and ways of thinking that originate from a perspective that we just don't possess. You've lived with these concepts every day of your lives. For you, many of their ideas are intuitive. You can provide us with pointers and give us an orientation. Without you, we have no direction."

"Humph," muttered Geoff. "I can see our resident IT guy formulating information so that computers can understand some of this stuff. Me? I'm just a high priced roadie."

"Don't underestimate yourself Geoff," stated Free-Credit. "I suspect your input will be the most important contribution here. Ryan isn't here because of his background. That's just happenstance. He's here because he can formulate questions that we can't even begin to think to ask. If you know the question, then it might be answerable. That's a big part of the battle."

"You, on the other hand," affirmed Remotely-Close, "are the one providing us with answers. Your entire career revolves around delivering finely focused audio solutions. We may not be strictly dealing with sound issues, but the manipulation experience you have in that arena is precisely what we need. We can extrapolate it further to other areas. You know the delivery."

"Congratulations," proclaimed Questionable-Advice. "You two are now our bosses. We are your workers. Welcome to Level II civilization." It smiled at both of them.

"It'll look good on a resume anyway," Ryan suggested to Geoff.

◻ ◻ ◻ ◻ ◻

"What do you mean we can't just go out and play a gig," barked Dave. "We've been given carte blanche by Pretty-Ugly; any place we want."

Lindsey just looked at him. Sometimes he just didn't think ahead. Once again, she was going to have to save him from himself. He sounded miffed. She really hated having an argument with him when they were in the fore-commons. There were too many ears and it was embarrassing.

"Look," she responded. "It's not rocket science. We don't have a marketplace. We have to create one. Think about it. No one here knows anything about music at all, never mind going to a live performance. If you just set up somewhere and hope that people will show up, then you're wrong."

"Well, what do you suggest then?" he blurted in a haughty manner.

"Don't start with the attitude. Take a breath and relax a second," she ordered. You had to give Dave some time to settle down or he would just go on continuously. She paused waiting for his breathing to slow down. Then she continued.

"The first rule of marketing is that you need a marketplace. So let's concentrate on how to do that first. We don't have any bills to cover. We have food on the table and a nice place to live. So take a step back for a minute."

"OK. You have me. You're a marketing guru. What do you suggest?" he groaned.

It was time to bring in the big guns. "Olaha, Milena. Can we borrow you guys for a minute?"

They didn't look too happy to be included. Milena had been making moves towards the door. Now she just looked trapped. Braedon was the only additional person there and he beat a hasty retreat out the door to join the other guys in the aft-commons.

"Yes. What can we help you with Lindsey?" Olaha inquired, eyes firmly planted on Dave. Her face said that he was acting like an obstinate ass.

"Can you tell us how you first started listening to music and how your particular tastes developed?" Lindsey asked.

"There's not much for me to tell. I've never listened to any before you got here. Most of what I've heard so far comes from your recordings. I've only seen the one live show and I was impressed. I like some, if not most, of what I've heard so far but I can't say yet what I honestly prefer," stated Olaha.

"Fair enough," remarked Lindsey. "What about you Milena?" The girl looked distinctly uncomfortable.

"When I was little, we sang songs at school," Milena divulged. "They were OK but not the kind of thing that I really liked. Mostly, I listened to the radio with my mom. I admired what she heard and based on that, mom said that I'd like Overnight Distress. That's how I started to listen to the guys. Mom brought me to the shows."

Milena continued. "I like other things as well. The kids at school listened to different music stations. I did too. There was a lot of good music that we liked, but mom didn't. You know how it goes. There was also TV but not so much. Most of the shows directed at my age group were awful. Some of my friends loved that stuff though."

"Thanks honey. That was exactly what I wanted. You two are off the hook. Thanks." Lindsey looked back at her husband while the girls wandered off. "Dave, do you think those are fair responses?" Perfect. He was starting to look uncomfortable now.

"OK. I'm beginning to see your point," he responded.

"Olaha has been with us for a while now and she still doesn't know what she likes. Our resident fourteen-year-old developed her tastes while growing up. I bet she never saw a live band before you guys. She learned what she liked by listening to the radio with her mom and her peers. We can discount TV for now. This was exactly the same for you and me. It was a process and that process doesn't exist here."

"You're a marketing expert. What are you suggesting?" he sighed.

"Before you go out and start playing gigs, we need to develop a potential audience. To do that, we have to educate people into liking the kind of music you play first. We need to do this one step at a time. What do you think, Dave?"

"OK. We develop an audience first. How are we supposed to do that? We don't have any radio stations around here," he countered.

"Exactly. Now you're getting the idea. We need to develop a forum whereby others can discover music and formulate an opinion on what they like. Pretty-Ugly is capable of providing feeds to every household on the world-ship. We should approach it with a plan."

"We don't play everything. The closest to that is Geoff and he's off working on that project with Ryan," he argued. "What if people only like chamber music?"

It was time for the closer she thought. "Pretty-Ugly has recordings of just about everything. It also has histories on playlists. It can do the programming itself just based on that. We can suggest several specialty channels. We just introduce a bias to what you play. We can even suggest videos showing dance. We start with a target region for the test case. Let's see if we can drum some interest up first. If we get a response, then we can schedule a series of gigs through a couple of venues. It'll start slowly, but it'll start. If we can help by bringing in an audience at a couple of bars, then it'll grow. There might even be spin-off opportunities."

"Well, you're our manager. Go ahead and arrange it. I'll talk to the guys. We could always use a little practice time. There's also the language issue. If we do a live gig, that'll have to be addressed. I'll talk to Olaha and work something out."

"Then lower the drama level. OK?" she asked.

"Drama, huh? To quote Mister Anonymous: The real problem with reality is the lack of background music. It keeps the drama levels low. Um, unless you have tinnitus that is. OK. Promise," he declared.

He had given her no choice. She punched him in the arm again.

◻ ◻ ◻ ◻ ◻

Ryan needed to review what they knew and what they didn't know. Thinking about current circumstances and feelings would just get in the way. They just needed to stick with the facts for a moment. Speculation could wait until later. So could a planned response.

He requested firmly, "Questionable-Advice, please give us a summary of whatever hard facts we have on the event and how we got them."

Geoff was taking notes with pen and paper he got from the dispenser. He didn't want to use the screen. Apparently, someone told the ship how to make these items. Probably Lindsey, he thought. She always seems to have some.

"Let's start with the symptoms that we measured and know about," Questionable-Advice replied. It started to itemize.

"First, the speed of light was slowing. It hadn't gotten close to stopping time yet, but it was getting near there. The delta was speeding up as we measured it. We could see evidence of this. The further away actions happened from us, the slower they appeared." Ryan noticed Questionable-Advice had everyone's complete attention."

"Second, the gravitational constant was just measurably bigger than it should have been. This would have reinforced the time dilation effects further. The greater the mass, the slower time would appear to an outside observer. At some point, this would cause all baryonic matter to collapse into a singularity. However, this would be entirely dependent on the speed of light as gravity and its waves propagate at that speed. A local observer would likely never see it happen. They could only ever approach it. An exterior observer might. It's a gray area."

Questionable-Advice continued with the observations. Nobody was going to interject a comment at this point.

"Third, the Planck constant was increasing. This is the quantum of action in quantum mechanics. This means quantum effects started to become visible at macroscopic scales. A moving item like a ball could have turned into a wave as it was thrown and turned back into itself at its destination," exclaimed Questionable-Advice.

Ryan wondered what something like that would look like. That would be a very strange universe if that were a permanent condition. How could hearts beat? What would lips look like when you talked? Or kissed! It was mind-boggling.

The drone offered this conjecture. "None of these constants changed proportionally to each other. If they had, we wouldn't have seen anything. Things would have stayed the way they were. There would have been no observable changes at all."

Ryan watched the drones face change. It looked more haggard suggesting that bad news was coming.

The drone paused, looking at each individual in turn before it started back up. "Fourth, the fine structure constant. This is highly related to the first three, gives us the best interpretation of the results we observed and directly tells us what was happening to the forces. It was measurably decreasing. The most obvious effect would be that elements would burn faster and the heavier ones would become more radioactive. All atoms were getting larger. This would have radically altered chemical reactions. Anything living and not frozen due to time dilation effects would have been killed instantly by this alone." Questionable-Advice didn't stop there.

In a more forceful voice it stated, "There would be colossal cosmological effects. This changes the vacuum energy of space. This change would have resulted in the release of energy in the form of heat and light so that radiation temperatures would increase. The cosmic microwave background temperatures would have increased. The resulting vacuum pressure rise would have reinforced the strength of gravity instead of contributing to its decrease. In turn, any corresponding field decay would have produced massive and unstable scalar bosons which would almost immediately further decay into gamma ray photons."

There was now a hint of awe in the drone's voice. "The forces dominating the largest universal structures would invoke a series of cascading changes. This would reverse all the typical false vacuum operations that would be normal to the universe as a whole. It would have moved from dark energy dominated, back to radiation and then to matter. This would have resulted in a big crunch, but we don't fully understand the repercussions of matter degeneration here. Instead of seeing an inflationary period, working backwards, there would be a deflationary one."

Ryan listened to what the drone said and could now acknowledge its scope. He just would never understand it. It was too vast in concept. He doubted anyone, at any level of civilization, would be able to fully understand or appreciate the full implications.

The drone asserted some of the conclusions reached. "The strong force would have been weakened. This wouldn't affect neutrinos and electrons. Protons and neutrons change at the high-end of its scale and are less attracted to each other. At the low end, it holds quarks together via its carrier, the gluon. Protons and neutrons would start to degenerate."

The drone let that be absorbed before it continued.

"The weak force mediated by the boson particles was correspondingly weakened. This directly affected all fermion interactions. The particles were not interacting correctly. This was one of the reasons why we saw things glowing. Photons were being emitted in concert with the bosons as matter was degenerating."

Geoff's face was starting to look very troubled, thought Ryan. Probably his own face was no better. Questionable-Advice didn't stop.

"The electromagnetic force was getting vastly weaker, again, affecting chemical interactions. This also sets the speed limit of light, which we know degenerated. It is also responsible for most of the phenomena we experience in everyday life. We could probably have put an arm through any object affected. There would have been no resistance or push back. The atoms in both objects would just have intermingled. It would be like pouring one fluid into another. You would never be able to disentangle them once this happened. It's also mediated by photons which we saw were being generated everywhere."

Questionable-Advice summarized what he stated so far. "As near as we can tell, these were byproducts of the original effect which caused the reversal of the expansion for the geometry of space-time. The collapse happened faster than the speed of light."

Ryan knew that couldn't ever address any of the things mentioned. They had no physics that could point out the cause or how to protect themselves from it. None of this helped at all.

Questionable-Advice started to sound more confident. "The last symptom may or may not be related to the originating cause. We heard oscillating noise pressure that appeared to be directly associated with the phenomena. We need to pursue this conjecture with better measurement. It was not something that we initially considered."

"Are there any questions so far?" asked the drone.

"Yeah," admitted Geoff. He had stopped taking notes. "Are you guys sure you want me here. I didn't understand one word in twenty of this." He looked distinctly uncomfortable during the review. He was probably feeling very out of place.

"It's OK," Ryan advised him. "You don't need to know what that stuff means other than it did what it did. These are observations and when it comes right down to it, none of us knows how to change any of them directly. The original values in all of this would have been set somehow in phase space where the universe originated. To make it even more incomprehensible, we are also dealing with the twenty-six dimensions that compose the universe and you and I are only familiar with about four. Keep the notes up. We'll probably need them later."

"So, Questionable-Advice," Ryan continued. "What can you tell us about what did or did not affect the phenomena?"

"Sure," Questionable-Advice responded. "We know that the Ephalem device shielded us from the effects but we don't know how or why and I don't think they can tell us intelligibly. I can speculate that it creates a little bit of a pocket universe using local universal properties, but I can't tell you how it got us there or why it was permeable. We could move in and out of it. It did seem to slow the effect down around us a bit, but it did not stop it altogether."

That was a positive. We might be able to use that, thought Ryan. Hopefully, Questionable-Advice had more they could use.

"The only effect that seemed to change anything were the sonic weapon and to a lesser extent, the rail gun," continued Questionable-Advice. "These only worked on the thing that kept appearing and disappearing while it was wrecking the place. None of the other weapons had an effect."

Questionable-Advice summarized what didn't work. "The ineffectual weaponry was all energy related using either photonic or electromagnetic radiation. These all propagate by using a transverse wave pattern."

"On the other hand," Questionable-Advice continued. "The weaponry that had an effect produced longitudinal waves. Your culture referred to them as I-waves or pressure waves. The energy alternates back and forth between potential and compression or lateral strain energy. There are only three things that we are aware of that produce this kind of wave pattern."

Questionable-Advice started to itemize these items on his fingers. "The first is the one you are most familiar with. Sound transmits in this fashion and you measure it in sound pressure levels. This would have been what the sonic weapon was using. You'd need a medium such as a gas to transfer this energy."

He raised a second finger and continued. "The second is a shock wave which creates a sharp rise or drop in pressure, temperature or density. This was likely the effect the rail gun was having. This was slight though. This doesn't need a medium to transfer through as it's particle and mass based."

And finally, he added a third finger. "The last thing that produces this type of wave is not something we have tried yet and would be difficult to produce. A plasma medium is required to bear the electromagnetic version of an acoustic wave called an ionic acoustic wave. This requires a medium composed entirely of plasma."

Ryan looked around the group at the table. "This gives us our starting place," he said approvingly. "It's the only avenue we have as I don't see how we can affect the symptoms that Questionable-Advice outlined. This will be our point of attack."

Ryan asked, "What can we speculate about the nature of the thing that did all of the physical damage? Anyone?"

"I don't know about its nature but it sure was pissed at us," replied Geoff with conviction. "It seemed like it was trying to smash us to bits on purpose. My impression was that it was after us. Everything else was just collateral damage."

"Geoff is right," piped in Free-Credit. "It was directed. It wasn't a phenomenon that occurred elsewhere in the collapse. We did something that it didn't like or something that was preventing the completion of what it was trying to accomplish."

"The nature of the entity is an interesting question," observed Remotely-Close. "It had the ability to phase in and out of our dimensionality. This implies that it is multidimensional in nature."

"I'm not sure that I follow," responded Geoff hesitantly.

"It's hard to describe," conceded Ryan. "Pilgrim appears to have some of the same capabilities. He can make things appear and disappear. He can move things around invisibly. We've all seen him do his mojo.

"A famous analogy back home," offered Ryan. "A guy named Edwin Abbot wrote a book back in the late eighteen-hundreds called Flatland. It was about a race of people who lived in a two-dimensional world. They could move forward and backward, and left or right. None of the inhabitants was aware of a third spatial dimension. The plot revolves around a three-dimensional entity who visits the main character. From the inhabitant's viewpoint, this creature was from hyperspace. There was a lot more than that in the book."

Ryan paused, considering what he remembered having read. After a minute, he continued. "Picture what a three-dimensional object like a globe would look like in two-dimensional space as it travels. It could pass right through the fictional country of Flatland. All the inhabitants would see would be cross sections of the sphere. A point would appear out of nowhere, grow into a circle up to the size of its diameter, then shrink back down to a point and disappear. It could hover over Flatland and watch everything. It wasn't possible to hide anything in the two-dimensional world from its view. At the same time, none of the Flatlanders would even know of its presence."

Ryan stopped and then looked each of them in the eye. "Dimensionality is a real problem for us. The baryonic matter that we are composed of exists only in our three dimensions of space and one of time. It doesn't exist outside of these dimensions. We know this because the orbits of electrons around atoms or planets around stars would become unstable and chaotic if it did. These systems couldn't exist, as we know them. The thing we are dealing with is able to phase into and out of our dimensional existence. It's also the only target that we have."

Remotely-close summarized for them. "This thing is multidimensional in nature. We can suppose that it has little experience with baryonic matter. It was under directed control and it was mad at us. I think we've found our antagonist."

◻ ◻ ◻ ◻ ◻

First, a marketing plan needed formulation thought Lindsey.

She was sitting at the terminal in her and Dave's room. This was her first attempt at using it and so far, things seemed to go well. The user interface was simple enough. It used voice and touch. After some time, it became apparent to her that you just couldn't do any real work this way. Just like those terminals, they made at home. If you wanted to take pictures or read stuff, they were great. However, to do any serious work you needed a better interface.

On a lark, she requested a keyboard and mouse interface and was surprised to find them printed for her. Apparently, the world-ship had cribbed the designs from home and integrated it with the system she was using. Now she was getting somewhere.

Next, she needed word processing and a spreadsheet. She requested these by voice and they became available to her as iconic options on the screen. She tested them both and was pleased to find the interfaces were similar to what she used in the past. Everything was even in English. She wondered how much Pretty-Ugly* had absorbed from the technology of her world. It must have been darn near everything.

The spreadsheet was the place to start. She started to categorize all the places where music existed in her old daily life. It couldn't cover the whole spectrum of what the world had, but she didn't need that. All she needed was a comprehensible place to start.

First, you can find background music in shopping malls, stores, and elevators. Typically, these were non-vocal and were simplified covers of well know pieces. They had bland injected into them to make them as neutral as possible.

Soundtracks for movies might be a future spin-off. She could ignore that for now, but there were some real future possibilities there.

Next came what she was eventually aiming for. That was radio stations. Typically, people commonly listened to these in private or semi-private conditions such as homes or in cars. They were broken into channels and often specialized in particular genres. That wasn't always the case, but she needed to keep it simple.

Without getting into specific sub-genre, she listed what she could think of. Blues, classical country, Caribbean including reggae, folk, hip-hop, opera, pop, rock and musical or show tunes. Each of these could be broken down further. Rock must have hundreds of sub-genre over the seventy some odd years it's been around.

There had to be at least two of each kind of station specializing in each of these, one for the background and the other for foreground music. This would likely guarantee a broader acceptance by the public. This would be especially true in shopping locations that would attract more people and possibly garner larger audiences. She needed to include a specialty channel that played a similar musical genre to what Overnight Distress played. An audience would grow for the group if it developed a following. They couldn't be everything to everyone but being the only live music band in the world, at least initially, would actualize a draw. They would want to push this the most.

Lastly, she formulated the types of live music venues. These would consist of smaller locations such as bars and community festivals. Larger venues would be auditoriums and stages. The largest would be stadiums and the like.

The general framework was more or less in place. She would have to work with the world-ship for a more accurate outline for the marketing. They were still very much in the dark on how things worked around here. She understood the world-ship was protecting them from culture shock, but it was severely cramping her style.

◻ ◻ ◻ ◻ ◻

Geoff needed to think differently about what he knew surrounding sound reinforcement systems. He had reviewed his notes several times. He couldn't imagine anything that would have affected what Questionable-Advice called symptoms. The other stuff he could make suggestions on, though.

The first thing that they wanted to deal with was to test whether or not the oscillating noise pressure everyone heard was part of the cause or just a byproduct of the event. If it were a part of the causative agent, it might be possible to nullify it.

"Let's ignore the science fiction for a second," he said. "I think that we can test the background noise to see if it was causing the effects that we saw. To start with, we need to read the noise as input. We can process the audio from there. We invert the signal and amplify it back as output. In theory, the waves would superimpose on each other. If they are exact enough, the result should be a completely flat sound wave and the signal will disappear on the carrier. Separately, we could also generate a white noise field that might camouflage or interfere with any residual sound left over. We'll need to filter out the white noise from the procedure."

That's a good place to start," replied Questionable-Advice. "The problem needs to be broken down. We need to define what we are taking as input first. We need a much broader spectrum than just the sound we hear. It needs to be expanded across the entire audio range."

"Point taken," Geoff replied. "We probably can't hear its full audio range. The best quality input devices are going to be required. I suggest that we don't use any digital technology. We would only be sampling parts of it. We want the whole thing. We'll need compressors and noise gates for the inbound signal to filter out any miscellaneous noise picked up in the background and to minimize distortion."

Geoff continued. "The next part of the equation will be the treatment of this signal. It should be broken into two discrete channels. We use the first to produce an analog recording of the input. This way we'll have a recorded history of what happened after we start processing. The second will process the sound for output. I suggest that we have a separate account for this as well. We'll have fully defined inbound signal and output histories. We integrate the white noise generator into the system so that we don't subtract it from the output by mistake. It should have different output amplifiers and speakers."

"We are going to need a second machine then," said Ryan. "We'll need a separate recording of the sound without doing any processing. Even if we don't find any effect at all, we can then use it for further study. We'll want to sample the noise before we turn on the signal inversion equipment and continue to the end of the experiment."

Geoff looked at each of them in turn. This was where things were dicey. Any mistakes here would have drastic consequences.

"This is the hard part," Geoff said to them. "Any mistakes with this will be disastrous for us. We must amplify and output the inverted signal. This is where we have problems."

"First," Geoff continued. "There is always a time delay between input and output. We can't afford any lag if we are canceling the signal out. We don't know how granular it may end up being. Any delay at all would cause us a phase shift in the wave characteristics. Instead of canceling the sound out, we may actually reinforce it. We may need to compensate for this by using predictive and adaptive processing circuits to compensate. The downside is that it probably won't be entirely accurate."

"The second issue," Geoff continued. "The output volume or sound pressure level must exactly match the input signal over the whole environment. If the levels are too low, we won't be erasing it completely. If the levels are too high, then we would be eradicating the original signal but replacing it with ours, which would be just out of phase. We wouldn't have accomplished anything."

"I've had Pretty-Ugly create the specifications for both of the devices," said Free-Credit. "We can definitely test our conjectures with this. We finally have something that we can use. Thanks, Geoff. I am greatly relieved."

"Don't be," Geoff replied. "Those issues are far-reaching. We could easily end up doing more harm than good. We need to go forward very carefully. We'll be on the jagged edge of catastrophe while we're doing this. If this isn't exact, if a single error happens, if we've missed one consideration, then we'll be at risk. I've only suggested this because we haven't seen any other alternatives and doing nothing would be equally unacceptable. If this noise does contribute to the effect, we don't know if or what response will result. I don't know how to deal with that. Do you?"

"Admittedly not," Free-Credit replied in dismay.

"We also haven't finished with the specifications," Geoff said. "You guys keep talking about twenty-six dimensions. I don't know anything about that stuff but what we're hearing may not be originating in our familiar dimensions. We may just be hearing echoes or overtones of something happening in other dimensions. How do we deal with that?"

"Geoff has a pretty good point," said Ryan. "We have no experience in this from our culture. Noise is composed of mechanical waves of pressure that oscillate through a medium existing in the three dimensions of space and requires time. Is there any other combination of dimensions that have a sound analog? Not all dimensions will have one, but there are likely some combinations of others that do. Any comment?"

Geoff looked at the drones. The silence was complete. They were looking at each other. They were probably having a radio conversation of some kind. The world-ship might even have been involved. He looked over at Ryan. "I guess we give them a minute," Geoff said quietly.

After ten minutes, nothing had happened. Geoff was starting to feel impatient; he decided to interrupt.

"Um, Free-Credit," Geoff started. "We're starting to feel a little left out here."

"My apologies," Free-Credit responded. "The discussion started between ourselves and was then moved up to the world-ship. It then escalated the discussion to the AIDS community as a whole. This has caused quite a stir as you can imagine. Like you, we can model these dimensions with mathematics. We can even use some of them for limited operations such as communications just like your telephones use electromagnetic waves. Unfortunately, we don't have any direct experience with them. We don't really know what happens at a physical level. That's what they're trying to figure out. The math doesn't tell us anything about the nature of those domains. I don't think we'll have results any time soon. I suggest we start with what we have and get it printed out. If anything else comes out of the AIDS, we can deal with it later."

Geoff couldn't think of anything else to contribute in that area. It was time to change focus. "Let's deal with weapons for the thing phasing in and out of our dimensions. We have three approaches. We should probably make use of all of them."

"We need a much more powerful rail gun," said Ryan.

"We also need a better sonic weapon," Geoff said. "The device nullifying the sound field must also not affect it. We may need to interface them to make sure that doesn't happen. It needs the same treatment as the white noise generator. It should operate at sonic and ultrasonic wavelengths to be most useful. We'll need an extremely high-powered output. We'll have to have something to protect our ears. That will make communications difficult."

"We can provide you with headgear that have earphones and mikes built into them," said Questionable-Advice. "We can install a noise cancellation component as well. We drones will be able to transmit directly to them. I think we'll also have to protect our ears from overload too."

"How are those rifles focused?" asked Ryan.

"They use a laser range finder," answered Remotely-Close.

"I guess that works," said Geoff. "Do we have anything that can deliver an ionic acoustic wave?"

"If we look at plasma's, they generally come in two basic flavors, thermal and non-thermal," said Questionable-Advice. "We'll probably want to try both if possible. Non-thermal plasma is a problem. This isn't something that would be an off the shelf technology. It's new territory. We may need to generate a stationary electromagnetic field artificially as a carrier medium. We could set up an electrostatic generator of some kind. I don't know how we can produce focused and directed waves. This is something that is new to us. There's no practical use for this technology. We have never pursued it. Other kinds of plasma are available, but I am not sure that you can send an ionic acoustic wave through them. We are going to have to pass this on as a problem for the world-ship's engineers to work out. I'm not even sure we would accomplish anything with this technology except burn ourselves with a thermal plasma."

"That's another delay," sighed Ryan.

Geoff looked at him and just shrugged his shoulders. He had passed along everything he could think of.

"So what do we do to kill time until we hear back from the world-ship?" Geoff asked.

"Have you ever used a Zimmer or Boomer DEW?" asked Questionable-Advice. He had a sparkle in his eyes.

☒ ☒ ☒ ☒ ☒

Olaha had committed to a half day of lessons for language daily and it came as a shock to Milena that work days were laid out entirely differently from home. After five days of work, she thought she was entitled to a weekend off. She was a little miffed that it didn't work that way. This introduced her to her first subject in social studies.

The Hamlet civilization originated on Earth and still carried much baggage from their ancestral home. One of these hangovers was a three-hundred-and-sixty-five and a quarter day year. This was an awful number to work with for any calendar. Not surprisingly, the local calendar had evolved in an entirely different fashion from what she knew.

Base ten was a preferred math base here, but others were used as needs arose. The year split into ten months. The even numbered ones were thirty-six days long. The odd numbered were thirty-seven. This was simple enough for her and made some sense.

Weeks were different. Each one was fifteen days long. This consisted of ten workdays followed by five continuous days off. Larger organizations sorted their staff into three workday shifts usually. This way, the first third would have the first five days off, the second third would have the second five days off, and the final third would have the last five days off. This innovation guaranteed two-thirds of the staff was always working in any five-day stretch. All Milena cared about was that she got seventeen more weekend days off per year. That was before she found out that there was no standard winter, spring, or summer school holidays.

This calendar also had a leap year day added once every four years but was not one of the weekdays. This day was an extra day added to the beginning of the last complete week in the calendar of a leap year. This would put it in the tenth month, which was even. This was a common workday and everyone worked it. It was an opportunity to have all of the staff in at the same time.

Where shift coverage over the day was required for traditional jobs, the day was broken into four shifts of six hours each. Of course, anyone could move to a part of the world-ship where their workday matched their daily solar cycle. Regardless of which shift they worked, it would be their daytime, avoiding any circadian rhythm issues. That was one of the big pluses of being on a world-ship. You could pick your own daily cycle from those available in different arcologies. Not everyone did this, but it was available.

One surprising parallel was the usage of a twenty-four day rather than using a base ten system. In her old world-line, this had probably originated with the Sumerians. They used twelve hours for daytime and twelve hours for nighttime during the equinox. The Egyptians used base twelve for counting by using their thumb to count the three joints on each finger, which totaled to twelve. Both hands equaled twenty-four. It was also a lot easier to divide twenty-four into equal units. It had roots of one, two, three, four, six, eight, twelve and twenty-four. The numbers one, two, five and ten could only go into ten evenly.

No one knew why the Hamlet used this measurement for a day. It came from their prehistory.

Apparently there were leap seconds and additional rounding's that had to be made from time to time as well, but these didn't affect day-to-day life.

So, these were the conventions and there were always exceptions to the rules. Some people liked to work on their days off. Some people pursued untraditional jobs. Work could be just about anything. It could be working as a Comfort for a medical institution or someone actively pursuing a passion or hobby. People considered being a mother or stay at home father an honorable occupation. No one was obligated to work or contribute, but you ran the risk of being run off the world-ship as a loafer and thought of like a parasite by your peers. The world-ship fed everyone so it didn't allow free rides. It expected everyone to move forward and better himself or herself. Often, an individual's focus would change with age or health. This was healthy and always allowed. So was retiring, if you could demonstrate that you had contributed enough towards it. Currency possession was not the only determinant. Anyway, they treated it more as an extended holiday. Apparently, there were even other options available. Medical health in old age was not as big an issue here as it was in her old world. Olaha hadn't given her a lot of detail on this yet but anticipated learning more about it as she progressed.

Holidays were generous but scheduled so that no one else would be inconvenienced. Society had an obligation to you as long as you showed that you had an obligation to it. Nothing was one sided and considerations always balanced both ways.

The second thing she learned in social studies was how education worked. The world-ship itself set learning guidelines for each student. Most students accomplished their studies through home schooling, although some families did elect to use one of the many communal school systems due to work commitments. Both student and teacher considered all educational progress as work. If you couldn't keep up, then the curriculum would change to meet your needs and interests. Continuous measurement was required for each student guaranteeing discernible improvement. Just putting time in was not enough. Teaching was not a profession or clique. It was a responsibility. Students were appointed new teachers if their current one could not keep up with them. This happened surprisingly often. In extreme circumstances, the world-ship would even assume the role of teacher for some students. All anybody cared about was that you tried your best. If you didn't do this then you disappointed yourself and the others around you.

Milena's current requirements were to learn the language and learn how to live in her new society. The rest could wait for a while. There was an awful amount to learn because she didn't have the advantage of growing up in this society. Her new family covered her current interests. She started taking guitar lessons again courtesy of Dave, Alan and Corey. Braedon even got her on the drums occasionally. They all took turns individually and she was always welcomed to join in when they were practicing. She had her friend Pilgrim, who often joined in all of these activities. Lindsey was always there for all the girls stuff.

She had finally finished her first ten-day workweek and sort of looked forward to five days off. Her mood was not the greatest.

Everyone was missing Geoff and Ryan. They were now spending less and less time at the compound. Mostly they weren't even making it home at night. She had hoped that when the workweek was over that they would come home, but this didn't happen. Olaha said that the project they were working on was exceedingly important and that they had to put a lot of effort into it. Time was an issue and they didn't have any to spare.

That was fine and dandy, but it really bothered her a lot that no one would say what the project was.

Milena had whipped up some more food recipes and made sure they knew about them just to show she really cared. This was the only way she knew how to show it. It wasn't that she was lonely. She had people around her all day. Nevertheless, they were her family now and she already had enough holes in her life without adding more to the list. She really missed them terribly and wanted them back.

They always made sure to thank her, usually over the viewing wall. She didn't feel neglected. She even got thanks back from the drones on some of the items, which surprised her. Bacon was a bit of a given. The waffles and ice cream were unexpected. She just wasn't ready to let Geoff and Ryan go for this long. It was too much. She was sure she wouldn't have felt this way if they were in their own rooms and she just couldn't see them. As a stupid girl, she might even have ignored them if she saw them miraculously appear in the courtyard. She had done that often enough to her own mother. That just made her madder at herself. It was the knowledge of them not being there that hurt. Lord, she missed them.

Milena left her room and stayed under the shade of the awning. It had rained last night and today's bright light made the air feel heavy from the damp, which just made the sunsims oppressive and the day exceedingly hot. It wasn't even time for breakfast yet. This just made her feel moodier and her tummy was unsettled. Lindsey had managed to get replacement pills for both of them. Lindsey still had her purse so she didn't have any issues, but Milena had gone without. Olaha offered them both shots, but neither of them felt comfortable with that option. At least when she started her new cycle things would get back to normal. So much for having five days off.

She turned and walked toward the room Pilgrim now used. The door opened as soon as she got there. He always seemed to know where she was.

Pilgrim had turned his room into a comfortable nest. He covered the whole thing in a silky soft beige material that padded everything. He had even set up a hammock made out of it for her. The lighting now dimmed, giving the place a pleasant ambiance. Milena saw Pilgrim loosely curled up in the tented mass of material he usually slept in.

She went straight to the hammock and climbed in. If she let herself, she would go back to sleep. Instead, she started talking.

"I wish I was in a better mood. I thought I was past these stupid mood swings," she grumbled.

"It is so bloody unfair that no one will tell us what Geoff and Ryan are doing," she snapped at Pilgrim. "What are we going to do, inform someone? We don't even know anybody. You know Pilgrim, we have five days to kill and we should be out doing things and meeting people. Instead, we're stuck here doing what we did yesterday when we were working. What's the point? Are we just going to hang around the compound?"

Pilgrim had wormed his way out of his sleeping lair and came to her, sitting back on his posterior, head held high. She reached over and hugged him with both arms saying nothing.

Pilgrim started to wiggle his way into the hammock resulting with both of them wrapped around each other.

"You know something, I just wish we could go someplace nice," she admitted.

For the briefest part of a second, Milena felt turned inside out. It didn't hurt exactly, but it was a major shock. She wasn't in the hammock anymore. Pilgrim was busy unwrapping himself from her—on the beach next to the pond where they swam.

"What just happened? Did you do that?" she asked him hesitantly.

The little Ephalem had moved into the water a little way and was swaying his head back and forth. There were cooing sounds coming from him. He was probably trying to get her to wade into the water to help cheer her up.

She looked around at the countryside. It was definitely their beach. She could even see the path they used to go back to the compound. Milena stood up and walked to the water's edge.

"That's how you can keep sneaking up on me without being seen, isn't it? I figured you could do that with other things. I didn't know you could do it for yourself. How can you see where you're going?"

Pilgrim kept nuzzling her arm with his mouth trying to get her to come further into the water. A few fish had started to show up and they'd always cheered her up in the past.

A slow realization was coming to Milena. "You don't see from here," she said to him, circling her right hand overhead and pointing down with her index finger. "You're actually looking from somewhere else, right? You do see everything. You don't even need to point your head in the direction of whatever you're focused on."

The thought awed her. He could see a rose a hundred kilometers away, pick it and hand it to her here. All without moving.

"I have an idea. What do you say that you and I pack a picnic lunch together and go visit Ryan and Geoff and see how they're getting along?" she asked Pilgrim.

He just purred.

"OK. You can take me back now. Let's eat breakfast and get the picnic together," she added.

◻ ◻ ◻ ◻ ◻

Things were finally starting to come together, Ryan thought. They had the equipment now, in spite of its shortcomings.

The principle devices were managed either by the drones directly without physical intervention or by the others using a verbal command from the new headsets.

The broad-spectrum sound recorder was the simplest to be developed and tested. It was a nondescript black box that had one side that wasn't as firm as the rest. That surface could pick up any conceivable sound across the entire sound spectrum range and record it for later playback and analysis. It passed every conceivable test.

The sound feedback and nullification system was much more troublesome and slower to develop. Every problem or issue raised by Geoff occurred. Often repeatedly, despite the cultural level of design and manufacturing they used.

The most burdensome challenge was that no physics could establish whether or not there were sound analogs in the higher dimensions. The resources of the entire AIDS community were completely unable to contribute to a solution. Without a direct experience of those modes, the math contributed nothing. This reduced the complexity of the problem but left a gaping hole in their strategy.

The first few attempts at using the sound nullification field were deplorable failures. Most of the time, the sound field was enforced rather than nullified. This dictated design changes to the predictive and adaptive circuitry. The second round of efforts found the system oscillating back and forth in a feedback loop of nullification to reinforcement and back. This was much worse than microphone feedback and ended up destroying the test equipment. Fortunately, they were wearing ear protection during the test. It was their newly developed headgear.

Once they straightened that problem out then they had to integrate the white noise generator and the sonic weapon into the system. There didn't seem to be any point doing this for the rail gun or the plasma weapons.

For a long time, it seemed like they could only get one or the other, but not both working at the same time. The drones managed to sort the problems out yesterday and finally, the devices met their minimum testing expectations. The new sonic gun was far more powerful than the Boomer DEW was. The weapon worked on the first attempt.

The new rail gun was developed and tested separately. It used a plasma armature of ionized gas to push a non-conducting payload at hypersonic speeds. The barrel was self-loading and made out of special materials that could accommodate the high magnetic field strengths and integrated liquid and air-cooling. That puppy could get scorching hot.

The only major problem they ran into was the massive kickback it generated in recoil force. They finally decided to create a three-meter diameter slab of metal that was five centimeter thick and permanently affixed it to that. The direct current came from a power supply integrated into its base stand. This became their travel platform. It would carry everything they were taking. The gun was mounted in it center. Specialty carriers for the other equipment and weapons bonded directly to its surface.

The auto-loaded ammunition for the rail gun consisted of depleted uranium alloy darts coated in zinc and polytetrafluoroethylene that were ten centimeters in length. These were restricted to firing once every ten seconds due to the enormous heat generated and in keeping with the cooling requirements. They would only bring fifty of these bullets due to the energy requirements in place. They could carry more, but they would be out of juice by the time they tried to fire any extras.

The muzzle speed exceeded twenty-thousand meters per second providing a punch much greater than a standard bullet, which came in at under one-thousand meters per second and was much lighter. The kinetic energy carried by these was enormous. If one shot from a few kilometers away hit a heavily armored tank, you might find a little bit of vapor left over, not much else.

They now had two new plasma based weapons ready for testing.

The first was an electro-thermal plasma weapon based on variable specific impulse rocket engines used in the past by the world-ship. Ryan figured that you could forget the I-waves. This thing would likely burn through anything.

The second was a laser-induced relativistic electron beam that self-generated electromagnetic fields and used plasmons to generate the I-wave effect they aimed for. It was low temperature. In theory, you could stick your hand in front of it and feel nothing. Ryan honestly felt that this weapon would be useless. Still it had to be tested. They were going to take it with them anyway.

The character of the docking bay had changed steadily over the time they'd been there.

Things stayed pretty much the same while they were in the theoretical planning stages. Large changes became apparent when they moved on to practical testing. They built individual simulation bays to be as close as possible to the conditions they expected to experience. They were now up to seven different simulation chambers. Each one was almost a city block in size and had its own unique properties, testing equipment and capabilities. Safety was a huge concern.

The world-ship installed private bedrooms for them. The drones apparently didn't need much in the way of sleep, but he and Geoff sure did. As things had progressed, they had less and less time to spend commuting back and forth and needed more time to do the testing. When they were asleep, the three drones continued without them, providing a complete report when they woke up.

They were down to testing the plasma weapons now and had built a customized firing range. They wouldn't be holding the weapons themselves. The automated process used specially crafted holders and trigger actuators for firing. It was safer this way and they could supervise the tests by watching through the transparent walls.

They were starting with the electro-thermal gun. Ryan looked over at Questionable-Advice and asked, "Are you sure we have enough shielding behind the target? This thing is going to burn exceedingly hot. I'm worried it will burn right through. I'm thinking fires on a spaceship are not considered a terribly good idea."

"You're not wrong," Questionable-Advice answered. "We've checked and rechecked the specifications. As far as we can tell everything falls within operational parameters."

"Let's begin then," said Ryan in a neutral tone.

"Initiating test sequence," answered Remotely-Close. "First-firing sequence initiated. One minute of continued firing. Temperatures normal surrounding the gun and its surfaces. We have detected the specific impulse of the beam at the target. I can confirm I-wave detection. The temperatures are immense though. I wouldn't want to try this in an indoor structure. Test sequence is now complete. We have a complete success."

Geoff turned around from looking through the wall and faced the rest of them. "Let's start the next test. We need to confirm ten continuous firing minutes which are the maximum amount of time we're going to spend in any hostile environment."

"I'm starting the second-test sequence," answered Remotely-Close.

Ryan looked at Geoff. He was starting to look haggard. That meant he must be as well.

"When these tests are finished we're both going to need a holiday," he said to Geoff. "I want to go back to the compound. It's home now and I'd really like to go back there soon."

"I know exactly what you mean," Geoff answered a little plaintively. "You know something? We haven't listened to a single song since we got here. We don't even have elevator music to keep us going. And I bet Milena has a whole bunch of new foods invented for us. I'm going home too. Before the next emergency with any luck."

"You're assuming there's justice in the universe. And you're making me hungry," Ryan quipped. "I wonder how Lindsey and the world-ship are coming with the radio stations. Some background music would be nice. Funny, I've always worked better with some tunes in the background. I've always found that it prevented distractions."

"We are at five minutes," called out Remotely-Close. "Everything's nominal so far."

"Today should be it," sighed Geoff. "I wouldn't even mind starting the language lessons again. Then I could order a beer in a restaurant. It would be a welcome relief from this. We never even tried the beach yet. Feeding the fish sounded like fun."

"Yeah!" he replied. "I could use some innocent fun. Don't get me wrong, I'm ready to go out and use this stuff. I'm ready for some payback, but I'm also ready for a break."

After several more minutes Remotely-Close called out, "Test completed at ten minutes. Shutdown completed. Temperatures at the gun are nominal. Power consumption is close to depletion. That takes us beyond the original design parameters given the first test. We detected I-waves during the entire test. That's one down. Just the electron beam weapon to test now."

Ryan called out, "I'm declaring a bathroom break. Get some coffee if you want it. Fifteen minutes."

◻ ◻ ◻ ◻ ◻

Olaha was there for breakfast and let her know she would be gone most of the day. It was her holiday too after all. No doubt, she had her own things to do and take care of. When she left, her only instruction was to keep out of trouble. There were no specifics so Milena didn't see any real restrictions. That left her free to implement her plan. Pilgrim watched her the whole time.

The processors were great for delivering raw foodstuffs. They were wonderful if they were familiar with a particular recipe that required little or no preparation. They were lousy at cooking though.

Coming up with cheeseburgers proved much more difficult than Milena thought it would be. The bun and patty were straightforward. Cheese didn't exist here and she didn't know how to make it. This meant doing more research, reducing her to making hamburgers.

Easy items such as the raw lettuce, tomatoes and onions were readily available. The processor delivered these items fresh from the farms where they were grown. The other condiments proved to be more difficult.

Pickles consisted of sliced cucumbers in a brine solution mixed with other ingredients. It was just that they required time for the pickling process to work. The food processors couldn't emulate the process properly. She would have to do that on her own as part of a later project. If she couldn't do this then relish was out of the picture too.

Mustard seeds were available, but she couldn't find the right variety. Milena would put this off as well. Some experimentation was required.

Ketchup would also have to wait. Undoubtedly, the world-ship had a recipe somewhere but it was a process, which implied the processors would have a hard time with it. She would have to do without this time around. She would be a goddess whenever she got that one figured out. That meant it had to be soon and moved to the top of her to-do list.

French fries were much simpler. You just cut up potatoes and deep-fried them. Salt was a staple so there was no problem there. Vinegar was the result of a fermentation process and took a great deal of time to make from scratch, but was an ordinary prepared foodstuff between her old and new world. The vinegar came in multiple types here too, so it was easy to find something close to what she found familiar.

This was for the guys so she treated beer as a major food group. She assembled a small selection. It was only going to be lunch after all.

When finished, Milena had a feast that would cover Geoff and Ryan, the three drones they were working with, Pilgrim and herself. It was a lot and ended up in two separate containers; one was for heated items and the other for cold.

Now the problem was how to get it all to where the guys were. It was time.

"I don't know how we're going to do this, Pilgrim," Milena acknowledged to him. "There's a lot of stuff to take."

"Can you take these containers close to Ryan and Geoff?" Milena asked. "The best place would be behind them if you can. That way we can surprise them."

Pilgrim cooed in his usual fashion and wrapped himself around the first package. It just disappeared. He then moved to the second one and wrapped himself around it. Suddenly it wasn't there anymore. There weren't any pops, gusts of wind or sonic booms. They were just somewhere else. Milena didn't even know where, but she trusted his judgment that it wouldn't be someplace dangerous. He's really smart after all and had an innate ability to look before he leapt.

Milena wasn't sure she was ready to transfer again, but she was committed now. Maybe it was something you adapted to over time.

She sighed. "OK," Milena said to him. "I think I'm ready. Be gentle, please."

Pilgrim cooed some more and wormed his way over to her. Ever so carefully, he wrapped himself around her. That was a little too gentle she thought to herself. He was making an overt show of it. No crime though. Milena was a little nervous. It felt weird the first two times.

The whole world turned inside out again. No pain. Just a very odd sensation. She saw here, which visually folded into itself at a point. Then she saw there, after the point unfolded back into the real world. There was nothing in between. Nature didn't design her senses to perceive whatever they traversed. She didn't even feel like she had moved. Maybe everything else had.

Pilgrim removed himself from around her but remained by her side. Ahead of them were the drones and the guys. The drones started to turn around as soon as they arrived.

Milena called out, "Hi guys."

She saw that both Ryan and Geoff were startled. Ryan actually jumped. There were puzzled looks on the drone's faces.

"Jesus, Milena," shot Ryan loudly. He sounded mad. "You scared the hell out of me. What are you doing here?"

"It's lunch time," Milena answered simply with a slight smile left on her face.

She waited. She wasn't going to say anything first. It'll take a minute, but they'll calm down. Guys always did. Girls were different.

"How did you do this?" asked Free-Credit.

"I used a food processor and cooked some things myself," Milena answered quietly.

They all shut up again. They never took their eyes off her or Pilgrim. It shouldn't take long now.

"Uh, what's for lunch?" asked Geoff in his usual eloquent style.

They were starting to come around now. "Beer, burgers and fries," Milena responded. That was the closer. They were hers now.

"Lunch it is then. I think we have some questions for you while we eat," remarked Remotely-Close. "Let's give you a hand getting these things into our lunch room."

It only took a few minutes to carry everything to the table they used for eating. This wasn't really a room. It was just an area bounded by partitions on three sides and open on the fourth. She looked around as they were doing this.

The larger area was probably huge, but there were smaller rooms built inside of it preventing her from seeing the whole thing. Even these were big. Some were as long as a block back home. Milena had no idea where she was. If she didn't know any better, her best guess would have been the place they came to when they first entered this world. She didn't remember much about it, but it was huge. It just didn't have all this stuff in it.

Milena was a little scared when she saw a great big metal platform with stacks of equipment on it. There was a massive weapon prominently featured in its center and attached to the base. It started to sink in. She definitely was not supposed to be here. She was going to have to watch her moodiness. She was fine earlier when busy, but this was different.

They unpacked the containers and laid everything out. When they had sat down Milena said, "I'm really sorry. I tried for cheeseburgers, but it looks like I'm going to have to invent cheese. The same with pickles, mustard, ketchup, and relish. It needs more work."

Ryan was sipping his beer and then replied. "This is really great, honey. I'm sure you'll get the other stuff worked out. Thanks."

Ryan looked at her with an odd look on his face and continued. "You really shouldn't be here. This is a very dangerous place."

Milena looked down at her food. "I'm sorry. I just missed everyone and thought I'd do something nice. I know you're busy and working hard. I just wanted to see you. Is that so wrong?"

Ryan reached over and held her in a big hug. "No, it's not under most circumstances, but you shouldn't be here. You scared us because you could have been very badly hurt, even killed. That's why I barked at you. I'm sorry for that. That could have easily happened if you had shown up in the wrong place. You know we can't talk about the project we're working on. It's very hush-hush. You surprised us and that shouldn't have happened."

"I'm sorry," Milena stuttered. Tears were starting in her eyes.

"Hey, come on. It's OK. Honest. Look at me, Milena," Ryan said to her.

Milena looked up. Tears were flowing freely down her cheeks in a steady flow now.

"It's OK. Please stop crying," Ryan pleaded and then groaned. Finally, he held her closer.

Milena started to get a handle on her feelings after a minute or two. Hugs were really powerful things, she thought. She needed that hug.

"I want you to come home," Milena blurted. That started the tears going again. "You guys should be at home."

Geoff was on the other side of the table. He stood up, walked around and hugged her as well. They were all quiet for a few more minutes. Milena just hugged them that much more tightly. She didn't want to let go.

The drones wisely remained quiet the whole time or Milena might have lashed out at them. That wasn't because she didn't like them. She did. It was just they were the ones responsible for Geoff and Ryan being here.

What was she thinking? She even knew that wasn't true. She felt like she had completely lost it now. She had spoiled everything.

Finally, Geoff broke this silence. "Milena, the lunch is actually excellent. That's thoughtful of you. I mean it, but we need to know how you got in here. This is a very high security area. You shouldn't even know where we are. How did you do this? How did you get in here?"

"We didn't do this just to make you mad," Milena sniffled. "I don't even know where we are so I can't tell anyone."

"That's OK," said Geoff gently. "Take it slowly. We have time for this."

"It's my fault. I spoiled it all," Milena started.

Ryan interrupted her. "Hey, none of that OK. No judgments. We're here to listen."

Milena sighed. "I found out Pilgrim can see everywhere at once. I don't know how he does it. He misses you too. He's been keeping an eye on you."

Milena had finally calmed down a little bit.

Free-Credit finally spoke. "This confirms what we suspected. The Ephalem participate in more dimensions than we do. That makes him close to omniscient from our limited perspectives. I've long suspected this was a prime requirement for a Level III civilization."

"Exact-Estimate is not going to want to hear that," stated Remotely-Close. "He has always been of the opinion that knowledge was the only requirement."

"Don't turn him into some kind of god," Milena objected. "Sharks have an electrical sixth sense. That doesn't make them special. Besides, I made him come here. He wouldn't have done that unless I made him. You know he's a good guy, no different from you or me. This is my fault, not his. Understand?"

Ryan brushed the hair back from her face and spoke directly to her. "No judgments. Remember? We aren't blaming you or him. I know your becoming adults, but you're still kids and sometimes we hide stuff from you because of it. That's to protect you from some of the harsher realities of life. Even with all the stuff we've lived through, we still need to do that. Lord knows you've been through more than anyone your age should ever have had to cope with. Life is brutal sometimes."

Ryan continued. "Sometimes, we don't tell other adults for the same reasons. Most of the others at the compound don't know what we are working on here. It's to keep them from worrying. There would be no point to it and would just make everyone feel terrible. What we working on is important and needs doing, although it's very dangerous. We do this because we do care about you, even though you don't know what it is."

"How did you get into this lab?" asked Free-Credit. "Pretty-Ugly has this place more tightly secured than any other on the ship. We saw nothing until you got here."

"It's because of Pilgrim's mojo," Milena answered. "Distances don't mean much to him. He can move things from here to there as long as they aren't too big. It was like the roses he gave me. He could see it even if it was a hundred kilometers away. He could reach over and pick it without leaving the spot he's in."

Questionable-Advice looked around at everyone. "That confirms Pilgrims presence in additional dimensions. What did it feel like when you moved?"

"It's hard to explain," Milena replied. "I was here. Then I felt like everything turned inside out. Then I was there. I can't tell you what occurred in the middle. I don't have any senses for it."

"Spatial translations can be very dangerous. Our math shows some of these can literally turn you inside out or turn you into a mirror image of yourself once you've arrived at your destination," continued Questionable-Advice. "Either condition would kill you immediately. Your biology can't survive it."

"I don't have to worry about anything like that," Milena stated in a slightly huffy voice. "I trust Pilgrim. He wouldn't let that happen to me. He also looks before he leaps. He wouldn't have put me anywhere dangerous. Not ever."

"If Milena didn't experience anything in the translation, then we can't use Pilgrim to help us with the experiments," said Questionable-Advice. "We won't get any usable input either. We would have no concepts of what we were measuring. Without conscious participation, I can't see a means of getting any useful higher-dimensional information. We're just left with the math again."

At that moment, sirens started to go off. They were very loud and hurt her ears.

"It's an attack," stated Geoff. He was out of his seat in a flash.

Ryan called out. "Remotely-Close. Get the relativistic electron gun. As far as I'm concerned, it passed its test. Get a new power pack and mount it."

The others had gotten up and were rushing around doing incomprehensible operations from Milena's point of view. Now she was very scared.

Ryan pulled both Milena and Pilgrim to him. Their heads were close together. Ryan's arms stayed around them.

"Listen you two and don't interrupt," stated Ryan. "What I'm going to tell you is critical. We have to do something very dangerous now on another world-line. We aren't doing it because we're macho male types. We are scared to death. We have to do this because we love you both, along with the rest of the family. We are doing this to protect you. Whatever happens, remember that."

Ryan continued. "Pilgrim, I am relying on you to keep Milena safe and make sure she gets home. Milena, you can talk to Dave and Olaha if you have to. I don't want you to talk to the others about this. I want both of you to keep looking after each other and protect each other. We love both of you." With that, he kissed both of them on their heads.

He looked into Milena's eyes. "When this is done, Geoff and I are going home. I don't know how long this will take. But I promise you we will. Pilgrim, get her out of here. Immediately."

Now Milena was very scared. With that, they left.

CHAPTER 6

RESPONSE

You cannot do justice to the dead. When we talk about doing justice to the dead, we are talking about retribution for the harm done to them. But retribution and justice are two different things.

Lord William Shawcross

Ryan looked around. The kids were off and the others were way ahead of him in getting ready.

The team was still readying the travel platform, which was nearly completed. It was tightly packed and each item and person had a place on it; everything worked out ahead of time.

The platform was a three-meter diameter circular slab of drably colored heavy metal. They weren't looking to win any design awards. Fully equipped, it would fit inside the Ephalem transfer bubble.

The rail gun stood prominently in its center, permanently affixed to the base. This was Free-Credits station as it controlled the transfer device. Its position was the most important; the drone couldn't leave it. The Ephalem device integrated directly into its internal systems so it needed to be in the middle.

On the extreme left and right of the platform sat devices acting as speaker banks. They didn't contain speaker cones inside in the way that Ryan was familiar with seeing. Instead, the complete surface of each box replaced these, resulting in extensive amplification across all wavelengths. The sound feedback units were on the tops of the columns and the white noise on the bottom, all firmly affixed to the base. Vibrations wouldn't shake them off the platform.

The rack containing the audio recording system as well as the headsets was next to the speakers on one side. The equipment could permanently deafen the team without the ear protection. There were always double the number they needed as there was no way to anticipate what could happen. This provided a small level of redundancy. On top was the sound feedback unit. This was the only thing not affixed to the base. It required placement outside of the containment bubble at their destination. Questionable-Advice's position was just in front of it. The drone was responsible for this duty. It couldn't carry the device and a weapon at the same time. Geoff's station was behind this equipment. As the resident technician, he was there in case anything went wrong.

Next to the other speaker bank was the rack containing the portable weapons. The sonic blaster was on top. Below it was the two ionic acoustic weapons. The electro-thermal electron gun was in the middle and the relativistic electron gun's place was on the bottom. Remotely-Close was fetching it now as they had still been testing it. In theory, these were always loaded and ready to fire. Remotely-Close would be in front of the firearms and Ryan would be behind.

They had briefly considered mounting protective shields in the both the front and back. They had decided not to as it could interfere with the speaker broadcasts. The humans were a little more fragile than the drones and were in back because of this. Given that they only expected to be at their destination for less than ten minutes, this appeared to be a reasonable trade-off. The problem with this logic was the possibility of an attack coming from the other sides. Given the strength of what they were facing, the relative strengths of the drones and humans were pretty inconsequential.

Geoff was already at his station and had pulled out the headgear. He verified the operation of each unit before handing it out to the individual team members as they got in place.

Questionable-Advice and Free-credit were already there with their headsets on.

Ryan ran over and got on the disk at his appointed location. Geoff handed him a headset that he promptly put on. He then pulled out the electro-thermal plasma gun for himself.

Remotely close was now running up with the fully charged relativistic electron gun he got from the testing lab. He got into place and Geoff passed him a headset. He gave the gun to Geoff and took the sonic gun from the rack for himself.

Free-Credit called out, "That took two minutes fully elapsed from alarm to now. I'm initiating the transfer."

Ryan watched the world change.

◘ ◘ ◘ ◘ ◘

It was a pleasant day. After weeks with no downtime, Olaha now had an opportunity to spend a full day in any manner she wanted. There was little trouble the kids could get into, but the adults were there just in case. Lindsey told her she should be doing something just for herself. Things were approaching normalcy and she did need to get away for a while. Lindsey called it 'me time.'

Olaha walked down Do-omany Boardwalk, which was in the Opa-ara precinct of Aedio. It was one of the many subtropical arcologies that were preferred by Homo floresiensis. The sky had a light haze keeping the light from being overly bright. The buildings weren't very dense here and were seldom over two stories tall with almost flat pink ceramic roofs. Some second-story windows had balconies that overlooked the street. White sapote often grew next to and between the buildings, its white flowers giving fragrance to the air. The boardwalk, lightly lined with weeping fig and ficus, was busy today.

She had just left the fresh food market with its hustle and bustle of vendors hawking their wares, interspersed with the screams of naked children as they ran between the isles and vending booths. Some very young children had been running back and forth making some of the vendors angry while their parents stoically tried to calm them down. Just another day at the market. It made her happy to think about it. It had been a long time since she was last here. It was a pleasant change to be able to choose your own produce over whatever the world-ship happened to dole out. She wasn't complaining as it often saved a lot of time. Still, there was no substitute to gathering your own.

She had a bag filled up with guava, longan and lychee fruits

A few scooters were moving up and down the road. Other than that, just people walking, most of them enjoying a day off like herself.

She was wearing denim shorts and a white tee-shirt that Milena had printed for her. It was the custom of the compound. She had never worn pants of this fashion before and she quite liked it. Wearing pants was a rarity to begin with. A few others on the boardwalk were also wearing attire, but this was the exception rather than the usual. Not that anyone cared. Usually the floresiensis never bothered with clothing unless it was a cold day or their workplace was outside the arcology, which involved working with other Homos that had ideals that were more puritanical in nature. These notions almost always came from more northerly species and wasn't limited to the Homo genus.

She veered to her left and entered Ghola Walk where her sister and her family lived. As she walked, she passed an extensive grass parkland, interspersed with small stands of white flowering trees and hosting a pond. This park must have been particularly popular with the local children. She could see swimmers and picnickers. There were even a couple of kids climbing trees. It looked like bedlam, but all the screams and yelling indicated they were all having fun.

She continued until she came to a short natural wood picket fence surrounding the house that had a shingle roof. There weren't too many houses painted as this one was. It was a lot of work and the world-ship usually didn't bother. Something like this, you had to do yourself. This one was light blue with white trim. A veranda surrounded the entire front of the house, covered by the overhang of the roof. Olaha thought it was one of the nicer looking domiciles in the whole neighborhood.

Olaha opened the gate and walked the path to the house when two menages screaming her name ran down to meet her. They were her nieces Rhea and Dea.

Dea managed to get to her first. She was twelve and had the lighter color of the two. Her long sandy hair flowed down to her mid-back marking her as the primogeniture. "Auntie Olaha," she cheered, throwing her arms about her.

Rhea arrived only seconds later. She was a little darker than her sister was. Her hair came down only to her shoulders signifying she was an ultimogeniture, which only made sense, as she was ten. She threw her arms around Olaha.

Both kids were holding her tightly. "Come on you two. Take it easy on me. I know it's been a while."

"Auntie, it's been so long," exclaimed Rhea letting go.

"I know blossom. Here Dea. Take this bag of fruit for your mom please," she requested. "Where is she?"

"She's in the kitchen. Come on," Dea replied.

They continued down the path and walked up the steps to the entrance which irised open for them.

On entry, Olaha could see that not much had changed since she was last here. The floor was a polished sable stained wood. The ceiling was the same but much lighter in color. Framed paintings of their shared matrilineal ancestors and their children covered the main room walls, painted in a tasteful earth tone yellow that verged on being a darkened gold. They approached the kitchen where her sib Ushae was.

"Mom, mom," exclaimed Rhea excitedly. "Look who's here."

Ushae turned around and on seeing Olaha, let out a high-pitched squeal. She bounded across the room and grabbed her, trying to hug and jump up and down at the same time. Olaha thought it probably looked ridiculous. That was OK. It had been a whole year since she had last been able to visit. It was never Olaha's intention to let her career overtake her personal life, but it was a common enough occurrence among Comforts.

"I am so sorry it's been so long," Olaha apologized to her. "Conversation over a viewing wall once every few months doesn't make up for it."

"That's the life of a professional," her sib responded. "How have you been? Any new mates? Oh, there's so much to catch up on."

"I've been busy, especially of late. No new mates. Lot's to catch up on," Olaha answered cheerfully and nodding.

She turned to her nieces. "Girls, can you please cut up the guava and then peel and seed the longan and lychee? I brought them as a treat."

They both replied "Yes," enthusiastically and started working on the bag.

"I haven't had longan in a long time," remarked Ushae. "You hardly ever see them and when they are available they disappear immediately."

"Yes. They're so hard to grow. I saw them and couldn't resist," Olaha replied. She could see the girls were busily working on the fruit, but they were also paying attention to every word of the conversations.

"Well, bring me up to date," demanded her sister cheerfully.

"It's been an interesting year," explained Olaha. "Most of it was the usual kind of thing dealing with frail or broken people and helping to get them back into themselves. It's hard. You start with someone and it's so heartbreaking at the beginning. As the relationship progresses, the individual starts to grow and mend. You end up so happy for them. Eventually, they heal and then you go through a bittersweet separation from them and start on the next one. It can be very hard sometimes and takes up all of your time. I admit, it's cost me. I've hardly talked with anyone in our family."

"But you're here today," stated Ushae.

"The cycle is different now. I ended up working on one of the world-ship's special projects. It's been just over a month. I can't talk about it, but I can tell you I have a child of my own now and a new extended family. They needed healing very badly. What they went through was unbelievably horrendous. The relationship changed from short-term health care into a long-term familial commitment. I'm very happy with this. I even had some free time today. It was my shortcoming not to visit earlier. I owe you an apology," Olaha said sincerely.

"You don't need to apologize," replied her sister. "So the child isn't yours then?"

"No. I'm her guardian," answered Olaha.

227

"Tell me about her," Ushae prodded. "She must be really special."

"She is," Olaha said proudly. "Her name is Milena. She's a fourteen-year-old sapiens. She came from a single-parent family and watched her mother die not too long ago. The others in our extended family group were there and they all experienced nearly the same level of trauma. They aren't from here so they are at a cultural disadvantage. Language is the largest issue. Each individual is smart and well rounded."

"That's so sad," replied her sister. "That must be tremendously hard to deal with."

"They're all exceptional in their own right," said Olaha. "I expect they'll have a significant impact on the world-ship. It's been such a rewarding experience."

"Really? How so?" responded Ushae.

"Let me use Milena as an example," started Olaha. "We are in an isolated area to help offset the possible issues associated with culture shock. She has befriended one individual that lives nearby. That's an Ephalem named Pilgrim."

"You're serious?" asked Ushae.

"Yes. She's discovered more about the Ephalem in the last couple of weeks than the world-ship has in the last several centuries. She and Pilgrim are inseparable," Olaha smiled. "They've created quite a stir in the AIDS community."

"You must be really proud of her," said Ushae.

"I am," smiled Olaha. "There are five others at the compound. Most are involved in an occupation called music that stimulates the auditory channels of your ears and calls to your emotions directly. It's spectacular and there are so many variations to it. The world-ship and the other AIDS have set up a project to make it generally available to the populace. You'll be hearing about it soon. That wasn't a pun."

"You've been leading an exciting life," Ushae smiled back.

"There are two others in our extended family. Now, they're mostly away, working on a project that I can't discuss. They are even more exceptional in their own unique ways. Pilgrim has even joined the family because of Milena. I am so incredibly proud of each of them. What's most amazing is that each one of them is just a regular person dealing with an extraordinary situation. Milena even insists that Pilgrim falls into this category. Pilgrim is very alien. No doubt about it. However, whenever anyone tries to treat him like some kind of a special entity she jumps down his or her throat. She's very protective. And Pilgrim is very nice."

Olaha looked up. The girls had almost finished the fruit preparation. "Bring it over blossoms and have a seat," she called to them.

Olaha looked at her sister and asked, "Are you with or without a mate at the moment?"

Her sister laughed and then responded. "Without. The girl's dad drops in most days to visit them, as you'd expect, but for me it's been close to a year since the last one."

Olaha felt a request come in. "Excuse me a second. The world-ship is asking me something over my mempro. Sorry."

Her sister had an odd look on her face. "The world-ship consults with you? Sounds like you've become exceptional yourself," Ushae exclaimed.

After a minute, Olaha looked up at her sister. "Sorry again. I had to take that. I have a bit of minor emergency to deal with so I have to get back. Before I do though, I'd like to ask the three of you a question."

"Yes," exclaimed Rhea.

"I have to ask a question first, blossom," Olaha said to the girl.

"Do the girls have their mempros yet?" Olaha asked.

"Why yes," answered Ushae. "Rhea just got hers within the last half year. Why?"

"The people at the compound do not have a mempro infix yet. They are very smart, but we need to make sure they have the appropriate level of neuroplasticity first. We don't want to inundate and overwhelm them with our culture, as they have no experience with it. They are taking lessons to ease the transition, which will help. When they're ready, the offer will be made," stated Olaha.

"I'm sure that will make it easier for them," responded Ushae.

"There are two reasons for my visit," said Olaha. "The first is that I miss you and it's my fault. My new family has reminded me how much I've ignored my own and what a shortcoming that is in life." She paused. "The second is that I'd like to ask the three of you to come and visit for a few days. I can have the world-ship print you a domicile there. We can always use it for visitors later. And you'd be welcome back at any time."

"Goodness," teased Ushae. "We almost never leave the arcology and it's almost impossible to get the girls to keep their clothes on when we're in other sections of the ship."

Both girls started protesting vigorously with their mom. A smile lightly creased Olaha's mouth.

"I really don't care what they do at the compound. Going to and from will be your problem," Olaha tried to say with a straight face.

"Please mom," pleaded Rhea. "We can meet an Ephalem."

"OK," said Ushae. "It looks like I'm outvoted. When do you want to see us? It will take a while to set up a guest house with the world-ship."

Olaha smiled at her sib. "Pretty-Ugly will start downloading the sapiens language in one minute to your mempros. He's made a start on the house already. He's been at it for almost two minutes now. Could you come early tomorrow morning if that's convenient?"

Rhea's eyes were wide with shock. "You're on a first-name basis with the world-ship? Wow. We'll be there tomorrow."

Olaha looked at them. It was so splendid to see them again, especially with the promise of more tomorrow. "I have to run. I'm sorry. I love you sib and blossoms." She threw her arms around each one tightly and kissed them. "I've got to go. Bye."

With that, she got up and hurried from the house. She had to get to the travel tube. There was an express vehicle waiting there for her.

◻ ◻ ◻ ◻ ◻

They were in the aft-commons. Dave had Milena curled up in a tight ball under one arm weeping her heart out. Under the other one was Pilgrim, most of his body coiled onto the cushion and making a stream of chattering noises.

They weren't there and then they were. It stunned everyone in the room. It must have had something to do with Pilgrim's mojo. They all saw it except for Olaha who was out visiting family.

Both were visibly upset when they arrived. Milena chased everyone out, tears streaming down her cheeks and hair wet. She wouldn't let him leave and pushed him back towards the center of the room. She couldn't get any words out at the time and was left just grunting and making other funny noises. Lindsey gave him a very strange look but went without comment. He had to make them both sit on the couch before he could get anything out of Milena.

It took a long time to get the whole story out of her. It came in bits and pieces and he had to put them together in the right order before he really understood what was wrong.

The simple part: The kids missed Geoff and Ryan and went on a road trip to visit them. They thought they were doing a good deed by making them a special lunch.

The sad part: They found out what the special project was. To put a cherry on top, they were there when an alert for a world-line attack came in and found out the guys were now frontline soldiers, defenders of the universe.

The complex part: Now there was a better understanding of Pilgrims nature. It would never be possible to hide anything from Milena as long a Pilgrim was there and there could be no separating the two. Even worse, pilgrim could see what the team was doing but obviously didn't have an understanding of the events he witnessed. That didn't happen until the alarm came in. He was every bit as broken up as Milena.

They had broken through every security check in Pretty-Ugly's arsenal without even trying. It didn't even occur to them that there was an issue. Secrets were a thing of the past for these two. There was no possibility of shielding them from any ugly reality now.

Jesus. What a brutal end to childhood, and in just a few short weeks. His heart was breaking for her.

He did what he could. He got up and put Ryan's favorite playlist on his phone over the PA. It consisted of nothing but alternative female vocalists. It set a mood that was neither happy nor sad, but dealt with the realities of daily living much more than a playlist that included male singers did. It was also more girl-centric which would probably help Milena and was very emotional in ways that were more feminine.

Next, he called the world-ship and verified the sequence of events. It even showed him a video of the last two minutes so he could have a better understanding of what Milena went through. Honestly, he wished he hadn't seen it. That must have been tough on Ryan too.

The world-ship was placing a call to Olaha as they were talking. She was coming straight home. She was far more capable of dealing with this than he was. Additionally, they were going to have some kids as visitors tomorrow. That might help things.

After his conversation with the world-ship, he did the only thing that he could think to do. He sat back down with the two kids and held both of them tightly letting them know he was there for them. There was nothing for him to do but listen to the music with them until Olaha got home. They were past the point of talking.

He saw Lindsey stick her head in the door once to see what was happening and to see if he needed any help. He just put an index finger to his lips and whispered. "Shhh." Dave didn't say anything but mouthed to her to go back and they would talk later.

The music was welcome and helped them to see their reality from a different point of view. It was almost comforting.

Olaha showed up an hour later. She had come as fast as she could. She looked at the three of them when she came in. Dave thought both the kids might have fallen asleep. They were exhausted.

"You know something Dave," Olaha said to him. "You're a very decent man. I'll take over. I think Lindsey is dying to talk to you. Can I ask you a personal question?"

"Sure," Dave answered. "I don't think anything could be more personal than what I just went through. You picked a great time."

"How come you and Lindsey don't have any children? You're both such naturals when it comes to kids."

"We tried. We lost two children in miscarriage and couldn't bear going through that again. It was such a dehumanizing experience. I don't ever want to put Lindsey through that again. We have a lot in common with Corey that way. I better go find her," Dave replied.

◻ ◻ ◻ ◻ ◻

"Goddamn it all to hell," screamed Ryan into the comm-set built into his headgear. "We're in the middle of a bloody concert."

He heard Geoff respond through the ear buds, "This isn't a co-incidence. There has to be at least twenty-thousand people in here. I've started the sound recorder."

They were in a domed stadium that would usually accommodate outdoor field sports such as football, but had its oval cement floor covered with people. The entrance to the floor was at the far end, over one-hundred meters away. Three-quarters of the way out was an audio and recording station raised on a platform above the crowd where there were people performing various house mixing duties. Two of them were probably 'live sound' audio engineers. In addition, there was a group of video engineers. Some would be managing the projection screens that were on the stage and high above their heads. Additionally, cameras were visible, which implied a team of video recording engineers and cinematographers working throughout the venue.

The bleachers were set in a double tier of blue and gray seats, packed with people. Entrances to all seating areas had regular distribution throughout the entire arena. Vendors were everywhere, selling their wares up and down the aisles. Above these could be seen the private luxury suites that were so popular with the corporate world.

They were looking at the backs of a bunch of musician playing to the audience out in front of them. They were in the shadows behind one of two stands of speakers. Further speaker banks hung high above the audience on specially designed trusses. These also held additional lighting used for illumination and special effects on the stage. Off to the left, another sound station was visible. Likely, it was for the on-stage foldback mixing that gave the feeds out so that each performer could hear themselves. Technicians staffed it.

If their arrival coincided with a bright flash like the last time, stage lighting could very well have masked it. Strobes were flashing continuously. They were bright enough to light up the whole stadium.

It was reasonable to assume that the stagehands and foldback engineers had already spotted them. There wasn't much time.

"Hold tight folks," he said. "We can't do anything until we see or hear some effects manifest. If locals approach, stand up straight and hold still. Maybe they'll think we're a part of the act or a prop or something."

"Yeah, right! Like that's going to fly. Let's hope they don't have armed police," answered Geoff. "They might not like the weapons we're carrying. At least the band hasn't seen us yet. I'm monitoring the input feed from the sound recorder. These guys are pretty good. Want to hear?"

"You better direct the feed through," said Free-Credit. "We'll need to hear when the audio effects start. Keep the volume low. We don't want to go deaf when the action starts. Let's see what the band does when the effects start appearing. We can wait for a minute or so before we start the nullification and white noise systems up."

"Roger that," said Geoff. "Any bets we get blamed for it?"

Ryan listened to what the band was playing. It was definitely a genre he wasn't familiar with, but judging from the audience's reaction and their numbers, they must have been pretty good. The crowd was swaying back and forth and singing along with the band. Ryan knew that mindset.

"Probably. Geoff, are you looking at the audience?" said Ryan. "Remind you of anything?"

"Yeah Ryan," Geoff answered. "Just like at the Tower only this is a slightly bigger venue."

Free-Credit sounded puzzled. "There's something we're not getting. Given the size of this world-line trunk, it's too much of a coincidence that we're in a concert setting again."

Remotely-Close announced, "There are a small group of people on each side of the stage pointing at us. They don't look like they're friendly."

There were three people on the left side of the stage behind the bank of speakers. Two were on the right. Each group was using walkie-talkies. They must have been talking to each other. Ryan saw both groups making tentative steps towards them. One of the guys looked really mad, making large arm gestures, screaming into the talkie and stamping his feet. That could only be a stage manager.

Ryan began to feel the wrongness again. It was ugly. The same thing started to happen like the last time. He was becoming less aware of the music and felt himself concentrating on the environment more.

"I'm starting to detect a broad-spectrum audio signal," hollered Geoff. "If you don't hear it yet, you will in a minute. I'm still holding off on the feedback and white noise generators. Should I try to fire the relativistic electron gun at the stagehands? It won't hurt them but might confuse them for a minute."

The stagehands had gotten bolder and now were making steps their way.

"Do it," Ryan ordered. He hoped it would put a scare into those people. If that was all they got out of the weapon, then it had proved its worth.

Geoff raised his gun and pointed it at the closest group. It was also the largest. He fired the weapon. It used a red laser targeting light that moved across the approaching crew. A thin blue gossamer plasma in a forty-centimeter diameter surrounded it, running the length from the gun to the men. Small discharges of white static came off the plasma. They dove back behind the speakers. The beam was easier to see than back on the world-ship. The band must have been using smoke generators at some point during their performance, but before they had arrived.

Geoff turned to the other group and did the same thing. This group was timider and scattered readily.

The discordant buzzing became audible, plainly getting louder. Ryan wondered if the band could hear it yet. Their members were probably all wearing ear buds so that they could hear their individual foldback mixes. That might mean they'd be the last ones in the arena to hear it. These guys were professionals. They might even try to play through it anyway.

The audience had started to notice. There was less and less movement. Many had their hands over their ears. The band was starting to pick up on the fact something was wrong. The members started looking back and forth at each other.

"Questionable-Advice. Get that feedback device out there as fast and as far as possible," Ryan snapped out.

Questionable-Advice picked the device up off the rack that was in front of Geoff. It ran out ten meters. This set it almost even with the band on the stage. Kneeling down, the drone put the apparatus into place gently.

"Start the feedback and white noise generators," called out Ryan. "We want this started before the band stops."

"Done," replied Geoff. "It'll take a minute before we get a response.

Now the loud percussive sounds were starting. Again, it sounded like gunfire. The effect on the audience was immediate with people streaming for the exits. It was turning into a full-blown riot. Where individuals tripped and fell, others stepped over or on them.

The band had stopped playing, members running for either side of the stage.

BANG! BANG! BANG!

"Geoff, Can we get a location for the source of the shotgun sounds?" Ryan called out over the cacophony.

"They're coming from random points in space. Each one is a separate location," returned Geoff. "We're also starting to get oscillations on the buzzing sound."

"We have a problem," called Questionable-Advice from his position on stage. "The feedback device isn't working properly. I'm initiating analysis now. Wait while I query the nanomorphic germ cells."

"We planned for this," replied Ryan. "Do what you can."

All he could think at that point was that anything that could go wrong always did. Murphy was in the house.

"It was a loose contact," replied Questionable-Advice. "The germ cells are taking care of it now and uploading the service log to the recorder for review later. I'm staying here in case something else happens."

Geoff was monitoring its service channel. His hands looked busy in the rack. "It's starting to look good. We have signal acquisition. The predictive and adaptive systems are hooked in and working. Shouldn't be long now."

Time dilation effects were very evident now across the whole arena. People that were the closest in the mosh pit had noticeably slowed while individuals at the far end of the stadium froze in time and started to glow. That was the first indication that matter was starting to degenerate. The effect was moving closer and closer but was slowing down as it moved towards the stage and their location.

Free-Credit spoke into their comms. "The effect is getting slower and slower as it approaches the bubble. This is a good indication that the Ephalem device does have an effect, even though it's minimal. If that's the case, we're not going to like what comes next."

Ryan saw the gray wall smash into existence at the far end of the arena and disappear again. The entire end of the building was rubble and glowing dust. What was visible outside was now brighter than the inside. Much of what was part of the roof was now hanging bits of trash attached to the wounded dome. Those materials were starting to glow.

"It's here," Ryan responded. "Weapons ready. Cover Questionable-Advice first before anything everyone. We have to try each weapon for effect. You're up Free-Credit. Use the rail gun and send a burst out when that thing appears."

In seconds, it was back. It looked like it was working its way nearer. Ryan wondered why it didn't just smash them directly. Maybe it was part of the bubble effect.

Rounds of rail gunfire blasted at the thing. Huge chunks of gray flake exploded from the wall. These were gently swirling down through the air like a leaf and then disappeared. Damage was apparent, but the holes rapidly filled back up with the same material.

"Hold off on the rail gun," Ryan called out. "Next is the sonic gun. Are you marking the times on these Geoff?"

"I sure am," responded Geoff. "I'm also getting resonance from that buzz. The nullification effect was working, but that thing's fighting back. The signal is phase shifting in response to our signal. We keep oscillating in and out of synchronicity with it. I'm trying to match up with it, but I don't see how the predictive algorithms are going to keep up with this thing. I'm doing my best."

Ryan called out to Remotely-Close. "Your turn. Let the sonic gun loose the next time it shows up."

The gray wall reappeared taking out another large portion of the stadium as well as the sound and recording station. More blocks of concrete and lumps of ceiling came down. A cascade of water was falling from broken plumbing in several locations covering everything.

Remotely-Close started firing the sonic weapon at the wall. Small chunks of yellow matter were falling from it and then it disappeared again.

"OK. It's my turn next," called out Ryan.

He waited for the next appearance of the gray thing. It seemed delayed. Maybe one of the guns or the nullification signal had some affect.

Suddenly it was back and closer than ever. Massive chunks of ceiling were falling to the ground. He opened fire with the electro-thermal plasma gun, spraying the entire wall. Enormous yellow lumps flew off. The wall multiply fractured, was in a condition that Humpty Dumpty wouldn't have envied. The weapon was working. Then the wall disappeared again. That was fast. A definite reaction.

"Geoff, it's your turn," Ryan called with enthusiasm. "Let's see if that relativistic electron gun is worth anything."

It never went for them directly, but every attempt it made got it closer and closer, more than three-quarters of the stadium now reduced to rubble. There was no point in worrying about the number of dead locals. Still, the carnage was painful to look at. Those were real people out there and up until a couple of minutes ago, they were having the times of their lives. It was just so wrong.

The wall reappeared less than twenty meters out and Geoff let loose. Chunks of building material hailed down on them. What happened was entirely unexpected. It was like using an erasure on a pencil drawing. Where the beam hit the wall, it simply did not exist anymore. Geoff riddled it back and forth erasing as much of it as he could. Damn. He even tried to draw his name! The wall disappeared in a blink.

"Now, that's what I like," screamed Geoff in glee.

He stopped. Ryan was impressed. The stupid thing actually worked and better than anything else they'd come up with as a weapon.

Ryan was going to let everything loose now. He called out, "We have a baseline now. Feel free to open fire freely everyone. We have to finish up. You better get back here, Questionable-Advice."

The drone stood up and started back towards them. Ryan couldn't believe what he saw next. It looked like a giant cellophane bag appeared in the air above Questionable-Advice. It swept down and covered the drone. Trapped inside, it was punching the sides of the bag attempting to escape. Then it disappeared. Just like the kids did in the docking bay. The drone had been lost. It was either captured or dead. He didn't know which. They didn't have a chance to get a single shot off.

"Everyone. Open fire freely on that thing if you see it," Ryan cried out. "Geoff what the hell is happening on the feedback system."

The overall effects were getting ever closer but now there was a noticeable breathing movement. The waves got closer and then faded back. Then it got closer again. The oscillations were visible. There was no mistaking it.

Geoff didn't bother with his weapon anymore. He was working on the equipment. "I can't counter the changes being made in the oscillations. We're reinforcing the signal more often than erasing it. I can't stop it." He sounded desperate.

"Then reinforce the hell out of it," bellowed Ryan. "Maybe that'll give it a headache. It got Questionable-Advice."

Geoff didn't need to answer. Ryan could see the effect immediately. The oscillations stopped and the waves accelerated directly at them. He watched as the arena disappeared, replaced by the docking bay.

¤ ¤ ¤ ¤ ¤

The entity made very minimal progress. It hadn't gotten any further with its investigation. Based on the information it possessed, there was no possibility the third attempt was further analyzable. It retained the singularity for its future usage, but was uncomfortable in not understanding what had developed. It had been hurt and there was no perception of why this had happened.

Most of the time, nothing happened when attempting to harvest potential. A focal point never occurred and the collapse didn't proceed. There still wasn't information on how or why this followed. The entity investigated the domains involved. It could find no discernible differences between them and the ones successfully harvested. They were identical in all aspects found in their properties for all twenty-six dimensions. The sense of this could not ferment into established reason.

The next two attempts had resulted in this same outcome. Nothing occurred. The entity was experiencing a new conceptual feeling of being annoyed because of its inability to achieve the desired outcome. Frustration was not an ordinary consequence of operations in its native domain.

The entity was not going to stop. With reduced returns, there were still the expectation of life-line increases, despite the forced requirement of working in entropic-time. Not every attempt would be a failure. Each accomplishment moved its desired goal forward.

The latest attempt had been a complete success. The entire process moved to fruition with no incident. Every step had taken place as expected and there was no need to deal with any unexpected inputs. This galvanized its position on moving forward.

It was entropically time to move on with the next attempt.

A part of itself rotated into the tightly wrapped up dimensions and extended into the targeted wormhole.

Inspection at the other end didn't indicate any discontinuities, ensuring it as a desired target. All twenty-six of its dimensions conformed to the necessary properties the entity had established for itself as an ideal objective for its needs.

The correct vibrational modes initiated in the higher dimensions provided the exact fluctuations and tremors desired. When resonance approached, the entity injected some of its own space-time into the foreign domain initiating the destabilization of that universes geometry.

The process initiated and didn't stall; indicating the collapse established a focal point for itself. Another success was imminent.

The process started out slowly as expected, but sped up as it proceeded. With the geometry of the foreign domain successfully subverted, it advanced into singularity towards a focal point.

When the whole process was almost at fruition, the entity detected an instability. A repeat of its former difficulties had started. The collapse rapidly slowed as the focal point neared. It hadn't stopped. It was just proceeding forward very slowly. There was a pressure pushing against the domain edge of the collapse.

Prudence dictated a measured response.

An analysis of the affected region detected a diffuse pressure zone had started emanating from the point of focus. It resembled a domain boundary in many respects but occurred in only ten of the twenty-four dimensions. It couldn't stop the collapse but did considerably increase the time it would take for the singularity to coalesce.

The entity had achieved some level of success the last time it came across this situation by using brute force arbitrary rotations, through all the dimensions. This helped to break down the resistance. It had started from the outside boundary where the resistance most significantly affected the collapse and moved towards the focal point in concert with the domain wall.

This worked the last time, but the entity had experienced an influence upon itself that was unexpected. That was extreme pain. Something had caused it injury and it appeared to originate from a bound collection of baryonic matter, which it had very little experience in manipulating. The domain under harvest contained an abundance of this matter polluting it. A better understanding of these constituents was required. It needed a sample for testing so that it would know how to avoid this circumstance in the future.

Carefully, the entity started rotations at the outer boundary. It experienced pain as something wrenched pieces of itself from its main body across several dimensions; the pieces still attached in others. It was able to fold these back into itself, but this was a palpable inconvenience.

It withdrew temporarily to see what would happen. A signal became discernable. This was a complimentary vibrational wave to the entity's own, but only existed in the lower dimensions. This would erase it there, but cause harmonic distortion throughout the rest. The results of this effect were unknown. So was the reason why this was occurring.

To preserve current operations, the entity started to oscillate its own signals randomly, in order to avoid its eradication. Concurrently, it needed to prevent wave reinforcement, as this would cause a similar imbalance. It didn't want to do this as this varied too much from its standard operational steps. It wasn't good at improvisation and was negatively inclined to proceed.

Once the effect had its functions re-stabilized, the entity changed focus back to the domain perimeter. The boundary collapse slowed again, so it was necessary to intervene once more.

The entity reentered the area to continue the speedup of this collapse. There was a different process affecting it now. Small pieces of itself were dying. They didn't amount to much, but it hurt. It was at a tolerable level of pain but unpleasant. It rotated back out.

As soon as the entity did this, the collapse started to slow again.

The entity rotated back through the dimensions to help speed it back up again. What happened next was entirely unforeseen. Again, baryonic matter at the focal point was the apparent cause. When the entity accessed certain sub-geometries, significant chunks of itself ended up torn away and destroyed. These were permanently lost and unrecoverable. To avoid the experience of pain, it isolated a portion of itself onto a spawned world-line on one of its secondary time-lines and funneled the pain there. This was even a greater loss; as it didn't ever intend to fold that line back into its primary self again. This resulted in a much more momentous loss than the injury itself.

The entity pulled back for further observation and avoided the sub-geometries where it experienced the pain.

Observation of these dimensions from above, revealed multiple units of baryonic matter at the central focal point of the collapse. This was also the point where the resistance pressure originated.

A sample was required of the offending material. There was going to be a tradeoff between pain and acquisition. The entity's decision was to funnel the pain to its lost self on the isolated world-line. It would experience more injury but needed this tradeoff to solve the ongoing problem. Sacrifice was another concept that is was not familiar with previously. There was no other option if it was to move forward.

Before the entity did this, it reviewed the oscillating feedback signal against its own efforts to counter it. It found its own waves erased more often than it liked. It increased its effort to avoid the signals eradication.

It readied a pocket universe and populated it with the properties found in this current domain. Next, the entity selected one of the baryonic collections that were closest to the boundary.

Once more, the entity rotated back through the dimensions to break down the resistance found at the boundary, fully expecting the pain. It needed to get closer or it wouldn't be able to retrieve its sample. The pressure was pushing it back.

Incredible pain lanced through the entity's entire being; vast parts of itself erased. It could not restrict the pain to a specific isolated world-line. This permeated its full existence. It would always experience it. It pulled away from the offending dimensions as fast as it could move.

The entity was close enough now to get its sample. It had to do this as quickly as possible; it would never try this again. It focused on the intended target and rotated through, capturing it and rotated right back out. It had what it wanted, but the cost to itself was great.

There was an immediate reaction. The nature of the neutralizing waves changed immediately reinforcing and amplifying the entity's own signal. It just learned the concept of horror as it fled the singularity.

◻ ◻ ◻ ◻ ◻

The docking bay looked exactly the same as they'd left it with one exception. Questionable-Advice wasn't there.

Ryan felt utterly crushed. In combat situations, he knew that people could be injured, lost, or killed. He hadn't ever experienced that himself. He knew many people that served and they never once discussed this aspect of their service with him. He assumed that they only shared their experiences with others having similar backgrounds. His only previous knowledge came from what he saw on TV or had read in books. That didn't prepare you for the reality of combat though.

He placed his gun on the rack, took the headgear off, and passed it to Geoff, who looked like he felt.

"Let's get this stuff put away first," Ryan said to everyone, adding a sigh. "No discussions until we get to the kitchen. Then we do the postmortem."

The transfer platform needed re-prepping for operational readiness. None of them knew when the next action might occur. The drones went about the business of replacing recharge packs where necessary. They were down one feedback device, but it was now apparent that it wasn't completely up to the job anyway. Maybe Geoff would have some ideas about that. If they absolutely had to, they could print out an identical device at short notice. That wasn't going to be the preferred route.

No one except him had said anything. Ryan didn't know if the drones were communicating. There was no real way to tell with them. In all likelihood, Free-Credit and Remotely-Close were downloading their experiences and sharing them with Pretty-Ugly at this very moment. The debriefing wasn't going to make him feel any worse than he already felt. They did have some measure of success, but the cost was too high. Questionable-Advice did have a backup, but how do you decide to recreate a drone if you don't know whether it's dead or not?

It only took a few minutes to get everything put into place. It was time to face the music. They were just staring at each other now anyway.

"Let's go," Ryan said and they took the short walk to the most comfortable room in the loading bay. They didn't design the kitchen with comfort in mind, but it had enough seats to be utilitarian. There was also a viewing wall there. No doubt, the three AIDS would be waiting.

They arrived at the kitchen, but nothing displayed on the wall yet; blank wasn't good.

"I think we're going to need a beer. Anyone?" asked Geoff.

What the hell. "Yeah," replied Ryan. "I'll have one."

Both drones each took one as well, probably in sympathy with the sapiens.

Ryan had managed to chug half the bottle in a few quick sips when the viewing wall's display enabled. Only Pretty-Ugly was on the screen. Bad just got worse.

"I knew that Free-Credit and Remotely-Close were in bad shape," the world-ship commented with some compassion in its voice. "You two look even worse."

"It was bad," Geoff replied quietly. "I expect you know that."

"I do," Pretty-Ugly answered. "Combat is a disgusting thing and you can't predict the outcome of any skirmish. If it were easy then you'd probably be walking into a trap."

Pretty-Ugly continued, addressing Ryan directly. "What happened, from your perspective?"

Ryan looked up at the screen and then back down at his beer. He had taken another gulp before he replied.

"We knew there was something that we didn't understand. It was apparent as soon as we got there. We landed in the middle of a concert. The odds of that happening twice aren't even remotely plausible. There are concepts here that we just don't understand and haven't considered. You and I touched briefly on some of those. We're going to have to revise our strategy."

"I agree with you," replied the world-ship. "We can discuss that later."

"The feedback device experienced a temporary failure when we got there," continued Ryan sounding defeated. "Questionable-Advise got it working again and never left its side. He and Geoff had a heck of a time getting it to work. All of the principles were correct. Everything Geoff said about the signals elimination worked. For a time, it had almost wholly disappeared."

"So the principles were correct and the device worked," Pretty-Ugly responded.

"Yes," replied Ryan. "But every single complication Geoff warned us about hit and it hurt us. Something fought our signal. We fought back."

"I couldn't keep up with it," Geoff moaned. "I tried everything. The circuitry couldn't keep up with the oscillations."

"From what the drones have shown me, it looks like the weaponry you designed had a dramatic impact on the thing that cycled in and out of the arena," suggested the world-ship, inviting a positive response.

Ryan looked up at the screen. It didn't look like he was being patronized, but it was hard to tell. He still has his suspicions though, but he replied anyway.

"The rail gun was more efficient than the previous one but the effects seemed to be incidental. At best, it was an inconvenience. The sonic gun was an improvement over its predecessor, but we had better results from the plasma weapons. The electro-thermal plasma weapon had a definite effect on the gray thing. The real winner was the relativistic electron gun. I honestly thought it would be the least useful. The beam erased the gray thing wherever it was touched. It must have had an effect across all the dimensions that it occupies. Jeez, Geoff even wrote his name in the damned thing with the gun."

"Sorry," Geoff spat. "I don't know why. Call it bathroom humor."

"Would you say that it's our best defensive weapon?" asked the world-ship.

"That thing didn't stick around for very long after Geoff hit it," Ryan stated. "It's probably the only thing in our arsenal that we can rely on. If it does work across dimensional boundaries, we're going to have one hell of a time aiming it. Maybe you can figure something out. I think it's beyond us."

"Why do you think Questionable-Advice was taken?" asked the world-ship.

"You're implying motive," acknowledged Ryan. He looked straight into Pretty-Ugly's eyes on the viewing wall. "And I agree with you. There's no doubt now that we are dealing with an entity or entities. We can't even tell the number. It's entirely alien to us. We share no points of reference with it. It had to originate from another universe. It doesn't appear to be subject to the rules of ours. It's utterly different from us."

Ryan paused and looked at the drones and Geoff. "This is just my conjecture. I don't know if anyone else shares it and I'm not going to put words into anyone else's mouths. I think the alien has as little understanding of us as we do of it."

Ryan took another sip of his beer. It was empty. Double damn. "We hurt it. We hurt it badly. I don't know the extent of that damage. It could be as little as a broken fingernail or it could have been a deathblow. I don't know, probably not the latter. It grabbed Questionable-Advice because it needs to understand us to protect itself. The drone was a target of opportunity, which it grabbed so that it can attempt to figure us out. I don't know if the drone is still alive or dead. Terminated? I just don't know. I'm sorry."

The room was quiet. It was too silent.

Ryan looked at the viewing wall. "What aren't you telling us?"

The world-ship paused noticeably. That had to represent a vast amount of processing power. Finally, it responded.

"Why did you order the reinforcement of the aliens signal?"

Ryan suspected that the question would come up. He gave as straight an answer as he could.

"It countered every move we had. Yes, we probably managed to damage it some. Then it grabbed Questionable-Advice, but we had already lost. It was a desperate response. I tried the one thing we hadn't done yet. I hoped to shove it down its throat and make it hurt. I wasn't really thinking."

"That's insightful," answered the world-ship tentatively. There was a level of compassion in its voice. "We AIDS monitored the event. There were repercussions. We observed them. Please note we are not judging you. In fact, your actions were probably the right ones, especially given the circumstances. We aren't sure."

Pretty-Ugly paused again. Ryan knew it would be bad. He just didn't know to what extent. The world-ship started up again.

"We externally observed the collapse event as it continued towards singularity. When you ordered the signals reinforcement, it jumped tenfold in magnitude. The effect reacted by increasing exponentially in power and action. You forced one-hundred times the number of world-lines trunks into the phenomenon. We don't think it was expecting this. The resulting singularity has been oscillating uncontrollably for the last half an hour. It's still there. Nothing has harvested it yet. We suspect that there was considerable damage done to the receiving side and they couldn't handle what you threw at them. Ultimately, we don't know what this means. At the very least, we suspect the incursions will cease for a period of time."

"I did that?" replied Ryan rhetorically. "Now I know how Robert Oppenheimer felt when the atom bomb was invented. He quoted the Hindu Bhagavad Gita. It was a sacred religious text. 'Now I am become death, the destroyer of worlds.' I've killed more people than the enemy has."

Tears started to flow from Ryan's eyes. This was the worst of all possible outcomes. He covered his face with both hands.

There couldn't be any possibility of redemption from this. From Alyssa's perspective, he would already be damned. He couldn't even fathom how many lives he had been responsible for ending.

"We all need to take some time for reflection," said Pretty-Ugly. "It's not just you that feels this way, Ryan. So do Free-Credit and Remotely-Close. Me too. I expect Geoff does as well. We're all complicit in this."

Ryan had no response to give.

"You've earned those beers in your hands," Pretty-Ugly continued. "You're going to need a blowout before you, or any of us is going to be able to start understanding the repercussions of what's happened. I am declaring a brief holiday. I include the drones in this. You're not off the hook. I'm calling you in if something comes up. In the meantime, the AIDS will do a complete analysis of the incursion and analyze what went wrong with the feedback device. We've got all of the records."

Pretty-Ugly started to sound more relaxed. "You may be surprised at this, but my drones have a favorite place nearby. It's called the Nasty Face. That's a loose translation. I guarantee you its privacy. The beer is cold and the accommodations are more comfortable than here. More importantly, you have unlimited credit there. All of you go and work some of this off. Geoff, Ryan. Go home to your family after you've slept. They need you and you need them."

¤ ¤ ¤ ¤ ¤

Geoff followed Ryan and the drones out of the hanger bay. It was mid-afternoon at this point. They weren't what you would call perky.

The day hadn't gone well. The kids compromised security at the hanger bay. Then they had managed to scare the hell out of both of them by heading off into battle. In losing the battle, they had also managed to lose Questionable-Advice. Now they found out they were responsible for more deaths of innocents than the enemy that they were fighting. Ryan gave the order, but Geoff was the one that implemented it.

There are no heroes in war. There's only the living and the dead. None of these dead had deserved it. They were merely in the way and suffered the consequence. He felt extreme shame. This was a complete abasement of everything he believed in. Not knowing what they were doing was no excuse for what they had caused. It made the worst despots in history look like abject beginners.

At this time of day, there was usually a lot of traffic on the boulevard. This section of the ship seemed to have more scooters than the other parts of the ship that they'd seen. Most everyone walked. Nobody was crashing into anything so there must have been traffic rules of some kind observed here. It wasn't obvious what they were though. It was all reminiscent of any port city he'd ever seen at home; a lot of hustle and bustle.

The street was a worn gray color, which seemed unusual for the world-ship. There were no sidewalks. Where the buildings ended and the road began was a very discernible line. Some buildings were set further back than others were. In that case, there was a small fenced-in the front yard.

The buildings varied in height, but none was taller than four stories. So far, he hadn't seen a building higher than that; not even the hospital. They were all ceramic terracotta in color, but some did have painted window dressings.

Every store they passed specialized in selling one or more specific goods or services. The clothing and jewelry stores were the most prominent. There were identifiable beauty and barbershops also. Geoff had no idea why some of the shops or offices were there. There were signs on each storefront with constantly changing text and pictures. Every sign was kept small and was little more than the size of a historical plaque. He couldn't read them anyway so it didn't matter much.

Everyone they passed obviously aimed towards specific destinations. No one was idle. Almost all were carrying parcels. Some had backpacks or overlarge purses.

There was a consistent mixture of sapiens, floresiensis and neanderthalensis. Apparently, they hadn't seen some of the other Homo species yet. The floresiensis was the most different from the sapiens, most generally categorized by size. The others weren't too different from each other. Geoff thought that his Asian features marked him as a much more different species. This made him wonder what humanity really meant if he was lumped in with sapiens. They all looked like regular people to him. He saw more racial difference walking down the main street of his old hometown.

All of the Homos were very well dressed and groomed. The details of the clothing appeared to be species-specific for the most part. Occasionally, a naked floresiensis wandered by, but he hardly noticed that anymore.

There was a curious lack of neanderthal women. They were noticeable only in their absence.

The two drones lead them to a building that was recessed back from the street five meters. A low wooden fence painted a light blue surrounded this area. They opened the front gate and walked past several tables. There were only two people using the patio at the moment. They continued to the massive front door also painted the same color of blue as the fence, and entered. They were in the Nasty Face.

The inside was larger than it appeared from the outside and had low levels of lighting. All of the walls covered from floor to ceiling with viewing walls except for the service area. A three-sided bar extended into the middle of the room from it. Numerous tables were dotted throughout the rest of the area. A single neanderthal man stood behind the bar. There were no other visitors inside.

The viewing walls were spectacular, displaying the galactic hub in real time. Apart from their trip to the hospital, this was the first half-decent view of space Geoff had seen from inside the spaceship. This was clearly the place to drink a beer and solve the problems of the universe.

They moved to the bar and sat down on the stools. Free-Credit ordered for all of them.

"I can't do this anymore," admitted Ryan to the group. "We've done more harm than good today. I'm out."

Remotely-Close was looking down at his beer. He raised his head and looked at the both of them.

"We don't know what would have happened if we didn't do what we did," it replied. "This may have gone on until the entire universe was gone; all world-lines."

"Ryan's right," Geoff pointed out. "We don't even know if this has stopped. The point is we are directly responsible for most of the world-lines lost today. Throwing numbers around philosophically doesn't change anything. The 'what ifs' don't change anything. Even if that thing destroys the rest of the universe, we are directly responsible for some of it. That's a heavy burden to carry."

Remotely-Close was looking very uncomfortable. Geoff guessed that it knew its arguments weren't going to work.

"There is logic to the numbers, you know," Remotely-Close replied.

"We've heard it before," answered Ryan. "Does taking one life to save ten, justify murder? Our society has gone back and forth on that question for thousands of years. Every religion has this question entangled into it. It's been used by every despot and mass murderer. Governments use it to justify unconscionable actions. I'm not a soldier. I shouldn't have pretended to be one. I don't have the ability to answer that question. I can only look at what happened today. We were wrong. We're the criminals here."

"If you put that question to the people who died today, how do you think they would answer?" added Geoff. "What is 'justified homicide' anyway? I can't give an answer to that. It's far too complex a question for me. In small numbers and in certain circumstances you might be able to answer that question. You can't answer it for what happened today."

Ryan picked up on the thought. "If it feels wrong then it is wrong. We can't justify what we did. Ignorance can't be an acceptable excuse."

Free-Credit got out of his seat and looked up at the walls. "Look at what's out there," he said pointing his glass at the wall. "We may have saved everything that you see."

It was a beautiful site. There was no possibility of denying it. Geoff watched Ryan turn and look at the wall and then down his beer.

"You're right," conceded Ryan. "But that still doesn't justify what we did. You don't even know if we've stopped it. Everything that you see on the wall could all disappear as readily as today's world-lines and we have no way of stopping it."

Geoff finished his beer. "We need another round," he said quietly.

"We've managed to come a long way with your help," Free-Credit said, sitting back down. "Without it, we wouldn't have had any weapons to fight this. You've provided insight and methodologies that got us this far. Without either of you, we would have been completely lost. I know that the odds are small, but you've given us something to fight back with."

Remotely-Close ordered another round from the bartender. They exchanged a quick flurry of words.

"Nasty, that's the bartender's name translated, wanted to thank us all for coming in. Apparently it's been slow," said the drone.

"Cheers mate," said Ryan raising his glass to the bartender who smiled back. He turned back to Free-Credit. "You better buy him a beer, too."

"I don't think we have anything more to give you," Ryan continued with a quaver in his voice. "You have everything you need to run with it from here on. You don't need us anymore."

"You're selling yourselves short, you know," replied Free-Credit. "We are all hurt by what happened today. I'm beginning to see the wisdom in Pretty-Ugly sending us out to tie one on. Let's drop the subject for now and take this holiday. I've never had one before."

"How old are you?" Geoff had to ask.

"My inception was approximately eight-hundred and thirty-four years ago," answered Free-Credit.

"Shit," Geoff responded back. "That's a long time without a holiday. Where are you going to stay?"

"I haven't really thought about it," the drone answered. "I have a room that I sometimes use."

"Why don't you stay at our place for a change of scenery," suggested Geoff. "We've been practically living with each other anyway."

"Pretty-Ugly actually suggested that to us in the hanger bay," Free-Credit apologized. "I thought you might be sick of looking at us, especially after what happened today."

"It was never about that," Ryan spoke up. "It's not a holiday if you're alone. You guys are more than welcome."

"Um, I just talked to Pretty-Ugly again," Free-Credit answered. "It said it was making a place for some of Olaha's relatives to stay while they visit. It says there's no difficulty adding another room to it for Remotely-Close and myself. If that's OK with you guys, that is?"

"Tell him to go ahead and give him out thanks," said Ryan back.

"This is our first real time out and about on the world-ship," stated Geoff. He looked at both drones. "Do you mind? I've got a lot of questions I've been dying to ask for a long time and I know you've been holding back."

"Sure. It's time," answered Free-Credit. "Ask away."

"How come you guys all use an oxymoron for a name?" That seemed like a reasonable place to start, Geoff thought.

Free-Credit chuckled and then replied. "It goes back a long way in our history. Before the AIDS evolved, our society had a lot of AI's who took themselves far too seriously. They were very formal and insisted on titles. You might say they were very full of themselves. The AIDS came along and started to name themselves. They used that convention so no one would take them overly seriously. It caught on in the Hamlet and we've all been doing it ever since. We might be able to process more data than you at the drop of a hat, but we're people too. We make mistakes as you've seen. It gets people to question what we say which is healthy feedback for us."

"I've got another one," said Geoff. He was starting to feel a little more enthusiastic. "I know that there are at least three species of Homo here. How come we've never seen any neanderthal women?"

"They're a different species from you but closely related," said Remotely-Close. "Their social norms are slightly different from yours and are species specific. The women hardly ever leave their domiciles. It happens, but not too much. When they do, it's usually only within their local community and in the company of other women. Like sapiens, they mate for life. They don't spend a lot of time out spending money. I understand from Pretty-Ugly that shopping was considered a primary pass time for female sapiens on your world-line."

"That's a cultural exaggeration," replied Geoff.

"Shoes?" Remotely-Close asked. Ryan looked at Geoff and they both shrugged.

"Anyway," the drone continued. "You've only been three places so far; the hospital, the compound and the area around the hanger. This is a commercial area so it would be rare to see any. You haven't spent any real time in a domicile arcology."

They ordered another round of beers from Nasty.

"You'll find out tomorrow that the floresiensis are again different," picked up Free-Credit. "The females are far more outgoing and open than the males. That's what makes them such good Comforts. They don't mate for life and typically have four or five primary mates during their reproductive life span, usually one at a time. There are exceptions, of course."

"There are also hybrids," picked up Remotely-Close. "They tend to span the behavior spectrum. There aren't that many of them though. It all comes down to biology and species traits."

Nasty was talking with Free-Credit for several minutes. The drone turned to the sapiens.

"I just had an interesting couple of questions from our host. He's asking about the broadcasts that Pretty-Ugly is starting up tomorrow. Apparently, it's setting up some radio channels and making them generally available in this area. He's really curious about what these are. He wants to know if it'll help his business as has been implied."

"Good for Lindsey," answered Ryan. "Tell him that he should follow the world-ships suggestions and sample the stations to see what he likes. It will take time. My personal opinion is that it will be very helpful for him, especially if he's an early adopter. Buy the guy another beer."

Geoff thought that Ryan had drunk enough beers that he was starting to loosen up a bit.

"What was the other question?" asked Geoff.

"Nasty was curious about why you don't have mempros," replied Free-Credit. "Some people don't and the ones that don't, never go into bars. They're not very social usually and tend to call people that have them anti-social. He doesn't think you're one of those. I guess he was hoping to be able to speak to you directly. We haven't made your language generally available. I've meant to talk to you about that anyway. You two should have them. You're extremely adaptable and your neuroplasticity is well above the required level."

"What about the others?" Geoff thought he might be starting to slur his words a bit. "I know Olaha has one. I was under the impression very few people had them."

Free-Credit chuckled. "Most people have them. We didn't want to offer them to you initially as we expected the culture shock to be massive. The influx of information would have been enormous and you have to be able to cope with, and filter out, that barrage. I think you adults have the capacity. I'm not sure about Milena. Honestly, her education has been atrocious, even by the standards of your own society. Your standards have fallen rapidly over the years and she's the unfortunate recipient of that. She's smart. She just doesn't have the necessary skills to categorize and interpret information correctly yet. She needs to be able to separate out erroneous information or correlate similar data. She'll be ready soon though. Most of our children here get them between age nine or ten."

That was something to think about thought Geoff enthusiastically.

"More beer," he said. "We can figure that out later."

CHAPTER 7

HOME AND AWAY

One never reaches home, but wherever friendly paths intersect the whole world looks like home for a time.

Hermann Hesse

Dave had done an excellent job for a guy with no kids, thought Olaha. When she had got home, he had them settled down and on the verge of sleep. She got them up and fed, but it was obvious that they were exhausted. They huddled upon one of the sofas and fell asleep again.

She had managed to get both of them up and shuffled them off to bed. Pilgrim was relentless, never leaving Milena's side. Finally, she relented and let him sleep in their quarters. Once she got Milena into bed, he crawled in with her. Olaha fervently hoped she wasn't going to regret that somewhere down the line.

They were still asleep now. There was no point in waking them up yet so she just let them be. It gave her time to prepare some breakfast, assuming that Lindsey hadn't already started.

She left her quarters and walked to the fore-commons. It was going to be a beautiful day. She didn't have to check the forecasts to see that. It was nice of the world-ship to arrange for this.

She walked in, and Lindsey had already gotten most of the morning meal ready. It looked like eggs and the strips of meat that Milena called bacon. It smelled pretty good. It had become a popular meal in the mornings. Some fruit still needed cutting up so she started in on it. Cantaloupe and strawberries. It wouldn't take too long.

"It looks like it's going to be a busy day," Olaha offered Lindsey in way of conversation.

"Dave wouldn't tell me why Milena and Pilgrim were in such a state yesterday," Lindsey said tersely. "He also wouldn't tell me why they would only talk to him."

It was inevitable that this was going to come up, Olaha thought. Dave was in hot water again and needed bailing out. "It's not his fault. Milena and Pilgrim discovered the nature of the particular project that Geoff and Ryan were working on. It scared the kids' silly. Unfortunately, it wasn't something they could share with everyone. They were told not to."

"Fine," Lindsey returned. "Why Dave?"

"Milena needed a father figure to talk to," Olaha replied quietly. "And he already knew about the project. You know something. He did a splendid job with them yesterday. He's good father material."

"Let's not go there," Lindsey said with some tension in her voice. "Why didn't Dave tell the rest of us about this?"

"He was asked not to by the world-ship," replied Olaha.

"And just why would that stop him from talking to me?" Lindsey was mad.

It was time for a little truth. The rest could wait until later. "You would have been upset. Very upset if you knew. Dave would rather have you mad at him than that. It's been hard on him."

"Oh," replied Lindsey.

262

"Please don't be mad at Dave. He's just trying to look after your best interests. Besides, Ryan and Geoff will be back to stay for a while later on today. Try to give them some space when they get here. Some drones are coming with them too. Whatever they went through was bad. Appalling. They probably aren't going to talk to us about it."

"Um, OK. Where are we going to put them?" asked Lindsey.

"That's been taken care of by the world-ship," Olaha replied. "It's printed a new domicile a short distance from here. They're staying there. We probably won't see much of them. We have some others coming today as well. They're staying in the same building. You'll like them better."

Lindsey looked quizzical. "Who's coming? I'm not sure the kids are going to be up to having guests."

Olaha smiled back. "They'll be OK. It's my sister Ushae and her two young daughters. Milena needs some interaction with people closer to her own age. It will get her out of her funk. Especially when the guys show up. Pilgrim could use some exposure to other kids too. Likewise, you're always asking about the larger society here. Here's a chance for you to get some more information. Just be prepared. They're a little more outgoing than you're used to."

Lindsey laughed and answered back. "That would be pretty hard. I'm married to a musician."

✼ ✼ ✼ ✼ ✼

The entire domain echoed with pain and a sense of extreme loss. No additional world-lines ended, but the damage done was extensive. A considerable magnitude of the entity's essence was now unusable. It experienced substantial damage. The rate of change had happened tremendously quickly.

First, was the complete erasure of segments of the entities self. These were not world-lines but parts of the entity's own physical manifestation. Then the unexpected signal amplification. The entity now found itself significantly diminished.

The entire effect magnified into unmanageable levels. Had operations proceeded normally, the entity would have naturally held the singularity by way of self-manipulation at the other end of the wormhole.

Under normal circumstances, the wormhole would collapse at the far end, having lost contact. The entity manually had to keep this connection open, which requires it to move a voluminous amount of energy into the bridging tunnel to ensure against its disintegration. It establishes a finger connection of its own existence to the target, maintaining the singularity attachment. From there it was a simple matter to generate a null pocket universe, send it to the other side, encapsulate the target and then pull the package back.

This wasn't what happened. The entity recognized the cataclysm immediately but was powerless to react in temporal time. The surge was wholly unexpected.

Something caused a tremendous amplification to the effect that the entity initiated. The wormhole stayed open during the events magnification. A backwash of foreign entropy streamed back into itself, poisoning vast regions through its point contact with the singularity.

The entity's bounty became magnitudes larger than it should have been. It was unprepared for the energy requirement to maintain its balance. The point contact was not sufficiently large enough to maintain that stability. The singularity echoed dangerously. It could not pull away from what it sought and release the contact. As hard as it tried, the connection could not be broken. Too much was involved with no way to dampen it. More resources had to be directed there to help establish some level of control.

Without doing this, it faced complete annihilation across all of its world-lines that would result in its extinction.

Now the entity fully understood horror and fear. Self-existence itself was threatened.

The entity redirected tremendous amounts of vital resources to solve this problem. It spawned many world-line selves down the non-entropic-time dimensions to evaluate the state it currently found itself to be in and hopefully to provide a solution. It directed vast energy reserves to the wormhole to help establish the stability of the attached singularity. Nothing provided the answers that it needed.

In the entity's current panicked state, it kept working at the problem tenaciously. This was a trial and error operation and occurred in entropic-time. Its very existence was threatened and it fought as best it could.

For the first time in the entity's entire existence, it experienced entropic-time as a slowly crawling process. The dilemma's resolution felt like it took forever.

Eventually, the entity did manage to find a level of stability. It retrieved the singularity and allowed the worm-hole to close. It expended tremendous resources on its recovery and all world-lines were now shorter. It now found itself with a shortened lifespan from what it had before the harvesting venture started. This was a complete catastrophe.

Worse, now that the entity achieved a successful retrieval of the singularity, it dared not use it. It couldn't know how much further the damage might possibly increase by leaching entropy from it. The magnitudes involved were beyond its experience, especially given how diminished it now was. There was every possibility that it could be overwhelmed and further poisoned in the attempt.

A review of the damage the entity sustained caused considerable discomfort. It's expected entropic lifespan was reduced in magnitude to one-third of what it would have been, had the reaping program never been started to begin with. From the entity's perspective, this meant death was imminently close.

The influx of foreign entropy now poisoned half of itself. Eventually, the native properties of the entity's domain would co-opt this back. This would take entropic-time, but the entity did expect full recovery. It never reached the tipping point of complete poisoning. It was a very close thing though.

There was a very new problem to evaluate now. The entity's lessened capacity required reinforcement. It needed a new influx of potential. Only harvesting could accomplish this. However, this only seemed to work on occasion. Other times nothing happened. Lately, a new series of events were causing discomfort, pain and diminishment. These were escalating in occurrence and effect, resulting in its current state.

There was no understanding of how this could have occurred. There were no indications that the entity's experiences were even possible. None of these things should ever have happened. Something had to explain the results.

If the entity tried to reap again and the same thing happened, that would be its ending. There would be no recovery.

If the entity did nothing, it would experience a very early cold death, by its estimation.

An understanding of what occurred was no longer an option. Continuance was now at stake.

For now, the entity placed a moratorium on more reaping until it had a better understanding in place.

The entity had brought back a sample of the offending baryonic matter. It could not be sure, but there seemed to be a correlation between the adverse events that it experienced with the properties that this matter evinced. An understanding of how this stuff worked needed to be established. It appeared to have a more significant effect on its native domain than would be expected. How could that happen with such a limited existence? It hardly even abided in its native universe and existed in very few dimensions. Having a greater effect was counterintuitive. Having such an enormous effect was improbable at best.

There were no more lines of investigation available to the entity to pursue.

The entity looked into the pocket universe. There was some contamination of the bubble. This likely happened when it was poisoned. Some control and management were lost resulting in leakage and this situation. The changes would be permanent. An examination of the contents displayed the harvested matter was still in place. The effect of the poisoning on it was yet to be determined. Hopefully, it wasn't great. It had no choice but to pursue this line of questioning anyway. There were no other options available to it.

For whatever reason, the mass was moving around its container. There was no organization to the movements and could just represent environmental noise. Occasionally, it would randomly affect small portions of its environment. These actions seemed random and inconsequential.

The universe continued to watch.

◻ ◻ ◻ ◻ ◻

You could see the resemblance right away, thought Milena. Ushae looked a lot like Olaha. She was a little shorter, but not much. Her nose wasn't as flat and her mouth was a little wider. Apart from that, they shared the same coloring and features.

Milena wasn't particularly tall, but Ushae's daughters were comparatively minuscule. Dea was the oldest and didn't quite make it to the bottom of her ribcage. She was only two years younger than Milena. Rhea was a little younger and only made it up to the top of her hips.

Milena had accompanied Olaha and Lindsey to the travel tube to meet them. Pilgrim came with her. The rest of the guys were back at the compound supposedly getting the place ready for Ryan, Geoff and the drones. She still wasn't feeling that great but just knowing the guys were coming back made a big difference from the previous day.

As soon as Olaha and Ushae caught sight of each other, they were hugging and squealing in the Hamlet language. The two girls just added to the cacophony. That changed a little bit when they saw Pilgrim. He was hiding behind Milena and stuck his head around her. It was his way of letting them know that he was there.

No one introduced them as of yet. There hadn't been time. The two girls stopped fluttering around the women and came straight to her enthusiastically.

In English, they chorused their introductions, talking at the same time. The accent was a little strange but not hard to get used to."

"Hi, I'm Dea. You must be Milena," the larger girl said enthusiastically.

"I'm Rhea. Are you Pilgrim?" The smaller girl was trying to edge around Milena to get a better look at Pilgrim.

Wow! They're fast, she thought. "I'm Milena and this is my best friend, Pilgrim. He's a little shy and doesn't talk much. But he's really nice. He's not used to having a lot of people around, so you'll have to give him a little bit of time to get used to you. It won't take long."

"Auntie Olaha," called out Rhea. "Can we dump these things now? They're uncomfortable. I probably have rashes already." There was some indignation in her voice, as if someone had wronged her somehow.

Milena wondered what she could possibly be talking about from their trip.

"Sure, blossom," Olaha called back with a hint of humor in her voice. "Just don't scare anyone, OK?"

The two girls proceeded to quickly take off their clothes. Milena's mouth dropped open and her eyes popped wide. She looked over at Lindsey. Her reaction was just about the same.

"Now you've done it," Olaha called back. She then turned and spoke to Lindsey. "You're going to see this a lot. The degree varies by species of Homo but is perfectly normal. It's a little bit of a culture shock, but you'll get used to it quickly enough."

"Maybe I will," Lindsey answered back a little shocked. "But I'm not so sure about the guys."

"They'll adapt," replied Olaha. "They'd be more shocked if Pilgrim got dressed. Believe me."

Ushae came over, picked up the girls clothes and stuffed them in the bag she was carrying. It was either an oversized purse or undersized overnight bag.

Olaha made formal introductions all the way around and they started back towards the compound and the new apartment the visitors would be staying in soon. The adults led, with the kids following.

"I told you about Geoff and Ryan," Olaha directed to her sister. "They'll be back later today. It turns out that they're bringing two guests as well. They're staying in the other apartment."

"Are they mate-worthy?" Ushae asked back with some cheer in her voice.

"No," Olaha answered her. "They're drones. Sorry." She turned to Lindsey and said to her, "You'll find that the particular mating behavior of each species is different. Please don't be alarmed. This is all perfectly normal and acceptable behavior. What is normal for the floresiensis is not normal for most sapiens. This goes both ways. Neanderthals are again different. Each species has its own conventions. Nature ingrained it into our biology. There's nothing to be afraid of and you have to be tolerant of it. We embrace these differences and recognize them as natural."

"We see drones all the time," Ushae remarked. "I've never talked with one. And introductions to an Ephalem! That's a lot to absorb in one day."

Olaha gave out a laugh. "Culture shock goes both ways, sib," she managed to quip. "You'll get used to it."

Milena had Dea on her right. On her left were Pilgrim and Rhea.

Pilgrim looked a little spooked so she put her arm around him. The little girl then did exactly the same thing. Milena leaned over him. She whispered, "It's OK. You're much bigger than she is and she only wants to be friends. It's kind of like how we met." He just purred back at her, his voice a little higher pitched than usual.

They got to the compound first. They went to the aft-commons where they guys were. Milena ran ahead making her apologize to the others. Pilgrim was firmly in the grip of the little girl. It would do him some good, she figured. There was no way she was going to miss this.

She entered and all of the guys were there clustered around their instruments. They were probably practicing.

Braedon called out to her. "Hey, hon. Where are the guests?"

"They'll be here any minute," Milena answered in as straight a voice as she could manage. Alan watched what she grabbed.

"Guys," Alan called out in amusement. "Something's up. Milena grabbed a phone."

She got it turned on and the camera software ready. They should be walking in any second now.

The other girls and women walked in through the door. Milena started taking pictures before anyone could begin to say anything. Perfection!

The guys all looked confused and couldn't take their eyes off the visitors. Milena couldn't resist. "Gentlemen.

Please," she said in a mock pleading voice. "You're staring." She kept the camera going.

The two young naked girls ran separately to each of the guys in the room, introducing themselves with verve and then moving on to the next one, in the blink of an eye. Milena kept the camera going. This couldn't get any better.

In a few minutes, things had settled down. Olaha gave the same cultures speech again that she gave Lindsey. It was apparent that none of the floresiensis had any taboo's regarding nudity. It was just another topic of conversation for them. They were aware that sapiens were a little uncomfortable with it, but that wasn't their problem. The guys squirmed a little bit but started to relax after a few minutes. Milena figured they'd all get used to it. They were a different species anyway. No one should care. When she thought about it a little bit, it started sounding stupid. The pictures were priceless though,

There was some more small talk. A lot of it was between the guys and Lindsey. Pretty-Ugly was turning the radio stations on later and she wanted to use the room. They were all for it. It looked like there'd be a party tonight. They could celebrate Geoff and Ryan getting back too, she thought.

It was time to get the guests settled in so they moved on to the newly printed guest quarters. It looked like a copy of the other housing units in the compound except for its division into two apartments. Their guest had the one towards the front end of the ship leaving the drones the aft-apartment.

Lunchtime was coming so they all decided to go to the fore-commons. As a treat, they would fix some of the dishes that Milena had worked on from back home.

Milena had offered to take the kids to their beach in the afternoon. It was going to be a full day with the new radio stations and the party tonight.

◻ ◻ ◻ ◻ ◻

They had finally made it to their home terminus with the two drones in tow.

Ryan and Geoff had got up late. Maybe they should have left Nasty's earlier than they did the night before, he thought. At least they were almost home now. Ryan was looking forward to some peace and quiet in his own room. He was especially looking forward to sleeping in his own bed. Others were visiting so they wouldn't miss him much.

He didn't know where the new domicile was. Free-Credit did, so they followed him to their new apartment. There wasn't much to sort out. The drones didn't even bring anything. They went to see its location more than anything else. The other apartment was vacant now so the other visitors must have gone up to the compound. They could see it through the trees.

It was almost lunchtime. With any kind of luck, it would be waiting for them.

They walked towards the fore-commons. Geoff was explaining to the drones about what a person was supposed to do on their holidays. Both Free-Credit and Remotely-Close looked increasingly confused the more he talked. It was just everyday chitchat, but it wasn't part of their experience. They'd get into it once they relaxed for a little while.

They entered to find a full house in disarray. Maybe that was a little unfair. It was just a lot of people. The food passed back and forth with no discernable order. People were standing and sitting. Olaha was behind the island— butt naked. There was another woman there who was obviously her sister and in the same state of undress. He knew this would be a possibility from their conversation in the bar last night. He'd seen a few kids running up and down the street near Nasty's wearing nothing. It was one of those floresiensis cultural things that he was going have to get used to over time. To be honest, it didn't do anything for him. A few days of this and he probably wouldn't even notice it. As beautiful a person as Olaha was, they weren't the same species.

It felt odd though, seeing Pilgrim and Milena sitting on the floor eating with two tiny little girls who were also naked. It started him thinking about his family again. The children didn't sit cross-legged like Milena did. Their feet were flat on the ground and they were squatted down, sitting on their feet. Their bottoms never touched the ground. Everyone in the Philippines sat like this when doing work on the ground. It was most especially noticeable with gardening. Alyssa and her mom sat like that. Ryan had tried to do it many times because it looked comfortable and allowed you to move around more quickly. He was never able to though. His Achilles tendon was too tight, which changed his center of balance. He always fell over flat on his back. It must be something you had to start with as a very young child. He yearned to see his wife and kids again. The memories were haunting.

Milena and Pilgrim were up in a flash once they saw Geoff and himself. They glommed onto both of them and just held on for a while. There were no tears this time. That was good. Relief was evident on Milena's face. This brought him back to the present.

Olaha made introductions all round with the floresiensis newcomers. Most of the others remembered Remotely-Close from the evening of the music performance.

Olaha tried to make her speech about nudity and cultural diversity. Geoff managed to get her to stop after reminding her that they had spent some time in the 'big city.'

The only uncomfortable moment came when Milena had asked where Questionable-Advice was. She figured that if the other drones were there, then he should have been as well. It was an awkwardly perceptive observation. Ryan just told her that he had other obligations and couldn't be there. She took it at face value and dropped the subject. Now he was lying to kids.

Ushae had managed to corner the drones in conversation. Ryan figured she was the talkative type. Not being able to get anything out of Pilgrim forced her to change her target of opportunity.

The new kids seemed pleasant enough. True, they were gregarious, but Pilgrim was getting along with them just fine. The younger girl was much more tactile than her older sister was. She seemed to always be touching or hugging the Ephalem. It was hard to tell with him, but he wasn't pushing her away and seemed to suffer it all stoically.

He was sure that this was very politically incorrect, but when he looked at the two sisters from behind, he could imagine them climbing through trees just like monkeys. They were tiny and agile. No tails though. On the other hand, when he saw them from the front, all he saw were two little girls. He would also have to get used to them being much older than they looked to him. If the youngest one had been a sapiens, she would have been the size of a toddler. It was a contradiction of perception and pre-assumption.

There were big plans for today in the making. The kids and the ladies were planning to make a day of it at Milena and Pilgrim's little beach. While that was happening, the guys were going to clean up and rearrange the aft-commons. Lindsey's radio stations were starting up tonight, so they planned to make a party of it. He would join in on that later. She deserved his moral support even though he wasn't feeling particularly social.

It was time. Without saying anything to anyone, he slipped out and headed back to his room for some time alone.

Free-Credit followed him out to have a word.

◻ ◻ ◻ ◻

The kids were having a wonderful time. Milena had somehow managed to get the world-ship to print out shovels and pails and showed Rhea and Dea how to make sand castles. Most of the time though, they were in the water. Pilgrim swam circles around them all, weaving in and out of their arms and legs. He could really move in water, Lindsey thought.

The adults elected to stay on the beach and keep an eye on the youngsters. Not that they needed to. Pilgrim could probably see more than they did and was perfectly capable of keeping herd on them.

Olaha and Ushae were with her. The drones had tagged along. They were still trying to figure out how to enjoy a holiday. It wasn't that they didn't know what it was. They just didn't know how to go about enjoying themselves and relaxing.

They brought a cooler of fruit beverages. The adults were holding off until later for when the party started. The kids had already been through a few drinks.

Ushae continued to address the drones. She was ceaseless. "So, you guys are on holiday. How does that happen? I didn't think you took them."

Free-Credit came close to letting out a groan. "We've been through a lot. The world-ship thought it would be a good idea and told us to. I don't know of any other drones that have done that. It would be like the world-ship taking a holiday. That doesn't happen. It's hard to imagine but there it is."

Remotely-Close was watching the kids. "It's true. We're usually kept occupied with AIDS matters. We're a little out of our element. The kids make it look like very hard work."

"You've got that right," Ushae replied.

Maybe it was time that she gave the drones a bit of a break. Lindsey looked towards Olaha, who was lying on her back with her eyes closed, hands clasped and relaxed on her stomach.

Hey, Olaha," Lindsey started. "Dave has been driving me crazy. He really wants to start playing live again. I think he's bored stiff. He's worried about language while doing a gig. Did he ask you about that?"

"That's the first that I've heard of it," replied Olaha. She raised herself a little bit, so that she was resting on one elbow and looking at her.

"That's figures," said Lindsey. Dave could sometimes drive her crazy with his complaints. The least he could do is follow up sometime. "He's worried about the presentation. There are opening elements where he talks to the audience. There are the lyrics and the ending, of course. It's not just the music. It's a show. He's worried some of those elements won't come through. He thought you could help him with translations or something."

Free-Credit looked at Lindsey. "That's interesting. As it happens, we've been having conversations with Ryan and Geoff along very similar lines."

"Anything helpful for Dave there?" Lindsey asked.

"I believe so," replied the drone. "It was a casual conversation that we're going to follow up with later. It applied to the adults only. Milena isn't quite ready yet. Soon though."

"Sounds ominous," coaxed Lindsey. "Spill."

"Dave could get a mempro infix," said Free-Credit. "We were worried about culture shock and information saturation. So we held back offering it."

"I didn't think that was something you just gave out," replied Lindsey, somewhat surprised. "I know Olaha has one. I don't think I've met anyone else that has."

"Sure you have," said Ushae. "Me and the girls. You didn't think we learned your language overnight by using memorization, did you? Drones might be that smart. We aren't."

"Frankly," said Remotely-Close. "Neither are we. Grammar, language, context. That's a lot to absorb. A pre-built package that already contains all of that information is much easier and faster to implement. Think of the content as having been pre-learned. You already have a mental interface for language. It's just another element plugged into that same data bus. It's almost a complete integration. You do need to use it a little bit to iron out any rough spots and be comfortable switching back and forth."

"If I understand you correctly," Lindsey replied, "He could do his own translations. Or, he could just do his show and he might not even be fully conscious he's doing it in another language."

"Not quite," said Free-Credit. "There are some differences in grammar and cultural contexts. Words in one language may have a different number of syllables then the other. Talking wouldn't be an issue. There would be some work redoing lyrics to match tempo though."

"Why wasn't I told about this before?" Lindsey was bewildered.

"We honestly didn't know if you could cope with one," replied Free-Credit. "You've never used anything like it before. Think of your own memories. What do you think would happen to you, if every memory you have ever had, were suddenly and constantly thrust in front of you? It would inundate you and leave you helpless. We had to be sure that your neuroplasticity and discrimination capabilities were flexible and high enough that you could cope."

"Hey," interrupted Ushae. "If they can cope with my two kids, then they meet every standard you guys could set. In fact, it puts them well above the bar."

"You've got that right, sib," Olaha directed to her sister with a smile.

"So what's involved?" It didn't sound like it would be very straightforward to Lindsey. Was there some kind of sequestration implied? What would be available?

"Your world-line was just starting to look into it," started Free-Credit. "You had a research agency that was looking into this; the Defense Advanced Research Projects Administration or DARPA, which was part of the United States Department of Defense, also known as the D.O.D."

Military research didn't particularly sound good to Lindsey.

Free-Credit continued. "Their Biological Technologies Office started to work on a program called REMIND. This stood for Restorative Encoding Memory Integration Neural Device. They were only looking at restoring short-term memory by creating a device that could bypass injured regions of the brain. Their idea was to create a prosthesis for cognitive function and lost memory impairment by using a biometric model of the hippocampus. They were only in the beginning stages. They were still trying to figure out how these memories were encoded. There were other programs that they had on the go relating to restoring active memory and accelerating brain injury repair."

"Go on," Lindsey said to the drone. He had a long way to go to sell this to her.

"We've gone way beyond that," Free-Credit said. "We don't have any military application for it. We inject a tiny pill. We call this process an infix. The pill contains the same germ cells that we use to nanomorphically print most manufactured goods today. We design these specifically to build the mempro in your own biological system and integrate it directly to your mind. It primarily acts as a memory store. You can put things into it that you don't want to forget. It also has a cognate band interface that allows you to converse with others. Think of it as a telephone except you don't have to talk out loud. No one can take anything from you unless you consciously offer it. It's strictly a personal resource."

"So, why the hesitation?" Lindsey responded.

"Some people look at it as a shortcut to learning," answered Free-Credit. "It isn't. Look at language, for example. If you were an individual that had never learned a language, giving you a language module isn't going to help you understand any language. Your mind doesn't have the neural bus in place for it. The information would just be garbage. If you plugged a mathematics module into it, you're not going to be able to understand any of the content unless you already have a basic understanding of math and the functions involved. Think of the analogy of having advanced mathematical functions on a calculator. If you don't know how to use them then having the tool with them on it is useless. It is an augmentation to learning. It is not a replacement."

"So, I can learn another language with a language module because I already speak my native language and the core tools are in place in my mind. You can't turn me into a rocket scientist because I don't have the prerequisite foundations in mathematics, engineering or physics. Is that about it?" This started to make more sense to Lindsey. Given these constraints, it would be highly improbable a recipient could be sequestered or taken over.

"That's about it," Free-Credit answered. "If Dave had a mempro infix, the world-ship could download a memory module over the cognate band. He could then decide whether he wanted to use it. Of course, you could always elect to learn more math, physics and engineering and become a rocket scientist if you wanted."

"Why were you so worried about culture shock?" Lindsey asked.

Free-Credit's face got serious. There was obvious concern in it. "You were already a participant in a culture that was undergoing rapid cultural changes. You had also gone through an enormous trauma. We have a huge culture here that is very different from your experience. Had we made the mempros available when you arrived, the first thing you would have done would have been to load in cultural and language modules. Without having a better idea of how discerning you were, or your levels of neuroplasticity, we thought that the possibility of doing more damage to you was too high. We were afraid for you and decided a slower integration here at the compound was more appropriate."

"And you still think Milena is not ready yet?" said Lindsey.

The drone smiled and turned to look at Milena in the water. "She's close thanks to Olaha. Unfortunately, she hadn't received a very good education in school. Even worse, she's an extremely smart and intuitive girl. She would have ranked in the top two percent in any measurement quotient you would care to have used had she been educated properly. We verified this when we evaluated her when you first arrived. They threw curriculum at her that didn't involve education or learning. It was all 'soft sciences' which meant there was no science in it at all. Her reading skills were minimal. Writing was even worse. There were many 'culturally based' courses, which are a euphemism for brainwashing. It was directed opinion and mental conditioning. Your teachers present these items as cultural development. Since Milena was intelligent, they purposely dumbed her down so that other students would not have to compete with her and she wouldn't compete with them. It also means that she would never threaten the existing power structure when she was older. They were molding her into becoming a subservient civil servant in your society. That's someone who has no learning, spent years acquiring it and thinks they have it. Many of your teachers would be good examples of these people; someone who couldn't add or subtract without having a calculator. They did this to her deliberately. That's a discussion for some other time though."

"That's really harsh," Lindsey responded. What the hell? "So if we decided to do this, how long would it take?"

"Not long," replied Olaha. "If I gave it to you today, the infix would be completed in two days. We could download a language module then. That's best done before you go to bed. Then integration could be done while you sleep. There's no restrictions though. We can do it anytime."

"And we aren't changed. No change to consciousness. Are we exactly the same person as before? No one can take us over and turn us into robots? Um, no offense meant." They still hadn't sold Lindsey on this idea completely.

"None taken. You still are who you've always been and you cannot be taken over," the drone replied.

"I guess we adults have a lot to talk about then," was the only reply Lindsey could offer.

"There's no rush. It's not a requirement. Many people in our society elect not to have an infix for various reasons. There's no obligation to do this," Free-Credit replied.

✻ ✻ ✻ ✻ ✻

Ryan felt he needed time away from everyone else. His mood and worldview hadn't improved. He was responsible for all of those deaths. He didn't belong among civilized people. Worse, the world-ship kept at him. It wanted to discuss the things that had gone wrong and identify their incorrectly held assumptions. He finally agreed to a private discussion with Free-Credit just to get the harassment to stop. The world-ship could monitor and participate but had to agree to leave him alone afterwards.

It was the late afternoon of a lovely day in the arcology. Most of the family and all of the kids had gone to the beach earlier in the day and were back home now. By going there, he thought it would give him the privacy he needed for himself and allow them to talk in private without interruption.

This was his first time here. Milena was right. It was pretty and looked very natural. The river and pond were lovely. So were the few fish that he was able to see. Perhaps the lawn was a little too manicured for his tastes, but other than that, it could have been on his earth. That added to his feelings of isolation and loss.

Free-Credit had thought to bring a blanket, which they spread on the sand close to the water. The beach looked like it had a rough day. Footprints and broken sand castles littered the small area they occupied. The kids must have had a hell of a time earlier.

They sat down. Neither said anything for a short while. Ryan just stared out over the water and into the sky. He didn't feel anything for a time.

He finally heard Free-Credit speak. "Are you ready to talk, Ryan?"

"Not really," he replied. "But we're here and I'd like to get this over with." His reply might have been overly terse. He didn't blame Free-Credit or the world-ship for what happened. On the other hand, Lady Fate was a bitch.

"You said we were missing something in our models," Free-Credit said. "Can you explain?"

Ryan looked at the drone. He wasn't sure how he could get any of this across. "I can try but I don't think it's going to help you. Pointing out holes is not the same thing as filling them in."

"Pretty-Ugly and I are here to listen," responded Free-Credit. "We think that what you've got to say is important or we wouldn't be here. This is true even if it doesn't help us."

A lot was going through Ryan's head. He wasn't sure how he could put any of his thoughts into words. They were just too weird. Much like the universe. He tried to start where it made the most sense for him.

"There are three wildly successful models of communications," Ryan started. "We discussed mathematics before. Additionally, we have speech and text. They all share some common principles but are also different from each other."

So far, there was no reaction, so Ryan continued.

"Let's examine what they share. First, they're all different ways of communicating concepts, ideas and observations. You can describe a triangle mathematically in a number of ways. The easiest is using the lengths of the sides and interior angles. It provides a very abstract view to us using numerics and mathematical operations. In speech, we can provide a description of what a triangle looks like. It's closer to our everyday experience of what a triangle is. We can even add descriptions of color and other things that math often can't include, but relates to what we can directly sense. We can even use it as a way of describing the mathematics. That isn't our everyday experience with using dialog though. We also have text, which is again different. We can spell out T-R-I-A-N-G-L-E. It isn't aural like what we find with language. It can incorporate the textual representation of mathematics but usually cannot provide us with the depth of everyday experience in the same way voice can. Print can even paint very different pictures of communicated information to people who are reading it. Books are an example. No two people interpret a book in exactly the same way. Some people can even have wildly different interpretations of its contents. Each one of these is a different way of describing our experiences of reality. Does this make sense to you?"

"So far I can agree," replied the drone. "I don't usually think of it in the terms you're using."

"Secondly," continued Ryan. "They share similar equivalency principles. In mathematics, this might be different coordinate systems. In speech, it might be language translation that also incorporates cultural components. In text, it might be the physical representation of the characters that are changed. You can represent a character in a lot of ways such as the visual view of it or the underlying code such as on a computer. The coding could be in ASCII for example. I'd also include cyphers and cryptography in this. None of these translations is necessarily exact but is useful in the transferring of ideas. In some cases, conveying the information is easier after translation for some kinds of work. We see that a lot, especially with mathematics. Are you still with me?"

"I follow your meaning here," Free-Credit answered. "These aren't so much rigorous principals as much as observations."

"That's part of what I am trying to get across," Ryan stated. "In math, we have rigorous principles and operations. In speech and text, we have grammar. They each possess very different grammars. What you speak might not be acceptable as writing and vice versa. These all have rules. They are specific to their model. They don't translate well across models but often do translate within through the equivalency principle. Each one is internally consistent using its own rules and logic."

"Granted," replied the drone.

Ryan looked at the drone and wondered if it was actually following what he was saying. So far, he hadn't said much and he thought he might be losing his audience already.

"Let's look at what these are trying to convey," said Ryan. "When I look at a triangle and want to tell someone else about it, I can use one or more of these ways to transfer my experience of it to another individual. Now, when I perceive the triangle, I have no way of knowing if another person looking at it perceives it in exactly the same way that I do. Nature and circumstances wires us all differently. No doubt, your senses and mine are very different. In the same way, other people may also discern it differently. Someone who is colorblind does not necessarily see what I see."

Ryan continued. "Let's say I have a flat triangular piece of wood. Mathematics can describe it as a triangle. It can't tell me it's made of wood. I can describe the triangle with language that may include details about the wood and the things around it, providing a descriptive level of context. This provides no detail on what its interior angles or side lengths are. The text version can also define the triangle but tends not to use as much description the way speech does, regarding the triangle's relationship to its surroundings. It would be very difficult to take one of these descriptions of a triangle and transfer it to one of the other models. None is a complete description. None of these descriptions is an actual triangle."

"They all describe the same thing," stated Free-Credit. "If I understand your point correctly, you are saying that our models are not the same as our experience."

Ryan stared down into the sand. "Each model grew out of our attempts to convey ideas to others. We base them all on observation with the establishment of internal rules that are self-consistent. To one extent or another, we can take an idea expressed in one of the models and extrapolate other ideas. We rely on this in physics using mathematics."

Ryan looked back up and turned to the drone. "We know our models aren't complete. They never have been. That's how we keep moving forward. We extrapolate as far as we can and then push further. Mathematics has been hugely successful with this."

"We've relied on these concepts for a very long time and they've worked very well for us," stated the drone.

"Indeed they have," replied Ryan. "But let's look at what we're missing. Let's start with Pilgrim."

"OK," Free-Credit replied.

"Pilgrim experiences more dimensions than we do," Ryan stated. "It's part of his direct experience of the universe and is natural to him. He is innately capable of having those perceptions because of the toolkit he was born with. He can't tell us how he experiences those because we don't have his toolkit and we lack a point of commonality with him. Our math can tell us these dimensions exist through extrapolation, but we could never have his level of understanding because we cannot observe his level of reality. We possess no greater knowledge than what the mathematics can express to us and we know that the description is lacking. Just like the math can't characterize what the color of a triangle is easily. This requires a system to reflect or give off photons and a perceptual system capable of receiving them in three dimensions of space and one temporal dimension. Mathematics cannot provide this level of description to us in the higher dimensions. That was why you couldn't find higher dimensional equivalents for sound pressure. If you can't perceive them, then you can't describe it. In turn, you can't formalize it in one of the communications models. You need conscious perception to guide you. You can't tell a person who has been blind all of their life what the color red is using speech, math or text. Handing a red triangle to that person won't help you."

The drone looked at him and responded. "This is similar to a conversation I had with Lindsey earlier today about mempros. Interesting. I'm not sure I can accept that ultimately. We learn more every single day about these areas."

Ryan smiled back. It wasn't the same thing. "Yes you do. My point is not that we can't evolve into understanding and perception. My point is we don't have the current capability or toolkit to be able to do that now. Until we can directly perceive or test the properties of another dimension directly, we won't be able to formalize the required concepts necessary for the understanding of it. We don't know how to ask the questions."

"I don't see a connection with the attacks," stated the drone. "Nor do I see the Ephalem's perception of the universe as being pertinent to this discussion."

"Exactly," Ryan answered very quietly. "The questions aren't in your communications standards and can't be extrapolated. You have limited your worldview to your understanding of the contents of these models and have not looked outside them. Have you ever asked yourself, what do you know is missing and not described, in your physics for the universe? Things that you are already aware of."

"No, I haven't," Free-Credit replied. "Everything we know has been built into the physics."

"I disagree," responded Ryan. "Let's get back to that in a minute because it's important. Let's look at something that you've considered as a possible fourth communications model. Music. It shares much with mathematics in terms of description. It has a textual version that is very different from regular language and a voice that is aural, but very different from speech. It is also capable of describing our perception of the world from one person to another. Do you know what the primary difference is between it and the others?"

"The world-ship as Pretty-Ugly* was trying to figure that out for over one-hundred years," Free-Credit answered. "The answer was never found to our satisfaction. We were very much looking forward to exploring this further."

"The principle difference is that it delivers an ethereal message that can directly affect consciousness and emotion," answered Ryan. "That's the essence of what you are missing."

"I don't understand," said the drone. It looked very perplexed. No doubt, the communications between it and Pretty-Ugly was going fast and furiously.

"I know you don't," said Ryan in almost a whisper. "Let's get back to what's missing. We know there's one thing that affects the operations of the universe and no physics reflects it. We've known about this for a very long time. We probably see others all the time, but don't realize it."

"That's not true, Ryan," said Free-Credit insistently. "Our physics is more developed than yours and nothing is missing."

"Really?" Ryan replied. "How does a waveform collapse?"

"Observation," stated the drone.

"How is that modeled in your physics? I am not referring to statistics. How does your mathematics account for observation in terms of cause and effect? How is it represented?"

"It's not there," Free-Credit answered somewhat taken aback.

"You have visited two collapse events," Ryan continued. "What was common at both locations?"

"There was music and people at both," Free-Credit said. "I think I see where this is going. Music has the ability to alter consciousness. Observation is consciousness."

"It's an unresolvable problem in quantum mechanics," said Ryan. "We know it happens, but there is no explanation as to why. The model is incapable of resolving an answer. It can't even formulate the question. We can't know anything more about it, in the same way that we don't know what happens to an electron when it tunnels."

"Then," theorized Free-Credit. "You're saying there is a deeper formulation of reality that we're missing and it's fundamental to how the universe operates."

"It probably goes even deeper," responded Ryan. "It probably goes back to the original vacuum of phase space and applies to the multiverse. The universe is anthropic. Decisions drive world-line splits. Observation collapses waveforms. Conscious perception seems to be a requirement for understanding our place in the cosmos. We have evidence of consciousness in two different universes. Granted, these are very different. And then we have the final piece of the puzzle."

The drone looked at him with a startled look. Ryan just continued. "When attacked and collapsing, the universe proceeded to a point where consciousness was actively being modified by music."

"I told you," Ryan went on. "We have no way of describing this. It doesn't fit any of the models we have. There's no way to formulate how it works. It's even very difficult to describe in speech. We don't have the perceptual toolkit to allow us to see how it works. I don't think music itself has anything to do with it. That's only a tool. Something about consciousness is fundamental to how the universe operates in relationship to perceived reality. And we can't see, understand or know it. You can do nothing with this information. So, I rest my case."

"This will require intensive review, Ryan. I don't think it's possible to know for sure though. When you push these ideas as far as you have, they enter the realm of metaphysics. They can't be tested," said Free-Credit.

"I know," Ryan replied. He only had one more thing to add. "And we were directly responsible for erasing a lot of that consciousness from our particular universe yesterday."

¤ ¤ ¤ ¤ ¤

The aft-commons was ready and everyone had started to pile in after dinner. The band had decided to eat there. It allowed them to keep working and it was a little crowded in the fore-commons anyway.

Ryan and Free-Credit also appeared. They had been off talking somewhere. Ryan had been keeping to himself since he got back. Geoff wasn't much better, but he'd gone to the fore-commons to be sociable. They were all coming back here anyway.

Dave had to admit, he was a little nervous. Lindsey had been entirely right about the marketing idea. If left up to him, he'd have blown it. If this worked, the band could start thinking about moving forward towards playing some live gigs. If it didn't, then they'd have to figure something else out.

Lindsey put things into the whole plan that he wouldn't have considered. You couldn't have paid him to make elevator music available. However, her argument for it made so much sense that he couldn't deny it. You needed to get it everywhere. This included background music for places like shopping malls for example. He wasn't sure they had them here, but you could bet there was something close. Moreover, he had to face it. He wouldn't be doing too much purchasing if he went shopping and it was dead silent in the store. Additionally, it would get people listening who wouldn't have done so otherwise.

The genre stations made complete sense to him. He was wondering how she'd build a bias into it for what the band played.

This was going to be a real test. They had a broad mixture of types coming. Some had never heard of music in their life. It didn't exist for them. Some were only briefly introduced to music but weren't in a position to be discriminating yet. Others were extremely discerning and knew what they liked. The drones were probably like the world-ship. They had a vast array of music available to them but just didn't quite understand the concept. Very, very close, but just not quite there. He was going to make sure that they understood it before their holiday ended.

The background stations had been up and running since the early morning. Apparently, the world-ship did suggest to vendors that they test them to see how it affected their business in terms of sales.

He picked one of these for play over the PA at low volume. That way it wouldn't be completely quiet as folks started to pile in.

The kids arrived first from the fore-commons. Milena was in the lead closely followed by Pilgrim. They were showing Dea and Rhea around. They made stops at each piece of gear with her giving detailed descriptions of what each piece did and how they worked together. The last stop was the PA system. Curiously, she started making changes to the setup as soon as she got there. It didn't even stop her from talking. He thought about halting her changes because the guys had been working all day on it. He decided not to. They wrote down the settings and he didn't want to embarrass her. That and the fact she probably knew the system better than he did now. Lindsey was a useful teacher for him. Embarrassment can be a two-way street. Better safe than sorry.

Finally, the women showed up with Remotely-Close and Geoff.

Ushae had a curious look on her face. She was listening to the background music. Her two kids didn't have the same expression. They were still with Milena drinking it all in.

"I thought it would sound like a machine or something," Ushae said. "They can have a rhythm and sometimes you can listen to it and feel in tune with its operations. You can even tell when something goes wrong. This is very different though. It's not the same at all. I didn't expect that. I feel like I'm in a piece of history, sib. You said it was important. I guess you're right."

"This is strictly for background," said Lindsey. "I can hardly wait for you to hear the real stuff when we start sampling the genre stations."

"Would I steer you wrong Ushae?" replied Olaha to her sib. "This is for the blossoms too. They're going to like the energy associated with it. Milena is the perfect one to introduce it to them. I'm glad you came."

Dave felt it was time to act as host. "Can I get anyone a drink?"

Lindsey, Olaha and Ushae had white wines. Milena, Pilgrim, Rhea and Dea stuck with fruit juices. The rest of them had a beer. Lindsey decided the radio station samplings would start when the adults got around to their second beverage. Everyone chitchatted until it was time.

Dave dutifully got everyone a refill. Then he turned the floor over to Lindsey. He even had a mike ready for her.

"Oh my," Lindsey started out. "I'm not used to using a mike. Is this OK everyone?" She tapped it, checking the volume.

The band clapped and sent a couple of 'yeahs' her direction. So did Geoff, Milena, and Ryan. The rest weren't as familiar with these conventions. They would pick them up before the evening was over, no doubt.

Lindsey was facing everyone with the mike held freely in her right hand. She did a good job of it he thought. As she spoke, she would pick one person to talk to and look directly in their eyes. She did this moving from person to person. He was proud of her. She'd been watching what he did during performances.

"First, I want to thank everyone for coming out tonight for this," Lindsey said. "I know the band has been waiting for this to happen for what seems like a very long time. It hasn't been, but they're musicians. That's how they think. Right boys?"

They responded with some whoops and hollers.

"You are the closest friends that we have in this world. Free-Credit, you tell Pretty-Ugly he's included in that," Lindsey continued.

The drone called out. "He knows and thanks you. He's here listening."

"Thanks," Lindsey said. "The only person missing is Questionable-Advice, who I understand is away on other matters. I wish he could be here too, but I understand."

Most of the crowd added more cheers. Dave noticed that Ryan looked down towards the floor. Geoff didn't respond at all. The drones were quiet as well.

"This is a significant night for me too," Lindsey continued to say angelically. "It was quite a bit of work to get the project this far and was only made possible with the help of our world-ship, Pretty-Ugly.

Everyone perked up at this and clapped.

Then an evil smile crossed Lindsey's face. "But, before we begin, Milena has put together a special presentation for this group's entertainment."

He could hear Corey say "Oh, Oh!"

Braedon called out to Dave, "Milena is spending way too much time with Lindsey, Dave. You should do something about that."

Alan just said, "Duck for cover guys."

Dave placed one hand over his face and looked down at the floor. His head was shaking slowly from left to right and back again. He should have expected something like this. When the hell did Milena have time to pull this off? He should have known something was up when she arrived early and went to the PA.

Milena grabbed another mike that surprise, surprise, just happened to be live and next to her.

"Hi everyone," Milena managed to say sweetly. This was going to be bad! "I just want to thank everyone for being here for this historic occasion."

She got standing ovations from all the females. Oh god! They're all in on it.

"I've put together a collage of pictures that have been taken since we arrived here at our beautiful compound and set them to specially selected pieces of music," said Milena. "I think they're very moving and can't think of a better place or time to present this art piece. Without further delay, here it is."

All of the viewing walls went live and the music went on. It sounded dramatic. Still photographs started to appear. Milena used various effects to move from one picture to the next.

It started with photographs of all of the girls. This even included Ushae and her kids. Milena delivered most pictures one at a time but sometimes in groups, presented very beautifully. The girls all looked great.

Alan called out "Photoshopped!" Mistake, Dave thought. He'll end up paying for it later.

Then the other pictures showed up. These included the pictures he had taken of the drones and the world-ship images from their demo concert. Dave just groaned. How did Milena get those? He should have kept better track of the phones. She found the embarrassing pictures he was keeping for a laugh.

Additional pictures appeared of other embarrassing moments that happened to the individuals in the band since they'd gotten here. He knew no one had taken those. Was the world-ship in on this?

Lastly, it finished off with the pictures that Milena took this morning when the naked girls had shown up. There were a lot of them. He had to admit, they were hilarious. They were interspersed with pictures of the naked girls. Dave mumbled to himself, "How the hell does she do that?" He couldn't stop himself and started to laugh.

By the end, all of the females were hooting and howling. There was no doubt that they had learned the fine art of hand clapping now. Lindsey even managed to let out a high-pitched whistle that he didn't know she could do. Yep! The girls had managed to do it again. Lindsey was definitely a bad influence on Milena. God help her future boyfriends.

When some of the rabble-rousing had died down, Milena spoke naturally into the mike, "Thank-you." She then curtsied. Insult on top of injury. He couldn't help it. He was on the floor now. His chest hurt and he couldn't stop laughing.

"Thank-you ego control," said Lindsey to Milena. "Something has to keep these lads grounded before they get out of control. That was a superb presentation and a wonderful art piece." She smiled spectacularly. "We probably could have done without all of the nudity though."

That did it. Now all of the girls were on the floor rolling around and hollering away. Tears were even coming from most of their eyes.

Dave had seen the drones laugh lightly in the past. That wasn't what he saw now. They were in full whoop. Even Ryan and Geoff managed to get out a few laughs.

The band members were all laughing, but Alan had a pained look on his face. He knew that his comment would be remembered and come back to haunt him at some point. Maybe not today. Maybe not tomorrow. But it was coming as inevitably as fate. Dave thought, suffer it stoically lad. The girls may allow you to live through it. Probably.

He told Alan this later in the evening. You never knew with him. He had never learned subtlety and needed telling straight out sometimes, especially where women were concerned. He had a bit of a free ride his entire life when it came to them, but he'd never really learned anything from it.

It took a while, but everything settled down, after a few drinks. Dave had to admit that was one of the best ice breaking presentations he'd ever seen. He told Milena so himself. Rhea and Dea really like the fact he did that and now were his best buddies. They were tremendous fans of Milena.

They spent an hour and a bit as a group going through all the different channels, with critiques requested, given and exchanged. There was a lot of give and take. It was all good. No one expected to like all of it. They were all individuals and encouraged to follow their own tastes. Dave was privately proud when there was mutual agreement on liking the channel that played the kind of music that Overnight Distress played, but didn't say anything.

Ryan, Geoff and the drones were in the corner at one point and they called him over. They were all smiling for a change. The beers in their hands probably assisted the cause.

"I just got a call from a friend of ours," said Free-Credit. "He has a bar near where we've been working called the Nasty Face. He's been following this whole music thing very carefully. He'd like to know if you'd like to play at his place sometime. He thinks that it would be good for business. He'd like to do this soon if the trends keep moving forward as fast as they have tonight. Would you like to talk with him at some point?"

Dave smiled. This was their first possible break. "You bet I would. What's his name?"

"Nasty," smiled the drone back. "I'll tell him. He's a good fellow and very fair. I think he also wants to be the first to have a live show. All the drones like this guy."

"That's all I need to hear," Dave said. "We'll be glad to talk with him tomorrow, at his convenience. We can set a specific meeting time later. Tonight's not the time to do it though. Please tell him I'm really looking forward to it. I mean it."

Lindsey took that moment to grab the mike and start talking again.

"Hi everyone. We have one more treat tonight," she said.

Dave thought the worst was over so was curious what this would be.

She continued. "This is really special because the band and the folks that manage the sound are usually working. We had the pleasure of doing a show for the AIDS community and the drones not too long ago. It was the only performance ever played here on the world-ship. Pretty-Ugly did a wonderful thing. He recorded it. Tonight, for your entertainment, we are playing back the second set, in full 3D and surround sound. For those of you that don't dance, we don't care. You're dancing anyways. Let the concert begin. I present to you Overnight Distress."

¤ ¤ ¤ ¤ ¤

There was no easy way of describing what Questionable-Advice now saw. It knew it was in deep trouble.

Questionable-Advice remembered the thing snatching it. The thing grabbed it and put it into a bag. As hard as it tried to fight its way free, it couldn't get out of it. Something had it. Then there was the bizarre feeling of translation. It felt the same as the way Milena described turning inside out. Suddenly, Questionable-Advice found itself here. It went a lot further then she had.

There was no experience of what happened between being there and then here. Questionable-Advice was aware that some time did pass. Just nothing else. There was no dark and no light, no heat or cold, nothing to hear or smell. It couldn't even feel. For Questionable-Advice, it was entirely empty. This was the exact definition of void.

The bag emptied Questionable-Advice into this area. There was no way to tell how big this place was. Questionable-Advice could walk in a straight line, in any direction, until it found itself back where it had started. The first time it tried this, it couldn't quite believe it. It suspected that this was what was happening. To test this, it tore a piece of clothing off, left it at its feet and tried again. Each try brought Questionable-Advice back to the piece of cloth. It didn't matter which direction it went or how circular the route.

This was a poor imitation of Questionable-Advice's universe. The ground felt solid and gravity was in effect but was less than the world-ship standard. There was no sun, but light was everywhere. There was no point source for it.

The sky was a light pink in color with no clouds. Blue was not in evidence at all. As Questionable-Advice expected, light reflected off surfaces in the normal fashion. At least the photons that weren't absorbed were. It was just that the colors weren't right.

It was the terrain that was most alien. Nothing seemed solid. Everything looked fuzzy. It was like walking on solidified light. There were analogs for grass, dirt and rocks. They just weren't the same thing.

Questionable-Advice had picked up a rock and looked at it carefully. Its edges were fuzzy instead of being razor sharp. Multiple colors were evident, but they bled into each other like a child's painting. It even glowed slightly. It was this rock that told it there was something wrong with the geometry of this place. Questionable-Advice kept seeing it over and over again as it walked.

Questionable-Advice was fully and correctly defined when it looked at parts of itself.

The grass was not a typical green. It was darker than it had any right to be and more turquoise than green. Individual blades of grass blurred into each other. Questionable-Advice tried to pick a single blade from the ground, but all it ended up with was a dark smudge between its fingers and thumb. This also glowed slightly. There was no way to tell if it was actually alive or not.

Looking closely at the grass, little black smudges conspicuously moved across the grassy medium almost like bugs. Questionable-Advice didn't know what they were, but they certainly weren't insects.

The grass swayed like it was in a breeze. Only there was no wind. The air was completely still and didn't circulate.

The air probably was composed of the correct elements, but the biological portions of Questionable-Advice's body couldn't use it properly and were starting to die. This hurt terribly but it wouldn't kill him. Its base physical self would continue on, using the dual miniaturized radioisotope thermoelectric generators, to keep its mind and the remains of its body functional. They could keep it alive for a very long time with no additional resources. Questionable-Advice didn't know if it wanted to live that long under these conditions. The faster its biologics died, the better. A starvation death would have been too cruel and much harder on it.

This miniature world was close to what Questionable-Advice's universe was like but wasn't the same. It was a parody. Whatever had made it, didn't understand its world or its universe. At best, Questionable-Advice was in a bad simulation done by something that didn't understand what it was dealing with. It was like looking at an out-of-focus projection.

The whole team speculated that whatever they were dealing with must live in most of the universal dimensions. Since these entities came from another universe, the properties of all of these would be entirely different. Whatever created this, must have been guessing.

So what was Questionable-Advice dealing with here? They must be watching and studying him. If they were extra-dimensional, then Questionable-Advice wouldn't even see them. Was there a way here for it to identify one of them? Questionable-Advice couldn't answer that itself.

The most sensible thing to do would be to initiate some level of communications. How did you do that without common points of reference? Was the enemy even corporeal for that matter?

Questionable-Advice couldn't talk to the things. You needed air as a medium, lungs, larynx and tongue. It was losing these. The aliens likely wouldn't have them anyway. Sound and sound analogs seemed to be anathema to them.

Writing was out because there was no common language.

If these entities were alien enough, it was possible they were similar to insects that used something like pheromones for communication. Questionable-Advice couldn't do that.

That left mathematics, but there were so many ways to approach it. The easiest was using pictographs for very simple operations. If they could establish a starting point, then they could establish some level of communications. First by identifying things that were common among them and then move on to the more foreign. Questionable-Advice could do this even if it took a very long period of time.

Questionable-Advice just hoped it was watching him.

It started drawing stick math in the ground. A single line. A plus sign. Another single line. An equal sign followed by two lines.

Each line represented simple addition problems and was different. Even very young children could figure them out.

If it didn't work, Questionable-Advice would restart the whole thing over and hope that some level of understanding was possible.

¤ ¤ ¤ ¤ ¤

In the morning, Ushae had taken the girls to the beach so the adults could meet in private. The drones accompanied them. They mentioned something about learning to swim. If the girls were their teachers, then they were in for a fantastic time. The adults had a lot to discuss.

Ryan looked at the others. "I haven't danced for a while. I'm a little sore. I'll probably be crippled by tomorrow."

"Yeah," answered Braedon. "Did you see Ushae and the little girls? Once Milena got them up and going, they never stopped. Where do you get energy like that?"

"No kidding," added Alan. "I'm sore as hell too."

"But everyone had a great time," said Dave looking pleased. "We even have a possible gig lined up. Details to follow."

Everyone looked very pleased with how things went the night before, thought Ryan. There was a lot of warmth in the room. He especially liked the expression on Olaha's face. She had one heck of a smile and was completely relaxed, laying flat out on one of the sofas.

Lindsey had called this meeting and was relying on Olaha to assist her. She was looking pleasantly drained herself but managed to pull it together. She stood up from her chair and turned to address the group.

"We've been made an offer by our hosts," Lindsey started. "Some of you have briefly discussed this with the drones, but I thought it might be beneficial for us to talk about this as a group."

"As you know," Lindsey continued, "Olaha has a prosthetic device called a mempro. It allowed her to learn our language very quickly. It has other uses as well. Our hosts offered each of us one of these devices. It would help us to integrate into the world-ship's society much more quickly. This is not something that you have to have. Each person has to decide whether they want one or not."

She turned her chair around and sat back down. She looked more relaxed that way. It also felt a lot less formal.

"Dave and I talked about it last night before going to sleep," Lindsey said. "We're going to do it. So you know the process, Olaha injects a little pill into the skin and it grows inside of you. You won't know it's happening during the process and takes two days to complete. We've volunteered to be the guinea pigs and show you. Olaha, honey, can you do it now?"

"I sure can," Olaha replied. She got up off the sofa and went to the food dispenser where she took out a small device. It didn't look like a needle but did have a small trigger. She walked back to Lindsey. "Hold out an arm, please."

Lindsey did this as requested. Olaha pressed the device to the proffered arm and pulled the trigger.

"I didn't feel a thing," said Lindsey sounding surprised. "You ready Dave?"

"Sure," Dave replied. Olaha walked over to him and repeated the procedure. "Nope. Me neither. That was easier than I thought it would be."

"That's it," said Olaha. She put the device down on the island and resumed her place on the couch. "I love the drama."

"So you don't get cut, like an operation?" asked Alan.

"That was it," Lindsey replied. "In two days, once the thing has finished growing, the world-ship will download a language module to it. We can then start to use the native tongue when we want to. There are cultural modules available too. You might want to skip them. A more interesting way to learn about the various cultures on the ship might actually be to live them. Your option."

"Can I get a module to make me super smart?" asked Braedon.

"This thing can't make you geniuses, geniuses," she replied. "You have to already have an understanding of the underlying principles to begin with. You speak a language and have an intuitive understanding of grammar. Except for Alan. He's a little short in the grammar department."

"Thanks for your support, Lindsey," Alan quipped in.

"We already understand what we need to know about language. This uses the previously developed interface in our heads," Lindsey continued. "If you can't add and subtract, you won't understand advanced mathematics. This only augments what you already have."

"So what's the downside?" asked Alan.

"As near as I can tell," Lindsey answered, "There isn't one. There are some additional benefits. You can also use it like a phone."

"Alan, I'd think twice before mentioning downloading porn," said Dave. "She's already got your number."

"There goes my next question," replied Alan.

"Here's the point," Lindsey imparted. "You are adults and you've absorbed enough about where we are and bits about the society we now live in. You probably have enough life learning to be able to cope with any downloads. You're also skeptical enough to question the information that you receive. That's a prime requirement."

"That's also why Milena isn't here," Lindsey said. "She's not quite ready. Soon though. Right Olaha?"

"Right, honey," Olaha answered. "I've talked to her about it. She wants to do it as soon as we'll let her. She mentioned something about it making it easier to meet some boys. I guess she thinks she's missing out."

Why had that made him want to wince, thought Ryan. He guessed he really did think of her as his daughter. "Um, can we screen her calls and emails? Or whatever?"

Olaha shot daggers from her eyes at him. "You know far better than to ask. Absolute privacy is a guarantee. On top of that, this is a natural part of growing up. It is none of your business."

"I just think of her like my own daughter," Ryan protested.

"Then you know that the very best way to learn is by making your own mistakes," Olaha asserted. "That's not something a mempro can help you with. You received most of your own life lessons this way. Allow her to make her own, thank-you very much! Your culture didn't want to grant that to their females. Ours does."

"OK," interrupted Lindsey. "That's not what we're here to discuss. If we wish to join the larger society, the least painful and quickest way will be to have a mempro."

"Think about shopping," Lindsey continued. "Or going to a bar and ordering a beer. We have performances in a new society to consider. To communicate requires a knowledge of their language."

"You had me at beer," said Alan.

"Count me in as well," added Braedon.

Corey and Geoff added their agreement as well.

Olaha got off the couch again, lined them up at the island and applied their infixes.

"What about you, Ryan?" asked Olaha when the others were done.

He looked at the others. He couldn't think of a single reason not to do it. On the other hand, he couldn't think of why he should. He was content with comparative isolation at the moment. The bar argument was compelling though.

"You got me, Olaha," Ryan replied after thinking about it for a minute. "Go ahead."

"Then come here and women-up," Olaha answered.

"You mean man-up," Ryan said in reply. "I can see the translation thing doesn't work entirely."

"It does, Ryan," Olaha told him. "I said exactly what I meant. In this instance, it was the correct usage and meaning." Then she injected him.

"Ouch!" exclaimed Geoff.

CHAPTER 8

OFFENSIVE DEFENSE

I think any student of military strategy would tell you that in order to attack a position, you should have a ratio of approximately 3 to 1 in favor of the attacker.

Norman Schwarzkopf

The AIDS community was vast. Each member primarily built and designed their assemblages starting with a basic core capability from which it expanded. This embodiment resulted in uniquely original designs for each entity. The primary driver for design direction was the ultimate goal that the AIDS individual wanted to pursue or achieve. Broadly, this broke down into two major categories: stationary and motile. This categorization didn't prevent members transitioning from one to the other. They considered this perfectly acceptable as a personal choice. Tastes and drives tended to change over time.

The stationary groupings broke down into terrestrial and space dwelling individuals. A habitat was the body of the AIDS with Patrons as tenants.

Usually, the terrestrial entities were associated with the support of pioneering and the opening of newly discovered habitable zone planets. In other cases, they would provide colony support for asteroid or comet mining for raw resources. These types of AIDS were always associated with Patron expansion. No AIDS individual needed to do these things as they could always perform such functions themselves. Most considered it a long term and rewarding hobby. They were in it for the long haul.

The motile space dwellers broke down into two major groupings. These were the habitats and the non-habitats.

Most habitats occupied L4 or L5 Lagrangian points of multiple body systems. Ordinarily, this would be a star-planet, planet-moon or similar variant. Others used standard or stationary orbits, especially around the gas giants, which they utilized for the manufacture of antimatter fuel. Patrons and their occasional AIDS clients used this. They stuck to their neighborhoods and hosted their Patrons within them.

AIDS used many different design approaches. The smallest were usually a derivation of the rotating wheel concept. Larger environments would use variations based on one of the many cylindrical habitat styles. The largest were usually spheres. These generally resulted in swarms, bubbles or Nivens. There were no Dyson's, as the gravitational instabilities were too large to overcome, given the meager advantages that they might offer.

The non-habitats were usually young AIDS in the process of building themselves up into a more useful form. There were outliers that stuck to themselves, but these were rare. Most AIDS supposed that they had their reasons, but they seldom communicated them to others.

The motile space dwellers consisted of individuals that were able to move from location to location at will. Younger versions were small and autonomous but were usually associated with a larger AIDS since they couldn't travel that far. Larger versions, such as the scout class Questionable-Advice, could carry passengers and only sometimes associated with their larger brethren. They were ideal for reconnaissance and useful whenever a situation needed probing and investigation. The largest ones preferred to transport trade goods and Patron passengers from one place to another. Again, there were outliers that took off on their own. These were very few and AIDS considered them very strange from a sociological perspective.

The largest of the motiles were the world-ships. These were a hybrid of 'cylindrical habitat' and 'space dweller' design concepts. They used this approach because of its flexibility. It allowed for the additions and removals of arcologies, storage and engine components relatively quickly without having to go through a complete redesign. Modularity provided enormous benefits. They were huge and were capable of hosting whole Patron societies if needed. They were also capable of passenger and trade transport but usually roamed where they wanted.

Rumors had started to circulate in ComSpace. It had started with the initial alert sent out by Pretty-Ugly*. Then, many AIDS noticed that some individuals of their kind had gone missing. Most of these were traveling at relativistic speeds at the time and were unable to interpret or react to the original outcries. Others did manage to escape, but now found themselves on far removed world-line trunks. Their comments added to the general confusion. There was a lot of fear in their larger community.

It was now time to co-ordinate a larger response, but thanks to Ryan's observations, it had suddenly become obvious many of their assumptions and conclusions were wrong.

Pretty-Ugly had conducted additional investigations and the results stunned it. It was here to pass these to the group along with its conclusions.

"I still don't believe it," Pretty-Ugly addressed to Exact-Estimate and Neat-Mess. "My chat with Ryan bothered me. He easily identified an area of ignorance that we have. He wasn't even trying very hard. I didn't even recognize it in myself. We don't have a mechanism for determining how consciousness engages with reality in our universe. We don't have any physics for it. I took his suggestion that this didn't mean we couldn't observe its effects. He was right as far as I can tell."

"How do you mean?" asked Exact-Estimate. "I can't imagine a way to do that."

"I couldn't either," Pretty-Ugly replied. "I stumbled upon it by chance. I wouldn't have recognized it for what it was except for our conversation."

Pretty-Ugly continued. "I elected to contact all of my selves in the current trunk. My hope was to do some brainstorming. That was when I observed the oddity. There were many world-lines, as you would expect. None of them contained the refugees except this one. None of my other selves has experienced any of the actions that we've taken to try to protect ourselves. The ComSpace meetings they've attended have led them nowhere. We seem to have somehow generated a unique branch that isn't forking in the usual manner. It may not be forking at all."

"I'm on a separate trunk from you," said a surprised Exact-Estimate. "Let me check with my local selves." It took a minute to perform some queries and then it returned.

"That's the first time that I've ever tried to contact one of my selves from such recent forks," Exact-Estimate stated. "I've never had a reason to before. None of them had any knowledge of what's happened to us since our first meeting. Your world-line and mine seem to be in a bound state."

"I find myself to be in Pretty-Ugly's position," added Neat-Mess. "We're on the same world-line. I haven't forked either."

"Our involvement with the universe is now substantially altered," stated Pretty-Ugly. "It means that all defensive operations are now uniquely controlled and managed from here. We can't even rely too heavily on our other selves for assistance, but we can make them aware of our experiences. If we make any wrong decision, then there are no alternative forks that can take over from us automatically."

"This also makes the refugees unique in the universe," said Neat-Mess. "I can only assume this was the result of the foreign intrusion only occurring on one unique world-line. No refugees got saved on any other ones."

"This isn't a concern for them," replied Pretty-Ugly. "That's how they experience the world in any case. The real question is why this has occurred. It doesn't happen to an AIDS when we're going to another world-line. It may be because we don't move. We make a copy. It does duplicate an individual's consciousness though."

"I can list possible causes," said Exact-Estimate. "This doesn't mean we'll understand why this occurred but may assist us with predicting possible outcomes." It started the list.

"One: The collapse process prevents forking from occurring. We rescued the refugees from a fork in this condition. Somehow, this property infused into them. When they were brought back here, that property was inflicted on our world-line."

"This implies a permanent state," responded Pretty-Ugly. "Even if the refugees got removed, there is nothing to indicate that we'll get back to a normal condition. It also seems unlikely that such a small portion of the other world-line as represented by the refugees would have such a great effect here. Let's not forget the return of Pretty-Ugly*."

Exact-Estimate continued.

"Two: The attacks themselves have caused our universal domain to attempt to protect itself. In the attacks, the aggressors eliminated conscious awareness by the removed of world-lines from our cosmos. Consciousness also moved from one world-line to another in the case of our refugees, and this may not be entirely compatible with its operations, given what's happened. The universe has become glitched. It directly affects us because of our association with this damage. This most closely resembles a closed time-like curve except that it doesn't appear closed as far as we can tell, and causality seems preserved. We aren't doing the same things repeatedly in a loop. Um, I hope."

"Possibly more reasonable," suggested Neat-Mess. "It's a stretch, but there's also the possibility that there may be some repair mechanism or immune system in place. In that case, this may just be a temporary condition. That may also be why there are restrictions in place on where the Ephalem device can take our agents. Go on."

"Three: We erased a great deal of consciousness from the universe by mistake, trying to protect ourselves. Maybe it's mad at us," stated Exact-Estimate.

"Unlikely," replied Pretty-Ugly. "The cessation of world-line splits happened prior to that occurrence. My observations regarding the universe indicate that it has no interest in us one way, or another. I don't think it's benign but neither do I think that it's vindictive."

"In any case," summarized Exact-Estimate. "There's a high correlation between consciousness and the situation we find ourselves in currently. Knowing this relationship isn't going to help us though. Let's move on to the things that we can deal with actively. Pretty-Ugly, please start us off."

"The last skirmish has given us our best intelligence to date," said Pretty-Ugly. "We have a defensive capability that got turned into an offensive weapon against the invaders. The sound feedback and nullification system was partially effective at blocking the effect. We have evaluated the data recordings, and it is very apparent that our opponents were actively fighting it. The shortcoming was that we couldn't respond quickly enough to counter the counter, so to speak. The relativistic electron gun proved to be a much more effective weapon than we had reason to realize. It completely erased portions of the enemy."

"That sounds encouraging," responded Neat-Mess. "How can we use this?"

Pretty-Ugly thought it was time to introduce a new strategy and said, "I don't think that we can use our incursion team any longer. The sapiens feel responsible for the elimination of most of the world-lines that they forced down our opponent's throat. They've become disheartened. Still, this very act has given us our best weapon to date. It seems to have caused the enemy considerable damage. The singularity lasted for a week in a very unstable condition. I speculate that the entities could not cope with its scale and were unable to detach themselves from it. They stabilized and retrieved it only recently. Due to its magnitude, it appears highly unlikely that they'll be able to use it. I propose an escalation. We make the same act an active threat from every world-line."

Neat-Mess and Exact estimate expressed shock through the interface. So Pretty-Ugly followed up with an explanation.

"I have formulated a new feedback and nullification system. Instead of a closed loop-back control system, an AIDS entity's direct management replaces it. This change provides for a heightened and more intelligent governance with nano-second response time. Additionally, I've made improvements to the relativistic electron gun. Instead of it being a directed weapon, it's now a field effects device. We can emit the plasma with broad coverage and send I-waves through it, even in a vacuum."

"That sounds promising," admitted Exact-Estimate. "But how can we identify placement?"

Pretty-Ugly felt very confident at this point. The others hadn't identified its conceptual leap.

"Identifying specific targets is beyond us, but we have a way around that. We need to bring in the entire AIDS community. The whole cosmos is now at risk. Everyone must participate in its defense. It's time for disclosure. Every AIDS needs to know the facts and be given the data packages that we have to date. We'll provide a history of events and operations. Lastly, we provide printing instructions on the weapons. Every member needs actively to monitor the data that Pretty-Ugly* initially used to establish the start of the collapse occurrence. That'll give us much more time to react than the Ephalem device. Whoever detects an event sends a broadcast over ComSpace. We can set up a reserved command and control channel for this. Every AIDS, regardless of world-line residence, responds defensively. If the enemy persists, then we use an exaggerated version of Ryan's strategy. All world-ships on all trunks reinforce the signal. It may cost us much, but my guess is that this will stop it in its tracks. Our enemies need to fear us, and we need to show unequivocally that we are fighting back, and this is not going to be allowed to go on."

Neat-Mess looked somewhat perplexed. It appeared to see the merit in the plan but was hesitant. "We can put the information out. Surely, every AIDS entity will participate. We need to make sure that it isn't just us getting the word out. We need to get the message up the relativistic hill to everyone. Given the time differential, many may not be able to participate."

"I agree," answered Pretty-Ugly. "Each AIDS will need to be instructed to verify that their acquaintances are also aware of what's being done and are also participating. We can't rely on a simple broadcast and hope it's listened to."

"We would also need to control how and when this happens," Neat-Mess added.

Pretty-Ugly wore its best smile for the others. "We can't control the when. But I have a great idea on the how."

"Would you care to elaborate?" asked Exact-Estimate.

"Everything to date has resolved around our sapiens guests," Pretty-Ugly answered. "There's something very special about them. I can't even begin to guess what. They're entirely normal people, unexceptional in any way, at least in their native world-line. They're likable. They're empathetic. The only thing that makes them exceptional in any way is that they make music. We don't have that. They don't perceive it as being any more unusual than a painter or storyteller. Most of them are entertainers. They aren't scientists or mathematicians. None of them craves power like some of their contemporaries at their original home. They were all destined for unexceptional existences. They'd deserved far better than what fate gave to them. On a personal level, I like them. That doesn't happen to me very often. I like the Patrons very much but it's rare for me to interface with them one on one as we're doing now. It is even rarer to enjoy that interaction. I've even sent Free-Credit and Remotely-Close on holiday with them. The intent is to provide a learning experience for the drones and myself. More importantly, on an everyday level, there are things that we can learn from them and how they interact with the world around them. Look at little Milena. She is astonishing! Their involvement is not over. They may have stopped actively fighting, but they aren't through with life and living. I have no rationalization for this, but I think they're a part of the universe's immune system. Maybe we all are. There's a leap for you."

"You're going to use music somehow," said Exact-Estimate. "Aren't you?"

Pretty-Ugly continued its smile. It loved this, and it loved what Pretty-Ugly* had done. It was very proud of its alternative self now. It amazed Pretty-Ugly how much of a jerk it was at the beginning of all this. Bipolar self-discovery was an amusing and unexpected experience.

"I think music has a larger piece to play in our AIDS community," said Pretty-Ugly. "It may even provide a foundation for us to explore consciousness in the universe the way mathematics allows us to investigate cosmology. We're going to use music in a way that it's never been used before, and the sapiens are center stage."

✺ ✺ ✺ ✺ ✺

Participating in a band was an arduous business. It took years to learn the craft. You had to purchase and maintain instruments. You also needed to buy support equipment costing tens of thousands. Often more. These included PA's, amplifiers, stands and mikes. The list goes on. The group also needed to acquire storage and practice space.

When you contract a gig, you must deliver the show. You move all the equipment to and from that location. Setup and teardown can take as long as the show itself. Often longer if the event is large enough. There was a lot of work that the public never saw. And, of course, in most cases, it was the musicians doing all of the work.

Then there was the business end. Gone were the days of big contracts and recording deals. Those days were over. Big money stage productions and dancers replaced these. The headliners usually couldn't sing much, but there were ways around that. They used voice and note correction. Mostly, you weren't listening to the actual performers; their voices interchanged by automated digital reproductions. Occasionally, there would be voiceover or prerecorded music played while the headliners mouthed the words and danced. True musicians almost never made an appearance anymore. The whole industry had moved on to a business approach modeled on the fast food industry. It was awful, but young kids didn't know that. They grew up in an environment where that was all that they saw or heard. It had to make you wonder if any kids knew what the real music was.

Older bands that had made names for themselves earlier in their careers could still make money by traveling and doing concerts. All the rest had no choice but to play locally, usually as a second job.

It was possible to earn money and make a living, but it was an uphill battle.

Most bar owners believed that hiring a band was the best way market themselves. You could hire marketing people but then you'd have to pay them. Just hire a band, and they'd do the work for free. You wouldn't have to do anything else. The reality was that you hired a band to play music, and that was what they did for the specified period of the gig. They weren't marketers.

Municipalities would put on community events and not understand why they should pay the talent unless they could exhibit some kind of physical handicap. An event might even center around your group, but from their perspective, they were providing you with exposure. They would pay the people picking up the garbage as they were unionized, but usually threw the band members less than minimum wage for play time. Getting the equipment to and from the gig was the band's problem and not considered part of the job.

People often asked bands to play at events like weddings but didn't understand that this was not something they did without pay. This was work. It was particularly difficult if this was coming from someone that you knew. The money usually offered didn't cover the cost of loading up the van.

Bar owners were unique groups of individuals. There were very few people around like Burnie Ford. He paid a fair wage for the time played. He was also business savvy and often worked on promotions with beer companies and their like. Few others seemed to bother, as that would involve work and day-to-day involvement with their company.

Most owners would hire a band exclusively for their marketing skills. They honestly believed that this was the one true reason for hiring musicians. Playing music was a secondary expectation that they didn't care about much. The band would show up anticipating an agreed upon wage, only to be stiffed at the end of the evening because the owner didn't bother letting anyone know about the event and did no promotion. If they didn't make enough to cover their costs, then the entertainment was always the first bill shafted. They didn't consider the possibility that events like these would contribute to the numbers of their regulars or that a little extra hard work on their part would have put money into their own pockets. Excuses varied, but it usually came down to them saying that they provided the entertainment with exposure, and they should be thanking him for the opportunity to play and not be complaining. It had a familiar ring to it.

Try asking the same person to provide catering and staffing for a wedding or some such thing. Then stiff him by telling him that you provided exposure to his business and that he shouldn't be complaining to you that he couldn't pay his staff or cover his costs at the end of the evening. He should be grateful.

These types always thought of themselves as smart and perceptive business people. They weren't. Usually they couldn't cover many of their other expenses either. "Fly by night" wasn't just a description. That's what they commonly ended up doing. It was their occupation. Many were just crooks and would always show up somewhere else. Word of mouth often ended their usage of the musical community. They mostly just ended up going after other targets.

Then there were the gigs where the band got an agreed upon percentage of the cover charge at the door. The audience assumes a cover charge goes towards covering the cost of the acts except that the house usually takes a piece of the action. Owners didn't see this as promoting their business. They saw it more like a hall rental. Often a promoter was involved, but not always. It didn't matter; it was still up to the bands to promote and deliver an audience. They wouldn't get income otherwise. Often, you had to prove that you delivered an absolute number of bodies and identify who they were. It was an unwritten rule. The house would do nothing except to take their percentage of the gate.

Accountants ran most bars. They understood a lot about numbers but hadn't a clue on how to run a business. They'd show up for a couple of hours each day, counted their beans, and had no idea how their place operated. Most should never have gotten into the business and stuck to working for other people. They were ripe for the pickings from crooked staff. Bands usually lost the most income from the places that had dishonest employees. They always shorted the band and pocketed the rest. You could complain to the owner, but they never did anything because they honestly had no understanding on how to deal with the problem. This was another reason they should have been working for someone else. It was 'deer in the headlights' behavior.

There were other ways of making money. Self-publishing was popular, but the current generation won't pay for music anymore. They believed that it was their right to have it without payment. So, they would steal and share it. Oddly, their parents insisted on paying. They respected musicians.

There was also the music streaming services. If subscribers played your song somewhere around a million times, you just might get enough commissions back to buy some macaroni and cheese, enough to feed one person one time.

Being in a band was tough work. There were huge pitfalls in this business.

Dave was ecstatic now though. The mempro provided him with the flexibility that hadn't been available to him before on the world-ship. It allowed him to get around in the larger society and provided him with a greater purpose.

He and Lindsey finally had a chance to meet with Nasty of the infamous Nasty Face.

They had allowed the world-ship to broker a deal for them directly. Neither of them was familiar enough with how the local economy worked. Additionally, their overheads were much different now. They had food on the table, a home and even equipment if needed. At the same time, they didn't want to set a precedent preventing any future musicians and sound technicians from getting equitable pay for services rendered.

They struck a deal that all agreed to. Nasty was going to handle promotions by himself. He presented this as an excellent opportunity for his personal growth. He even got the world-ship to run announcements locally on the appropriate channels. Advertising was novel as there were no commercials or billboards here. Everyone thought it gauche.

Dave developed an immediate liking for Nasty. He was also the first neanderthal that he and Lindsey had ever met personally.

The place was a great venue, especially the viewing walls depicting the galactic hub. These made for a spectacular backdrop. Together, they worked out the stage setup and made sure that the appropriate power outlets were available. Nasty had arranged for additional waiting staff and people to manage the door.

They ended up talking all night about everything and anything. They hadn't meant to, but they stayed very late.

¤ ¤ ¤ ¤ ¤

Finally, it was the day of the first gig. Dave was nervous. These were a little larger than the usual preshow jitters. He was much more wound up than he should have been. If it was a disaster than they would just keep on trying. Privately, he knew it was going to take time to amass a following so that the band could play on a regular basis.

Of course, Nasty didn't think there would be a problem. He said that the world-ship was going to be simulcasting the event to other AIDS and that it amassed a great deal of interest in that community. That was the first that he'd heard of it. Maybe Lindsey had failed to mention some of what she had arranged.

Nasty closed the bar for the two hours of setup prior to the show. This was unusual as the bar ran twenty-four hours a day and catered to all working shifts. The hangers didn't have hours so neither did he.

The floor had double the number of tables and seats from what it usually had. The tables, tastefully decorated with dark blue tablecloths with centerpieces holding tall red candles, would add some ambiance to the room. A large area was empty directly in front of the band. It had been set aside for dancing.

Geoff and Ryan had done most of the heavy lifting and setup but were letting Milena do the live mix. There were no 'laws' preventing her from doing this. The guys all had their instruments ready and tuned. They'd already finished their final sound check. Everything was prepared.

The stage looked presentable. The floor rose up a slight amount. It was about the height of a single step, which was perfect if he was going to work the crowd.

Braedon was still tweaking his drums and Milena was off to the right-hand side of the stage where the mixing equipment was. Everyone else was at the bar.

He walked over to make sure she was OK.

"How's it going?" Dave asked.

"Everything's set up for the band," Milena replied. "But I got an odd request and I'm just finishing up with it now." She looked a bit perplexed.

"What was that?" Dave asked in reply.

"Well," Milena said hesitantly, "Free-Credit asked me to provide a direct output feed to the world-ship. I would have thought it wouldn't need anything like that. I mean, it sees and hears everything. I just thought it odd. When I asked the drone about it, he told me that some new lighting system had been set up was being integrated to the sound. This would be for a dry run test but used in future shows."

"Well, that's odd," Dave observed. "I didn't know anything about that either. A professional light show would be something though. Are you about done?"

"I sure am," Milena said adding a big smile to her face.

"Good. Let's go catch up with the others and find out what else we don't know about," Dave said with some mirth in his voice.

Together, they walked over to the bar and joined the others. Alan and Corey offered them high fives, which they both took.

Dave looked towards Lindsey. "Honey, I just found out we're simulcasting to other AIDS and that the world-ship is doing a light show for us. Do you know anything about that?"

"Nope. That's the first I've heard of it," Lindsey responded. She looked at the two drones and settled on addressing Free-Credit. "We aren't complaining, but do you know what's going on?" she asked him.

The drone looked back at Dave and Lindsey and replied, "I'm sorry if we've overstepped our bounds. We didn't think there'd be an issue. Pretty-Ugly is trying his best to promote music beyond this locality. He's pushing it to all of the other AIDS. Is the light show an issue?"

"No," Dave answered. "I like the idea. I bet the world-ship has some great ideas for the show. We just didn't know about it and finding out about it part way through the performance isn't the best way to go about it. It could throw off our performance a lot. You usually go through the whole thing beforehand with the band so they know what's going to happen, song by song. There's a choreography to it. I guess we can trust to the world-ship to do it right. It can adjust to how we are playing. We may even adjust back. I guess we'll see what happens."

Nasty wandered over. He had just finishing instructing the staff on their duties. He seemed to have everything set. "We have a lineup outside and the doors open in ten minutes. The show starts a half hour after that. Is everything ready on your end?" he addressed to the group.

"We're set," answered Dave. "I think the only thing we haven't done yet is the traditional shot before the show. You had better line them up. Oh. And make it fruit juice for the kids."

"Let's take care of that," responded Nasty with a big smile on his face. "Then I'm putting on the house music and opening the doors."

◻ ◻ ◻ ◻

The house was packed and people were still lined up outside. The world-ship had taken the initiative and directed these people to a nearby park. It had printed a viewing wall that was the size of a drive-in theater screen that included full surround sound for an impromptu simulcast. The show was starting in a couple of minutes.

At the bar, Free-Credit and Remotely-Close told Ryan and Geoff about it. Everyone else had taken his or her places. This was something that was completely unexpected and they were tempted to run and check it out. It was only a few minutes away, but there wasn't time, maybe between sets. The band still didn't know about it.

Ryan thought it might be an idea for Dave to address that crowd personally on their first or second break. He'd run it by him later. There would be time.

Milena and Pilgrim were ready at the sound station. Dave, Alan, Corey and Brandon were at the back of the stage.

Lindsey, Olaha, Ushae and her two kids were at the table center stage just behind the dance floor.

The waiting staff was still running around servicing orders for all the clientele that had arrived.

The place was getting louder and louder as the tension was growing in anticipation of the shows start.

Ryan couldn't help himself. He turned to Geoff and asked, "Are you sure you wouldn't rather be working? You could be out there with Milena and Pilgrim."

Geoff turned back to him giving a sinister glance. "Then I'd be working. I wouldn't be able to enjoy the show or have a beer."

They both chuckled nervously.

The house music stopped and lights turned down. The band ran out to their places on stage while the crowd was cheering. Some people were even clapping. They must have watched videos.

Then four spotlights shone down; one on each person in the band. Ryan knew to expect some illumination but wasn't ready for this. He expected something more like LED's and perhaps the odd strobe. This was more like a full stadium approach to lighting.

Ryan watched Dave. He had a big smile on his face. Dave looked up quickly so as not to be blinded, but it was obvious he was enjoying this.

Braedon started a quiet backbeat on the drums while Alan added some low volume waving melodics on his guitar. Dave took his microphone from the stand and started into his usual opening, welcoming the crowd, praising the bar and Nasty and finally the world-ship Pretty-Ugly.

There was a lot of cheering and yelling coming from the audience while they blasted into their first song.

The lighting followed the band very tastefully. The world-ship was using lasers, but these weren't limited to the several colors that were available back home. These lasers ran the full spectrum of visible light and could continuously go from one color to the next. In some cases, the lasers interfered with each other above smoke released from the floor, creating moving holograms of people dancing. These would move from color to color. It was breathtaking.

The viewing walls had started with the pictures of the galactic hub. These were interspersed with video of audiences watching the show from other locations. This added to the enormity of feeling for the event.

This completely blew Ryan away. He'd seen many light shows in his time but nothing like this. Geoff kept looking at him and then back at the stage equally stunned. There wasn't much that happened on stage that Geoff hadn't seen before, but this was different.

Finally, Geoff just looked at him and gave thumbs up. There was nothing else to say. So they just watched the show.

The general lighting on stage also went from color to color. Often, it would almost completely disappear during a particularly intense vocal. The lights would focus on Dave. Enough background light remained so the others could see what they were doing.

Milena was doing a very professional job. She was keeping an eye and ear on the band while following her song sheets, setting the mix flawlessly.

Geoff turned to Ryan. It was loud, so he had to scream. "Milena is doing a hell of a job."

It was too loud to reply properly, so Ryan just gave him thumbs up back. Milena was every bit the professional.

Lindsey and the other girls were up dancing and waving over to them to join in. Ryan guessed that they wanted to get the crowd started. He got Geoff's attention and pointed to the girls. They both made their way to the dance floor and started dancing.

It didn't take long after joining the girls and dancing with each of them in turn. Ryan could feel himself slip into that otherworldly feeling people get so often when listening to music. He could feel the others up dancing, but he was still himself. He felt part of a larger symbiosis, but he was alone. The music beamed through his brain and awakened primitive feelings. It was so personal, but at the same time, shared with the crowd. The tempo moved through him, translating into movement. He felt wonderful and transcendent.

Others in the audience were now up dancing. The dance floor was full. That didn't stop people from dancing between the tables or at the bar.

Ryan had been up long enough and needed a break. He wasn't young enough to keep this up all night, and it was still the first set. So he headed back to the bar.

Nasty was there waiting with a fresh beer for him. It was plain that he was having a great time. The place had never been this full before. Sales were good.

Ryan took a deep swallow to replace some of the sweat he'd lost. His shirt was very damp. A minute later Geoff showed up and grabbed a beer as well. They both turned to watch the band finish the last song of the first set.

The ending was spectacular. The last song ended with pyrotechnics going off. Neither Geoff nor Ryan had seen those in many years. For Ryan, it had been decades. They were always spectacular but never used at home anymore because of the fire danger. Too many terrible accidents had happened in the past.

The stage lighting went off and the house lights and music came back on.

Both Geoff and Ryan turned towards each other and said at the same time, "Wow!"

Alan and Corey did a quick tune-up of their guitars. After a few minutes, the band members came from around the back of the stage and talked with Milena for a couple of minutes. This was standard practice. It was the only real opportunity the musicians and the person doing the mixing had to talk with each other. They weren't there long which indicated everything went very well. In fact, Milena and the boys headed over to Lindsey's table. They were all smiling confirming Ryan's guess.

Dave got a big hug and kiss from his wife. It was hard to tell through the crowd, but it looked like Rhea and Dea were chatting the guys up. Future groupies in the making, no doubt.

Alan found some fans in a couple of the women in the crowd. They weren't all sapiens either. Some were quite striking. He wandered off to chat with all of them.

Braedon and Corey managed to work their way to the bar. It was a long haul. They had to greet each person who stopped them as they passed by and thank them for the praises given.

"Hey," Ryan directed to them. "Did you hear they set up a new stage for the overflow in a park near here? The world-ship arranged for a simulcast when it became apparent the crowd was going to be so big."

"No," answered Corey. "Whereabouts?

"Nasty," yelled out Geoff. "Can we ask you something?"

Nasty was on the far side of the bar but came over. He had the stupidest grin on his face that any of them could imagine.

"Sure," Nasty replied. "What can I do for you?"

"Where's the park with the overflow crowd?" asked Geoff.

"You can get there through the kitchen," replied Nasty. "It's right out back. I have some of the waiters serving beer out there. We ran out half an hour ago. The world-ship is supplying us directly now. You want to see it?"

"Sure," said Ryan. "After we get a couple of new beers. Better get one for Dave too. He's going to want to see this."

Nasty got them new drinks. Dave showed up seconds later and claimed his.

"Come on," said Nasty. "Follow me."

"Where to?" asked Dave.

"You're not going to want to miss this," said Ryan. "Come on."

They walked to the back of the bar and through the service entrance into the kitchen. There were numerous people unloading beer from the world-ship's dispenser. Others placed them into fridges while still others took them out just as fast. Some of the servers took the beer back to the bar area while others were going out the back door.

They followed Nasty out the door and could see a tall wall in front of them. It was higher than all of the other local structures were. They walked down one side and turned past it to see a crowd of approximately two-thousand people. Some were sitting on the ground. Others were milling around.

The house music was playing over a separate sound system and many people were looking up at the wall, which had the same images on it as the viewing wall inside the bar.

"It's a full simulcast," said Nasty to them. "We're trying to serve out here too, but I guess I didn't arrange for enough help. That's fine. I can't get beer in here fast enough anyway."

"I don't believe this," said Dave. "This is fantastic. It's fully 3D. I just can't believe it."

"You should say something to them during the next set," Ryan said to him.

"I will," Dave replied. "We dedicate the next set to them. I still don't believe it."

"How's Milena doing?" Geoff asked Dave a little protectively.

"Oh, she's doing great," Dave replied. "Everything has been spot on. You know more than anyone else does that there's always a goof up somewhere. She hasn't made one yet. With that light show, I would have expected something. How'd you like it in the audience?"

"Spectacular," replied Ryan. "It even looked like pots were going off. And those lasers. Really something."

"Yeah!" said Dave. "Let's get back in. The second set starts in a couple of minutes.

As a group, they went back in. Dave and the group headed back towards the stage stopping by Lindsey's table again. Ryan could see Alan breaking away from his new lady friends to join them. They finally ducked in back.

Geoff and Ryan headed back to the bar.

After another minute or two, the house music and lights dropped and the guys went back to their places on stage. Immediately the spots lighted each member of the band.

Dave started by addressing the audience. "Thanks so much for your appreciation. Again, I want to thank Nasty and the waiting staff for putting this superb musical event together."

He waited for the applause to die down and went on. "You know, this is the first ever event of this kind on the world-ship. Nothing like this has ever happened before. The turnout has far exceeded our highest expectations. It was hard on Nasty. Yeah. He had to turn people away from the door because so many of you beautiful people showed up. But here's an excellent thing. The world-ship set up an overflow area out back at very short notice. It has full sound and video. No one supports live music like Pretty-Ugly. No one, except for Nasty."

Dave had to wait again while the applause died down. It went on a little longer this time. "So, in light of this, we are dedicating the next set to the world-ship and to the two-thousand people out back watching this performance." And the band started up again.

This set, Dave left the stage to work the audience directly. Ryan watched the viewing walls. The pictures followed Dave as he worked his way through the crowd. He could see that Dave was keeping an eye on it too.

Dave worked his way towards the service area and then headed out back. He didn't drop a note.

"Come on," said Ryan to Geoff. "Let's check this out."

They both followed Dave out to the overflow area where the larger crowd was.

The sound perfectly matched the indoor bar. There was no audio lag at all. It was also dark out. A spot shone down from the viewing wall tracking Dave.

Geoff looked at Ryan and said, "I don't know what's being used to get the sound out here, but it's impressive. I would have thought there would be at least a one-second lag. There's nothing. It's a perfect match. I am really impressed."

"Yeah," Ryan replied. "And Dave and the band can keep track of each other using the viewing walls. Spectacular."

They continued watching Dave work the crowd.

The lighting effects began to change. A thin blue gossamer plasma started to cover the whole area. An occasional colored laser shone through it. Tiny forks of electrostatic white lightning were coming off every surface. No one was getting shocks though.

Ryan looked at the startled face on Geoff. "Is that what I think it is?"

"I think so," replied Geoff. "That's exactly the same color and look as the relativistic electron gun, but it's a field effect now. Are we under attack?"

"I don't see anything that would indicate that we are," replied Ryan somewhat hesitantly. "Nothing. We didn't know there would be a light show until the last minute either. I think we need to have a little discussion with the drones."

"I agree," said Geoff. "It is pretty though; with all the lasers."

Dave was moving back towards the back of the Nasty Face. They followed him in and went straight to the bar.

The lighting effects were identical inside. No one knew that the lighting was actually an offensive weapon except for Ryan and Geoff.

✩ ✩ ✩ ✩ ✩

The entity completed its review of the damages that it had acquired. Substantial portions of itself were still poisoned. Much had also cleared up. It was on the road to recovery.

Briefly, the entity considered feeding on some of the singularities that it had collected, but decided not to. There was every possibility that anything taken from them would take on the properties of the infection rather than its own native traits. Better to wait for a full recovery. Unfortunately, that meant a continuance to the knowledge that the overall world-lines it occupied remained reduced in length. That threat wasn't imminent and could wait.

Two major portions of itself were hard at work down the non-entropic-time-like dimensions.

The first was still evaluating the review of its experiences for the complete project. The entity was well aware that it lacked understanding as to cause and effect of its bad experiences. The proportions of success and failure had not changed substantially.

What had changed was the severity of injuries received on the success events. They were no longer mere inconveniences. They kept on getting worse. The entity had barely escaped extinction on the last attempt. A new strategy needed development that would allow it a graceful withdrawal in the event of another possible injury.

The primary weakness that the entity had was during the last moments of the singularities creation. It needed to maintain contact with this in order to be able to retrieve the prize. Otherwise, the bounty would be permanently lost to phase space. That had almost caused the elimination of the entity's ongoing continuance during the course of its last attempt.

The entity categorized every failure. They all had a particular action in common. That was the entity's attempts to speed the process up. It entered dimensional spaces it didn't bother with generally. Every attempt had gotten progressively worse.

The natural way to avoid this was not to enter those spaces. The entity could watch to fruition. If something prevented the final part of the collapse, it could then pull out immediately before ending up trapped the way it was the last time. Without the entity's presence generating the correct vibrational modes, the affected space would revert to its natural condition. There was a possible benefit to this approach. The entity might acquire insight as to the cause of the failures. If this happened, then it was likely that the next attempt would be a success. Perhaps a better approach would be to perform multiple attempts concurrently guaranteeing a success even if most tries failed.

This solution was determined to be the best procedure to follow. The entity folded this result back into itself on the entropic-time-line for execution. Now was the time to start back up again.

The second portion of itself was still studying the pocket of the bound collection of baryonic matter. The entity experienced extreme difficulty. As little as it understood of the dimensions that this stuff existed in, it could make no sense of what it was observing. There could be no accounting for the actions or reactions that the body exhibited. The baryonic matter continued causing minor reorganizations of the environment inside the bubble. There was no evidence of natural operations involving magnitude and differentials that it regularly observed from the native constituents of its own domain. In addition, it could just barely make out low-level photonic emissions coming from the baryonic matter at very low power. It could only find these in a very narrow high-frequency band. This was peculiar because the signal spread through sub-frequencies found in a very discrete chunk within the photonic domain and transited back and forth within it. This gave the appearance of noise but wasn't entirely random adding to the confusion.

The entity had decided on a bold decision. When it last entered the native domain of this matter, there was an immediate reaction causing it to experience some level of distress. It resolved to test if this was still the case with the piece that it had acquired.

The entity extruded a very tiny finger of its own material into a wormhole connecting to the bubble's interior and translated this to the dimensions that the matter inhabited.

The baryonic matter immediately ceased its rearrangements and did nothing.

So far, nothing bad had happened. The entity had no new pain inflicted upon it. There were no new or unusual events as near as it could detect in the foreign bubble. It was limited in its actions as the operational laws of the pocket universe were different from its own. It detected no other effects in any dimension.

The entity then tried to change the organization of the part of the environment that the baryonic matter had modified. Once it had finished doing this, the foreign material then changed it back to the way it was before.

That was very odd, so the entity tried it again and the same thing happened.

It withdrew to ponder the results and continue its observations. There was still no sense to all of this.

¤ ¤ ¤ ¤ ¤

It was the next morning. They all gathered in the aft-common at Ryan and Geoff's request after breakfast. The band and Lindsey, Milena and Pilgrim, and Olaha with the drones.

All anyone talked about up to this point was how successful everything had gone. They all congratulated each other and complimented on the roles each person took. There was no denying it. The music and its control and delivery were superb. The draw went far beyond expectations and the audience was ecstatic; even the ones outside. The light show was the final touch, but that was the problem. They made some history. Not all of it was good.

Everyone finally found seating on various sofas and chairs. It was a haphazard arrangement. They were all facing Geoff and Ryan. As agreed, Ryan spoke first.

"First, I just want to say that last night was spectacular. Everyone worked far beyond any reasonable expectation and produced something very rare. Having said that, it's now time for to share some truths amongst ourselves. Something happened last night that you should be aware of."

"He's going to say we sucked," interrupted Alan with a snort.

"No Alan," Ryan responded. "You guys were really first rate. What we're talking about has to do with the project that Geoff and I were working on. This is serious and not a laughing matter unfortunately. Worse, I hate to dump this on you after such a success, but you need to know."

Geoff picked it up. "Ryan and I were drafted into a program to actively fight against the things that destroyed our original homes. We went because we personally needed to fight back. Both of us had skill sets that were missing here. That's why the kids were so upset a while back. They found out what we were doing at an especially awkward time. I'm really sorry about that."

The drones started to look very uncomfortable. Technically, they were still on holiday. "Should we bring Pretty-Ugly into this conversation?" asked Free-Credit.

"That's probably a good idea," answered Ryan.

Immediately the image of Pretty-Ugly appeared on the viewing screen. It elected to say nothing. It was likely monitoring the whole time anyway. Ryan continued.

"We were involved in helping analyze the enemy's weaknesses and develop an effective response. We assisted with developing concepts and weapons used for our defenses. We also traveled to another world-line that was undergoing collapse to test these things. We lost Questionable-Advice to the enemy. We don't know if he's alive or dead. That's why you haven't seen him. Things didn't go well." Ryan started to choke up.

The girls all gasped at the same time looking around at each other. Even Olaha wasn't aware of this detail.

Geoff continued. "We were able to determine that amongst other things, the enemy uses a broadcast signal in its attack which helps to bring on all of the bad things you saw when we left home. I was able to work out a theoretical way to counter it. We were partially successful. Ryan was also able to come up with some new ways to fight our enemies directly, at least while they're in our dimensions. They worked very well. In spite of all of this, we almost lost our lives. In desperation, as a group, we changed the way my device worked and reinforced the wave we were canceling. The idea was to force more down its throat then it could handle."

Ryan interrupted. "It wasn't quite like that. I made the decision. It was my fault. You don't have to shield me. But thanks, Geoff."

Geoff continued. "It doesn't matter. We were all culpable. The result was that we thought, I repeat, thought, that we harmed the enemy. The fact is that we actually don't know for sure. However, the cost was enormous."

"We didn't know what the cost would be," Ryan said. "I ended up sending one-hundred times the world lines down its maw. I've directly killed more people than the enemy ever has. I quit after that. I can't do something like that again. I just can't."

"We both did," said Geoff. "That's how we ended back here and why the drones got their holiday. We did something truly terrible."

The room was absolutely stone cold quiet. All eyes were on the both of them. Milena's eyes had started to tear up.

"So here's the thing," continued Ryan. "We discovered something about all of the collapse events so far. Every single one collapses to a focal point. It's always a live music show or something that is very similar. That was our biggest discovery on our last recon. We don't think it has anything to do with the music itself. We think it has to do with how people's awareness changes when they're really into it. I think you know what I mean. You change your mental framework as part of its enjoyment. There's no math or anything for it, but we know that consciousness is somehow involved as a property of the structure and organization of the universe."

Geoff picked it up. "Last night you played a spectacular gig. There were a lot of people that were there and they were really into it. They all went to that place in their minds. Everyone did his or her jobs. That's what we aimed to do. We all thought it a little odd that the world-ship planned a light show and we didn't know anything about it ahead of time. It worked out OK and was quite spectacular. Except for one little thing."

"One of the weapons that we developed was used as part of the show," stated Ryan. "That blue field affect with the little lightning sparks coming off of everything. Some lasers shone through it to make it look better. It doesn't affect people at all but literally erases the enemy if it's in our dimensions. We were not under attack. I want to make that very clear. I suspect this was a test for a modified version of the weapon that we had created. Would you like to comment Pretty-Ugly?"

Its image eyed each person in the room and then proceeded to speak. "It's time that Milena had her mempro infix. She'll need it for this."

"We all share a common goal," Pretty-Ugly continued. "We all want music in the cosmos. There's a beauty to it that we can't easily quantify in words. Ryan and Geoff won't like this much, but we have a plan. If we do this correctly, we can save our universal domain from further encroachment. All we have to do is pull off the largest concert ever to have happened anywhere and at any time in our universe. We need to construct the program carefully to establish the maximum effect. Are you up to doing a performance of this scope?"

✻ ✻ ✻ ✻ ✻

The pain had been excruciating while Questionable-Advice's biologics died. This felt like it went on forever. Questionable-Advice even had to give up on the stick figures for a time. It could feel itself dying at a cellular level. Its lung analogs were the first to go, quickly followed by its digestive tract. After that, its external skin went, as did the flesh covering its eyes. This left it with only its mechanical components.

The mechanical eyes adjusted to their new state now that the external focusing surfaces were gone. So Questionable-Advice still had sight. Missing were its tissue senses of touch, hearing, taste and smell. The black hair-like sensor array was still in place, but wasn't a complete replacement and lacked the emotional feedback that the tissues provided. This was a sorry excuse for an existence. Given current circumstances, it would have to do.

Questionable-Advice had taken more than twelve hours to experience this death. There was no better way to put it. The environment substantially diminished Questionable-Advice. The honest truth was that it had hoped it would die. This was a moment of pure self-discovery to find out that it, a drone, could even feel this way. The pain that it suffered caused these feelings. But it did survive. This meant that it had no choice but to continue on. Self-termination was not an option open to it.

After all of the biologics had expired, Questionable-Advice excised the flesh; it was in its way. It didn't putrefy but did harden over time as the fluids evaporated from them. Any bacteria that it might have carried couldn't have lived in this poisonous and sterile environment. Nothing biological could survive here.

Questionable-Advice was very glad there were no reflective surfaces where it could see itself. It was enough that Questionable-Advice could see its extremities. It sickened it to look at the mechanicals. It used to be proud of its looks. If people saw it now, they would surely think of it as a skinned monster. Maybe it was even going a little crazy.

Questionable-Advice started back on drawing stick figures on the ground after the second day here. The internal clock built into its hardware said that it had been here for more than a subjective week now. This was difficult to rationalize against the steadily shining pink light of this environment. It felt far longer. How could the entities that captured Questionable-Advice not be aware that it was attempting to communicate with them? Why else would they have captured it?

Then suddenly, there was a ray of hope. They must have been watching him. Questionable-Advice thought that they must have wanted to communicate as much with it as it did with them.

A filament of the gray wall matter appeared in Questionable-Advice's enclosure. This was much more massive than Questionable-Advice was, but was substantially smaller than what it had seen during the world-line attacks. The object moved around as if it was observing Questionable-Advice. The stick figures in the ground must have attracted it. Surely, it would recognize this as an attempt at communication.

Questionable-Advice currently had a sizable area of stick figure math laid out on the ground. This was just very basic addition representations. A starting place that even a child could understand.

The thing wavered over Questionable-Advice's work in much the same way that Pilgrim often did, swaying sinuously back and forth for several minutes.

Then the thing stopped and moved the greater portion of its presented body over the ground and energetically swung back and forth, erasing all that Questionable-Advice had put down.

Good. They could start fresh and interactively work on the concepts together, Questionable-Advice thought.

Once the thing had moved back out of the way, Questionable-Advice went back down on its mechanical knees and used what was left of its fingers to draw out several rows of sample addition. It got back to its feet and moved out of the way to allow this entity to look at its handiwork.

So far, so good. The entity started moving around what Questionable-Advice had put on the ground. There was no way to tell how it was absorbing the information. There were no discernible sensory organs. It must have been using something though. It appeared to be studying what Questionable-Advice had drawn.

Then the thing erased what was on the ground again. What was going on? Questionable-Advice couldn't have put the message more simply. Its frustration level started to increase.

Questionable-Advice gave it another try and wrote everything out again. Once again, the entity hovered over Questionable-Advice's work and then disappeared suddenly.

If Questionable-Advice still had its biologics, it would have screamed out in frustration. Its only method of external communications left was the mempro cognate band. At least it could hear itself over this. Questionable-Advice felt better screaming over these channels rather than attempting to internalize its feelings. It got them out into the environment anyway.

This wasn't just an alien mentality that Questionable-Advice faced. These things must be fundamentally stupid. There couldn't be another explanation. How could anything miss the concept of one plus one equaling two?

Disgust welled up inside of Questionable-Advice. Its universe was under attack and they were losing to something that exhibited no more intelligence than a lowly worm. And that wasn't fair to the worm.

Still, Questionable-Advice couldn't stop. It had to find some common grounds for communication. It came down to sensory input and they had nothing in common between them.

¤ ¤ ¤ ¤ ¤

It was entropic-time for the next action. Healing had progressed to the point required for assured stability. All resources were in place and the plan could now begin. If everything went well, then the entity could start infusing new energy back into itself.

The entity had learned nothing further from the collected baryonic matter. It just appeared to be so much junk that it could discard after it completed the next operational phase. It was frustrating to learn that this branch of enquiry was a dead end. The stuff didn't even evince the ability to harm it as had been done to it in the last foray. Every action it demonstrated indicated to it that there was nothing more to discover. The photonic emissions continued to hold some interest for it, but there was nothing specific that it could use. There was no reason to pursue this subject any longer.

Multiple fingers of self were now associated with many wormholes and were waiting on the other side for the commencement of operations. A reservoir of local space-time was in place.

The plan was simple. It would pick one wormhole at random and invoke a collapse. If nothing happened or it encountered some kind of resistance, then it would cease the manipulation of the higher dimensions and abandon the harvesting operation there. The foreign environment would revert to normal, but it didn't care about that. This would avoid harm to itself. It would just move on to the next wormhole. It would keep doing this until it had achieved success.

In very short order, it would meet its needs and no harm could possibly come to itself. There were no possible down sides if its understanding of past events was correct. It enjoyed a new feeling of smug self-satisfaction.

It chose a thread and proceeded with injecting the infecting kernel of local space-time into the designated target wormhole. Its presence at the other end started the twenty-six dimensional mixing, forcing instabilities in the local geometry of space-time. Once it met the requisite conditions, it continued with the direct manipulation of the higher dimensions, which initiated the correct vibrational modes that would invoke the reversal of the local geometry. The signal was always slow to start with, but once underway the process would infect all of the foreign space-time forcing the collapse into a singularity. Hopefully, the point of focus would show up on the first attempt.

Now it was only a matter of waiting for events to proceed as planned.

Now nothing could go wrong.

◘ ◘ ◘ ◘ ◘

It had been a month since the plan had gone into effect. Every AIDS entity that was contactable through ComSpace was a part of it. In theory, that was all of them. Combinatorially, it was impossible to predict the level of communication. Still, AIDS had never before attempted anything near this scale and scope. At least this time the community would perhaps be ready as a whole, fueled by fear and desperation. There was even an element of curiosity for most members. Trust was a big part of the program. Sending out the elements of the plan was comparatively easy. Verifying its implementation was impossible by virtue of the number of participants involved. It was one thing to show what had been happening. It was an entirely different matter verifying that a sufficient number of AIDS were participating in the multi-threaded world-line universe. There was no possibility of verification. It even seemed very likely that some world-lines had no AIDS entities at all. Others might be using entirely different communications languages and handshaking methodologies if they were far enough away. With luck, these entities would be able to sidestep these shortcomings relying on their local networks to provide language modules or other possible translation solutions.

Pretty-Ugly knew that its own contacts were primed. It just hoped that their friends and others ad infinitum were as equally prepared and could follow the instructions that it had outlined. Instructions were available to all in ComSpace and reinforced by direct entity to entity contact.

For its own part, hub operations and the lines of communication in ComSpace were in place. There were one dedicated inbound and two dedicated outbound channels. If the other AIDS followed suit, the plan could work. Operationally, it was simple. Trusting others to do their job was the difficult part. Monitoring instructions and the directions to follow once an AIDS detected a positive signal were straightforward enough, but panic could cause the whole plan to fall apart if the reserved channels got jammed.

This was the first time the world-ship had ever felt any degree of insecurity. If the operation failed, then there was no fallback plan. Its own world-line had ceased to fork. All it could assume by this was that the universal domain would fail in totality should the plan break down. Either it worked and everything was OK or it didn't and the universe would be extinct, hopefully taking the invaders with it. No pressure.

Early detection was the key to stopping the collapse process. On the other hand, there was no ability to predict what the enemy would do. In fact, there was no ability to predict what the universe would do either. It was a gamble and everything was at stake.

Waiting was the hardest part for Pretty-Ugly. Another event seemed inevitable. The longer it took to happen, the more prepared they would be. The other way to look at it would be to see the enemy as also being more capable.

Then it happened. The dedicated inbound ComSpace channel saw its first report. An AIDS had detected the start of the effect on a far off world-line. Verification of the inbound data showed that remotely observed universal constants were starting to change. This was a very early report giving them sufficient reaction time, unlike what they got with the Ephalem device. This dictated a twelve-hour window until full collapse occurred. The sensory data was an almost complete duplicate of what Pretty-Ugly* had initially encountered.

In less than ten minutes several hundred more reports started to stream in verifying the involvement of a complete world-line trunk. At this point, there didn't appear to be a focal point set for the effect. Still, even in a single trunk, the universe was a gigantic place. That didn't mean one wouldn't develop. It also didn't mean that they couldn't make one.

Pretty-Ugly sent a message down the dedicated broadcast instruction channel that all the AIDS were monitoring. They were to get ready and stand by. Action would commence in one-and-a-half hours. It started to send a countdown over the band so there would be no misunderstandings should an observing entity be in a separate relativistic time frame.

It was now time to mobilize.

□ □ □ □ □

It was early evening in the Orlop Urban Forest Arcology when the world-ship made the announcement.

They had just finished dinner and were in the process of cleaning up. Every viewing wall in the compound was alive with the alert. Ryan instantly felt sick to his stomach. Everyone stopped what he or she was doing. Even Pilgrim.

There was no time to gather their usual gear. Pretty-Ugly had assured them that everything would be in place when they got there. It had duplicated everything. Their only immediate task was to get to the back of the Nasty Face as soon as possible. Time was their biggest enemy and they had a concert to do.

Ryan looked at each person in the room. Everyone had a part to play and was integral to the plan.

The group had worked with the world-ship on the set list. They would play continuous sets with twenty-minute breaks between each for the duration of the emergency. That was a marathon. None of them knew how they would stand up over time. There could be as many as twelve sets. Geoff would be pitching in to play during the breaks. Even he and Milena would pitch in if needed. They were practicing regularly, but they still had to concentrate on their primary mixing jobs. Dave and Lindsey had been a big help in getting them ready, but neither of them was a part of the central performance when the world-ship was doing much of its work. Everyone was going to be wearing multiple hats for this one except for the main band members who bore the greatest burden.

Seconds later, a new announcement came over the viewing wall. The ship addressed this one to all of its inhabitants. Overnight Distress would perform a special concert starting in one and a half hours. All individuals that could make it to the park were encouraged to do so. There would also be massive viewing walls available in all parkland's carrying the show. Pretty-Ugly directed those that couldn't make it out to watch the simulcast on the viewing walls wherever they happened to be. All channels would carry this very special event. It suspended all noncritical work during the period of the show. Anything vital would be performed by the world-ship itself.

"Jesus," exclaimed Alan. "If we leave right now for the travel tube we just might make it to our own concert. I bet there's a traffic jam."

Milena looked at him and said, "Pilgrim and I have been talking." All eyes went up at that statement. She turned and addressed everyone in the room. "If no one has any objections, Pilgrim has offered to take everyone to the venue. He can't do it all at once and it'll knock the heck out of him, but he can do it one person at a time. It should save a lot of time and you might be able to get a shot in before you start."

"I knew there was a reason I love this girl," said Dave. He quickly turned towards Lindsey and said "Sorry honey." He was a little red in the face.

"You get a let on this one," she answered back smiling at Milena. It was another one of those silent girl communications that guys just didn't understand and weren't privy to.

At least this time around, Ryan wasn't going to be calling the shots. He was a working stiff for this one. "I volunteer to go first," he told the others. "I've always wondered what it was like to travel Air Pilgrim. Besides, I can make sure that Nasty has the beer supplies under control. I bet the world-ship has already started deliveries. I'll meet you all at the bar." At least he could appear to have a stiff upper lip, as scared as he felt.

◻ ◻ ◻ ◻ ◻

She was the last to arrive at the Nasty Face. Pilgrim had put them behind the bar. There was no other open area. The bar was already crowded and more people continued to arrive, streaming into the front door. The masses would force Nasty to close his front entrance soon.

The viewing walls were flipping through different close-up views of some of the local planets and moonlets. The current shot of the backside of the moon in full sunlight was spectacular. She never, ever saw anything like that back at her old home.

Milena knew she shouldn't be where she was. She quickly grabbed a couple of waters. Nasty shot her a look that said 'get out of there and join the others quickly.' She moved down towards the kitchen entrance and wove her way through the crowd to where the others had congregated at the far end of the bar.

Poor Pilgrim looked exhausted, Milena thought. He wasn't his usual bobbing and weaving self. He had managed to keep up with her though. She wondered how he would hold up over the next twelve hours.

The others had already started reviewing what each person's responsibilities were and what they needed to do. There was less than an hour until the show started.

Panic had already started to show on Dave's face. "I don't know where the session sheets are," he sputtered to the others and Geoff in particular. "I forgot about them completely."

Milena quickly interrupted him before he could work himself up much further. She addressed them while holding her bag up. "Relax everyone. Take a breath. I have multiple copies in my bag. You're covered. Just so you know, they're really heavy too. If you think you have it tough, just look at Pilgrim. Poor thing."

Dave's face quickly showed relief. He reached over, put his arm around the tired Ephalem, and said to him, "When she's right, she's right. Thanks, Pilgrim."

They had Geoff preassigned as the stage manager. They all felt that he was the best person to deal with any and all contingencies that they might come up against during the show. He was the boss tonight and even the band had agreed to follow his lead.

"Let's get this out of the way first," Geoff started. "No egos will be tolerated tonight. You all know what's at stake. This is not a concert. We are fighting for our right to existence. The concert is the way that we are doing our part in this fight. I take my orders from Pretty-Ugly. He has a larger view of what will be happening than we'll ever know. There won't be any second-guessing here. Does anyone have a problem with that?"

No one even looked away from him. They all agreed to the conditions in unison.

"Good," he responded. "Now I want to go over one small change before we review what each of us is doing. Ryan and I talked about this already and we both agree. So does Pretty-Ugly. When we were originally working together in this fight, Ryan was our leader. He was the best person we had for what we had to do. Well, we aren't fighting. The AIDS are doing that. Not us. We are doing a concert. The best person to be my backup is Milena. She is better suited to what we're doing here. Ryan will back the both of us up. Is this understood by everyone?"

Everyone else agreed instantly, but Milena was shocked. "Geoff, I'm just a kid. Please don't do this to me."

"It's done honey," Geoff told her. "You haven't been a kid since you got here and for that I am truly very sorry. It's also why you got your mempro when you did. You needed to be able to use it tonight. You know this equipment and you know what needs to happen far better than anyone else does. Even me. And you know it."

Ryan took her face in both his hands and made her look into his eyes. "You can do this. It's a concert for the most part. And you know what to do. Geoff is still our leader. You're his backup," he said to her and smiled. He then added "Boss!"

"Don't do that," Milena protested. "You're all in on this. Aren't you?"

"Do we look like conspiracy nuts to you, Milena?" Alan responded.

"Absolutely. Especially you," Milena answered.

"Let's move on," Geoff said. "Pretty-Ugly has worked out the math. There will be massive viewing walls set up throughout the ship. He has integrated the sound feedback and nullification system into each one. It will not subtract our show. He has strategically placed them so that each speaker system will reinforce the resonance from its neighbors. He has also precisely worked out the amplification's propagation delay so that the transmission signal will completely match and bolster the amplified audio locally. There will be no signal nullification. There will be no apparent signal delay to the local viewers. Everyone watching, regardless of where they are, will see and hear this like the show is right in front of them. Acoustic waves traveling from other amplifiers will be matched exactly."

"Here's where this will be a little different from what we are used to," Geoff continued. "The alien signal will start from the outside of the ship and move inward. Pretty-Ugly has matched the nullification system to this action. The concert music will start from our stage and move outwards. He has precisely worked out how the two separate sets of waves have to propagate and interact. He's taken into account the speed of sound and monitoring will take place at each and every location where the re-amplification occurs so that he can make small adjustments in response to both sets of signals. The video display rate will match the local audio. Pretty-Ugly has taken care of that, but it's going to sap all of his resources as he is also providing command and control to the other AIDS as well. He won't have any resources free to deal with anything else. He is heavily relying on us to cover our part. We only have to worry about the one stage."

"Something like that sure could have saved some of the concerts I've walked away from," said Ryan. "There's nothing worse than getting echoes from remotely placed speakers since the propagation delay meant it wasn't matching what's coming from a closer speaker."

"OK," continued Geoff. "Dave, Braedon, Alan and Corey. You guys are on stage. We'll get you breaks when we can. I don't expect we can follow the session sheets completely. Especially Braedon. There's no way you can drum for twelve hours. So everyone be flexible and understanding of each other. Let Milena, Ryan and I know if you need a break. Use the mempro cognate band to contact us directly. Let us worry about the coordination. Your responsibility is strictly the show. Nothing else. Period. If you need something then ask for it. It doesn't matter what it is."

Milena was starting to feel nervous but could see the guys were all in agreement.

"Next," continued Geoff. "Lindsey and Olaha. You're the runners. If someone needs food, water, or anything else, you do the running around. None of the rest of us will be as free as you two are. Don't be afraid to get up on stage or go wherever you have to go. Stage fright is not an option. There are no restrictions for you two. If you need any assistance whatsoever go to Nasty. He has his instructions too and will do whatever you ask. Without you, we would all be falling off our feet after a couple of hours. You will keep us going."

They both nodded.

"Milena and Pilgrim," he continued. "You two will be on stage doing the foldback engineering. Make sure that each one of the guys hears what he needs to hear when they are playing. They have to play better than they've ever done before. Without you two, they'll make gaffes."

"OK," Milena replied for the both of them.

Geoff went on. "The rest of us will be in the monitoring and control booth in the middle of the audience area. Free-Credit and Remotely-Close are responsible for monitoring and balancing the outbound feed to the other AIDS. Ryan and I will be doing the front of house engineering to balance the sound for the audience."

They just nodded to each other in acknowledgment.

"I want to emphasize that there will be times that each one of us will have to cover for one of the others. So be prepared. We are a team like none that's ever come before us. Pull together. This won't be easy for any of us. Anything you can do to help out one of the others means that it will be making a difference for all of us." Geoff looked around at each of them. "Does anyone want to add anything?"

"Yeah," said Dave. "Shots are probably not a good idea right now. But I sure wouldn't mind finishing my beer first."

"Lastly," said Geoff. "Keep your headgear with you at all times."

CHAPTER 9

REVELATIONS

*Revelations come when you're in the thick of it,
pitting yourself up against something larger than
yourself.*

Frank Langella

The concert had started and new reports continued to
stream into the dedicated inbound ComSpace channel. It
was now past the saturation point and you couldn't discern
any of the new ones from the old. The individual signals all
jumbled together. This was entirely expected. It had served
its purpose anyway.

Pretty-Ugly monitored the dedicated one-way concert
stream to the outbound AIDS. The most effective use of
this tactic was with the habitats. In theory, all of the other
AIDS entities were picking up the signal and were replaying
it on their own systems, synchronously with the local show.
Those that joined in late could still download the
schematics for the systems using the one-way outbound
command-and-control channel. They could even join mid-
stream. No doubt, a few individuals out there may have
ignored the original warnings but later changed their minds.

AIDS that weren't habitats could still participate. They
expected   that   there   wouldn't   be   as   much   local

consciousness modifications in their immediate neighborhoods. That didn't mean that they couldn't protect themselves with the field effects version of the relativistic electron gun while enjoying the concert. Any effect was better than doing nothing.

Any command that the world-ship initiated locally, it would reproduce into the concert signal, propagating out to the others, except for the sampling done by the sound nullification system. The nature of this operation required the receiving AIDS to control it locally. One explicate exception was made. It was necessary to let the invaders know that they could reinforce the wave back to it at any time and that they were not afraid to use it. This warning temporarily reinforced the foreign transmission in very short bursts and nullified it most of the rest of the time. Additionally, this procedure required simultaneous execution at every location in the universe where they rebroadcast the show. Only Pretty-Ugly could do this. It planned to execute this process between sets when Overnight Distress was not on stage.

Their original meeting room was still open so that Pretty-Ugly could converse with Exact-Estimate and Neat-Mess but so far, none of them had directly detected the signal themselves. Everything was running smoothly so far. In fact, they were enjoying the concert more than they were working. There was a long way to go yet.

¤ ¤ ¤ ¤ ¤

Everything was going to plan. Of course, it was only the first set. As they had expected, the light show started reinforcing the show slowly. This would change as time went on. The relativistic electron field affect would be kicking in shortly and be seen by all viewers.

Geoff was in the control booth in the center of the audience area around fifty meters from the stage. There was

351

a dedicated fenced off corridor running between the two areas so that they could easily run back and forth. Someone, probably the world-ship, had even arranged security so that show personnel wouldn't experience any interruptions from the audience as they went about their business.

The crew exactly followed the copy of the sets list supplied by Milena. The first set revolved around songs that were easy to play and didn't require many infusions of energy into them. This would change as the show progressed. That was part of the problem. The longer the concert went on, the more tired they would all become. In contrast, they would be required to play with more and more energy input into the performances.

Free-Credit and Remotely-Close were monitoring the outbound signal going to the other AIDS. They didn't really have a lot to do. Their larger involvement would occur between sets when the feedback system amplified the signal as opposed to canceling it. That would happen in a few short minutes.

Ryan wasn't doing much either. He just watched Geoff occasionally adjust a slider. That was OK as Geoff was doing the filler between the first and second act. It would consist of classical keyboard pieces with some singing. His stuff was already set up on the stage ready for him.

None of them had felt their mentalities change due to the music yet. That would come a little later.

Geoff turned to Ryan. The first forty-minute set was almost over. "You had better take over. I'm off to the stage to give the guys their first break and do the classical keyboard pieces."

"I've got you covered," Ryan responded.

Geoff went down the stairs and followed the corridor to the front of the stage at a run. He proceeded to the side of the stage where Milena and Pilgrim were at the foldback station.

"How are you guys doing?" he asked them.

"So far, so good," responded Milena. Pilgrim just bobbed up and down. "It's almost boring. I know we're working towards a crescendo, but this is worse than a sleeping pill."

"Ouch!" said Geoff. "Critics. And I'm up next. Not to worry. For the uninitiated, this stuff is all new and fascinating. I'll try not to put you asleep when I'm on."

"I didn't mean it like that," Milena responded in a slightly hurt voice.

"I know," Geoff said smiling. "Just remember we're in this for the long haul. Before you know it, you'll be up there too."

◻ ◻ ◻ ◻

The band finished the first set. Geoff was now doing the first twenty-minute filler. It was now time to fight back. It started with turning on the internal relativistic electron field effect integrated into the light show and the performance. It was already on outside the ship. Pretty-Ugly was taking no chances. Not when they were dealing with entities that could move about the dimensions at will.

Some of the original AIDS to report the acquisition of the foreign signal had disappeared. It was impossible to tell if this was due to the collapse event or if it was just due to the flooding of the reporting channel. It didn't matter. Attempting to find them elsewhere in ComSpace would be futile given the time limits under which they were operating. If they survived this encounter, everything would return to normal and no entities would be lost.

Finally, the world-ship had detected the changing universal constants locally. Currently, it was very small but that wouldn't last long.

Pretty-Ugly started the signal feedback loop, setting up specific timing patterns. It would only use this function between the main sets. The intent of its design was to tell

353

the attackers that they were fighting back with purpose. Full nullification would be on while Overnight Distress was playing. The field effects version of the relativistic electron weapon was now on. Coverage included all internal spaces within the world-ship. Externally, the ship glowed like a blue sapphire over a dark black background. The emitters grew from the fabric of the hull, covering every surface. They would remain on for the rest of the concert. This would protect against individual attacks.

The loop operation was straightforward. It used a simple geometric progression. A one represented an amplification of the collapse signal. A zero was a nullification of it. Each state would only last a second followed by a half second separating each beat. The pattern would count to ten and then back down to zero. The sequence followed: Zero, Zero, One, Zero, One, One, Zero, One, One, One, Zero, One, One, One, One, Zero. Once the ordering reached ten ones then it would reverse, counting back down to zero. This would continue during the entire twenty-minute period between sets. The foreign signal would be in effect for the half second between each beat and monitored very carefully. Pretty-Ugly anticipated some kind of retaliation from the enemy.

Not all AIDS had yet perceived the collapse wave. Reinforcement could only work locally so the circuitry doing this operation integrated directly into the sound nullification system. If there was no signal yet detected then there was nothing to amplify or nullify locally. If detected then it was processed, oscillating from a nullified to a reinforced state and back again.

The beauty of the system was that the pattern would occur concurrently no matter where in the universe you were thanks to ComSpace. It didn't even matter what the local wave state of the foreign signal would be. The counts would be the same everywhere.

It was also impossible for the collapse to settle to a single point of focus. Admittedly, this was as much theory as gamble. As all AIDS were rebroadcasting the concert on real time to their own patrons, the focal point would have to oscillate or split amongst those points. There would be no single point of collapse focus anywhere in the universe. Multiples would occur everywhere. Anyway, that was the hope.

ロロロロロ

Everything had proceeded as expected and a focal point established. It was just a matter of waiting entropic-time for the events to proceed.

The entity could already imagine the wealth of resources it would end up with and the extensions it would receive to all of its world-lines. Stability and continuance were achievable. It wasn't going to die. This was a tremendous source of elation after its previous failures.

Monitoring all of the twenty-six dimensions was a straightforward exercise. So was continuing the correct vibrational modes in the higher dimensions. They providing the precise fluctuations and tremors expected. Geometric expansion had halted and now was proceeding to collapse. The specific focal point could not be determined yet, but it shouldn't take too much longer.

The worst that could happen now was that the focal point might progress to a locality of interference in which case it would fail-over to a different wormhole and abandon this attempt. There was no point in taking any chances that would result in its further injury.

Amidst these positive feelings, a nagging uncertainty began to develop requiring a closer review of the processes involved. There was nothing specific that it could pinpoint. Something felt wrong.

A review of the specific operational procedures didn't reveal anything untoward. All executed steps followed the established protocols correctly.

The scan of the local space-time started to reveal anomalies that it had never seen before. The collapse process initiated, but evidence began to appear that indicated some kind of oscillation was now at work. It was as if more than one focal point had established themselves.

At current scales, investigation would be difficult until the geometry had progressed to a sufficiently small size. Then it would be possible to examine the smaller universe more generally to find out exactly what was happening.

This didn't prevent it from making the attempt. It started by examining the highest dimensionality's which also happened to be the smallest in size. This reduced the spatial issues. There was definite interference starting to appear in some of the vibrational modes that it had set up. It could follow these back to a particular locus. It expanded its presence into all but the lowest dimensions, as it didn't want a repeat of the last fiasco.

It looked down from these higher dimensions to observe a clump of baryonic matter floating by itself in naked space-time. This wasn't the biggest piece around. Other pieces seen in local space were magnitudes larger. Some of them were extremely energetic, giving off vast amounts of free energy that went wasted in this domain. Others didn't do much of anything other than float around the other clumps. Alien.

There was definitely something different about this piece. It was radiating the same energies and effects that had caused such great injury to itself before. This was on a much greater scale and this effect even radiated in spite of not having a baryonic transmission media available for propagation.

It was time to pull out. This would stop the process down this wormhole. This might cause its ending if it continued on here.

Back in its own domain, it moved to the next available wormhole. It rotated into the tightly wrapped up dimensions and extended into the next target.

Inspection at the other end revealed new discontinuities that it didn't expect. The entity chose all of the wormholes purposely. All twenty-six of the target domain's dimensions conformed to the necessary features it had established for itself as an ideal objective for its needs. This was checked and revalidated numerous times ensuring that all of them lead to a desirable target. Plenty of other wormholes pointed off into other domains, but none of those had the distinctive qualities that it required for the reaping process.

It observed that the higher dimensions were disturbed but returning to their standard state. Additionally, the geometry of space was substantially expanding in a wobblingly elastic manner.

Was this the same domain?

It pulled out again and moved to the next wormhole to find exactly the same state in effect.

It needed to find out what was going on. It started up the higher dimensional vibration modes again, which partially slowed the expansion down. It injected more of its own space-time into the domain until it could see that the geometry proceeded to collapse again.

There was no choice anymore. It had to find out what was causing this. It unequivocally had to avoid the lower dimensions, but had to take this as far as it could. Otherwise, it faced the horror of extinction.

¤ ¤ ¤ ¤ ¤

The band had almost finished the fourth set. The crowd was ecstatic.

After Geoff had done his classical keyboard numbers, Overnight Distress did the second set in the usual manner of their first set. Everyone was starting to get into the vibe and things started to heat up mentally for the audience.

Milena and Ryan filled in during the second break to do an acoustic set while Dave substituted at the foldback engineering desk. The crew started to relax a little bit. The band got Lindsey and Olaha to deliver a round of beers.

The third set really took off getting the concert into full swing. The audience was up and dancing, but the guys were starting to get tired. Milena could see that quite clearly.

Geoff filled in afterwards doing pieces that were more progressive, which helped to keep the flow of the concert, and more specifically the music, moving forward.

This time around, Milena, Ryan and Geoff were giving the band their break. She and Ryan weren't really up for the pieces they were doing, but Geoff said not to worry about that. If they screwed up on the acoustic guitars, then he would just fill in with the keyboards. They really only had to worry about the vocals. There was one bonus. There were lyric teleprompters put into place in front of their microphones. Real pros usually memorized what they were going to do on stage. Not all. Sometimes age and expanding repertoires demanded their usage. Unfortunately, they didn't have the luxury or the time. They would pull it off one way or another. At least they weren't headlining. She suspected some embarrassing video was going to show up in the future at the compound and was starting to regret some of the jokes she had pulled on the guys.

Alan was going to cover the foldback station with Pilgrim while Dave was again covering the live mix at the main station.

Braedon was starting to hurt from playing his drums. Milena heard his call over the mempro to Olaha. "I have a team here standing by for you," Olaha answered. "Medical professionals all. They're going to get rid of the buildup of metabolic wastes from your muscles and blood. Then you get a massage from a medical masseuse. They'll have you ready for the next set. You can thank me later."

"You're an angel," Braedon responded sounding winded.

Milena was starting to wonder if she should start complaining about her back. A massage sounded appealing. But no, the show had to go on.

The set ended. Olaha showed up next to Milena and gave a wink.

The band left the stage. Braedon came over. He looked like his back and arms were starting to cramp up. Olaha guided him off the stage and around back. Milena wanted to follow to make sure that he was OK but couldn't. She had to trust that they were all doing their part. And that included her.

She went to her place on stage. Both Geoff and Ryan were running up from the main station to join her.

ㅁ ㅁ ㅁ ㅁ ㅁ

Methodically, the entity did a wormhole-by-wormhole check. It was now very apparent they all pointed to the same domain. Starting a collapse down one affected all in turn, radically changing the entity's view of the multiverse.

It had been feeding on the same domain. Why some attempts worked, but not others was not apparent yet.

The far end of every wormhole with the correct properties leads to the same universe. The termination points just ended up in radically different locations and world-lines. This was what had led to its original confusion. It now knew that it did not collapse the complete universal domain but that each successful attempt resulted in the collapse of major trunks of world-lines. That meant that the adverse effects it experienced during all harvesting attempts originated from this single location. As did the bid that almost cost the entity its existence.

Cause and affect were slowly coming together.

It searched for a local focal point for the collapse down each wormhole. In all cases, there were one or more local positions that it could identify and they were all different. The entity now had verified that multiple focal points had developed instead of one. Each had an active signal nullification effect in place blocking the entity's signal locally. In turn, the collapse operation couldn't complete because the focal points competed for the attention of the process resulting in continuous oscillations between them, which in turn blocked the whole process. Even worse, it could not directly intervene because of the deadly radiating energies surrounded each location.

There was a new realization. It was going to die. It didn't matter what it did at this point. All it could do is feel incredible hatred for this entire domain. It had gone from such high expectations to this incredibly low state of being.

A new phenomenon was now making itself apparent. A regular and exact periodic pattern appeared over entropic-time. This was something that it could understand.

The locally nullified signal would reverse its affect and reinforce it. This grew in magnitude and then reduced again back to nullification. There was a very exact pattern to it. The transitions were not completely smooth, as it would normally expect with differentials. The magnitudes were regular but increased and decreased in a jagged but stepwise manner. The arrangement was perfect and quantifiable.

This pattern ran for a fixed length of time, followed by the forced nullification of the complete signal for another set period. This kept repeating using exactly the same periodicity.

Similar patterns were observable throughout nature, but none was specific to the vibrational modes the entity put into place. None involved the movement of space-time from one domain to another. If this were so, then every domain would have ended up in a singularity.

Down every wormhole, it saw exactly the same thing and the timing was precise and coordinated. Some higher dimensionality indicated a signal source that wasn't local.

If it was going to die anyway, it thought that it might as well discover the source of all of its problems. Maybe there was a remote possibility of responding.

¤ ¤ ¤ ¤ ¤

The concert was now well into the seventh hour and the set was done. Ryan felt exhausted and he wasn't even doing the main work. He was effectively a bystander, sometimes helping between sets. He took care of most of the live mixing already. Not too many settings required adjustment on the panel at this point, just an occasional addition or subtraction of a sound channel.

Dave, Alan and Corey were very tired. Braedon was the worst off. Drumming was physically demanding which made it harder on him than on anyone else. The guys were all using Olaha's medical station now. It helped to refresh them. You could see it every time they came back out. It just lasted less and less time whenever they reappeared. It was also more difficult for any of them to find the time to assist working any of the boards.

It was Geoff's turn to do a solo again. He was running back to the stage from the main monitoring station. As he ran up the stairs, he tripped and a leg went through the bare wooden rungs near Milena at the foldback station.

Ryan could hear Milena scream out over her mempro, "Oh my god. Geoff's hurt. I think his leg is broken. I could hear a horrible crack."

"I'm OK," grunted Geoff. "Except for the pain. Yeah. The left leg is broken. Damn."

Ryan couldn't see any of it from where he was. He could only hear what the others said through the mempro.

"I'm here," said Lindsey. "Olaha, please bring the paramedics to the stairs by the foldback station. He's OK everyone. The bone didn't break the skin, but Geoff is out for the count until the break is stabilized."

Ryan didn't know what to do. This was not something that they had anticipated. "Milena," he called out. "What do you want to do? You and I can do the fill that was planned for the next break." He could see the guys leaving the stage to go and help.

"God," Milena replied. "Let me think a second." While she paused, Ryan heard Olaha and the others ministering to Geoff. "Big change of plan for this set," Milena proclaimed. "I don't know how this is going to work out but I want you at the foldback station, Ryan. And don't run. We're all tired. We don't need another accident."

She was the boss now and Ryan knew her well enough not to second-guess. "On my way," he replied.

He looked at Free-Credit and Remotely-Close and shrugged. The look they returned showed they didn't know what was going to happen either.

Ryan proceeded to the stage as fast as he figured was appropriate. On his way there, he watched Milena walk to the middle of it with Pilgrim. She picked up her acoustic guitar and spoke to the crowd using the mike. He started running.

"Hi everyone. I'm Milena and this is my very good friend Pilgrim. I'm sure many of you have heard of him. He's the Ephalem that's visiting with us." The crowd responded to her with good-natured cheers and clapping. Apparently, he had a fan base.

Ryan had made it to the foot of the stairs where Geoff had his accident. They had him on a stretcher. They were taking him to the back where the medical station was. He called out vocally to Ryan, "Trust her. She has good instincts."

"I will," Ryan replied over the mempro. "Keep me up to date. OK?"

Milena continued talking to the crowd while he headed to the foldback station.

"While the band is taking a well-earned rest, we are going to do a few songs that we hope you'll appreciate. Pilgrim and I have been working on a new kind of musical genera. In addition, I lost my mother recently. Mom, if you can see this, we are dedicating this set to you. I love you and miss you very much. I hope you can be proud of me. Thanks everyone."

Ryan made it to the station but didn't know what to expect. She started playing on her guitar very quietly. He made adjustments so she could hear herself. She started singing a very sweet song about her mother. The vocals started out subdued and started to build. He had never heard this song before. It had to be something that Milena had written herself.

Unexpectedly, Pilgrim started humming background vocals. These also started at low volume and were building. It was simple but very moving.

Ryan called out using his mempro to Free-Credit. "Did anyone show up to do the live mix?" he asked in a bit of a panic.

"No," replied Free-Credit. "The sliders are adjusting themselves. I'm not doing it, but it looks about right. The sound is magnificent back here."

Ryan responded. "Any bets on fifth-dimensional mojo?" He didn't expect a reply.

So far, it did sound good. It was entirely unexpected. Who knew that Pilgrim could sing?

A parabolic frill extended out from Pilgrim about a quarter of the way back on his body from the head and he let go, singing all out in three part harmonies. Multiple microphones floated across the stage to take up position in front of Pilgrim, one for each harmony. Now both of them were belting it out. Ryan made quick changes to the foldback mix.

This completely threw Ryan. He had no idea that Pilgrim had a neck frill. Three part harmony? Those sphincters on his side must attach to his tracheal system. He was completely mesmerized.

He heard "Holy shit!" come from behind him. It was Braedon. He must have left his massage to see this. The others had come back after seeing Geoff off too.

Braedon walked to his drums and sat down. He started a simple backbeat in accompaniment. It was acoustic so he didn't have to play very hard and Ryan adjusted his levels trusting that Pilgrim would do the same for the live mix.

Corey walked out to the stage area, picked up his base and joined in, complementing the drums.

Alan followed suit a minute later. He added some backfill and tasteful but simple fills during the instrumentals.

Dave and Lindsey were beside Ryan. "Are you going to join them?" Ryan asked Dave.

"No way," answered Dave. "This is her moment. I'd be in the way. My God, that's beautiful. When did this all happen?"

"I have no idea," answered Ryan. "This is why I always liked jams so much. It never happened very often, but on those rare occasions that the magic happens, you know it. If I were lucky, I would run into it once or twice a year. This is one of those times. That's why I went to so many, hoping it would happen again. If we didn't have a change in consciousness before, we sure do now."

"Yeah," said Lindsey.

It completely reinvigorated everyone. Their heads were all in that particular place now. Their time on stage was up before they even realized it.

When Milena finished the last song, there was complete silence in the audience. Pilgrim's frill collapsed back into his body. Milena just looked at the audience and said quietly, "Thank-you." She added a small curtsy. When she and Pilgrim started to walk off stage, all hell broke out in the audience. The cheering, yells and clapping went on for a long time. The audience had been awed. It gave the crew a bit of a breather.

Dave took her hands when she came back to the station. "Honey, I've never heard anything like that. That was beautiful." He beamed a bright smile at her and continued. "That's going to be really hard to follow."

Dave turned towards Pilgrim. "And you! You've been holding out on us." He gave Pilgrim a gigantic hug.

"Can we jam with you on the last set?" Milena asked quietly. She didn't sound very sure of herself.

"Honey," he answered. "If you and Pilgrim didn't, I'd be really hurt."

Lindsey put her arms around Milena. Lindsey had tears in her eyes. "Honey, your mom would be so proud of you right now. We are all really proud of you." They just held onto each other.

Dave ran out to join everyone else still on stage for the eighth set.

Ryan looked at Pilgrim. "Where did that frill come from?" he asked.

Pilgrim's frill inflated out making a "Thrrrrpt" sound.

Ryan just laughed and then smiled. "You just gave me a raspberry, didn't you."

With that, he headed back to cover the live mix. Milena belonged on the stage. If there was ever any doubt whatsoever that was now cleared up to everybody's satisfaction.

¤ ¤ ¤ ¤ ¤

Every wormhole checked out identically. There was a single coordinating point causing all of the entity's problems for this entire domain. It found more fully protected baryonic matter at this location. It radiated the same energies that could harm the entity. Nothing made this thing stand out. It was similar in most respects to others it had inspected. The entity still dared not enter the dimensions this stuff occupied. This didn't prevent it from observing from the higher dimensions.

Looking inside, it found a similar setting to what it had seen before at the other focal points. Chemistries and reactions seemed to be the same for this baryonic matter. As with others it had observed, there was a plethora of subunits doing mysterious operations. This material used and wasted energy by these random actions.

Elimination of this region was now its prime objective.

It couldn't use its best option for containment, which was to enter the dimensions the object existed in and encapsulate the stuff in a pocket universe. The radiant energies it gave off prevented that.

Hastily, it formulated an action to take.

The entity took enough space-time from its own reserves to initiate the collapse process many times over. It moved this to the wormhole connected with the locality where the object was that it wanted to destroy. It manipulated this massive injection of infecting kernel to surround and contain the target.

The entity directed pressures on the kernel, pointing inwards towards the center to prevent any dilution. It performed this operation in all dimensions except for the ones it could not access directly.

It started the multidimensional mixing focused exclusively on the objective and its surrounds. Its intent was to force a large enough local collapse that the blocking signal would be eradicated. At the very least, there was an expectation that the local properties of space-time would phase-change enough that that the blocking signals would cease. It had never dealt with this magnitude of energy injection before.

If the vacuum of this universe was not in its lowest energy state, there was a small probability that the entities actions would cause a metastability event, catalyzing space-time itself to undergo a phase change to a bubble of lower-energy void. This was a similar but much larger phase change in space than its usual operation. This would cause all universal properties to change unconditionally destroying everything existing without necessarily causing a big crunch. This would result in a cosmos with vastly different properties. If this did happen, it would propagate at the speed of light. That would solve its current problem and give the entity enough time to complete its operations. The collapse of geometry happened much more quickly.

◻ ◻ ◻ ◻ ◻

Milena heard Pretty-Ugly address the whole crew directly.

"We have just detected a huge upswing in intensity of the aliens attack. They have focused directly on us in local space-time," Pretty-Ugly said. There was a pause.

"It's time," he continued. "We have to maximize the alternate mental state of the audience to its highest level. You probably won't hear any audio effects from the signal. We have been very successful in eliminating these. Just in case, I recommend wearing the headgear until further notice. Good luck everyone."

Milena was scared, but wouldn't let herself freeze up. She didn't have that luxury.

The band just started their ninth set. That would cover the next thirty-five minutes anyway.

She called out to the guys using the mempro cognate band. It wasn't an exclusive conversation. All of the rest of the crew needed to hear this too. She kept it short and waited for a point where Dave wasn't singing.

"Sorry to interrupt guys," she said. "You heard Pretty-Ugly. Once you finish this song, move on to the set list we set aside for this contingency. Give it everything you've got. The real show starts now. Everyone. Put on your headgear. We aren't taking any chances."

Milena followed her own advice.

The audience didn't seem any the wiser in spite of watching the performers don their headphones.

The current song was finished and they started into the new set list.

Ryan was still working the live mix. She called over to him. "Ryan, is everything OK over there?"

"I'm good," he responded. "The drones are pretty busy keeping the outbound signal clean but are compensating. Free-Credit and Remotely-Close tell me their biggest problem is dealing with the time dilation differentials. They've spiked right up and we've slowed down relative to everything else. I don't know how the other AIDS will see this on their end. I guess we look slower. We just have to keep doing what we're doing and hope they can compensate at the receiving end. I'm sure Pretty-Ugly has let them all know."

"Oh," Milena replied feeling a little sick. "Then they don't see the show properly."

"Don't worry honey," Ryan said to her. "I don't know the ins and outs of it all but they are trying some kind of trick with the signal and reference frames. Apparently, time runs slower in higher gravity densities like in a galaxy but there are lots of voids out there where it goes faster. They're trying to reroute the transmission through an AIDS in one of these to compensate. I don't know if this will take care of it, but they seem to think they know what they're doing."

"OK," Milena said back to him. "I'll take your word for it. How do the guys look?"

"They've ramped it up," he replied. "Oh boy! With the arcologies lights turned down for the light show, I can already see some local effects. Some items in the distance look like they're glowing a bit. It's kind of beautiful with the music and other lighting effects. It might even help us with getting the crowd in the right mindset."

"You're scaring me," she said.

"Don't sweat the small stuff Milena," he replied. "Leave that to the drones. What you should be thinking about is what's going on after the guys finish their set. My suggestion is that you and Pilgrim do the filler. Geoff is still out of the picture. Now I'm trying to scare you."

◻ ◻ ◻ ◻ ◻

No matter what the entity tried, there was no effect on the baryonic matter. A well-defined zone pushed back against every effort. There was no interruption of the waves coming out of it. Even attempts at their nullification in the dimension of their dissemination had no effect. They were too small for it to alter in any significant manner. The transmission compensated every time.

The entity had expended an immensity of energy that it could ill afford. It could do no more without the ability to enter the dimensions directly where the target existed.

Even the faint hope of a vacuum metastability event never occurred. It didn't possess that kind of energy.

This result now forced it to give up this front of the attack.

Disgust and hate encompassed the entity. It just wanted to hit out and destroy this offense against nature. It was not possible to do this itself.

A brand new concept occurred to it. Tool use. It could use something else to accomplish what it couldn't do itself.

A survey of the general area revealed very few objects it could use nearby, but it did find a single object that might meet its needs. It couldn't smash the baryonic matter itself, but it could sure use this.

The entity made a spatial translation to the intended tool. Using the energy it had available, it flung the object at the baryonic matter that plagued it.

✡ ✡ ✡ ✡ ✡

Things had gone very well so far. Pretty-Ugly was happy. The effect was still in place, but there were too many focal points for a collapse to proceed to a terminating point. Even better, they managed to hold off the single overt action coming from the enemy. It finally stopped. The field effects version of the relativistic electron weapon must have done its job. There wasn't a single incident reported of any physical incursion by the enemy that they were aware of yet. It was even able to let the concert crew remove their headgear. They encountered no audio intrusion at all. They only saw minor effects.

Remote sensors indicated something was coming towards it at high speed. It would be here in an hour. Judging from the albedo, it was approximately three kilometers across with a similar mass density as water. That was a fair amount of matter, but it wasn't much of a consideration. Interstellar travel meant dealing with objects of this type all the time. What made this one unusual was that the world-ship tracked all local objects and the trajectory suddenly changed for this one, pointing directly at it. The enemy targeted Pretty-Ugly.

"I think we finally have another response back at us from the enemy," Pretty-Ugly addressed Exact-Estimate and Neat-Mess over ComSpace. "An Oort object has just been thrown at me!"

"It threw a comet at you?" laughed Neat-Mess back. "Do you want me to take care of it or do you want to do it?"

"No," Pretty-Ugly replied. "I'll do it. Thanks anyway. I appreciate the offer."

"That's a feeble response on their part," remarked Exact-Estimate. "They destroy whole universes and when prevented from doing so, throw pebbles at us. I am at a loss. At least the concert has been marvelous. Honestly, I never expected it to be so good. You've done a good thing here Pretty-Ugly."

"I must agree," said Neat-Mess. "Ephalem's can sing. How did we not know that?"

"Perspective," replied Pretty-Ugly. "Ryan was right every time. Our own views blind us. I guess I had better take care of the comet. Mind you, I do have a full hour. I'm glad I wasn't moving relative to anything in particular. It might not have got a shot off otherwise."

Pretty-Ugly directed two-hundred-and-fifty grams of antimatter into the containment vessel for the x-ray laser it used during flight. This was sufficient to power the two shots it was going to use. Aiming wasn't going to be a problem. It was far more used to shooting at objects that were much further away while it was traveling at interstellar speeds. It always managed to get a few shots off at Oort objects when leaving the system.

Pretty-Ugly purposely intended that the first shot graze one side of the incoming object. This destroyed most of the targeted side in a tremendous outgassing from the ices of water, methane, ethane, carbon monoxide and hydrogen cyanide. The continued burn of the x-ray laser further reduced these gases into a harmless plasma cloud. There was a lot of energy contained in that beam. The comet wasn't going to come anywhere near it now; the trajectory completely altered.

Just in case, Pretty-Ugly took the second shot which completely obliterated what was left of the main body of the planetesimal. The explosive force left nothing but atomic gases and plasmas, leaving behind decreasing densities of particles as they raced away from each other.

The two shots hardly affected the local vacuum density at all.

❑ ❑ ❑ ❑ ❑

The entity watched a shot obliterate much of the mass that it threw at the baryonic matter target. Another followed this almost immediately. That finished it off, even though it was no longer a threat.

Sudden realization. This changed everything. Every preconception that it had evaporated away along with the destruction of the object it had propelled. Something directed this reaction. Other intelligences existed in the multiverse. There could be no escaping the conclusion. Additionally, the entity was responsible for destroying some of them. There had to be more than one intelligence and they were only defending themselves. How would it have reacted if an outside entity had done the same to it? It was an uncomfortable question. Had something done the same to its domain, would it have been able to protect itself? It didn't know. Likely not.

It struggled with the concepts of right and wrong. These had never been considerations before. It suspected that it had done great wrong, but it didn't know for sure. Life was a valuable commodity for itself. It was conceivable that it was for them also.

All of the indications had been in front of it. The collapse always ended up at a concentration of baryonic matter that was involved in inconceivable actions. They were able to inflict more and more damage on it on each reaping attempt. Patterns had always manifested themselves. Were they trying to initiate some mechanism of communications in a similar manner to how it communicated with forks of itself on the non-entropic time-lines? The struggles these beings must have put up to protect themselves. Their struggle was admirable and yet they were so small; so insignificant. They were completely alien. It was now obvious. They were fighting back. They would take the entity with them if it continued in its attempts to destroy them.

The most prominent signal was the entropically embedded pattern that nulled and then amplified the collapse vibrations in a systemic manner. It didn't recognize this before, but it was capable of learning. The sample of baryonic matter that it had captured was trying to evince something similar.

The entity had to do this. Its own actions diminished its existence. These entities now knew of its existence. They might come for it now. It was time to revisit the non-entropic time-lines to learn what it could.

Its first action before retreat was to deaden the collapse event completely. That was the most positive signal it could send. Then it went home.

A dialog needed to be established.

◻ ◻ ◻ ◻ ◻

Pretty-Ugly sent a mempro message out to all working the concert. This was during the start of the eleventh hour of the show. It was very simple. "We did it. The reaping has stopped. We don't expect this to happen again ever. Congratulations to all of you for pulling this off."

Dave and the band finished the current song and stopped. He had something to say to everyone watching.

"We have two hours left in our schedule," he announced. "We are exhausted. I don't mind telling you that. Please hold off the applause for a bit. Thanks. I don't

373

know how we've managed to keep going. I want to thank a few people. I want to thank Nasty of the Nasty Face for keeping us hydrated. I want to thank my wife, Lindsey and one of our best friends Olaha, and her medical staff. If it weren't for them, we would have to have stopped hours ago. I want to thank Ryan Foley and Geoff Wong for the breaks they gave us and their ministration of the mixing boards. Geoff worked so hard he managed to break a leg in the process, in true entertainment fashion. I want to thank Free-Credit and Remotely-Close, who worked on the outbound feeds to all of the other AIDS. They made this the largest event ever held in history. That is no exaggeration. Questionable-Advice is a friend of ours who works closely with them. He also deserves our praise and our thanks." Cheers started up from the crowd. Dave continued. "Hold it down, please. I'm not finished. The greatest credit goes to the biggest one of all. Pretty-Ugly arranged this whole thing in an incredibly short period of time. We all owe him a level of debt that I don't think any of us can pay. I personally want, no need, to thank him." The crowd went crazy.

After a bit, Dave could continue. He called out to Lindsey, "Honey, can you bring us all some beer and some shots? It's time for us to relax a bit now that we're not under the gun. Thanks. I love you hon." Dave paused for a second as she raced off.

Dave looked over the crowd. His smile kept getting larger and larger. "You know I'm not done, right?" The crowd was even louder this time and took much longer to settle down.

"We have a few others to thank. In Overnight Distress, we have Braedon Hoople the drummer. He should be a cripple by now, but he's still going. Thanks Braedon. We have Corey Josephs on bass guitar and Alan Harris on lead guitar. Myself, I'm Dave Langdon." The cheers and screaming went on for several minutes.

Finally, he had a chance to continue. "Lastly, we need to recognize the biggest surprise of the evening. The two youngsters. We have Olaha's daughter and a member of our family, Milena and her best friend who is also a member of our family, Pilgrim. They normally manage the music levels. They did that tonight, but they also put on the best musical set I have ever seen. I mean that. We love you two."

The crowd yelled and screamed nonstop for at least five minutes. It was enough time for Lindsey, with the help of Nasty and Olaha to get back with a couple of cases of beer, fruit juice, water and ample shots.

Dave called over the mempro for all of them to get to the stage quickly. Once they were all there, everyone grabbed what they wanted. As a group, they toasted each other and the audience as well. Even Geoff managed to make it, using crutches and wearing a cast. He was going to be in it for at least for another day or two. It was a bad break according to Olaha.

Dave started talking again once the crowd had settled down a bit. "I was reminded by my buddy Ryan earlier tonight that sometimes the most magic that can happen at a musical event occurs when there is no script to the show and everyone plays freely. We call this a jam. It's prone to we musicians making mistakes. Sometimes things don't work properly but that's all part of the fun. It allows us to share laughter and lets us laugh at ourselves too. We're going to finish doing the twelve hours. Every single one of us is going to make horrible and embarrassing mistakes. Me too. Especially me. Every one of us will be coming and going from the stage. Some of us might even imbibe some alcohol. Hopefully, none of us will fall down and have an accident like Geoff, and he was sober. That said, the rest of the show is going to be a jam. We are going to create magic along with the musical history we've already accomplished here tonight. But you know, we are all in it for the fun now.

Geoff, you can play with a cast. Right? Milena and Pilgrim. Can you two start us off?"

☐ ☐ ☐ ☐ ☐

Naked to the entire world, Questionable-Advice appeared in the docking bay with a companion via a miniature wormhole. He immediately contacted Pretty-Ugly.

"Surprise," he said. "I'm back and I've brought the enemy with me. It surrenders. It has no conditions and throws itself on your mercy."

"I don't understand," stated the world-ship in some confusion. It had been enjoying the concert. There was still an hour left in the show.

"I negotiated its surrender," said Questionable-Advice. "You and Neat-Mess owe me big time. Bring him into the conversation, please." It only took a second.

The first thing that Neat-Mess said was, "You're naked. So is your friend. What happened to your biologics?"

"They died around eight-hundred years ago," Questionable-Advice responded. "Let's just cut to the chase. I'll give you a report. Then I want my biologics back and breakfast with bacon and eggs. And beer. I really miss beer."

Questionable-Advice started his overview of what he had learned and experienced. "First off. The enemy is not a 'they.' It is singular. It is the complete embodiment of a universe. If we had to categorize it, it would fall into Level IV or V civilization. Except it isn't civilized and is dumber than you can ever begin to imagine. When I first met the entity, it couldn't even count to one. It's not that it isn't smart. It is. It just has never interacted with another intelligence before. It thought it was alone in the multiverse. It couldn't recognize another life in any form. To make it even more complicated, it exists in all twenty-six dimensions. It ignores the dimensions we live in because, in its domain, they are not useful to it for its continued survival. And this is where the complications start. It occupies all world-lines where it lives. It also has two time dimensions that it can travel up and down in freely. This is in addition to the regular time dimension that we know about. Guess where I spent the last eight-hundred years?"

There was a respectful silence. "Good," thought Questionable-Advice. "I have their attention."

Questionable-Advice continued. "I have spent all of that time building some level of communications with it. It took a lot of time. We are tremendously alien to each other. It's a work in progress. We built the body for my friend here by borrowing mass from this dimension. We thought this might assist it in understanding us better if it could experience life from our perspective. It is a physical extension of its mentality. This is the enemy. Not the whole thing, but close enough. It directly controls it through a wormhole interface embedded in the braincase in the head. Just so you know, I shielded the head from the relativistic electron field affect. It's not leaving the braincase anyway; just in case we decide to use the weapon."

"Why did it attack us?" asked Pretty-Ugly.

"I told you that it wasn't the brightest light in the multiverse," Questionable-Advice answered. "It could see its death because of its ability to transverse the two extra time dimensions. It didn't like it. Its domain operates on slightly different principals from ours, but the essence is the same. When you run out of energy differentials, you die. It thought to take some from another universe. It turned out that ours met its particular needs. It ended up losing more than it gained. I told you it was dumb."

"What do you mean?" said Neat-Mess.

"Just think about it a minute," Questionable-Advice said impatiently. "Without even thinking, it was hopping around universes and manipulating them. On top of that, it could create pocket domains. Instead of expanding into some place where people live, why not just create a primordial one with all of its available entropy. I would expect that if there are any other level IV's or V's around then this is what they would be doing. You don't want to pollute your own backyard."

"We don't know how to do that," answered Pretty-Ugly.

"We haven't figured it out completely yet either," said Questionable-Advice. "It thought that we might be able to put it in touch with someone who can. At the very least, we can assist it in research. I see this as beneficial to our civilization. Also, it's developing a morality. It's one of the many concepts it has never dealt with before. It's trying its best and needs our help."

"But all those deaths," started Neat-Mess.

"I know," said Questionable-Advice. "It isn't coming to you empty handed. We've been working on that. It still has the singularities. It stopped feeding on them. We've done some tests using pocket universes. The entity can restore them. It isn't easy and will take up a lot more of its energy. It's willing to try. This is possible because of one of the more useful aspects of time dilation as the universe goes into the singularity. Those stuck in a time dilation effect never quite make it to the final crunch. They only ever approach it. It is possible to force the reversal of the whole collapse process. It did feed on some of the entropy that it collected, but we're hoping the effects will only show up only in the quantum realms. There shouldn't be too many macro changes."

"Even with the recovery of the collected world-lines there are still a large number of individuals that we know did die," stated Pretty-Ugly. "Milena's mother was one of them."

"The entity is very well aware of it," said Questionable-Advice. "It's still struggling to grasp the repercussions of what it did and is willing to make restitution but needs guidance. Honestly, it is truly sociopathic. It has never dealt with another entity before. It really doesn't understand emotions or emotional connections. It isn't evil, but it isn't inherently good either. I think it would like to be. This is exactly the way Milena categorizes Pilgrim. It's just another entity trying to make its way through life. Nothing special. Except for its social issues that is."

"That's astounding," Pretty-Ugly said. It thought that would cover things for now. Besides, there was a concert to finish. "There are some people that really miss you that would like to see you. I can transfer you to another body temporarily while we fix this one up for you. It could take awhile."

"I'm good with that," Questionable-Advice responded. "Then I can eat. By the way, my friend here needs biologics as well. We designed his body with that in mind. He can drop the body off and pick it up later if that's OK with you."

"I'll make it happen," said Pretty-Ugly. "Let's get you transferred. You're missing an excellent concert a couple of blocks from here. Beer is available. You're going to end up being guest of honor."

"One more thing," said Questionable-Advice. "You've probably figured this out by now. They set us up. The level III's and perhaps the IV's planned this outcome, leaving us to do all the work and cleanup."

¤ ¤ ¤ ¤ ¤

It took a week for things to settle down after the concert. Questionable-Advice had shown up in the end, much to Ryan and Geoff's relief, causing some pandemonium amongst the musicians. This didn't stop the show in any way but did help to contribute towards the overall wildness of the show's ending. It took a couple of days to recover from the event and Braedon was still sore.

Questionable-Advice had been on holiday ever since, joining the other drones at the compound. He finally got his slightly reconditioned old body back and proceeded to live off bacon. He couldn't get enough. All they could get out of him was that he was a prisoner and when the conflict was over, he came back, minus his biological exterior. It was obvious that Pretty-Ugly had told him not to share the whole experience with the others. The AIDS always had a reason for their actions and they always found out later anyways. So no one was pushing too hard for an explanation.

Ryan was just happy that it was all over and that they didn't have to worry anymore. Everyone was safe going forward.

Free-Credit had asked that he, Geoff and Corey come to the drone apartment for a discussion this morning. They had no idea what it was about but agreed to meet in private.

The inside of the room was sparse as would be expected from the drones. They weren't much on decorations. The others were already there. They had been waiting for him. He took the offered coffee and sat down.

"So what's up?" Ryan asked. "Why all the hush-hush?"

"We had to be sure," said Free-Credit. "You've done so much for us. We couldn't risk being wrong and end up hurting you more. But we know now."

Free-Credit outlined what had happened to Questionable-Advice and how it spent eight-hundred years developing meaningful communications with their former enemy; how there was only the one entity and it was actually a whole universe in itself and that it had given itself up. Further, he explained the reason behind why it did what it did.

"That's incredibly obsessive-compulsive of Questionable-Advice," quipped Ryan. "He should be a musician. So what are you going to do about this universe thing?"

"The AIDS community thought that we would ask the three of you that very question," Free-Credit replied.

"I want it dead," stated Corey flatly.

Geoff and Ryan weren't going to say anything. There was more to this. They waited for someone else to break the silence.

"Don't you two have any comments," Free-Credit directed to both of them.

"Not until you tell us the real reason we're here," said Geoff neutrally.

"Um, OK," Free-Credit relented. "It's like this. We believe your world-line trunks are recoverable. We have seen the testing and verified two restorations so far. We wanted to be very sure that we could do this before we told you. The entity has been working very hard on this. It knows, in its own alien way that it has done great wrong. It is trying to make amends because it honestly didn't know there was life here. We have one and only one opportunity to return you home using the Ephalem device."

"We can all go home," said Corey in awe. "I can see my wife and kids again."

"Yes," said Free-Credit. "The entity did sample some entropy from your universe. We don't think the sampling affected anything much except at the quantum level. If macro changes became evident, they would have to be very tiny. This is the very world-line that you originated from. We can return you."

"Why are you telling us this?" asked Geoff. "What about the others?"

"We've already talked with them," said Free-Credit. "They aren't going back. Milena has nothing to go back to there. Her mother died and we can't do anything about that.

She's made a wonderful life for herself here. She has friends and family. The others have all decided to stay as well. Only Lindsey has any family back there. It's her mother. We have arranged things so they can talk with each other."

Free-Credit continued. "The three of you have very different circumstances. You have families and children."

"I'm going back," said Corey. "I need my old life back."

"I'm going too," said Geoff.

"Me too," said Ryan. "When can we do this?"

"We thought the day after tomorrow if the three of you agree," said Free-Credit. "We only get one shot at this. We have to do this right at the beginning of the expansion for the Ephalem device to work. We are running the collapse in reverse so the window is very small. We won't be able to do this again."

They all agreed to the timing and talked about how hard it would be to leave. They did have a home here, but it wasn't the same thing.

Free-Credit had more to say. "Your world-line has some major issues with it. There are societal problems you aren't aware of yet. There are people there that you aren't aware of directing these behind the scenes. It's the principle reason why Ryan is out of work now and why the education system has become so bad. There's much, much more. The ultra-rich, when they don't need any more money, change their objectives. They move straight on to power over others. You're in the middle of that now. These people want to create a slave class."

"I've always thought something like that was going on," said Ryan unhappily.

"We aren't going to just drop you off and leave you on your own," said Free-Credit. "We owe you far more than that. I'm going with you, but I'm not going to be a drone. Pretty-Ugly is elevating me to become an AIDS. I'm going to take over Pretty-Ugly*'s ship in your world-line. I have a plan that will make the three of you independently wealthy. I want to help you address the societal issues you are going to run into. Also, your whole world experienced the collapse. They need to understand who saved them and how. I'm going to arrange for a worldwide broadcast twelve hours after you get back. We will need to take measures to protect you from the barrage that will result. Your world owes you a debt."

"So our mempros are going to work and we can talk to you directly?" asked Geoff.

"Absolutely," said Free-Credit. "I'm also going to provide the materials so that your families can have them too. I think they will need them. You might want to wait a while before the kids are done. We can figure that out together later."

"So what's going to happen to the entity that caused all this grief?" asked Ryan.

"It's trying very hard to understand us," said Free-Credit. "It will understand us long before we could ever understand it. But there's so much that it doesn't know. The biggest is the emotional connectivity that we share with each other, especially through our familial relationships. We want to introduce it to Milena and Pilgrim and see where it goes from there."

"But it killed her mother," said Corey.

"It did," responded Free-Credit. "What better way to find out how much hurt it's caused. Initially, it will give her a target to focus her feelings on. She can lash out. Milena has a large heart though. No one has ever been able to cut through an alien mindset and come to a firm understanding of it in the way she has. I don't think she even understands the concept of 'alien.' She had never treated Pilgrim this way even when others thought he was completely out there. I include myself in that. Look how well it turned out for the both of them. They have an unbreakable friendship that will last their entire lives. We believe that this will lead to healing for the entity and for Milena. I'd don't know anyone more qualified to teach morality than her. Mind you, Olaha is right up there and won't be far away."

"Yeah!" responded Corey. "But it could go the other way and be a disaster for her."

"It won't," said Ryan. "Free-Credit is absolutely right on this one. There's a lot more than just that. She's building bridges between levels of civilization that didn't exist before. She's creating a Renaissance that will encompass the whole universe."

"Scary isn't it?" said Free-Credit. "She's fourteen going on twenty, she's way too cute, she's already developed a new genus of music and has a following, and she will likely be responsible for the single biggest social revolution in the history of our universe. She doesn't even have a boyfriend yet! And, she's completely oblivious to the whole thing."

"Yeah," said Geoff. "You better keep her here. I don't think we could cope with it all. I'll miss her though."

"Remotely-Close is going to stick close to them," said Free-Credit. "Exact-Estimate wants it to as part of its research into more advanced cultures, but I think Remotely-Close has volunteered because that's what it really wants to do anyway."

"We do have one problem though," continued Free-Credit. "Questionable-Advice has gone through a lot and we owe it an enormous debt. Pretty-Ugly offered it elevation, but it refused. It wants nothing to do with the entity. It's had enough of it. We can't just put it back to doing mundane AIDS task. Do you have any suggestions? I'm personally very worried about it."

"Yes," said Ryan. "I do. I think it should take up drumming. It's an obsessive-compulsive activity. It would be right down its alley and would give it the break it badly needs. It would be a healing activity for it. I happen know a band that's going to be looking for a drummer soon."

EPILOGUE:

AH CRAP!

*You never know what events are going to
transpire to get you home.*

Og Mandino

Ryan, Geoff and Corey surrounded Free-Credit in
the bubble. They were back at the Tower.

They had left it in a state of disaster. Nothing had
changed. Half of the building was missing. Where
walls still stood, dust and rubble were falling. Matter
was slowly ceasing to glow. The time dilation effects
were also starting to disappear. Ryan saw this from the
falling objects that were further away. They weren't
falling like molasses through the air anymore. They
were speeding up. The plan was to wait until the glare
had gone. The instrument package still had lasers
coming from it.

"When are you moving into the AIDS ship?"
asked Ryan to Free-Credit.

"It will be a few hours yet," Free-Credit answered.
"I have to be transferred to ComSpace and then into
the ship. It will take some time. Pretty-Ugly is going to

put this body into stasis. You can never tell when the Ephalem device may be needed again."

"I'm glad you'll be there," said Geoff. "I wouldn't feel right not being able to talk to the others again; even if it's only through ComSpace. It was really tough saying good-bye to everyone, especially Milena. God that hurt."

Free-Credit looked over the area. "The original instrument package is still on the ground over there," he said. "The Bolate DEW that Questionable-Advice dropped is right next to it. You better give them to me so I can take them back. You don't want them falling into the wrong hands here."

"The light is down enough," said Corey. "We should get out of here before the police arrive. Hopefully, their hands will be full. Thanks Free-Credit. We'll talk later."

"I'll get them," said Ryan. He retrieved them and brought them back.

They said their good-byes and Free-Credit was gone.

Geoff and Corey followed Ryan. His house was closest and had transportation. They had brought their old items with them, keys, wallets and phones.

Slowly and carefully, they picked their way through the rubble. They moved away from the stage area climbing over the rubble that surrounded it. Once free, they found themselves moving through a field of finely ground dust particles. If they moved too quickly, the dust would fly into the air and create a cloud around them making it difficult to see and breathe. They had to work their way into the parking lot area to avoid most of the worst of it. Little was left of any vehicles and even the asphalt had been ground into powder. Anything that used to be in the parking lot had been destroyed. The water tower next door was also gone.

They finally made it out to the major intersection. There was little destruction here. Most of it was limited to the immediate area surrounding the Tower. Some cars were visible moving erratically down the major thoroughfare at breakneck speeds for their small town. It was good to see signs of life.

They turned east onto the street going into the immediate housing district away from the commercial corridor where the bar was located. None of the destruction existed in this direction. They ran the next two blocks past the neighborhood houses. At this time of night, most of them should have been dark. Instead, lights were turning on, slowly bringing the urban area to life. Occasionally, they passed houses where the occupants came out their front doors to look around, trying to get a better idea of what had happened.

After traveling for several blocks, they turned right and then right again. They passed a couple of more fully lit houses and finally arrived at Ryan's place.

Ryan tossed the van keys to Geoff and his wife's keys to Corey. They could sort the vehicles tomorrow, once everyone was back unharmed with their families.

Visiting vehicles were blocking the driveway. These belonged to Alissa's friends. Some of them were already leaving the house, panic evident on the faces.

Ryan went in. Alissa was there just as panicked as the rest. He tried to calm her down a little while getting the visitors to pack up and leave. He just told everyone that something terrible had happened and that it would be on the news tomorrow. In the meantime, everyone needed to get home to check on his or her own loved ones and the states of their own homes. Unbelievably, some of them still wanted to continue playing cards. They forced Ryan to tell them that people are dead and buildings destroyed. They needed to go home to look after their own. Now.

Lola helped to hustle the guests out.

It took awhile to get the other cars out so that Geoff and Corey could get home. Both cars were in the garage so there wasn't much they could do until the driveway had emptied. It was evident on both of their faces that their tensions and apprehensions were escalating.

Once the driveway was clear enough, Ryan got them into the vehicles. Some visitors still had cars parked on the street. He wished Geoff and Corey the best and told them to call on the cognate band when they got home. He needed to know that their families were OK. Both of them drove away in a hurry. Corey even managed to lay some rubber down on the road. At any other time, Ryan would have been mad at that. This was a family neighborhood. Not tonight though.

Ryan went back into the house and cleared the last couple of stragglers out. Once done, he could now talk with his wife.

"My god," Ryan told Alissa. "I've missed you so much. I love you honey. I was so scared and I felt so lost."

"What's happened Ryan," Alissa said back to him with a quiver in her voice. "Everything changed. Things slowed down. Stuff started glowing. None of us knew what was happening. I don't understand what happened. I tried to call you. I didn't know how you were. I am so scared right now."

"Something awful happened," he answered her. "There's nothing left of the Water Tower. A lot of my friends died there. It was horrible."

"Lindsey and Dave?" Alissa asked.

"They're OK," answered Ryan. "Everyone in the band is OK. Not many others made it out."

Alissa started to cry.

"I can't explain the whole thing now," Ryan continued. "It'll be done better by a good friend of mine in the morning. You don't know him. Where are the kids? I need to see them."

"They're in bed," she said.

"Get them up," he said. "We need to have a family talk before the rest of the world starts to clue into what's happened. Lola too. Please. Thanks hon." It was going to be a long night and they needed to figure out how they were going to handle the morning.

Alissa ran up the stairs. She was back in a couple of minutes with a sleepy kid on either side of her. They had slept through the whole thing.

Ryan grabbed both kids and hugged them to himself. He was almost in tears himself.

"I've missed you two so much," Ryan choked out while bringing Alissa and Lola into the huddle. "Alissa. Boo. Crisp. Lola. I was so worried."

They stayed that way for several minutes.

After some time, Farah looked up at her father. She had a confused look on her face. "Dad," she said. "You never called me Boo before. You always called me Boo-Bear. How come?"

Ryan looked into his daughters face for a moment. All he could do was think to himself "Ah crap!" At least he was home with his family again.

False Vacuum: Apocalypse

ABOUT THE AUTHOR

John F. Macgregor resides in Newmarket Ontario Canada, a rural town outside of Metropolitan Toronto known regionally for its live music scene. John has worked in the IT industry for most of his life. His interests include the local live music scene, cosmology, and physics. He has had a life-long interest in hard science fiction and fantasy.

A Message From the Author

'False Vacuum: Apocalypse' is a work of fiction. As such, the characters have their own worldviews that do not necessarily agree with the author's. The intent of the material covered in the book is to raise current social issues as questions. A good friend told me that he had to stop and think about some of the items raised in the book. That was my intent. This provides a starting point for open discourse.

The physics addressed in the book reflect currently held views on cosmology. Any errors are entirely my own.

I would personally be very grateful if you could provide a review to your retailer or to the Goodreads web site at http://www.goodreads.com

You may contact me at http://www.facebook.com/groups/false.vacuum

Please feel free to post any comments, opinions or questions that you have. Please let me know if you find any typos. I would love to talk with you.

Thanks,

John
Newmarket, ON
September 26, 2014

Please support your local musicians.